THE ENEMY OF MY ENEMY

The Mafia chieftain stood in the center of his cell like a dark statue. Parnell faced him, stared into those solemn black eyes. The man's neck was as thick as his head.

"You are Don Vincenzo Caprano?" Parnell asked in Italian.

Don Vino nodded, a single dip of his head.

"I'm Lieutenant John Parnell of the United States Army, sir." He withdrew a square-folded piece of fabric, snapped it open. It was a yellow silk handkerchief with the letter L on it in script. "I was instructed to give you this."

The L stood for Lucky Luciano, the New York mob boss. A silk handkerchief was the traditional Mafia way of introducing the representative of one capo di capo to another. Fiercely patriotic to his adopted country, Luciano had offered himself as a link between the United States and the Sicilian Mafia. When Mussolini came to power, he had sworn to wipe out the deadly, secret criminal organization. As a result, all mafiosi hated the fascists.

Don Vino silently studied the handkerchief in the half-light. If he decided to keep it, it would signify that he would commit himself and his men to assist anyone who had brought it to him. This promise was binding, locked in by Mafia honor.

Don Vino nodded to Parnell, again a mere dip of his head, and shoved the handkerchief into his pocket.

"We must leave the prison immediately," Parnell said.

The Mafia chieftain stared at him without expression, then tilted his head slightly. Finally he said, "Yes, we go."

<u>BOOK YOUR PLACE ON OUR WEBSITE</u>
<u>AND MAKE THE</u>
<u>READING CONNECTION!</u>

We've created a customized website just for our very special readers, where you can get the inside scoop on everything that's going on with Zebra, Pinnacle and Kensington books.

When you come online, you'll have the exciting opportunity to:

- View covers of upcoming books
- Read sample chapters
- Learn about our future publishing schedule (listed by publication month *and author*)
- Find out when your favorite authors will be visiting a city near you
- Search for and order backlist books from our online catalog
- Check out author bios and background information
- Send e-mail to your favorite authors
- Meet the Kensington staff online
- Join us in weekly chats with authors, readers and other guests
- Get writing guidelines
- AND MUCH MORE!

**Visit our website at
http://www.kensingtonbooks.com**

RECON FORCE

THUNDERBOLT

CHARLES RYAN

PINNACLE BOOKS
Kensington Publishing Corp.
http://www.kensingtonbooks.com

To Punahou,
which has the greatest friends
and the prettiest girls
in the world

"You have come to conquer this great city simply as soldiers. You will accomplish this task within a year."

—*Marcus Cicero, 63 B.C.*

SICILY
Operation Husky

One

The eighty-foot Elco PT-207 slowed as it drew within sight of Isole Marettimo, the outermost of the three small Égadi Islands located forty miles off the coast of Sicily. It lay out there, the long, jagged ridges of its Mount Falcone black shadows resting on the moonlit sea.

The PT, from Motor Torpedo Boat Squadron 15, had made good time, skimming across what had started as a calm sea from its secret base on Cape Bon, Tunisia, her three big-bore Hall-Scott gasoline engines screaming, props cutting a white wake in the ocean. The boat's skipper, a navy lieutenant named Broadhouse, had held to a northerly heading for half the trip to avoid German picket subs prowling the waters off the southern coast of Sicily.

With him up on the control deck was Lieutenant John "Red" Parnell, leader of a small insertion force that would be put ashore on Marettimo. The force consisted of seven men, designated Blue Team, which was part of an elite company of specially trained soldiers called the Mohawkers who conducted clandestine operations behind enemy lines.

Beyond Marettimo, the other Égadi Islands, Levanzo and Favignana, were lost in the larger shadow mass of Sicily, itself completely dark under German blackout. But to the east, the eleven-thousand-foot-high open pit of Mount Etna cast a soft orange glow up into the night sky.

Lieutenant Parnell was a broad-shouldered man, six three, linear-muscled with crew-cut red-blond hair and a wide, athletic face that carried high cheekbones, a remnant of the Sioux Indian blood his mother gave to him. Now as he scanned the ocean ahead, Broadhouse abruptly came off the throttles and the roar of the engines died away. Instantly the deck tilted sharply forward as the drag from the ocean surface began pulling against the boat's hull.

The skipper said, "Best get your men ready, Parnell. We'll be making the run-in in about fifteen minutes." He glanced toward the southeastern horizon. "Damn it, I don't like those cloud banks out there. They're moving in faster than forecast."

"Will that be a problem?" Red asked.

"It's chopped up the surface already. I don't like working shallows in chop. Besides, the wind effect could mess up the water in those caves."

Red looked eastward. For the first time since leaving Tunisia, he felt the premission tension starting in him. It was an energy that wasn't really like energy at all, rather more a stillness or silence that actually held the real energy tethered.

He went aft along the fire barrier to the forward hatch of the midhouse, gave it a couple of slams with the back of his fist. After a short delay, it swung open. He quickly slipped down the ladder into the dark mess compartment. The hatch closed behind him and someone turned on a red battle lantern.

"Everybody up," Parnell snapped. "We're closing on fifteen."

His team rose and began gathering gear from off the mess

table and deck. The small room was cloudy and hot with cigarette smoke and smelled of weapon oil and fresh paint.

Most of their equipment had been tightly wrapped in waterproof oilcloth: Thompson submachine guns with spare clips taped to their stocks, handguns in shoulder holsters, demolition packs and timers, rolls of wire, underwater flashlights, and a long, folding steel auger with a roller bit and two extensions. One of the packs also contained several deflated goat bladders and diving goggles.

Loaded down, the men trooped up to the main deck and hurried past the PT's torpedo tubes to assemble beside a large rubber raft strapped to the deck just aft the bow. Besides Parnell, Blue Team consisted of Master Sergeant Wyatt Bird, Staff Sergeant Sol Kaamanui, Corporal Billy Fountain, and Pfcs. Weesay Laguna, Smoker Wineberg, and Angelo Cappacelli, a new replacement. All except Cappacelli were veterans of North Africa.

One other man would be accompanying them ashore, a short but heavy-boned Sicilian with deeply tanned skin and tattoos on his thick forearms. His name was Marcuzzo Vassallo, a *tuffatori* or lobster diver, and he would act as their guide. All the men wore swimming trunks, tennis shoes, and black T-shirts.

Moving slowly now, the PT rolled gently in the increasing chop from the approaching storm. It created thousands of dancing, moonlit spangles on the surface. They cleared past Point Mugnone, the northern tip of Marettimo, and swung beyond Point Raroia before turning south, holding a mile offshore.

A few dim lights were scattered along the coast, kerosene lanterns from small fishing villages. But back toward Sicily were dozens of tiny flickering orange lights bobbing on the ocean, tuna fishermen working the huge schools as they headed north after breeding off the African coast.

Lieutenant Broadhouse came forward. "We're at the shallows," he told Parnell. "I'll need your lobster diver to get us through the outer channel. Who translates?"

Red sent Cappacelli. Although the entire team had gone through a crash course in Italian at the Office of Strategic Services in Cairo so as to be able to work with Italian partisans, Sicilian was an almost different language. It was always spoken rapidly with enigmatic and heavily accented phrases, which made it very difficult to understand. Although Angelo had been raised in New York and San Francisco, he was originally from Sicily.

With engines idling, they passed through a series of reef channels and entered a small bay. Rocky gullies and hogbacks came directly down to a narrow rim of beach. As they neared it, the higher ridges began to emerge, tufa rock cliffs and jagged ridges silhouetted against the sky. To the left, on a two-hundred-foot-high headland, stood the dark outer wall of a seventeenth-century Capuchin monastery called Il Posare de Nerovento, the Place of the Black Wind.

The monastery's monks had been famous throughout the Mediterranean as embalmers, preserving the bodies of hundreds of wealthy Sicilians and Italian aristocrats for nearly three hundred years. Many of their mummies were still in the catacombs beneath the main building. When Mussolini seized power in 1925, he took over the monastery and converted it into a prison for political dissidents and members of the Mafia, which he had sworn to crush.

Blue Team's mission was to rescue two mafiosi still being held there, a powerful capo di capo or chief of chiefs named Don Vincenzo Caprano and his brother Santegelo.

High above them, Don Vino was not asleep. Instead, he lay on his filthy straw bunk and gazed stone-faced at the dark ceiling of his cell. He waited with the motionless, primitive patience of a leopard at a water hole.

A small light played for just a moment through the steel grating of his cell door. Then came a soft whisper, a man speaking in hill-country Sicilian: "Your Lordship, the time approaches."

Don Vino rose to his feet. He wasn't a big man yet he bore an unmistakable aura of power. His face was round, jowly even, his hair thick and black and, unlike the other prisoners', uncut because even in here, fear of him prevented the guards from touching his person. He had a heavy, unkept mustache and beard, and his eyes, even in the dim light, were carbon black and cast with a cold, lethal glint of pent-up violence.

He stood at the door. "You have it?"

"Yes." The man in the corridor passed a revolver and a box of cartridges through the grating. The revolver was a 10.4mm Bodeo with a ring on its grip.

"Santegelo?"

"Yes, Your Lordship. He too is prepared."

The night was silent save for the vague murmurings of sleeping men in the cells lining the inner wall of the corridor. The hall was cobblestoned and perpetually wet. Each day the prisoners emptied their slop buckets into it and then it was washed down with strong hoses. Still, the stench of excrement and disinfectant lingered in the air.

The man who had brought the weapon was a soldier-guard named Ermenio Silone, a Sicilian from the town of Valdibella who had been drafted into the Italian army. Like all Sicilians, he despised the mainland Italians who considered anyone from Sicily an ignorant peasant to be treated no better than a dog.

The guard asked permission to leave. Don Vito dismissed him with a jerk of his head and returned to his bunk. He sat examining the revolver, felt of its weight, and then loaded the cylinder. He didn't like handguns, they were too imperfect for killing. He had killed many men in his life but always with a knife or a *lupara,* a sawed-off shotgun. You knew a man's death was certain with these.

He lay down again. He held the gun on his chest and stared at the ceiling, waiting.

* * *

The team gathered on the beach below the prison. The PT had retreated back through the reef and was now anchored about a mile offshore, nearly invisible with its blue-and-white hull merging into the pattern of whitecaps.

Parnell huddled with Bird, Laguna, and Fountain, going over their orders and synchronizing watches. The three were to climb up to the approaches of the prison and lay numerous small demo charges along its outer wall. At precisely 0200 hours, these would be detonated, each blast followed by a thirty-second pause. They hoped the explosions would create a large enough diversion to allow the incursion team into the prison from below.

As they disappeared into the rocks, Vassallo led the others along the beach to a rocky alcove with a high back wall. The water was deep but glowed with moonlight. Beyond the alcove wall lay a vast labyrinth of marine caves. In order to reach them, the team would have to swim underwater for about a hundred yards.

Parnell quickly broke out the goggles and goat bladders and passed them out. The goggles had wooden eyepieces linked by leather tie-thongs. With their gear strapped to their backs and the bladders blown full of air, they slipped one by one into the water and went under, Vassallo leading the way.

The water was warm and clear, the shafts of moonlight shimmering, forming a distinct shadow line near the wall. Red flicked on his flashlight as did Vassallo, their beams playing against the face of the rock. It was pockmarked, the color of solidified lava. It was flat and partially covered with seaweed, which swayed gently in the current.

Parnell trailed the Sicilian down, feeling the upward pull of his goat bladder. Ten feet, twenty. His ears began to ache. Forty feet, then fifty. He saw the bottom of the rock face, which ended three feet above a sandy floor that was merely an indistinct blur of gray white.

He watched as Vassallo disappeared under the wall and

then followed. He found the diver squatting on the sand beyond the opening, pointing ahead and up. Parnell's lungs were beginning to ache with oxygen need, but he knew he couldn't yet breathe from the bladder. At this depth, the pressure would prevent his lungs from expanding.

He shone his light on the backside of the wall, which sloped upward sharply. Vassallo pushed off the bottom and went past him, headed up. He stayed close behind him. Twenty seconds later, the Sicilian drew up, floating. He pointed at Red's bladder and made signs for him to breathe. Although the overhead was still submerged, they had reached a shallow enough depth to let their lungs work again.

First releasing air, he unwound the nipple of the bladder, stuck it into his mouth, and sucked in. The bladder air was warm and tasted the way rawhide smelled. Breathing evenly, he waited for the others to come up.

Sol Kaamanui was the first, rocketing by sleek as a seal, the onetime hard-hat diver for the Corps of Engineers in his element now. Next came Cappacelli and finally Smoker Wineberg, who shook his head at Parnell, his eyes glaring behind his goggles.

It took them eight minutes to reach an open pool. Red came up last with everybody already sitting on the rim, panting. Wineberg, his taut, wiry boxer's muscles showing cleanly through his wet T-shit, spat disgustedly. "This suckin' on goat guts is *bullshit*. I fuck near *drowned* down there."

The air in the cave was dank and cold and held the odor of spawning fish. Water drained slowly from the walls. Each day at high tide the entire labyrinth of caves was inundated by the ocean. Calcite stalagmites rose from the floor like stacks of rust-colored artichokes and veins of obsidian, locked in the rock, sparkled like black glass whenever the flashlights hit them.

The men quickly unsheathed their weapons and moved out, going in a line with Vassallo in the lead. He was intimately familiar with the cave system, having explored it many times during lobster-hunting dives.

Parnell checked his watch, hissed. They were falling behind schedule.

A woman's voice suddenly cried out, moaned, then dropped,
sliding down into an urgent Sicilian obscenity.

Instantly Bird, Laguna, and Fountain dropped to the ground.
They were on the lower prison approach road, the front of
the main building about seventy-five yards away, rising huge
and stone-dark and looking like a fort.

They lay absolutely motionless, listening hard. Another
cry came, then a man's voice, incoherent. Bird lifted his head.
Wild grass lined the road, about two feet tall. Off to the right
were olive and orange groves long gone to seed, the citrus
trees skeletal like blackjack oaks. Now came a riffle of laughter, female and throaty.

He signaled the others to remain and crawled off through
the grass. The blades were thick, dry as fall hay. He reached
the edge of a small gully and looked down the slope. There,
clear in a pool of moonlight, a man and woman were fornicating on a blanket.

"God *damn!*" Wyatt murmured softly.

The man was naked from the waist down, the woman's
legs wrapped around his back. His buttocks glowed white as
he thrust steadily back and forth. One of his collar insignias
glinted suddenly, indicating that he was a soldier, up here
with either his sweetheart or a whore from the nearby village.

Wyatt returned to the road to wave the others in, told
them they *had* to see this. They all crawled back to the gully.
Squinting down, Laguna swore and lasciviously sucked spit
through his teeth. "Look at that goddamn *hijo de puta,*" he
murmured. "Poundin' pussy while on guard mount?"

After a few moments, Bird tapped his shoulder and they
returned to the road. Cowboy chortled. "Hey, *chico,*" he whispered to Weesay. "Wait'll them charges go off. If that ole
boy's still stickin' her, she's gonna clamp up on him. Flat

squeeze his dick off." They both got to giggling until Wyatt gave them the cutthroat sign.

They continued on up the road, doing leapfrog dashes and going to ground, until they reached a flat, sandy area directly in front of the prison's main gate. The gate itself was made of weathered wooden crossbeams bound with rusty iron bars.

They lay in the grass to check everything out. There were no guard towers along the wall and no visible lights. The entire place had the medieval look of a Norman keep. Dozens of seagulls were perched along the top of the rampart. Occasionally one would lift off and hover on the wind. The air had turned gusty over the last half hour and now held the warm, moist odor of a storm.

They left the grass and worked their way to the left corner of the structure. Jagged cliffs on this side sloped down to the beach. The wall was fashioned out of roughcut sandstone and was heavily coated with bird guano. They could see the PT out beyond the reef, a vague block of white lines, stationary and oddly out of synch with the rest of the whitecaps.

Bird said, "Y'all take the gate, Weesay. Cowboy, you got this corner. I'll lay the seawall. Remember, thirty-second intervals on the fuses. Anybody spots you, duck and withdraw without firing. And watch out for that Wop stud comin' back in."

Laguna spat. "I feel good I shoot that fucker."

A twisting blast of wind lifted sand against their faces. Wyatt checked his watch, luminous little dials indicating 11:31. "Okay, let's do it," he said and shoved to his feet.

Down in the caves, they were lost, the continually upsloping walls and narrow, water-worn passages all starting to look alike. Vassallo was agitated, cursing, saying in Sicilian, "I *know* was here. Look, look, this place. To God I swear it."

Parnell glared at him. "I think maybe there never *was* a plate, *l'amico*," he said to him in Italian.

"Che? Che?" the diver cried excitedly. "This is what you

think?" He shook his head stubbornly. *"This* the place. Hey, I no hold the knife by the blade."

Red turned to Cappacelli. "What the hell does that mean?"

"You've insulted him, Lieutenant," Angelo snapped. Cappacelli always had a hint of cockiness in his tone, even when speaking to officers. He was of medium height and compactly built with tightly curled black hair and a broad, thick-skinned face. Although a trained Mohawker, he hadn't seen combat yet and was not completely accepted by the others. "The knife phrase means he doesn't lie," he said.

"Goddammit," Red hissed. "Then that means the son of a bitch really *is* lost."

For the last forty-five minutes they'd followed the diver all over hell searching for a brass plug plate he claimed he had seen many times. According to OSS premission research, an Egyptian archeologist named Massar had actually placed such a marker in 1920 after drilling into the cave system from the catacombs. To prevent the tomb area from being flooded, he had put in the plug and then backfilled the ten-foot-deep drill hole with cement.

To break into the catacombs, Parnell intended to drill a blast hole beside the cement seal, going in at least eight feet before placing charges. With the noise of their detonations covered by those from Wyatt and his men, they would enter the catacombs, quickly locate and retrieve the Caprano brothers, and then return through the cave system.

But now they had a major glitch, added to the potential ones that were already a part of the mission. What if the marker plate had somehow disappeared since Vassallo last saw it? It could have been washed away or stolen. Without it, there was no way to tell where the caves came closest to the tomb area. Or, what if the catacomb wall was thicker than ten feet and they weren't able to drill deep enough to blow through?

Red kept looking at his watch, trying to will the damned thing to slow down. It was almost midnight already. That left them only a three-hour window in which to drill and blast, locate the two mafiosi, then get back through the cave system before the tide flooded it. According to oceanographic forecasts, the tide would begin turning by 0300 hours. If they weren't clear by then, they'd be trapped between the impassable caves and the roused Italian prison detachment.

Sol came up. "Maybe the guy's just disoriented, Lieutenant. OSS was pretty strong the plate'd *be* here."

Red nodded. "All right, we'll give her one more sweep. Everybody spread out. But stay within light distance."

Parnell moved off along a drift to the right, the walls lined with jagged strips of anthracite. Unconsciously, he began really examining the stone surfaces. He had a degree in mining engineering from the University of Colorado and now his geological curiosity kicked in.

He saw that the walls were made of tightly compacted sandstone and shale, pinkish in color. It was called graywacke sandstone. Interspersed with the main matrix were feldspar and quartz along with a skeleton of silica. Precisely like the Old Red Sandstone of the ocean bottom during the Devonian Age. That turned him cold. This kind of rock was going to be a bitch to drill through.

Someone shouted, "Here, over here! I found the sumbitch."

The auger bit kept overheating, smoking-hot all the way back and up through the men's gloves as they worked the crossbar. Parnell instructed them to drill on a down slant so they could pour in water to cool the bit and shaft. Each time they did, a burst of steam blew back out the drill hole.

It was three feet to the right of the archeologist's cement plug. The continual emersion in salt water had turned the brass plate a dull green, and seaweed dangled from its seams. The inscription was barely readable. It said: *placed by dr hafazah massar 9:22:1920.*

The work was grueling, everybody pouring sweat, taking turns, even Vassallo, until their arms and shoulders grew numb. It was now 1:34 A.M. Thus far, they'd drilled only four feet into the rock.

Parnell ordered Cappacelli and the diver back to one of the tidal pools to get sand to tamp the drill hole before they fired. When they returned Angelo said, "The water's rising back there, Lieutenant. Looks like the storm surge's shoving more water into the caves than usual."

"How much has it risen since we came in?"

"A foot, maybe two."

Parnell tried to figure. They'd already used up an hour and a half to get just four feet into the stone, with at least five feet more to go before reaching a point close enough to the catacomb side to punch through. *If* the wall really was ten feet thick.

He waved Sol over. "This is getting dicey," he told him. "We better double up on the explosives. If it makes too much noise, tough shit. Can you boost that shape charge?"

Kaamanui nodded. "Yeah, I can rig something with one of the extension caps." He tilted his head. "Maybe we'll hit soft stone deeper in."

"Don't count on it. This rock's braze strata, tight as shit. I'll tell you the truth, Horse. I'm not sure we got enough charge to blow through at all." He looked into the big Samoan's always-placid brown eyes. "And once that tidal flood comes in full, we've got a problem."

"Yeah," Sol said evenly.

They drilled on.

Bird and Fountain sat in the sand in fading moon shadow. High overhead, a thickening cloud cover was damping the moon's intensity. In the bay, the PT had edged back through the surf line. It looked dark and sinister sitting out there.

All the explosive charges around the monastery wall had been set and timed, everything still quiet in the prison. They hadn't even seen the Wop lover. Now the three men relaxed, that part of their task over. But inside they were still tuned tightly with that continuous overalertness of an operation in progress.

Laguna had idly wandered down to the water's edge, where crabs clicked among the rocks. Here and there the tide had deposited tiny dots of phosphorescence. When he returned, he had one on the tip of his forefinger, the thing glowing a bright green like a speck of radium.

"Hey, check this," he said, holding up the finger. "Ain't that pretty? I wonder what it is."

"A crustacean," Wyatt said.

"A what?"

"A crustacean, a tiny crab. The things float round in the ocean. Back in Hawaii they shine pure blue." Bird had once served with the old 25th Infantry Tropical Lightning Division in Honolulu. Deadpan, he said, "Them little bastards is poisonous as hell, boy. You get their juice in your blood, we gonna have to cut off your finger. Maybe your whole goddamn arm."

Weesay stared. Finally, he said, "You shittin' me?"

"Hell, no."

"Aw, fuck!" he blurted and dropped to his knees. He began furiously dragging his hand through the sand. Bird exchanged grins with Cowboy. Laguna glanced up and saw their faces. He stopped, glaring at them. "Assholes," he croaked, sat back in the sand, and spat angrily.

Bird's grin faded. He looked out at the ocean, the tide visibly higher now, then swung his gaze back to the monastery and down along the rocky slope, scanning all the way to the beach, figuring possible attack lanes and firing positions.

Cowboy said, "What kind of weapons you figure they got up there, Sarge?"

"Probably just rifles and sidearms," Wyatt answered. "They ain't set up to defend nothing from the outside, jes' keep them poor-ass bastards on the inside." He glanced at his watch, cupping a hand over it so the dials would show brightly: 1:41. Their charges would start going off in nineteen minutes.

He eased himself to his feet. "All right, let's get the raft out and then set up security positions." He lifted his chin, indicating the north wall of the monastery. "I figure them Wops'll come down that main beach trail. We can set up fire-bases on both sides of the ridge. That one looks like a tit."

They moved off along the beach to where they'd hidden the raft back in the rocks.

The drill bit was in a little past eight feet, two more feet of solid stone between it and the catacomb wall. Everybody was getting visibly jumpy over the incoming tide, the water already midway up their calves. Even Vassallo was shooting frowns toward Parnell.

After his final stint on the crossbar, Red had gone back to have a look at their entry pool. He had a difficult time finding it. The water now covered the entire chamber where it was, its surface rising and dropping as if it were breathing. His flashlight shimmered on it.

Once more he checked his watch. In sixteen minutes Wyatt's charges would go off. He experienced a moment of claustrophobic anxiety, like a rat trapped in a drainpipe with someone about to open the floodgates all the way. Dismissing it, he turned and headed back.

At the drilling face, he told Kaamanui, "Start loading the hole now. We got about twelve minutes." He knelt down to examine the jury-rigged, shaped charge. Sol had added one of the auger extensions to the original explosive canister. Inside the canister was a copper cone that would channel the full charge into a single point, creating a focus of highest pressure. By adding the hollow extension sleeve, the charge would be doubled in force.

They quickly extracted the drill and doused down the shaft. Then Kaamanui wired up the shaped charge and shoved it down into the hole, making certain it didn't butt directly up against the bottom. Next he laid in the string of three, three-stick packs of DuPont Hi-Vee straight-granular dynamite and tamped sand around them until the hole was filled. All the charges had electrical blasting cap igniters and were wire-linked to a battery-and-plunger detonator.

Five minutes to 2:00 . . .

Parnell began placing his men into their assault positions, first Smoker, then Cappacelli and Vassallo, the three smallest men, with Sol and himself going in last. They checked their weapons, the soft metallic clicks of actuators flipping into full auto, safeties coming off.

The Sicilian diver stood there looking dumbly at Parnell. Slowly, he began to understand what this American lieutenant was ordering him to do. He began shaking his head and jabbering at Angelo.

Red frowned at him, turned to Cappacelli. "What the hell's he yelling about?"

Angelo was arguing with Vassallo, waving his arms. He swore and turned to Parnell. "The guy says he ain't going in there. It's a place of the dead and nobody told him he would have to go in."

"Then get him out of the line."

Angelo translated. Vassallo crept off.

One minute . . .

They waited. The air in the labyrinth had changed subtly as fresh ocean water was being flushed into the caverns. The suck and hiss of it filled the silence, intensified the passage of the seconds.

They didn't hear the first diversion explosion, but they felt it, a soft tremor in the floor and through the walls. Two seconds later another explosion came and Parnell thought, *Somebody's timer screwed up.* He looked up the line, everyone's head turned, watching him. Seconds snapped past. Another tremor came, this one stronger. It made the surface of the water riffle.

Red yelled, "Fire in the hole!" and rammed down the plunger of the detonator.

Two

The charges made a resounding crack that echoed through the cave system, explosive energy racing through stone. Chunks of cement and limestone were hurled back out of the blast hole, slicing across the surface of the flooded cave. Before the last echo vanished, Parnell was up, bellowing, "Go! Go!"

The explosion had blown a four-foot hole in the rock face, narrowing down toward the head of the shaped charge. It fumed with smoke and rock dust. Wineberg was the first man in, crawling, holding his weapon out in front. Then Cappacelli and Sol and Parnell, each shuffling forward to the blast hole like paratroopers leaving a plane.

The rock fragments inside the blast hole were jagged, sharp as knife blades. They cut at Red's legs and shoulders as he started through. The hole stank of fumes, was dim with drifting stone dust. Ahead of him, he saw Sol, carrying two satchel charges and his weapon, struggling to get his big body through to the other side. He finally did and disappeared into darkness.

Parnell also had a hard time getting those big shoulders of his through, wiggling and squirming until he was finally able to drop down to the catacomb floor. It was pitch-black.

Two flashlights snapped on, then another. Their narrow beams, looking solid in the dust, crossed each other like clashing swords. As Red flicked on his own light, another blast sounded faintly from the monastery's outer wall. Its small concussion made the drifting dust tremble.

He looked around. They were in a narrow crypt shaped like a corridor. Over the smell of explosives and stone dust, he caught a denser, more acidic odor like ancient vestments found in a basement. The walls, bearing chisel marks, had dozens of two-foot-high shelves cut into them where mummified bodies were stored. Each was encased in a cerecloth embalming sheet that made it appear like a giant chrysalis. The sheets had turned black and were as dry as dead leaves. The sharp edges of bone joints and skull holes showed clearly through the fabric.

The end of the room broached into a central rotunda from which other crypt rooms extended like the spokes of a wheel. In several of these, the corpses were hung from the walls instead of being placed in shelves. These were not bound in winding sheets but instead wore clothing from the eighteenth and nineteenth centuries. Some of the colors were still bright in the light. The faces of the corpses were devoid of skin and each had its head bowed. They looked like skeletal puppets put away in a closet.

On the far side of the rotunda was a small anteroom containing an iron railing, a tall stone crucifix, and an arched doorway. They hurried through it and into a larger room that felt quite cold. The walls were made of precisely fitted stone blocks seamed with a yellow mortar. A stairway led to a landing with a wide bronze door. The door had frames of Gothic bas-reliefs of saints. Beyond it, they could hear men shouting, the crack of boots on stone, and then the distant popping of small arms fire.

Blue Team had trained for this mission at the H-School of the OSS in Cairo. While there, they'd been given blueprints of the monastery. So Parnell knew that this particular door opened onto the north side of the arcaded cloister, the monastery's main courtyard. He had been told it would not be locked. By ancient Sicilian custom, the entrance to any catacomb or mausoleum was always kept open, to allow the spirits to wander the land freely.

Now he listened beside the door, its cold bronze aged to the color of green agate. Another of Wyatt's charges went off. "Kill the lights," he snapped. Total blackness again as he felt the others came up behind him. He pushed against the door. It didn't move. He pushed harder. It still wouldn't budge. Using his shoulder, he shoved with his full weight.

It was locked.

He turned on his flashlight, ran the beam along the edges of the door. There were no lockboxes or sliding bolts. He checked the hinges. There were four, made of two-inch steel. "Sol," he said.

"Yeah, Lieutenant?" Kaamanui answered close beside him.

"Those OSS pricks were wrong. This son of a bitch is locked. From the *outside*. Can we blow those steel hinges?"

"No problem, I'll use the ninety-one."

Bird was pissed, sitting out there in the rocks watching the Italian guards firing randomly from the prison's ramparts and listening to his own charges going off. Unfortunately, his first charge had been two seconds late. Goddammit, he hated glitches, even though this one didn't make that much difference. Still, it was a matter of pride. He was the best land demo man in the team, the professional, a thirty-year man. To be embarrassed by a malfunctioning timer? Bullshit!

He, Laguna and Fountain were now set out in good defiladed positions halfway up the rocky slope that abutted the north wall of the monastery. From there, they could lay out interlocking fields of fire against anyone coming down the main pathway to the lower beach.

For the last three minutes, small searchlights had been probing the building's approaches. Now a larger light came on, from the other side of a bell tower located on the northeast corner. Its beam was as thick as a Roman column and looked smoky from ocean mist. In the gusts of wind, he could hear the hot hum of the light's filaments. Its beam swept along the beach and then out across the bay.

It pinioned the PT.

Instantly the boat's twin .50-caliber machine guns opened up, their spaced tracers arching almost casually up off the sea as their deep, throaty muzzle bursts echoed off the limestone hogbacks. There was a bright flash and the shatter of glass from the big searchlight. It went out. The .50s fell silent.

In that buzzing silence, Bird detected another sound, a metallic jingling. It came from the right. He swung around. Forty yards below his position the rocks formed a shallow dish with its far edge rising into a sharp ridgeline. He saw a dark figure dart into and then out of view. Directly behind it came two others.

He cut loose with two quick five-round bursts. A man yelled and then bullets came sizzling past him and slammed into the rocks above his head. He threw out another burst, turned, and scurried to a different position just as the deeper, slower rap of Weesay's and Fountain's Thompsons came.

Abruptly the firing stopped, leaving only the sound of the wind up high, sighing like a sorrowful giant. Then it started up again, coming from the north wall, the rounds striking with a flat, chipping sound like pottery shattering. Once more the PT's .50s opened up, laying in suppression fire. Their rounds tore lines of holes just below the top of the wall.

Under their momentary cover, Bird shifted his position, shouting for the others to do the same. He found another rock hollow and went to ground. From it, he could survey both the main trail and the ridge beside the rock dish. He scanned it, letting his eyes fix slightly off-center to make silhouettes stand out stronger.

He saw Weesay and then Fountain skittering among the rocks. They were unwounded. He relaxed, nestled the Thompson against his arm only to feel its still-hot barrel on his skin.

Always a comfortable sensation. Another explosion went off, on the other side of the monastery, near the gate. It was the last of their charges.

The two top hinges of the catacomb blew off cleanly, the lower ones still connected but allowing the door to hang with a two-foot-wide space between it and the frame. Kaamanui had used a new plastic explosive called BG-91, a dense, rubbery combination of nitroglycerin, nitrocotton, and chalk, which had not yet been issued to regular infantry. To trigger the charges, he'd used a length of detonating cord half-hitched around each quarter-kilo lump of explosive.

Cautiously Parnell peered through the opening into the courtyard. There was neither movement nor firing there. That surprised him. He'd expected the guards to open on their position as soon as they heard the door being blown. He figured they must have assumed it was simply another of Wyatt's charges.

He quickly squeezed through the door space and dropped into a squat. Again he scanned the courtyard. Lights were on along the inner arcade. On the other side of the cloister was a wooden stairway up to a parapet that ran along the front wall. He could see soldiers hunkered down up there, now and then nervously lifting up enough to look down onto the approach road.

A large fountain stood in the center of the cloister, its pond clogged with weeds and wild vines, its tall stone statue covered with bird guano. The lights from the arcade cast the shadows of its columned arches across the flagstones.

Red waved to the others. One by one, they came out into the arcade and gathered beside him, down on a single knee. Wordlessly, he chopped the air with his hand, indicating for Sol and Fountain to move that way, toward the front of the monastery. They went, hunched over, their tennis shoes making no sound. He turned, slapped Cappacelli's knee. Together, they moved off in the opposite direction, deeper into the building.

From in-country agents, the OSS had pinpointed the Caprano brothers' position. They were housed in underground cells on the south side of the building, beneath what had once been the monastery's stables and workshops. The small cells had been the first living quarters for the monks who had built the structure in the seventeenth century.

To reach the two mafiosi they'd have to go through the main chapel and dining hall to a small wine cellar near the kitchen. The Italian guard, Silone, would meet them there, direct them to the cell area, and unlock the Capranos' doors.

By the time they reached the inner angle of the arcade, the heavy firing from the PT had grown sporadic. Sniper shots continued from the north wall. They reached a small room beside the chapel. From it were steps that led up to the main dormitory. The room contained carpenter's tools and metal boxes of 6.5mm rifle rounds. A double door opened into the chapel itself.

It was dark in the church, only a faint light coming from a sacristy off the chancel. The chapel was large with a high ceiling braced by thick, interlocked wooden beams. Most of the pews had been removed and the space filled with pallets of foodstuffs and crates of military equipment and stacks of raw timber. The air smelled of packing grease and sawn wood and the faint scent-memory of candle wax.

They crossed through the stored gear and went up onto the chancel platform. The altar was large, made of dark stone. It had been stripped of all religious items except a three-foot-tall crucifix made of anthracite. As they passed it, Cappacelli paused long enough to genuflect and make the sign of the cross.

The dining room was just on the other side of the sacristy, brightly lit by a string of bare bulbs down the low overhead. Three long, whitewashed tables with attached benches ran the length of the room. Holding close to the front wall, the men sprinted across the room and into the cooking area. It had three large, brick ovens, the bricks scorched black, stacks of dry grape branches for kindling beside it and pots and long-handled frying pans hanging from the walls.

The wine cellar was behind a black steel door and down several steps that were worn with age. Red flicked on his flashlight. The cellar was narrow, about thirty feet long, with another steel door at the other end. Alcoves and floor-to-ceiling wine shelves had been carved into the walls. All the shelves were empty of wine bottles. They could hear the soft, furtive chirpings of rats.

Something moved. The unmistakable leathery scrape of a boot against rock. Red snapped off his light as he and Angelo hit the floor. It was dusty, the stones peppered with rat shit. Parnell pulled his feet under him and began to crawl forward.

A man's voice whispered, "Yankee?"

He stopped.

Again: "Yankee?"

"Rebel," he answered quietly. It was the countersign he had been instructed to give to Silone.

"Sì, sì," the man said. "It is I."

They found him huddled in one of the alcoves near the door. His brown uniform was drenched with sweat. He looked very young and his face was pale, his eyes hollow and dark. He was trembling visibly and kept trying to see around the glare of Parnell's light.

Red waved his light toward the second door. "All right, buddy," he snapped. "Let's do this fast."

Sileno frowned. "You are all?" he asked fearfully. *"Santo Dio,* where the others are?"

"Never mind that," Red said. "Just get us to the Capranos."

The man's face jerked back from the vehemence of Red's voice. Then he sprang to his feet, nodding anxiously. *"Sì, sì, signore.* You are most kind."

There was another explosion from somewhere in the cloister, most of its sound absorbed by the rock walls. Still, its vibration triggered a chorus of rat calls while Silone's shaking hands attempted to unlock the door. Furious gunfire erupted outside, the tinny pop of Italian field rifles, then the deeper hammer of two Thompsons.

Oh, shit, Red thought. *Sol and Smoker just got discovered.*

Wineberg had broken the guard's neck with a sharp twist, the bone cracking as if he had snapped a large tree limb. The man went still beneath him, flat against the cloister's flagstones. The twin searchlights high on the parapet instantly began probing across the courtyard.

The light swept past him, came back, holding. He rolled to his feet and headed back toward the arcade. Bullets slammed into the flagstones around him with sharp, stinging collisions. He reached a column and dove behind it, found Sol's big body already there in the shadows, giving covering fire with his Thompson.

After leaving the others, they had stealthily worked their way to and along the front wall to a point near the main gate. They could hear guards up on the parapet, calling to each other. The back glow from the searchlights filtered down through the cracks in the wooden planks, stipling their faces and shoulders with shadow lines.

Kaamanui quickly laid out two charges banked against the wall, dynamite sticks this time with minute fuses. They quickly retraced their steps back to the side of the arcade where the catacomb door was. Just before they reached it, a shadow appeared deeper in the arcade. It was an Italian, still in his underwear. He spotted them, stopped, puzzled, then broke out into the courtyard, screaming and waving his arms.

"Stop that son of a bitch," Sol growled to Smoker, who was closer to the guard. "He'll expose us."

Wineberg was already moving, his Thompson on the ground, going up into a full sprint within a few feet of the arcade. Two seconds later he intercepted the Italian, smashing into him from an angle, going for his head. Their momentum carried both men down hard onto the flagstones. Smoker grabbed hair and jerked the man's head back, slammed the crux of his elbow under his throat and hauled back, twisting sharply at the same time. He could feel the bristle, waxy-sleekness of the man's hair against his cheek as the vertebrae snapped.

Now he hunkered down behind the column as Sol tossed his weapon to him and they both raked the parapet and the opposite arcade, orange-white muzzle flashes flicking in the half dark over there, the enemy rounds coming in hot and thudding into the massive column. The wild crescendo bounded and rebounded off the ancient walls.

Don Vito stood in the center of his cell like a dark statue.

Parnell was the first through the cell door. Before he could say anything, both Cappacelli and Sileno jostled past him and dropped to their knees before the Mafia chieftain. Humbly, they took his hand and kissed it, murmuring, *"Bacciamo le mane."*

Red stared dumbfounded at Angelo. Then he bent forward and jerked him to his feet. "Go get the other one, damn it," he barked into his face. Cappacelli and Sileno rose and darted back into the corridor, the other prisoners calling out now, shouting questions in their thick dialect.

Parnell faced Don Vino, stared into those solemn black eyes. The man's neck was as thick as his head as the flashlight beam illuminated the thick angles of his features, casting them into a molded image of stolid, almost mindless malevolence.

"You are Don Vincenzo Caprano?" Parnell asked in Italian.

Don Vino nodded, a single dip of his head.

"I'm Lieutenant John Parnell of the United States Army, sir." He withdrew a square-folded piece of fabric from his trunks, snapped it open. It was a yellow silk handkerchief with the letter L on it in script. He held it up. "I was instructed to give you this."

The L stood for Lucania, Salvatore Lucania, better known as Lucky Luciano, the famous New York mob boss. A silk handkerchief was the traditional Mafia way of introducing the representative of one capo di capo to another. Luciano, himself born in Sicily, was now serving a life sentence in New York's Donnemora Prison. Yet he was still the most powerful leader of the American Cosa Nostra.

Fanatically patriotic to his adopted country, Luciano had offered in early 1943 to help the government fight the war against the Axis. First off, he boasted, he would bring about a complete halt to the sabotage the Germans were conducting on the New York waterfront. He did exactly what he said. Next, he offered himself to act as a link between the United States and the Sicilian Mafia.

For generations this deadly, secret organization had exerted a near-total control over all of Sicily. When Mussolini came to power, he swore to wipe it out. By the mid-thirties, hundreds of its members had been killed or imprisoned. As a result, all mafiosi hated the fascists.

The Allies quickly recognized a rich opportunity, use the Mafia as a source of intelligence on the island and as a stimulus for revolt among Sicilians who had been drafted into the Aosta and Arsietta Divisions of the Italian Army. Most importantly, the organization could act as an interim government to maintain civil order once the fascists were driven out. So, they quickly accepted Lucky Luciano's offer.

The two most powerful capo di capi in Sicily were Don Vincenzo Caprano of Camporeale in the midlands, and Don Giovanni "Gio" Borgo in the Nabrodi Mountains west and northwest of Mount Etna. Luciano chose to deal with Don Vino. There were rumors, still unsubstantiated, that Borgo had been instrumental in the arrests of the Capranos and was now openly helping the Nazis.

Don Vino silently studied the handkerchief in the half-light. If he decided to keep it, it would signify that he would commit himself and his men to assist anyone who had brought it to him. This promise was binding, locked in by Mafia honor.

At that moment, Cappacelli returned with Santegelo Caprano. He was more slender than his brother, with a shaved head and probing eyes offset by a surprisingly warm grin. He and the don did not touch each other but exchanged a long look.

Abruptly, Don Vino nodded to Parnell, again a mere dip of his head, and shoved the handkerchief into his pocket. He said something in the Sicilian dialect. Red turned questioningly to Cappacelli.

"He says he must kill the prison commandant before we leave, Lieutenant," Angelo translated.

"There isn't time."

"But this is a matter of honor," Angelo cried. "You can't interfere."

"Like hell I can't." He turned back to Don Vito. "I speak with great respect, sir," he said in precise Italian. "But you must understand my situation. We have very limited time and must leave the prison immediately." Don Vino seemed about to speak. Parnell cut him off: "I'm sorry, sir. We will leave *now.*"

"Jesus Christ, Lieutenant, you can't do—" Angelo protested.

"Shut up, Cappacelli," Red hissed. To the elder Caprano he spoke again: "You are my responsibility, sir. If I say we leave, we leave."

The Mafia chieftain stared at him without expression. Beside him, Santegelo's grin disappeared. He whispered something to his brother. Vino continued to stare, then tilted his head slightly, as if appraising Parnell. Finally he said, "Yes, we go." He moved quickly out the door.

The other prisoners were calling out loudly, begging to be released. Don Vino raised his arm. Instantly everyone fell silent. The five men, moving in single file with Sileno leading, went back through the wine cellar.

* * *

Corporal Angelo Cappacelli was shocked clear down to his Sicilian roots. Holy Mother Mary, this crazy lieutenant had just insulted a capo di capo. A terrifying, unthinkable act! Deep, inbred fears, absorbed into his consciousness from the moment his mother, Antonietta, had popped him from her body onto a dirt floor in the tiny upland village of Morello twenty-two years before, now rose out of the marrow of his bones to constrict his stomach muscles with dark apprehensions.

He had left Sicily when he was eight, gone to live with relatives in New York, in squalid tenements on the Lower East Side. Two of his uncles were members of the old Ciro Terranova gang. As he grew into puberty, he idolized them, relished their flashy lifestyle. By the age of thirteen he was regularly being arrested for ticket-running or rolling drunks outside the speakeasies and horse poolrooms in Mulberry Bend.

Afraid for his future, Antonietta shipped him off to her oldest brother, who lived in the Italian conclave of North Beach in San Francisco, California. His name was Joe "Shoes" Calugia, an odd-job man with Joe Adonis's organization on the coast. He oversaw shakedown operations in the city, collected the *pizzu* or protection money from Italian businessmen, Nevada-based pimps, and the fishermen who ran their crab and cod boats out of the bay.

After high school, Angelo worked on the docks and aboard fishers until the short mob war of 1939 when his uncle garnered him muscle work, "putting the spurs" to recalcitrant clients. Soon he was on the brink of becoming a *piciotto,* a mob apprentice who would eventually have gone on to earn his bones and become a full-fledged member of the Cosa Nostra. But then Pearl Harbor happened. The next day, filled with outrage and a splendid sense of patriotism, he enlisted in the U.S. Army and asked for immediate combat.

Now, bringing up the rear of the small, hurrying group,

he felt an ominous pull back in time, to the terror-filled whispers and the sounds of dark horsemen in the night and the chilling realities of *omerta*.

Lieutenant Broadhouse, squatting on the coaming of the PT, listened to the firing coming from inside the monastery, thinking, *Jesus, they're into it now.* He turned, squinted toward the beach, then scanned slowly outward, trying to read the chop pattern over the reef line on the south side of the bay. The wind had picked up considerably, now little flecks of rain in it. Wires of lightning showed far off along the southern horizon. He was unable to see a pattern in the waves.

He climbed over the transom and dropped down onto the conning deck. Above him, the two gunners were still in their swivel seats, now and then throwing out short bursts. "Give 'em some heavy suppression fire," he shouted to them. "Along the top of the wall. Make the fucking Wops keep their heads down."

The .50s opened up, both going, their muzzle blasts like shotguns in rapid fire going off, cartridge casings flinging hot from the receivers and pinging down onto the cockpit deck. He waved the boat's boatswain, Chief Warrant Officer Stone, to him, bent close to his ear to shout, "Juno, get those anchors raised. Then put out a leadsman with a power phone. I'm going in as close to the reef line as I can."

Using only his middle engine, he got the boat moving slowly toward the southside reef. Up on the bow the kneeling leadsman called back the bottom depths through his power phone, continually heaving the hand lead out ahead of the boat and then retrieving it, its leather markers dripping as he relayed, "By the fathom three," and then, "By the fathom two and a half."

The bottom was shallowing quickly. The minimum depth the PT could cross without scraping or beaching was eight feet. "By the fathom two," came with a crackle through the phone. Broadhouse eased the throttle until they were barely moving against the tidal current.

Now the leadsman shouted, "Reef visible dead ahead!"

The lieutenant shoved the running engine's synchro-meshed shaft chain into reverse and slammed on the throttle. The boat trembled as the Hall-Scott came up into power. But it was still moving forward on momentum. There was a solid jolt as the cutwater struck coral. Then the prop grabbed, pulling backward. Slowly they drifted back out into deeper water. Broadhouse eased off, letting the PT drift. The rain peppered his face and the heat coming off the barrels of the .50s warmed his neck. He made another run and finally took up a position thirty feet off the reef and less than a hundred yards from the beach, all three of his engines on idle now to counter the drift.

He waited.

They reached the arcade in the middle of a full firefight, Sol and Smoker behind their column, illuminated by a search-light out of their view beyond the overhang. The other one had already been shot out. Red tracer rounds from the PT burned past over the north wall.

Angelo stepped into the arcade and spotted something. He ducked back, held, then went out again, firing along the outer wall of the dining hall. Red came out behind him, also firing. Two guards were down just beyond the light.

He pointed at Don Vino. "You and your brother head for those men down there. You see them?" Don Vino nodded. Both mafiosi had their revolvers out. Red whistled. Kaamanui looked their way, turned to say something to Smoker. They immediately began putting out covering fire across the courtyard.

"Go!" Parnell shouted. He and Cappacelli opened up again.

The Capranos took off, Vincenzo lumbering, his brother loping easily, both firing across their chests. The small pops from their handguns were nearly lost in the thunder of the

Thompsons. They quickly reached Sol. He waved them through the catacomb door. In a moment, they were gone into the burial chamber.

The firing stopped, leaving only the whistling of the wind. With their clips spent, Red and Angelo quickly tore off others, the spent ones clinking onto the flagstones, rammed them in, and charged the weapons.

"Signore, when is my turn?" Silone said.

"You don't come."

The little Italian guard's face went white. "Oh, please, *tenente,"* he pleaded, "do not leave me here. They will kill me."

"No."

"Prego! Prego! Oh, mi Dio!" He began to weep. He fell to his knees, his palms together in supplication.

Parnell looked at him, swore. He reached down, grabbed the sweaty shirt, pulled him up. To Angelo, he said, "You ready?"

"Let's do it."

They opened up again. From the center of the arcade came more Thompson rounds. "Go!" Parnell shouted and leapt forward, firing, the spent cartridges tinkling onto the flagstones. He still had hold of Silone's shirt, pulling him along, the man blubbering, *"Oh, grazie, mi tenente, grazie."* Two bullets slammed against the inner wall. A sliver of stone struck the Italian in the face. He yelped but kept running.

They reached the catacomb door. Another bullet struck it, made the bronze ring. Parnell shoved Pinole through, then twisted and continued firing. He waved at Sol. Kaamanui darted past him, went through the doorway. Next was Smoker. Red pointed at Angelo, jerked his hand back. Cappacelli quickly disappeared beyond the door.

Red gave one final burst, his receiver locking back on another empty clip, then dove for the doorway and also disappeared back into the catacomb.

                              *   *   *

The outer room was still dry but there was water in the rotunda and the catacomb spokes, about two inches, the sound of the ocean coming in back there through the blast hole.

As planned, Sol remained behind to lay a trip-wire charge at the door, a quarter-kilo of Ninety-One with a spring-activated fuse. Once everybody was through the blast hole, he'd lay another beside where the brass plate had been, catch anyone coming through behind them.

Parnell herded the others along. "Move it, move it," he bellowed. Once he actually shoved Don Vino. The Sicilian boss said nothing, but Red noticed Cappacelli in the flash-light shadows looking aghast. He thought, *That little guinea's beginning to piss me off.*

Don Vino went out first. Like Sol and Red, he had trouble squeezing through. Santegelo followed, then Silone, Angelo, Smoker, and finally Parnell. The water level in the cave system was now waist-high, everybody wading around. He put his light back through the blast hole, Sol over there finishing the trip charge, then leaned in and pulled him through.

The lobster diver, Vassallo, was obsequiously begging the don's forgiveness for the discomfort of the high water. "You!" Red shouted at him. "Get us the fuck out of here."

They could feel the surge and suck of the tide as they moved along, Silone in the lead with the don next and the rest strung out in a line, each holding the shirt of the one ahead like kindergarten kids crossing a street. The air felt impacted, filled with the scent of open ocean.

Although Vassallo's instincts were perfect and he took them directly to the pool where they had entered the labyrinth, it took twenty minutes. The water level was now up to their chests and they stumbled about as if walking on a flooded reef.

They had left the bag containing the goat bladders and goggles on a high shelf, but the water surge had set it afloat. It took them another four minutes to find it, wedged into a crevice. The gear was quickly handed out, Wineberg grumbling, the Capranos and even Silone seeming already familiar with the makeshift breathing apparatus.

With bladders inflated, they went underwater one at a time. Their flashlight beams were diffused and made the water glow faintly green like a hotel swimming pool. Red was the last one. He swung his light around to make certain everyone was out. The water level was nearing his throat. The caves seemed to moan softly from the darkness and he could feel a breeze against his face, the air being compressed and forced out through seepage cracks in the rocks.

The muffled crack of an explosion sounded like a large firecracker in a metal barrel. Someone had just triggered Sol's first booby trap. Parnell took several deep breaths to oxygenate his lungs. Then, holding his bladder under his arm, he dropped off the rim of the rock pool, went down a few feet, somersaulted, and began kicking toward the bottom.

When Wyatt heard the soft, hollow blast of Sol's plastic, he knew they were on their way out. For the last several minutes, he'd been content to lie back, listen to the PT throwing heavy grazing fire up along the rampart, keeping the guards' heads down while the firefight in the monastery went on, things popping in there now, more firepower and determination from the Wops than anybody had expected.

His first instinct had been to charge up the hill, get up on that damned wall somehow, and take the dagos from the rear. But that wasn't his assignment. Parnell and the others could handle the inside; it was his job to secure the outside.

As soon as that trip charge went off, all firing had ceased from both the monastery and the PT; now there was just the sound of the wind and rain. The rain had turned squally, coming in quick, hard rushes of sea-smelling water, warm as urine from the desert winds straight out of North Africa. The moonlight was completely gone.

He shifted slightly so as to see the south end of the beach, a vague, gray curve. Then he checked Weesay's and Cowboy's positions and moved his gaze up to the monastery. Soon as the guards figured out that the raiders had gotten in through the caves, he knew, they'd come down to try and take them on the beach. If they still had fight enough to leave the monastery grounds again.

He ticked his fingernail against the Thompson's clip to test how close to empty it was. A thick *ping*. Still half a load. He sat forward and squinted out there, waiting.

They emerged into a full squall, the huge drops dimpling the surface of the reef pool. By the time Parnell came up, Sol already had everyone moving back toward the beach, the men going hard against the deeper water and the hiss and surge of the waves.

Reaching the tide-narrowed beach, they double-timed it in the wet sand, everybody shaking water from their weapons. The rain had momentarily tapered off and they could see the PT close in, faintly hear its idling engines and the burble of the exhausts.

They reached the raft and quickly slid it into the water. Waves jostled them and buffeted against the raft as Sol and Parnell held it while the others climbed aboard. Red glanced up at the monastery, its outlines dim in darkness. It was silent. Too silent. He had expected sniper fire at least. The Italians knew precisely where they were now and should be firing.

He whistled. Seconds later, Bird and his men emerged from the rocks, coming down fast. No one spoke. Swiftly they got into the raft and took up paddles. He and Kaamanui heaved the raft forward and leapt aboard, its bottom rippling unstably.

The Italians opened on them in one heavy volley, all their rifles going at once like a firing squad, a sudden, flashing crack and then bullets zipping and whipping into the water all around them. Someone grunted and air began hissing out of the raft. There was a momentary halt as the Italians cranked back rifle bolts to ram in new cartridges and then another volley came. By then the PT's .50s were going and sailors were kneeling on the deck firing rifles along with the team's Thompsons, everybody hammering away.

There were no more volleys.

The raft began to deflate rapidly, going flaccid and filling with water. They struggled with the paddles, trying to reach the boat before the thing folded completely. Even the two mafiosi stroked with their hands. Water sloshed around in the bottom. Parnell saw that someone was lying limp-dead against the center seat. He felt the warm sleekness of blood around his ankles. The man had a brown uniform. It was Silone. He was dead, shot in the back of the head.

They had to swim the last thirty yards. Hands pulled them up the side of the PT, its wooden hull smelling of new paint under the sharper stench of cordite smoke. A few sniper rounds started coming in. One ricocheted off a torpedo tube, another slammed into the conning barrier. Each was answered by bursts from the .50s.

Lieutenant Broadhouse already had the PT moving, playing his engines and rudder blades as he took them into a sharp turn. He got his bow pointed directly at the reef. The engines increased in their rumbling, gently at first as they headed out of the channel. Vassallo and Cappacelli were up on the conning deck with the captain.

Five minutes later they were through the reef. Broadhouse rammed on full power, sending the Hall-Scotts up into a wild roaring. The PT lifted its head up onto the step, water hurling off the chines and a tall roostertail curling white astern as they headed due east into open ocean, straight for Sicily.

Three

Camporeale, Sicily
9 July 1943
1818 hours

In the Capranos' home village a long procession wound down the dusty road from the church to the cemetery. Men in collarless white shirts and vests, women in black dresses like widows' weeds, and children carrying plaited palm leaves, everyone as solemn as mourners. A fat priest in green vestments led the procession. Close behind him came a bier of straw and wood with the erect statue of Saint George, carried by several young men in red sashes.

Blue Team and the two mafiosi, now on horseback and trailing several mules packed with their gear, drew rein beside a stand of Tuscan cypresses downslope from the town's cemetery. The night's storm had quickly moved out earlier that morning, but by late afternoon a new front had come in, winds strong enough to create twisting dust devils across the golden, sun-seared hills of western Sicily. The new overcast was thick and gave the twilight a purple-gray glow.

Someone in the procession suddenly spotted Don Vino and cried out his name. The front of the long line halted, those behind bunching up, glancing to see what was happening. The priest turned, the saint's bier paused. There was a moment of absolute silence.

Then the people rushed down the hill toward the horsemen, the animals snorting and sidestepping. They gathered around the don's horse in an excited clot. The women curtseyed, the men dropped into obsequious half kneels, reaching out to touch his hands, the flanks of his mount.

Wordlessly, his reptilian eyes expressionless, Don Vino nudged the horse forward through the crowd, the people scattering out of his way and then reforming behind him. He and Santegelo moved up toward the town.

Parnell and his men hung back. They were now dressed like peasants, baggy trousers with puttees and work caps. Their wore their American uniforms underneath and they'd scuffed up their jump boots and rubbed mud into the leather to hide their military appearance.

Earlier, just before first light, Broadhouse had deposited them on a lonely stretch of beach north of the port city of Marsala. Inland of the beach were large salt-drying ponds and short, squat windmills and a matrix of levees. Two OSS liaison agents met them, standing in the wind and rain with the horses and mules.

The lead agent's name was Biagio Fericinni, code-named Silver. He owned a small jewelry shop in Palermo, a stiff-faced, rapid-talking man. The other was simply called Pino, a slender, effeminate youth who grinned in quick flashes. Until Parnell and his men linked up with American units after the invasion, Fericinni would be their only contact to the OSS and their direct commander, Colonel James Dunmore, creator of the Mohawkers, who was now G-2 for Omar Bradley's II Corps of Patton's Seventh Army.

All through the long day they had ridden inland, across endless low hills of wild grass and scattered villages like scabs nestled among huge fields of wheat and corn and lemon and orange groves and vineyards, the sun searing hot and the air misty with dust.

Now Cowboy turned to Cappacelli. "Hey, *paisano,* what's *this* bullshit all about?"

Angelo gave him a sharp look. "What're you over here, a smart-ass?"

Fountain drew back, grinning icily. "Whoa, boy, back off."

Snorting, Angelo heeled his horse and cantered on up the road. Next to Fountain, Parnell and Bird exchanged glances.

From a distance, the town of Camporeale looked like every other small western Sicilian town, as if generations ago men had stacked rocks together to form a simple pile. It sat halfway up a hill with stands of cork oak and pine at the top.

In close, it wasn't much better. Narrow alleyways and *bassi* houses built of umber-colored stone blocks, blue or green doors on leather hinges, a small town square with a fountain and a stone lion's head in its center. Heaps of animal manure were piled in corners and there were shallow sewer-channels down the center of the cobblestone streets. The air was dusk-hot and stank of shit and lemon blossoms and cooking cabbage.

Neither Caprano brother had made an appearance since disappearing into Don Vino's house, a small stone building with peeling, sun-bleached stucco and the butt ends of oak beams protruding from its outer walls.

It was now nearly eight o'clock at night. For the past two hours, many men on horseback and carrying gun belts and sawed-off shotguns had visited the don's house. Most would remain a short time, then leave, loitering about the square, watchful, giving the Americans the dark eye. Cappacelli said they were called *bravi* and were Don Vino's "soldiers" come to pay obeisance to him.

Parnell and his men lounged around the square's fountain, their horses and mules grazing down in a field of tare grass nearby. They had watched as the procession finally reformed and continued its journey down to the cemetery where the priest prayed for a few minutes. Then everyone came back to town, their mood totally different. Now they sang as they walked up the hill, accompanied by an old man playing a goatskin bagpipe that Angelo called a *cerontella*.

They carried the saint's bier back into the church and then came down to the square, everyone gathering branches and armfuls of hay, which they used to make a bonfire. Food and bottles of wine appeared and several young men with bells on their knees danced and a gnome of a puppeteer put on a show in a wooden box with a red curtain using marionettes dressed as Saracen devils and the Paladins of Saint George and Charlemagne.

Cappacelli explained: "It's a festival for a good crop. *Santo Girogio* is *padrone* of the harvest. The moon saint. They rub holy sweet oil on his face and hands and then the priest says prayers." He shrugged. "So God will give a good harvest."

"Which harvest?" Laguna asked him. "Them lemon and orange groves?"

"No, this is for the wheat and corn."

Weesay laughed. "Hey, this year God and Blue Team gonna make their prayers come true, huh?"

Two years before, as the war in North Africa deepened and the need for military food stores increased, the fascist government had begun confiscating the wheat and corn harvests and shutting down the independent mills. Now everything was being processed in two huge milling complexes outside Palermo and the finished grain was locked in huge silo parks. With corruption rampant in the government, many people in western Sicily were now actually starving.

The larger of the two milling complexes was located at Altafonte, ten miles south of Palermo. This was to be Blue Team's second mission. Accompanied by Don Vino's mafiosi, they were to raid the complex and blow open as many of the storage silos as they could, let the people get at their own harvest. More than a humanitarian gesture, it was to show the Sicilian people the Allies could be trusted to help them.

Hopefully, they'd assist the incoming troops once the invasion started.

Two women finally came down to the square with food for Parnell and his men, plates of braized goat meat and eel, raw snails with thick slices of onion and tomato, and stone bottles of a thick, sweet wine made from raisins. Across the square the wind made the fire roar, sent sparks whirling and coiling up into the darkness.

Several little boys had been solemnly watching the Americans. They were dressed in ragged knickers and knitted peaked caps with colored puff balls at the tips. Every one of them had the sniffles. Now, as one wiped his hand across his nose, he drew something from one nostril, peered at it, then tossed it to the ground.

"Holy Christ Almighty," Fountain cried out. "Did y'all see *that?*"

"What?" Weesay said.

"That little bugger jes' pulled a goddamned *worm* outta his nose."

"Oh, yeah," Laguna said nonchalantly. "I seen that in Mexico. They's belly worms." He shrugged. "No big thing, *meng.*"

Cowboy disgustedly studied the food in his plate. Except for Laguna and Cappacelli, the others had also instantly stopped eating. "Y'all think there's worms in *this* shit?"

"Goddamn!" Wineberg said. He laid his plate on the ground.

"Look at this," Weesay snorted derisively. "What're you guys, fuckin' cherries?"

"Cherries, my ass," Cowboy said. "Y'all can eat this if you want. Me, I just lost my goddamn appetite."

Parnell decided he wasn't particularly hungry either. Instead, he watched the dancers for a few moments, then motioned Angelo over. "What do you know about this Don Vino? I look at those people, they treat him like a goddamn king."

"That's what he *is,* Lieutenant. Hell, he was famous even before I *left* Sicily. *Uomini rispettati,* a man of great respect."

"I thought the Mafia was a *bad* thing over here."

"It depends on who you asking. To these people, Don Vino's a saviour, a *pezzo di novanta.*"

"If he was famous when you left, how the hell old is he?"

"I'm not sure. Maybe sixty. He started young, as a *campiere.* You know, like a security boss? On the big estate of Baron Di Falmi." He laughed, slapped his hands together, a glancing blow. "Man, *nobody* fucked with that estate afterward. One time he faced down a hundred bandits, all by himself. He just *looked* at the fuckers, rode his horse back and forth, and give 'em the evil eye. You know? They backed off quick, man."

Near the fountain, the bagpipe screeled suddenly, a bottle broke. People began tossing carnations, the people getting drunk now.

"Finally, he went on the Maquis, too,*"* Cappacelli continued. *"He* became a bandit. The *best.* I heard stories he whacked at least a hundred men, one-on-one combat. I seen his crew one time when I was six. They rode black horses and used skulls for their guidons and lances.

"He got into vendetta with two mafiosi. *Capofamiglias,* subchiefs, from Giammaria and Roccamena. Popped 'em both. The Organization figures, Hey, we can use this guy, so they make him capo, and bada-*bing,* pretty soon all the *capofamiglias* in western Sicily vote him boss of bosses."

Bird turned aside, spat, came back. "What in hell's all this Mafia shit anyway?" He pronounced the word may-fia.

Angelo turned a cold eye on him. "It ain't shit, man."

"Then what *is* it?"

"A secret organization."

"Like the goddamned Masons?"

"Fuck no," Angelo snapped. "Listen, I can't tell you about it. But all you gotta know is don't never rat-shit one of 'em."

Wyatt chortled.

"Somebody's comin'," Wineberg said. He pointed downslope. Moving lights were visible down there, torches. They came from several directions and seemed to be converging onto the town road out beyond the cemetery.

Cappacelli stood up, grinning. "Hey, it's the horse racers," he cried. He started counting torches. "Sixteen . . . no, seventeen this year."

Fountain's head came up. "Horse racers?"

"Yeah. Whenever there's a festival, they hold a challenge race. The best horsemen from the other towns come in to ride."

"Well, cousin," Fountain said, getting up. "now y'all talkin' *my* gait."

The two riders fought in the street, both shirtless as were all the other horsemen. No one knew exactly what had started it. A slur, an insult to a man's mount. But then they were fighting and the women and the children withdrew into their houses while the townsmen stood and silently watched the battle. The horses, all stallions, stamped and snorted nervously under the roar of the fire and the grunts and heaves of the two combatants as they pummeled each other and rolled on the cobblestones.

Then a knife came out and another and the two circled each other, darting in, lunging and parrying, their blades floating back and forth, catching the firelight. Soon, both were cut and bleeding. Now one man suddenly feinted to his left and immediately slashed at his opponent coming in with a sweeping backhand. His knife sliced through the other's lower stomach, drawing a thin red line in his skin that quickly erupted with blood. It ran down into his trousers. The man's teeth chattered. He held his free arm against the wound and tried to step in to counter another slash but lost his balance and fell to one knee. He stared motionlessly at the ground, then slowly fell onto his back. His knife clattered away and he lay there holding both hands over his wound.

The other riders carried him to a wall and propped him up against it. A woman came out of one of the houses and examined him. She was skeletal and her black hair was tightly braided. Angelo said she was the *strega,* a woman who concocted potions and medicines and practiced black magic.

She swabbed something onto the man's wound and then wrapped it in a large white cloth. The blood immediately seeped through. She ordered the other riders to lift him and followed them as they carried him into her house. Almost immediately, the women and children came back out into the square and the music and festivities began again, as if nothing had happened. No one spoke to the winner of the fight. He walked over to his horse and laid his forehead against its neck, panting.

"Damn," Fountain said, grinning. "These old boys take their racin' almost as serious as back home."

"The one got shanked was from Montagnola," Angelo said. "They say he was pretty good."

"Who gets to run his mount now?" Cowboy asked.

"Nobody."

"Hey, *chico,*" Weesay teased. "Why you no race him? You're like Gene Autry, right?"

Cowboy turned and looked at the horses, the riders beginning to mount up and the animals shifting, stamping their hooves loudly against the stones, their eyes excited, showing white. He'd watched them coming in earlier, moderate-sized animals running about fifteen hands high, compact with deep chests and sturdily muscled hindquarters.

Good quarter horses, he had thought. There were sorrels and blacks and chestnuts and one bay with a blaze on its face and white stockings. None had saddles, only cotton blankets draped over their backs. They wore snaffle bits and simple rope bridles and tasseled headbands, each a different color.

He'd also noticed the riders, the way they sat their mounts, far back like children new to riding, no unity of balance, no smooth oneness with the animal. And they hard-bitted them, jerking and shouting. Born and raised in eastern New Mexico, Fountain had spent his whole life around horses and cattle, just like his daddy, old Johnny Glenn Fountain. Like him, he'd ranched and wrangled mustangs and worked the rodeo circuits, bulldogging and riding the wild broncs, and possessed a special touch with horses.

Johnny Glenn had always told him, "I don' never like no one to work a horse over with a trace iron. There jes' ain't no need. All you gotta do is get inside his head, figure out what he's thinkin' before even he does his own self. You do that, he'll flat follow you anywheres." It was said he bonded so well with horses, they'd even follow him to the shit house and wait while he did his business.

Cowboy swung back. "Hey, Cappacelli, can anybody race?"

Angelo shrugged. "I guess so."

"Go find out if I can use that old boy's horse," he said and felt his blood rising.

The horse's name was Scioperante. It meant Striker. It was a red bay with a small head, deep chest, and finely muscled hind legs. Cowboy gently walked up the reins, murmuring softly to the animal. It snorted and tossed its head and eyed him nervously. He touched it, as lightly as a breath, its shoulder, then its neck and cheek and muzzle, stilling it. He leaned his weight against it, a mutual touch of flesh and breath, beat and thud of heart as he continued speaking to it softly, calling it Chipper.

The other riders had moved to the lower field and were dashing their mounts, warming them up. Men with torches went down the road to lay out the course. It would extend beyond the cemetery, curve around through a small stand of cork oak, and return to the town square. People had already begun stationing themselves along the track.

Fountain, shirtless now, continued whispering. The horse quivered. With a single leap, he mounted, Scioperante rearing back and sidestepping. "Shoo, shoo," he cooed, running his hands down the thick neck. He turned the animal with his knees, letting the rein go loose. They moved across the square and into the field.

They started it with a whistle. The riders let out a shout and the horses squatted and leapt ahead, everybody bunched together. Cowboy jerked his knees and leaned forward as his horse sprang out, jostling for a moment against another and still another and then lengthening its stride as space opened.

Down the road they pounded, the first torch coming up. Quickly the faster animals forged ahead, forming a line. Cowboy leaned forward, up off his haunches, his face down close to the horse's crest, feeling the bristle of its mane against his throat, hearing the heavy blow of its breath and the thunder of hooves coming up to him in a joyous, heated rush.

He passed a horse on the inside, the rider twisting his head to look at him. Veering slightly with a shift of weight, he went hard by a second one. He was now five off the lead, the front-runner a black horse with a flowing mane. They passed the second torch, the road curving slightly, and then the third that stood just before the cork oak stand.

Under the trees the shaking rumble of the horses was like the roaring of wind. The riders and their mounts were large black shadows finely flecked with torchlight. Coming out of the stand, he quickly passed two more horses as they went into the stronger curve on the south side of the cemetery.

The horse directly ahead was the one with the blaze. Its white stockings flashed and glowed as they swept past the next torch. He could hear the horses' breathing deepen and shorten as they began the climbing pull back toward the town, the lights of it like fishing boats on a dark sea and the fire, halved now, casting a false sunset.

He drew abreast of the blaze. Its rider was furiously lashing it with a short quirt. As he cleared by, he put his forehead against Scioperante's neck. It was tight with muscle, hot as if it were fire-warmed. *"Now,* boy!" he shouted. *"Take* 'im!"

He felt the animal respond, a lift along his thighs, a surge. He closed with Black Mane. The fire was 150 yards out there. He saw the churning haunches of the other horse off his left

side. The rider turned his head back once, then again. He bellowed something and began furiously slapping his hand back
and forth across his animal's mane.

Seventy-five yards . . .

They were nearly abreast now. Cowboy felt a stumble
come and a quick adjustment, coming up through his horse's
right shoulder. They had fallen back slightly. As if in self-
rage, Scioperante's ears were laid back flat. Once more, they
came nearly abreast.

Twenty-five yards . . .

When they crossed the finish line, they were a foot behind Black Mane, both animals curving to the left, out into
the field, and the others coming up behind, everyone easing
down until the animals were trotting, blowing hard. Black
Mane's rider swung back. He was grinning. As he passed
Cowboy, he said something and cut his fist through the air,
nodding.

The rest of the team came down with Fountain's shirt and
a bottle of wine. They stood around slapping him on the
back. "Chu almos' take that black *figlio di puttana,* baby,"
Weesay cried.

Smoker said, "Twenty more yards, you'da had the fucker!"

Cowboy wiped down Scioperante, talking softly to him.
The horse shook its head, its lungs still heaving. Afterward,
he walked the animal down the road to cool him off completely. The torches were almost out now, their tiny flames
snapping in a strong wind that smelled of dust and ocean and
storm.

He drank from the bottle. It tasted thick and syrupy.
When he came back up, he paused beside the cemetery and
sat on a stone while the horse cropped in the tare grass. He
took another drink and closed his eyes, remembering home.

The sound of distant gunfire began around 11:30, deep-
throated big guns like kettledrums under the wind. It had

begun to rain just after the horse race and had increased rapidly. Soon the town square was empty, the fire smouldering and seeping the stench of wet ashes.

One of Don Vino's *bravi* had come and sullenly informed them they were to be bunked in an old stable. He brought them pallets of straw and cotton blankets stuffed with dried lentil leaves. The stable was merely a stone room made of piled slate with a weathered Dutch-type door. It had straw on the floor and melons hanging from the beams that lent a cool pungency to the other, staler odor of horse and pig manure.

Parnell laid his pallet near the door. The rain made only a soft hiss against the stone. He pushed the door open and sat looking out at the dark fields stretching mistily away into the night. It suddenly reminded him of another moment, he and his father on a hunting trip near the Blue River in the Arapaho National Forest in Colorado when he was still in high school.

During a heavy downpour, they'd come onto an old miner's cabin in a meadow. Like this stable it was made of stone. Inside was a wooden bunk and a metal stove and empty sugar and coffee cans stamped with the logo of the Silverthorne Mining Company. During the night the rain turned to snow. He awoke just before dawn and crept out and saw an eight-point white-tailed buck and four does crossing the meadow in the snowfall, their breaths smoking. He could easily have brought down the large male but he didn't fire, the animals out there running and bounding with such grace and purity.

It struck him now how different these two structures felt: the miner's cabin with a sense of frontier, of crossing into lonely, unseen places; this Sicilian rock stable filled only with the sour heaviness of an unchanging, unchangeable enduring.

He looked at his watch. It was 12:41. Soon, he thought, soon.

His men were asleep, grumbling with wine snores. The rain began to ease and then it stopped completely. Even the wind dropped. He could hear the distant explosions of guns and the thudding crack of bombs clearly now as Allied aircraft of the North African Air Force hammered Italian targets to the east.

Fatigue finally took hold of him and he fell into sleep, rolled into his blanket, its rough cotton like soft wire against his throat. Suddenly, there was a crash, like a faraway cracking in the earth. He jerked up, peered out through the open door.

Along the southern coast that lay seventy miles off, the sky was lit by huge flashes that made it appear like a vast umbrella through which showed bursts of gray sunlight. It would fade into darkness for a few seconds, then light up again. Now flares burst into life, like high stadium lights, unmoving and glistening with deadly serenity. Then came the huge candle-shaped tongues from naval guns offshore and the intricate matrix of rockets and hot tracer rounds, the rumble of it all rolling across the hills, dipping and surging in volume.

Someone moved up behind him. It was Bird. He said, "Well, Lieutenant, looks like them ole boys finally got here."

"Looks like," he said.

Silently, they watched the invasion of Sicily begin.

Among the many items covered by Roosevelt and Churchill at the Casablanca Conference in early 1943, one of the most pressing was where to go after the defeat of the Axis forces in North Africa. The Americans wanted to assault Fortress Europe across the English Channel immediately. The British, primarily for their own purposes, desired the focus of the war to remain in the Mediterranean. Eventually Roosevelt conceded and plans were ordered for the invasion of Sicily.

After heated debate, the Combined Chiefs of Staff chose one plan, code-named it Husky. It was scheduled for 10 July 1943. General Eisenhower was again appointed supreme commander, with British General Alexander as his deputy.

Following the surrender of German and Italian forces in

North Africa on 13 May 1943, Allied ships, men, and matériel began pouring into six major staging ports in Algeria and Tunisia. Two Allied armies would be involved in the invasion: the U.S. Seventh now under the command of Patton, recently promoted to lieutenant general, and the British Eighth under General Montgomery.

Patton's force included his old II Corps now commanded by General Omar Bradley, the 36th and 45th Infantry Divisions, the 2nd Armored Division, and the 9th Infantry, along with elements of the 82nd Airborne in reserve. The British Eighth possessed the XIII and XXX Corps, with two divisions in reserve.

Husky called for two invasion sectors. Patton's three main assault forces, code-named Joss, Dime, and Cent, would strike Licata, Gela, and Scoglitti on the southwestern coast, while Monty's two assault groups, called Bark and Acid, would go ashore at Portopalo Bay and Formicette to the west and at the Avola coastline in the east.

Once beachheads were firmly established, the Brits would race northward to the key port of Messina, a hundred miles away and only eight miles from mainland Italy across the Straits of Messina. Patton's primary target was Palermo on Sicily's northwestern coast.

When initially informed of the Husky plan, Patton was furious. He knew the Brits still considered the Americans mediocre fighters and had pressured Eisenhower into using them merely as a covering force to protect Montgomery's western flank. Uncharacteristically he held his tongue this time and accepted the inferior role. But he confided to his staff officers that once he took Palermo, he'd send his armor racing along the northern coast and "beat that goddamned Limey bastard into Messina, come shit or high water."

The Axis Order of Battle included the Italian Sixth Army composed of the XII and XVI Corps, and the German XIV Panzer Corps with crack elements of the 15th and 3rd Panzer Grenadier and Herman Goering Divisions. Overall Axis commander was Italian General d'Amata Guzzoni.

By midnight of 9 July the Husky armada had reached assault positions off the coast despite having had to fight rough seas and forty-knot winds since Africa. Suddenly and almost miraculously, the storm abated. Preceded by air strikes and airborne assaults by troopers of the 82nd and British 1st Airborne Divisions, most of whom landed far from their designated jump zones, the main invasion waves began streaming shoreward by 0200 hours of 10 July.

The initial opposition was weak and by dawn all Allied forces had established solid beachheads. But throughout the day, enemy resistance stiffened. Strong counterattacks developed all along the Allied perimeter, mostly spearheaded by German tank units. The most concerted was against the Dime force at Gela, where the Americans nearly got driven right back into the sea. Fortunately heavy artillery barrages and pinpoint fire from naval support ships decimated the German advance.

By evening of 11 July, a forty-by-twenty-five-mile-wide beachhead had been secured in the American sector. But the British, although their Bark and Acid groups had successfully linked west of Avola, began encountering ever-increasing opposition, particularly as they neared the ancient port city of Syracuse, twenty miles up the east coast.

Patton, always at the hottest place along the line, had set up his headquarters with Bradley's II Corps at Gela. As his own sector became solid, he began noticing the battle and intelligence reports coming in from the Brits and realized Montgomery's thrust northward was apparently stalling. Jumping at this opportunity, he immediately ordered his forward units to begin moving inland, one into central Sicily toward the western slopes of Mount Etna, the other along Highway 115 to Agrigento and then Palermo.

The race for Messina was on.

Four

Waffen SS Sturmbannfuhrer Witt Keppler sat watching the Allied bombers, American B-25s, pounding hell out of the city's waterfront, black smoke boiling up into the sky over the Bay of Palermo. Now and then tactical escort fighters, Spitfires, thundered close overhead, coming off strafing runs along the inner harbor.

He was at an outdoor café called the Birreria Italia, a Mafia *circolo* or social club in the Quattro Canti section of central Palermo. It was a slum area of dark, narrow alleyways and shabby tenements interspersed with the pink domes of Moslem *kubbas* and minarets from the Saracen occupation in the tenth century. Parked up the block was his VW-82 *Kubelwagen* staff car, his driver sitting at attention behind the wheel.

Although the late morning was already stiflingly hot, Keppler seemed to have maintained his cool, Nazi arrogance. He was dressed in a walking-out summer uniform of light green, chest medals glistening in the sun and his *Dienstmutze* cap bearing the SS Eagle and death's-head in gold pulled low on his forehead, shading his eyes. Beneath the cap, he was completely bald, the result of scarlet fever when he was nine. A black briefcase sat atop the tile-covered table.

Suddenly another Spitfire came over the water, guns going. Bullets slammed into buildings, stitched lines of holes in the street. The dun-colored aircraft flashed past, pulling up and away. Undisturbed, the major idly noticed it had pulled to the right. On the Eastern Front, the Russian fighter pilots always pulled to the left, going with the torque of their counter-spinning props.

He shifted his body slightly, aware of the stickiness of his skin. God, how he hated heat like this. Born in Bavaria, Witt much preferred icy marshes and snowy woodlands. Until six months ago, his *SS-Freiwilligen-Gebirgs* Division had been posted in the Carpathian Mountains in eastern Czechoslovakia. Then suddenly it had been ordered to western Yugoslavia to hunt down Communist Partisans.

It was well skilled in such work. Earlier, in Poland, its brutal *Ensatzgruppen* or Action Groups had slaughtered Jews and mental patients. "Useless eaters," they called them. In Yugoslavia, they quickly captured and beheaded over seven thousand Partisans, men and women, in two swift operations called "Black" and "Snowflurry."

During these huntings, Keppler had proven himself exceptionally adept and ruthless. This caught the eye of a high-ranking officer on General Kesslering's intelligence staff. Since Keppler spoke fluent Italian, he was immediately reassigned to Italy to help eradicate a highly active group of Communist resistance fighters known as the Corps of Volunteers of Freedom who were being supplied and armed by the British intelligence section called the Special Operations Executive.

The CVF had been created by a doctor from Milano named Constantine Fratoni. One of his ardent followers was a young Spanish Jew student named Augustin Friedl-Real whom *Abwehr,* German military intelligence, had found was operating with several bands of the CVF in Sicily. Keppler and his company of *Waffen SS* troopers had been dispatched to hunt them down.

Sicily was critical to the Germans as a defensive barrier against Allied penetration of mainland Europe. When word of the freeing of the two Caprano brothers by a military-style strike force reached Kesselring's intelligence staff, they immediately realized the Allies intended to use the Mafia against Italian and Nazi units on the island. When the invasion started, the Germans immediately sent two fresh German divisions to Sicily. And ordered Major Keppler to use whatever means necessary to stop any linkage between the CVF, the Mafia and the Allies.

He was at the Berreria to meet with the other most powerful capo di capo in Sicily, Don Giovanni Borgo. Operating from the town of Capizzi in the Nabrodi Mountains, Borgo and his son, Tino, controlled all black market, protection, and prostitution operations in Sicily. He also owned politicians and fixed prices on hundreds of commodities simply by controlling the production unions.

When Mussolini began his initial attack against the *Unione Siciliano,* the public face of the Mafia, Don Borgo had openly cooperated with the Fascist regime. It was even rumored he had been instrumental in the capture of the Capranos in 1938. Now he was the toast of Palermo, hobnobbing with Fascist and Nazi military leaders and Sicilian aristocracy.

Another Spitfire swept past. The downdraft of the plane's props stirred the torpid air that stank of dust from bombed-out buildings and rotting produce and dead animals, all of it merging into the sweet, cool scent of the ocean. He checked his watch. The don was late. He ordered another cognac from his waiter, an old man with one eye and a limp.

The outer street was air-raid empty, but he saw faces peering furtively from windows. He studied their dark, flat eyes. He despised these people, a base and uncivilized race who had been enslaved for nearly twenty-five hundred years.

They were too stupid and docile to deserve anything besides death.

Suddenly, two black Fiat Topolino sedans swung around a distant corner and raced toward him. They screeched to a stop in front of the café and five armed young men in dark suits leaped out and took up positions fore and aft of the cars, scanning the street.

A moment later, two other men emerged from the second car. The first was Don Gio, dressed in high style, a Norfolk jacket and riding breeches, glistening foxhunt boots, and dark glasses. He was taller than the usual Sicilian with a shock of thick, prematurely gray hair.

Keppler rose, stood at casual attention, appraising the man as he approached. The broad face, slightly lined, carried strength in a gross, earthy way. The second man was oily-skinned, his sweaty, bulbous body in a suit that appeared too small. His name was Pasquale Triolo. He was mayor of Palermo.

Keppler clicked his heels together, bowed his head. "Good morning, Don Borgo," he said in precise Italian. "You honor me with your presence."

Borgo's face broke open into a broad, startlingly gracious smile. "Ah, *Majore,* yes, yes." He nodded and sat down. Triolo sat to his right, Keppler to his left.

Don Gio gazed at him, still grinning. "Your uniform. Is good looking. I like it." He spoke with the heavy slurring of the Sicilian dialect.

"Thank you."

"So many pretty medals. What they all for?"

"Merely military designations."

Borgo said something to Triolo, pure dialect, too rapid for Keppler to follow. He thought he caught the word *fita,* cunt. Both men laughed. Triolo glanced nervously at the officer. Witt showed no reaction. The one-eyed waiter brought a pitcher of lemonade and gold-rimmed glasses. When the don drank, he made slurping sounds.

"So," he said, smacking his glass down loudly, "now we talk."

Keppler launched into his presentation. He would give Don Borgo five hundred thousand British pounds, he said, tapping his briefcase, for his assistance. "To do what?" Borgo asked. To create a mutual trust between the *Unione Siciliano* and the Germans. "It is stupid to trust *anyone*," Borgo said. But when trust is mutual, Keppler countered, both parties benefit. "How do *I* benefit?" Borgo demanded. By obtaining complete freedom of operation in all levels of Sicilian life.

Don Gio laughed. He had large teeth. He drank another glass of lemonade before answering, "I *already* possess that."

"Unfortunately it is now shared."

Borgo's eyes instantly went hard as flint. *"Rifiuto!"* he snapped. Then he and Triolo again exchanged words, Keppler catching the name Caprano several times along with obscene, enigmatic metaphors. Finally the Palermo mayor turned to him, saying in faulty German, "Be careful, *Sturmbannfuhrer.* This gentleman is . . . easily insulted."

"I apologize for that. But does he know Don Caprano is free?"

"Of course. He is not particularly disturbed over that."

"But does he also know Caprano is now working for the Allies?"

Triolo's face went pale.

Don Gio waspishly snapped his finger. "Enough German shit," he growled. "What? What?" When Triolo explained, Borgo again cut loose with another stream of Sicilian profanity. His bodyguards turned to look. The don glared across at Keppler, then rose and walked out to the sidewalk, stood for a moment, came back. He placed his palms on the tile table, leaned forward. "You know this thing for true?"

"Yes, Don Borgo. It's very dangerous for you now."

"Then what I must do?"

"First, kill the Capranos," Keppler answered quickly. "Second, help me capture members of the CVF."

"What is this fucking CVF?" He turned to Triolo. "You know of these?"

The mayor explained. When he was finished, Keppler said, "Unless these matters are resolved, Don Borgo, you will never be absolutely secure. If the Allies are victorious, they will protect Caprano and come after you."

A motorcycle came roaring up the street, a British BSA, the throaty rap of its engine bouncing off walls. The American bombers had left but distant explosions could still be heard out on the freighter docks. A young man and woman in leather racing togs were on the cycle. They stopped behind the don's Topolino. The young man climbed off and came to the table.

Keppler knew who he was, Tino Borgo, the don's twenty-five-year-old son. He was extremely handsome with classic Greek features and thick, curly black hair. His shoulders were broad, showing through the leather, and his eyes were a watchful green. He walked into the café patio with a sailor's swagger of arrogant self-assurance, then stood and studied the German major coolly.

Mayor Triolo rose. "Come, *Sturmbannfuhrer,* we walk?" he suggested in German.

Keppler deliberately left his briefcase on the table. They went up the block and stood beside a bomb-shattered church with beggars sleeping among the rubble, the Sicilian talking nervously of when he had visited Germany and of the beauty of the linden trees on Strasse Hindenburg. Back at the café, the Borgos were in a heated discussion, both flinging their arms about. Tino's leathers shone in the sun like a seal's skin.

Witt moved his gaze to the woman on the motorcycle. She combed her hair, one shapely, skintight-encased leg up on the protector bar. Her hair was long, down over her shoulders, the rich glossy color of polished ebony. It had been aerated by the wind and framed her beautiful face and dark, flashing eyes. She was Countessa Erice Salici, the twenty-seven-year-old wife of Count Rudolpho Salici, heir to vast Bourbon estates in east central Sicily, twenty years her senior.

German Intelligence knew all about the countessa. Born of Veronese aristocracy in northern Italy, she had attended finishing schools in Zurich and Paris, had known only luxury and pampering all her life, was strong-willed, occasionally used opium, and possessed a wild, impulsive nature that prompted her to perform bizarre things like swimming naked in the fountains of Rome, drunkenly riding on the hoods of Parisian taxicabs, and indulging in sordidly orgiastic affairs with artists in Venice and Ravenna.

Don Borgo waved them back. Tino and the countessa left, hurtling past the two men, Erice's newly combed hair flying as she gave the tall German officer an aloof, sleepy look.

The don came right to the point. "Show me your money."

Keppler unlocked his briefcase, opened it, and turned it around. The British pound notes were wrapped in *Waffen SS* bands. Borgo lifted two, smelled them, replaced them, and closed the case. "One thing," he said. "I want good German guns. And soldiers to show my *bravi* how to use them."

"Agreed," Keppler said.

He watched as the mafioso and the mayor sped away and then ordered another cognac and looked at the smoke still rising into the clear, hot Mediterranean sky over the harbor.

Altafonte, Sicily
16 July 1943
2216 hours

Blue Team and a single mafioso *bravi* named Alessandro were strung out along a railroad track, a double line that curved down out of a beech forest. Just over the ridgeline on their right the waning moon looked like a lopsided white basketball in the sky. The night was still save for a low humming that came from their target three hundred yards downslope, the government grain-milling complex.

The installation covered about ten acres with twenty storage elevators looking like dark, sixty-foot flashlight batteries in two lines just inside the western rim of the complex. There was also a power station, three processing mills, several outbuildings, and a small guard barracks. Two tall stone aqueducts crossed over the rail tracks on the south end, carrying water from a reservoir higher in the hills down to the mills and electrical-generating water turbines in the power station. The complex was now under total blackout with only tiny blue marker lights showing along the buildings.

While training in Egypt, the team had run sand table exercises on the installation using data collected by the OSS agent Fericinni, which fixed the positions of key buildings, guard posts, and operational timetables. Parnell also had schematic printouts of the elevator foundations that showed the precise spots in which to place their demo charges.

Since four of the silos were ancient and made of stone blocks instead of steel sheeting and circular girders like the others, there would be two demo teams. The steel structures could be brought down easily. As they toppled, they'd knock the others down like a deck of cards. But the only way to get to the grain in the stone silos was to blow huge holes in their bottoms and let the grain's own weight force it out onto the ground.

Cowboy came running along the track. "We've spotted the GPs, Lieutenant," he said. "Two men in each."

Parnell consulted his watch. It was 10:19. He looked down into the complex. It was blanketed in a thin haze from the smoke issuing from the mill stacks. He cursed. According to Fericinni's last report, the mills were supposed to be temporarily shut down for cleaning before the spring crop of corn and wheat came in and not restarted until midnight.

Red knew that floating particulates from grain processing could be as explosive as gasoline and set off by the smallest spark. Now they were going in there to set off demo charges! *Well,* he thought, *maybe the cleanup crews're just giving a final flush to the blower systems.* Either way, they couldn't scrap the raid now. This might be their only opportunity.

"All right," he said. "Hit 'em."

Fountain ran off.

From far away came the sudden rumble of artillery fire. Red glanced up in time to see the tops of the trees on the upper ridge silhouette for a moment against flashes of light. He took a deep breath, felt himself perfectly calm. The air coming down the hill carried the turpentine scent of pine bark.

They had left Camporeale in the midafternoon, the team along with Don Caprano and six of his *bravi,* all on horseback, avoiding the small, bleached-looking villages. By evening they had begun climbing steadily into the foothills of the Cuccio Range, which eventually became the Concha d'Oro, the Golden Shell, which ringed Palermo. Soon they passed through pistachio and walnut plantations and scattered stands of pine and beech. The 2,500-foot elevation turned the night chilly.

Parnell had divided the team into three crews. He and Kaamanui would hit the steel silos, Bird and Laguna the stone units. Meanwhile, Wineberg, Fountain, Cappacelli, and Alessandro would first neutralize the two guard posts on the southern rim of the complex and then set up security. The two demo crews would quickly enter the complex by using the water flume to the power station and cross to the elevator banks. Once all the charges were set and timed, they'd withdraw through one of the guard posts and link up with the don and his men and horses waiting in the forest.

Red shifted his explosives bag and the reel of detonating cord on his shoulders, checked the safety of his Thompson. He and all his men were dressed in dark paratrooper jumpsuits that carried no insignia. But around their necks they wore their rubber-rimmed dog tags, and small U.S. flags were sewn on the inside of their collars to identify them as American soldiers, not spies.

They waited, Red slowly beginning to feel his blood moving faster, coming up to it. Ten minutes passed. Twelve. Then a pinpoint of blue light flashed twice down the slope, then twice again. The two guard posts had been neutralized.

"Let's do it," he said, and came to his feet, running.

* * *

It was Cappacelli's first kill. *Jesus Christ Almighty!* Made his mouth dry, his hands tremble slightly. Nothing like when he was in San Francisco, the City, laying muscle to those stupid *bichero* rat fucks who were too slow paying their *pizzu* or getting cocky and hard-assed, him putting the spurs to them. But that had been simple: a little blood, some broken bones. This was different, man.

He and Alessandro had come up on guard post three from out of the dappled moonlight, the little thing looking like an outhouse with the two soldiers sitting inside with their heads down as if they were sleeping, both wearing fruity red fezes. Alessandro scuffed pebbles, which made the two guards look up. One stood and came out, a *soldato scelto,* a senior private.

Alessandro took him instantly, a clean slice across the throat, the guy gurgling for a moment with blood shooting out, while Angelo charged through the little door at the other as the man came up off his stool, his broad face suddenly drained of blood. Cappacelli put his boot knife right into the man's chest and hit bone. The guard shouted and then the knife found softer flesh and went right into his heart muscle.

Now Angelo stood over the body, the blood all over his knife hand and on the dirty wooden floor, bright in the glare of the twin bulbs. Beside the guards' stools was a field telephone and a small power box, probably for the electrical fence. He turned and looked at Alessandro, the mafioso calmly wiping his knife on the leggings of his victim.

The guard shed was already beginning to smell of fear and raw flesh, like dog piss. He stepped around the other dead guard and looked up toward guard post four, Smoker and Cowboy up there. He flashed his tiny blue vest light: twice. Again. Two double flashes came back.

Alessandro was going through the pockets of the dead guard inside the shed. He pulled a silver ring from the corpse's finger, turned, and held it up to Angelo, offering it.

Cappacelli shook his head. The mafioso shrugged, put it into his own pocket, his crude face as devoid of emotion as a stone statue.

And Angelo thought: *Cool, cool.* This one had steel *coglioni,* all right. Gonads the size of fucking grapefruits. It was the pure Sicilian don't-give-a-shit face of a mafioso he remembered. The steel of *omerta.* He felt a surge of affection and pride rise in him. Alessandro was of his people, himself. A *villano,* a countryman. Angelo looked up at the moonlit ridge, the flashes of artillery still highlighting the treetops, and inhaled, feeling the sweet rush of coming home.

He hadn't noticed that the field telephone had been knocked off its cradle during the attack.

The water was cold, the four of them going down the aqueduct on their backs, legs out front to take any hit of an unexpected crossbeam, Parnell in the lead, then Wyatt, Weesay, and Sol trailing. The aqueduct was old, built in the Roman style of cut-and-fill stonework with arches. The water trench was about four feet wide. The interior stones were water-smoothed as polished granite and filmed with a slimy layer of moss and bacteria.

They were in the one that led down to the power station. They'd had a time getting up into the water trench, nothing protruding to hook a line to. They finally had to toe-climb the side, holding on to the edge of an archway. Once they were immersed, the water made only a faint rippling sound but contained a strong grade-line pull.

Sol gazed up at the sky. The sides of the trench were faintly etched with moonlight. He grinned. The surging of the water reminded him of something, bodysurfing in Hawaii. As a teenager he'd lived there for two years with relatives on the island of Oahu. They taught him how to bodysurf, the real surfing, riding the big waves off Makapuu Point and Makaha Beach, not the way Californians *haoles* played in the beach break and thought they were natives.

The island combers had always come in in sets of seven, glassing up smoothly so he could ride in tight at the very edge of the curl, his down shoulder slicing and hissing through the water. Sometimes he'd miscalculate the speed of the break and it'd catch him, sucking him forward and down with a scary *ooooh, shiiit* feeling gripping his stomach as it broke completely and slammed him into a wild, whirling chaos of white water where he didn't know which way was up.

That same liquid, drawing-forward feeling was what he was experiencing now, skimming through the darkness as the pull of the water increased, the aqueduct's grade line steepening as it dropped toward the entry tunnel to the power station. That was going to be the tricky part. According to Tericinni, there was a heavy wire screen just inside the tunnel. If they missed grabbing the cement crown of the entry, the force of the flow would suck them against the screen where they'd be trapped underwater.

They had worked out a system, practiced it back in Egypt. Each man would hit the screen flat-footed, letting his legs take up the shock. As the water pressure instantly built against their backs, it would force their bodies upward. Shoving against the screen at the same time, they'd be able to surge high enough to grab the crown edge and pull themselves free.

Kaamanui tilted his chin, looked along the line of his body. The power station was less than fifty yards away. Its sides were dirty white. He could feel a gentle vibration in the water now, like a tiny electrical charge. It was coming from the rapidly turning vanes of the water turbines inside the power station.

The flow was beginning to hump slightly as it picked up more speed. He saw a dark shadow suddenly rise in front of the entry tunnel. Parnell. In a second, he was gone, to the side. Next appeared Bird, up and out. Then it was Laguna's turn. Sol saw Weesay's back and head lift partially out of the water. For a moment, the young Mexican struggled. Then his hands slipped from the cement crown. He fell back into the water and disappeared into the tunnel.

A second later the dark half dome of the tunnel loomed over Sol. His boots rammed into something soft, Laguna's body up against the wire. The water pressed powerfully against him, lifting. He went with the vector of its force, shoving, and cleared the water, blindly fumbling for a handhold on the tunnel's crown. There, he got one hand secured and held on with all the strength in his arm and shoulder.

Fighting against the heavy rush of the water, he twisted back into it and began searching for Laguna with his other hand. He touched canvas. Laguna's explosives musette. He clamped down on it and began hauling back. The water was like a powerful wind that buffeted and curled around him, made his ears flutter. His back and arms began to burn. For a second, he saw Weesay's shoulder break the surface. But his grip on the cement was gradually slipping. Growling, he gave it all he had, forcing strength into his fingers.

Suddenly his own weight began coming off. Bird and Parnell had hold of him and were pulling at him and reaching beyond for Laguna. They finally got them both over the side of the water trench and down onto a metal parapet that circled the power station.

They sat against the wall, panting. The vibrations of the turbines and the softer humming of the generators riffled through the cement. Weesay coughed and hacked and vomited water. *"Madre de Dios!"* he finally managed to gasp. "I thought I was fuckin' *gone, meng."*

Sol glanced at him. He reached out and slapped the back of his head lightly. "You clumsy little *fuck,"* he growled.

Weesay grinned, then started coughing again.

Parnell crawled over to him. "You okay?" he asked.

"Yeah, Lieutenant." He took a deep breath. "Yeah, I'm fine."

"Then let's move," Red said.

The forward grain elevators were made of steel sheeting with welded seams in sections, round as water tanks. They were streaked with rust. Built atop large cement slabs, they had external web-and-flange I-beams around the bottom and ground struts affixed, four of them each on a cardinal compass point.

Small drifts of fallen grain were banked around the bottoms of the elevators. They were filled with rat tracks and holes and the grain smelled sour from mildew. A small metal lean-to stood on the side of each silo. These housed electric motors that operated the tall flight hoppers, belt booms that lifted the grain out of rail gondolas, bringing the processed grain from the mills on the other side of the installation.

Leaving Bird and Laguna to handle the stone silos, Parnell and Kaamanui quickly worked their way along the spur tracks that ran between the elevators. A line of empty, badly weathered gondolas was parked at the south end. They were hooked to a fireless switch engine, stubby as a toy.

They paused beside the first silo in line, both sniffing at the air. In the night's stillness, the milling rollers and blowers generated a soft rumble. They couldn't see the haze in the moon shadow down here, but the air smelled of flour smoke and warm grain husks, a fall odor.

Kaamanui glanced over, said, "Those mills are operating already."

"Yeah, that fucking Fericinni."

They scanned the area. No visible movement. Parnell checked his watch: 11:14. He tapped Sol's arm. Kaamanui rose and sprinted across the tracks, his boots making soft scuffing sounds in the gravel.

Their demolition plan was simple. Two charges on the flanges and angle plates of the I-beams on the south side of the first two silos in each line. Another would go on the struts on that side. Since the flanges controlled weight stress, once they were blown out, the full weight of the silo and stored grain would instantly shear the beams' webs and struts, causing the entire structure to topple toward the blast. As each fell, it would smash against the next one in line, forcing it over in the same direction.

Parnell had difficulty squeezing his big arms between the beams and silo bulkhead. The metal felt warm from the weight of the grain. There were nets of wheat moth floss everywhere on the bulkhead, fine as spiderwebbing.

Each of his charges was made up of two three-pound bundles of DuPont Toval ammonia granular dynamite sticks taped in opposition. The firing system was ordinary blasting caps connected to a detonating cord trunk line and acid-pencil timers set on ten-minute delays.

He finally completed the base charges, started on the strut set. It was 11:36. He heard the sound of a truck far down along the approach road to the granary, probably the start-up workers coming up. Suddenly there was the sharp rattle of a motorcycle starting somewhere inside the complex. A moment later, its headlight flashed up against the buildings near the mills.

"Shit!" Parnell murmured and speeded up.

Cappacelli heard the cycle start and then spotted its headlight coming across an open equipment storage area straight toward them. He instantly switched off the light, plunging them into darkness.

Both men watched through the small guardhouse window. The two dead Italian soldiers were now propped up against a wall. Angelo's mind flew through options. He realized the cyclist was probably the sergeant of the guard. An idea occurred to him. *Maybe,* he thought, *just maybe.*

He felt for one of the soldier's fezes, took off his own watch cap, and put it on. Outside, the motorcycle bounced over tracks, its light dancing. Swinging into a turn, it pulled up in front of the shed. The bike was a Moto Guzzi model with a sidecar and a Breda 30 machine gun mounted on its handlebars. Cappacelli took a deep breath and poked his head around the corner of the shack.

"Aiy, cazzone cafone," the rider called sharply. "Your fucking phone isn't working."

Angelo squinted. In the back glow of the headlight he could see the man was a lance sergeant. *"Spiacente, Sergente Maggiore,"* he said, keeping his face in the shadows, his hand over his mouth. "My asshole *compagno* broke the receiver."

"Can you repair it?"

"Sì."

"Then make it fast."

"Sì, Sergente." He ducked back in.

The sergeant didn't move. They could hear the cycle's grumbling idle. They waited, Cappacelli's heart going cold. Seconds went past. Five . . . ten . . . At last the sergeant gunned his engine and roared off.

"Shit!" Angelo snapped. "The prick didn't buy it. Get out!"

They ran up into an outcropping of rocks near a stand of birch up the slope. The sound of the cycle bounded and echoed through the silence. Then lights started coming on, tall stanchion lights, section by section, gradually throwing the entire complex into misty brilliance.

Thirty seconds later, a machine gun opened up, its rounds tearing the little guard shack into shreds.

Parnell had just completed his last charge on the second silo and was tying it into the detonating cord line when the lights began coming on. He could hear the switches clicking overhead. Soon the entire complex was washed with bright light, softened slightly by the thick haze. He caught sight of Sol kneeling behind a silo lean-to. A hundred yards beyond, the Italian machine gunner was hunched over his cycle-mounted Breda still throwing bursts toward the guardhouse. A siren went off, then another. Three Italian soldiers came running up to join the machine gunner.

Almost simultaneously the other team members outside the fence began laying in cover fire. Their Thompsons sounded deep and slow. The Italians immediately withdrew behind several piles of wheat fodder. Now Kaamanui cut loose, raking them from this side. Two men went down. The machine gunner instantly swung his weapon around and fired two bursts at Sol. The bullets *whanged* dully into the steel sheeting of the elevators.

Parnell snapped his timer fuse, felt the thin metal instantly warm up as its acid capsule broke inside. Dropping it, he began blowing out the nearer stanchion lights. A few seconds later, Kaamanui came running across the tracks, hunched over. From the corner of his eye, Red saw two Italian soldiers running in from the number-two guard post. He swung on them. One man fell to the side, the other dove behind the base of the first silo.

He'd managed to take out four stanchion lights. Now he and Sol were in a semidarkness among the silos. Red waved Kaamanui past while he laid in covering fire until his clip was gone. He ejected it, popped in another, turned, and ran past Kaamanui, who was now on one knee, firing. By covering each other, they reached the cluster of stone silos where Bird and Laguna were anxiously waving them in.

The firing from the Italians stopped abruptly. But Parnell's group could see soldiers fanning out, slowly working their way to the south fence and toward the silos. Parnell leaned out, pointed at Weesay. Laguna turned and disappeared beyond the last stone elevator. Next was Bird, then Sol. The Italians were closing in quickly, less than fifty yards off. Red went to the ground and crawled into the shadow of the silo.

The machine-gun fire had torn out the gate of guard post three. The two electrical fence wires were severed, too, and sparked against their mounting brackets. He rose and lunged through and went up into the trees, seeing two shadows off to the right, lifting his weapon but then seeing they were Smoker and Fountain, coming in. Together they reached the beeches, the others already moving back up to the railroad track and the wailing of the sirens riffling through the trees.

The charges went off with muffled explosions, all sixteen, right on the button, everybody checking their watches, grinning, going *Bingo!* They heard debris hurtling against fencing, through tree branches. There was a momentary pause, maybe four seconds, slipping past. And then the hard, snapping crack like ice breaking up on a river in spring and the rumbling, rising thunder of heavy metallic crashes as the silos began coming down. A huge cloud of dust and grain smoke lifted into the air, underglowing from the stanchion lights.

There was a massive *whooshing*, sucking sound and then the whole sky seemed to light up, all yellow and red, as the cloud of wheat smoke and corn dust exploded. The detonation rolled, not like a clap of thunder but more like the sound of great rushing waters. A pressure wave swept through the trees, made the men's ears pop. Then a sudden wind came, blowing toward the granary as the superheated air over it lifted, creating a vacuum.

Everyone stopped dead, looked back downslope. All across the installation were huge islands of fire: buildings, the released grain, even the piles of stored wheat fodder. Men ran wildly, their clothes aflame. A truck exploded, hurled chunks of metal into smoking spirals. The men turned, stared at each other, shook their heads. The main purpose of their mission had just been canceled out.

Parnell inhaled, sighed disgustedly. "Well, *shit!*" he said simply.

By 0400 hours they were nearly fifteen miles south of the grain complex, down out of the high country and into the endless grass hills of central Sicily. Behind them the light from the fires had dimmed down to a soft blushing, like a foredawn.

They kept their horses at a steady pace, all strung out in a single line with Don Caprano in the lead, silent and grim as a mummy. They passed through orange and lemon groves and across fields of durum spring wheat, the stalks still half grown and the floral bracts scenting the air with a greenness.

The whistles came drifting eerily out of the darkness.

Amid the sound of the horses' hooves and the jingle of harnesses, none of the Americans except Cappacelli hearing them. Abruptly Don Vino hauled his animal to a stop. His men and then Blue Team pulled up, too.

Everyone sat listening. The whistles were coming from several directions: long trills and warbles, flutterings, twits, clear and precise as little threads of phosphorescence in the night. The *bravi* began moving silently up beside their don. Parnell watched. They all seemed suddenly *too* quiet.

He waved Cappacelli up. "What's going on? What the hell's that whistling?"

Angelo's head was tilted, listening. "That's how Sicilians communicate, Lieutenant." He sat up, sucked air through his teeth. "Oh, Jesus!" he gasped.

"What?" Red asked. Angelo didn't answer him. He listened intently, frowning. "Godammit, what the hell is it?"

Cappacelli turned to look at him. He seemed stricken. "Camporeale was hit last night," he said slowly. "Mafia raiders. Don Vito's brother Santegelo is dead."

Five

The riders had come in out of the moon's glow, ironically just at midnight, the same time the Fascist grainery was going sky-high. Forty men on horseback, the thunder of their animals coming across the night sounding at first like the distant artillery. Then the people realized what was coming and retreated to their homes.

Eight of the don's *bravi* had remained in the village with Santegelo. Now they came running with their *lupara* shotguns and old 1892 bolt-action rifles stolen from Carabinieri barracks, some even armed with the traditional peasant weapon, the oversized nail-plow like the one the priest had carried during the festival for Saint George.

It was a lost cause. The riders came in like a hurricane, right up the cemetery road where the race had been run, and into the square. By then a decent firefight was going on, Don Vino's men firing from stables and rooftops. They brought down two horses and a couple of riders, all of them dressed in red bandannas and goatskin vests.

But then the attackers opened up with automatic weapons, German machine pistols that went *thwappp,* fast as a single burst of air that stitched holes all over the walls of the town. A few grenades went off and the attackers began breaking through blue doors into *bravi* houses and finally into Don Vino's and Santegelo's.

The don's brother was able to kill two of them before they shot him, standing on his straw bed firing his shotgun and then slashing with his long knife like Jim Bowie at the Alamo. They dragged his body out to the fountain in the square and, still alive, sliced his throat from ear to ear. Then they cut open his scrotum, took out his testicles, and shoved them into his mouth, his body bent back over the side of the fountain with his blood turning the water an oily black in the moonlight.

The rest of Don Vino's men who were still alive, even the wounded, were put against a wall and shot. The last thing the attackers did, an ultimate insult, was to ride around and tear out all the statues of the town's patron Saint Teresa of Labon and replace them with black statues of another, Saint Lazarus, the patron of their own town. Then they rode off into the night.

Now it was 8:30 in the morning, the town as empty as if it were the middle of the night. People stared out windows but there was no sound. Even the animals seemed stilled. The corpses had been removed but their blood remained on the fountain's sides and on the firing squad wall.

Blue Team stood around on the cemetery road, Parnell not quite knowing what to do for the moment. The ride back to Camporeale had been fierce, everybody pushing the horses, the Sicilians grim-faced. Finally, he sent Cappacelli up into the town to find out what was going on. He hoped that these normally tight-lipped people would openly talk to him, one of their own.

In twenty minutes, Angelo came back. "The bastards were from another capo di capi's *coche,*" he told Red. "Don Giovanni Borgo. His son, Tino, was their leader." He shook his head angrily. "I know about this Don Gio. From back in the States. They say he's a Mussolini collaborator. They call him *infamito.* I even hear—"

"Cut the fucking goomba jazz and speak in English,"

Parnell snapped, cutting him off.

"They say he ratted out Don Vino."

Red grunted, squinted off toward the town. "They were using automatic weapons and grenades. Looks to me like Kraut ordnance. Are Vino's men armed like that?"

"No. Just old rifles and sawed-off shotguns. Maybe a few pistols."

"Unless they were stolen, either the Fascists or the Germans are arming Borgo's men."

Angelo nodded.

"So what does Caprano intend to do about this?"

"What else?" Angelo answered brusquely. "Him and his men'll go track down those rat-shit *squarest*. Kill the fuckers, bring their goddamned heads back on poles. He don't got no choice."

"Go on back down there. See what specifics you can get."

Angelo turned and jogged back toward the town.

Wyatt turned his head, spat. Like the others, he was covered with dust from the night's ride. It showed up the tiny squint lines around his eyes. "If'n them boys go up against German weaponry," he said, "they gonna get cut to ribbons."

Red nodded. "That's for sure." He gazed up at the empty square, then shrugged. "Well, that's too bad. But this isn't our fight. Get the men geared up. It's time we got back to our own war."

In the boiling heat of mid-July, Patton's Seventh Army had moved west and north with lightning speed against moderate resistance. General Alexander, fearing a prolonged battle in the west that would force American units to be withdrawn from Montgomery's flank, had specifically ordered him to bypass the major southern port of Agrigento. Patton got around the order by going at it in what he called a "reconnaissance in force," technically not a tactical assault.

Using armor, artillery, and naval gunfire support, his 3rd Rangers of the 3rd Infantry Division were able to take the port by 0300 hours of 17 July. Shortly after sunup, other elements of the 3rd Division invested Raffadali and San Cataldo, which put the Americans only ninety miles from Palermo.

In central Sicily, Bradley's II Corps was steadily driving toward Enna, Italian General Guzzoni's headquarters and the geographical center of the island. His forward elements had already taken Sommatino and Pietraperzia and were now nearing the main railhead of Caltanissetta, only twenty miles from Enna.

The Brits, however, had run into ever more savage opposition. German General Kesselring had flown into Enna on the fifteenth and immediately realized Sicily couldn't be held. His only option was a delaying action to allow Axis forces to withdraw across the Straits of Messina to mainland Italy before the Allies overran the island. Guzzoni agreed. A new defensive line was formed, which ran from St. Stefano di Camastra on the north coast, then to the mountain town of Leonforte, and finally due east along the southern flanks of Mount Etna to the port city of Catánia.

General Montgomery, frustrated that his Eighth Army had been brought to a halt with mounting battle casualties and hundreds of cases of malaria, decided to replay the strategy he'd employed at El Alamein. Instead of driving directly for Catánia, he'd left-hook through the arid Catánia Plain and strike at the Etna sector defensive line. Once through, he could roll it up all the way to the coast while Bradley continued protecting his rear and flank.

Unfortunately, before he could complete the redeployment, he had to rest and replenish his troops. He immediately brought his reserves, the 78th Infantry Division, from Africa. But he would not be ready to go on the offensive again until at least 1 August. Patton relished *this* news. With Monty bottled up for nearly two weeks, his chances of reaching Messina before his arch rival were looking better and better.

* * *

II Corps Headquarters
Gela, Sicily
18 July 1943

Mohawker Colonel James Dunmore, now attached to General Omar Bradley's intelligence staff, read the teletype message twice. It was taglined *OSS Section F, Haifa*. It informed him that agent reports from Palermo indicated Blue Team's raid against the grain complex at Altafonte had been "disastrously unsatisfactory."

The silos were adequately blown, the report stated, but a subsequent explosion of flour smoke had destroyed much of the processing facility and nearly all the released grain. Subsequently, the mission's main purpose of winning over the native populace through the release of grain had been a complete failure. Moreover, the extended loss of the facility would create long-term problems of food distribution for the occupying Allied military government.

"God dammit to hell," he blurted.

Dunmore was in a small secondary office of the Gela Archaeological Museum. The entire four-story building had been commandeered by II Corps. This particular room was now filled with teletype and encryption machines, dinging and clacking continuously. A helter-skelter pile of ancient Mediterranean artifacts lay in the back: red and white Hellenic *krater* vases from 400 B.C., trays of leg bones from Greek soldiers killed at Syracuse, Etruscan bronze jewelery and hand weapons. The place reeked of the perfume of antiquity and shellac.

An American major poked his head through the door. "Ah, here you are, Colonel," he called. His name was Max Nunn, Dunmore's in-county liaison with OSS. "Might I have a word with you, sir?"

Dunmore went to the door and into the hall. It was busy with scurrying officers and staff enlisted men. Nunn nodded at the teletype in the colonel's hand. "You received the update, I see?"

"Obviously." Dunmore disliked Nunn, a supercilious ex-lawyer from Detroit who had an annoying, smug smile when he talked.

"An unfortunate miscalculation of your team leader, I'm afraid," Nunn said.

"That's bullshit. Your operative said the mills were on night shutdown."

"Indeed. But your team leader should have opted for another attempt at a more appropriate time."

Dunmore stared balefully at him through his studious-looking glasses. "More bullshit, Major. But I don't have time to debate tactics. Get on with what you have to tell me."

"I'm afraid there's more bad news, Colonel. The younger Caprano brother has been murdered. A raiding force from an opposing capo mafia attacked Camporeale at precisely the same time Blue Team was at the granary. They also killed ten of Don Vino's men."

Dunmore grunted. This was not good.

"Two things about the situation are dire," the major went on. "First, this other capo mafia is Don Borgo. As you know, a strongly suspected Fascist collaborator. Second, the raiders were armed with German automatic weapons."

Again he grunted. "Well, I'd say that's proof enough. So what we've got here is a Mafia gang war with this Borgo in the driver's seat."

"Precisely."

Frowning, Dunmore walked to a window, looked out. Fifty yards away were tall rock walls built in the first century A.D. to hold back the sands carried in on the *sirocco* winds out of North Africa. He came back. "Can Caprano defeat this Borgo?"

"Not without our help. That's why we've decided to keep Blue Team with him."

The colonel's eyes narrowed. "*We've* decided?"

"Haifa headquarters, yes."

"Listen, Nunn, my team's officially attached to Second Corps and under my direct command. General Bradley and *I* say where it goes. The team's mission task has been completed, satisfactorily or not. Either way, the TM specifies Parnell is now to proceed south and link up with forward elements of 3rd Division."

"Parnell's already been ordered to remain in Camporeale," Nunn said, quickly adding a snide "sir."

Dunmore tilted his head and looked sideways at the major, like a bull about to charge. "You little weasel son of a bitch," he growled softly. "I ought to put your goddamned head through that wall."

"I wouldn't advise that, Colonel," Nunn said smugly. "I'm afraid OSS takes precedence in this matter."

Dunmore knew what *that* meant, some *personal* intercession by one Major General Wild Bill Donovan, creator and director of OSS and handpicked by Roosevelt. Well, screw the bastard. "You know what, Major?" he said, leaning down close to Nunn's face. "Let's just find out who has the most juice."

"As you will, Colonel." Nunn nodded his head, turned, and walked away.

Two hours later Dunmore was informed by Bradley's adjutant, Lieutenant Colonel Chet Hanson, that Blue Team would remain with the mafioso boss "for the time being." The order had come directly from Allied Supreme Headquarters, Algiers.

The touch of the knife blade across her throat sent a thrill through Erice Salici's body, hardened her nipples. So brutal, so savage. It was part of a little game she and Tino often played: her the helpless slave girl, him the wild Arabian creeping in the night. Rape and rapine in the midst of gentility.

Tino whispered, "Do exactly as I say or your blood will flow." Harsh, throaty voice close to her ear. How lovely, how absurdly melodramatic. Yet her body flamed at the sound of it, the thought of it, the hot, wine-scented smell of his hot breath, his skin still bearing the musk of horse sweat.

They were in the bedchamber of her *villa rustaca* in the wooded hills of Mount Pellegrino six miles from Palermo. It was a replica of the famous Villa d'Este by Ligorio in Tivoli, nestled among pines and water gardens and reflecting pools. The bedroom was in dim light, walled with black-and-white Roman mosaics of hunting scenes, lesbian orgies. Above them hung an ornate chandelier of crystal and gold medallions bearing the crest of her husband's ancestors.

Tino carried her to the bed, hurled her down onto it. It was a cloud of silk. He quickly tied her, legs and arms spread. In the dimness, he cut and ripped her clothing from her, the riding clothes she had worn on the raid on Camporeale, peasant garb, her hair wrapped and hidden beneath a red peaked cap. Now she was naked to him. She writhed in terror and arousal.

Gently at first, uttering Arabian obscenities, Tino molested her. Suckled her breasts, tongued her flesh all the way to her toes, returned to taste and snuffle her vagina. She did not believe she could hold climax off. Yet she made no sound, only stared at the dark shadow above her, watching with flashing eyes as he finally took off his night-black sheik's *bernoose* and stood with his member throbbing. She felt the peaking of her heat, that same heat that had burst into her the moment she killed the two men during the raid, her German MP-40 machine pistol going off in a single explosive breath and the men falling backward, their clothing fluttering slightly as the bullets went in.

He cut her free. Hissing, she was on him, biting, dragging him down. He lay beneath her. She hovered for a brief moment, savoring some inexplicable rush of power. Then she rammed his penis into her and began a wild, lunging coupling.

Afterward, they bathed together in a marble pool, soaping each other with pink soap and bran wrapped in silk, and drank sweet Silesian wine mixed with liquid opium. Erice's crazy eyes lost their flash and dropped into a sleepy, expressionless look of calm boredom. Her mind drifted through colorless vaults filled with the sound of the sea. She nodded.

A door slammed somewhere. Another. A moment later, the one into the bathing room was flung open and Don Gio walked in. Behind him were two bodyguards in their tight suits. The don wore evening dress, looked like a Chicago hood at his daughter's wedding.

Tino grunted and pulled himself out of the bathwater, sat on the edge of the pool giving them a drugged grin. His father glared at him. The bodyguards' eyes scanned, held briefly on Erice's nakedness, moved on.

"Dress!" Don Gio ordered. He swung around and moved out into the hall. Tino rose serenely and pulled on a silk bathrobe and followed. They stood on a landing of blue tile. A clock chimed from deeper in the building. The two bodyguards went farther down the hall and stood studying the wall.

"A horse's shit fool you are," Don Gio snarled in crude dialect. "Why? Why you do this way?"

Still grinning, Tino said, "It was the best way. The quickest."

"Stupido!" The don seemed about to strike his son. Instead, he made a harsh sound deep in his throat. "You transgress *rispetto*. Even you steal the saint? No! no!"

"You say we kill Don Caprano."

"But no like this."

"Sí, like this. *Cosí sí fa. Non di dietro.* Face-to-face."

"But Don Caprano is no *dead.*"

"Soon. Soon."

Don Gio seemed about to speak again. He didn't. He turned and walked away, paused, came back. His expression had softened. He shook his head, reached out, and took hold of Tino's cheek, shook it. *"Bel giovane,"* he said and smiled. He shoved his son's head. "So, go back to your whore." He and his bodyguards left, their shoes clacking on the tile.

Back in the bathing room, Tino sat on the edge of the pool. Erice opened her eyes, smiled dreamily. She touched his arm. Her fingers were cool. "Come back, *amore mio.*"

He nodded, then looked thoughtfully at the door. "You know, someday I will kill that man," he said.

* * *

For two days and two nights people had come to Camporeale to look at Santegelo Caprano's home and the scenes of the killings, men and women all in black, moving silently through the town like the sluggish blood of a dying man, staring at the bullet holes, touching the cobblestones where blood had flowed. Other men came, too, armed with holstered revolvers and bandoleers and *luparas*. These stood about in tight clots, their faces dark, giving everyone watchful, icy stares.

Now and then *capofamilias* from other towns accompanied by their *conciliari* and other subchiefs came to pay their respects and pledge allegiance to Don Vino. They disappeared into his house as stealthily as thieves and the lights inside burned throughout the night.

Meanwhile, Blue Team was forgotten. Women still brought food but no one spoke to the men. Even Angelo encountered a new resistance, as if the shock of the murders had gone deep and the people were once again plunged back into the ancient, dark tyranny of *omerta*.

Parnell grew more and more frustrated. Adding to it was the order from the OSS agent, Fericinni. He'd radioed a curt, coded message late in the evening of the day Comporeale was raided. Decoded, it said: *Attack on grain complex failure* . . . *Remain Comporeale till new orders*.

Now he and his men lounged in the sweltering heat of the day before their stable-barracks, played a Sicilian card game called *ziganet,* and watched at night the distant engagements and the faraway artillery, feeling useless and marooned as the war went right past them.

Santegelo and the other *bravi* were buried on the third day. The townspeople gathered at the church as the nine biers were taken inside for the funeral mass. It lasted two hours. Then they were brought out again and a procession formed to take them to the cemetery. The bodies were almost completely covered with flowers, carnations and roses and asphodel, with rosaries and imitation religious relics, bloody bandages from saints' stigmata, and slivers of wood from the crosses of crucified saints, all laid among the flowers.

The priest led the procession to the slow, dry, metallic tolling of the church bell. Behind him came the hired mourners, women in flowing black dresses and shawls. They wailed and beseeched the heavens with maledictions against the killers, calling out in the names of Gabriel, Michael, and Samuel. They broadcast salt and coral and amber powder across the ground to ward off any wandering evil spirits.

Then came Santegelo's family: his wife, Crofissa, moving upright on the arm of Don Vino, who walked with the enormous, expressionless presence of a Japanese samurai. Then Santegelo's twelve-year-old son, Mariano, and the other *capofamilia* and their retinues and Don Vino's own *bravi* and lastly the townspeople, everyone's boots shuffling heavily in the dust.

Parnell and the others followed at a distance to witness the burying. The nine graves were in a single line beneath two cork oak trees. The earth was pale, moistureless, and rolled away to the horizon, the tare grass hills bleached white and the outcroppings of stone dazzling in the heat. The priest recited prayers and the mourning women shrieked on cue. Beyond these sounds, only the bell and the high-up squeal of falcons.

Then the rite of vendetta began, the ritual as old as Sicily itself, medieval, born of ghosts and legends. Crofissa came forward and knelt beside the corpse of her husband. She touched his face, his lips, and then her own. Gently she laid two scapulae of the Madonna over his eyes. Leaning over the body, she began delicately removing the flowers from Santegelo's chest and drew back his shirt and coat, exposing his wounds.

One by one she kissed them, lingering as if actually sucking at their decaying tissues. Now Don Vino stepped up beside her and also knelt. He too kissed and suckled the blackened skin. Both he and Crofissa placed their left hands onto Santegelo's wounds while she intoned the symbolic entrusting of the act of vengeance to her husband's older brother. "In full sunlight," she intoned, her voice strong and precise, "may he drink the blood of the men who killed you."

And it was done.

That afternoon the OSS agent showed up. He came riding up toward Camporeale on a donkey, looking like a pilgrim out of *The Canterbury Tales.* He stopped near the cemetery, seemed hesitant to come up into the town.

Weesay told Parnell, who had been trying to sleep in the stable, his clothes drenched in sweat. He walked down the road to talk to Fericinni. They sat under a wild lemon tree while the donkey drowsed in the sunlight.

"This is bad," the agent said in his rushing way. "Very, very bad."

Red waited for him to go on. Instead, the man sat there wiping his sweaty forehead and frowning anxiously. Finally Parnell said, "You're taking a risk coming up here."

Fericinni nodded. "The Germans have detection crews all over picking up radio transmissions. In the future, be very careful if you must contact me."

"When do we get the hell out of here?"

"Not until this situation is secure."

"How do you mean secure? I don't think it's *likely* to be. You *know* Caprano's going after Borgo, don't you?"

"Of course."

"And he'll get his ass whipped."

"I know that, too. The Germans have given Borgo automatic weapons. He was recently observed with a *Waffen SS* major named Keppler." He slapped the dust from his cap and put it back on. "I also believe this Nazi has assigned German soldiers to instruct Borgo's *bravi.* I believe they might even have field mortars."

"Mortars?" Red snorted. "Caprano and his men are really in for it now. They attack this Borgo frontally and in the open, it'll be bloody."

"Yes. Sadly that is true."

"Then get OSS to supply him with weapons."

"Impossible. There isn't enough time. Nobody could foresee such a bold attack. Mafiosi have always struck with stealth, not like this." He turned to look up toward the cemetery. Four grave diggers were slowly filling in the graves. The scraping of their shovels drifted down clearly. He swung back. "That's why you and your team are to remain with the capo di capi."

Parnell gave him the narrow eyes. "What you're saying is you want *us* to fight his war for him?"

"No, just help *him* fight it."

"No. Our TM's completed here." Red saw Fericinni glance at him. "Hey, you don't really want to talk about *that*, do you?"

"I'm sorry."

"My orders are that we move south. It's up to you and OSS to help him."

"No."

"Godammit, Fericinni, this is purely a private war. I didn't come to this fucking sweatbox to risk my men's lives in a goddamned gangster rumble."

"Don Caprano is much more than a gangster, Lieutenant," he said stiffly. "His assistance is absolutely essential for the coming occupation." He gave Red a sly look. "Besides, he will soon be your immediate superior. OSS has given him the rank of a major in the United States Army."

"What?" Red cried, dumbfounded. "Are you shitting me?" He stared at the agent for a long moment. "And just what in hell does Dunmore think about this nonsense?"

"I'm not informed as to the feelings of your colonel. All I know is that your orders were cleared directly through General Bradley's headquarters."

"Whoa, that sounds like Dunmore's no longer in the loop?"

"Loop? What means this loop?"

"The chain of command. *Is* Dunmore out of it?"

"No, I do not believe so. More accurate to say he has temporarily been superseded."

Red dropped his head, gazed at the ground. "I'll be a monkey's asshole." He sighed disgustedly, then looked up again. "Does Caprano know he's now an American officer?"

"It isn't official yet. He will be ordained when representatives of the Allied Military Commission arrive on the island."

"Yeah, right, *ordained.* So what am I supposed to do till then, take orders from him?"

Fericinni managed a quick smile. "Of course not, Lieutenant. No, you are the professional soldiers here. You will simply give tactical advice and an equalizing firepower."

Parnell jumped at that. "Hold it! You expect us to share our weapons with his *bravi?*" He shook his head emphatically. "No way, buddy."

"I only meant you give him your military expertise."

"What if he doesn't want it?"

"He will. He's committed to us by his honor."

"I don't like this, Fericinni."

The agent shrugged. "I'm sorry. But we all must do what must be done."

Wyatt couldn't believe it. "Us take orders from that guinea?" he said. "This is bullshit, Lieutenant. They're flat puttin' us in the middle of a gawddamn civil war."

"I know it." Red looked around. "Where's Cappacelli?"

"In town somewheres. He's still tryin' to find out when the head honch's gonna make his move."

"Go get him."

Parnell and Angelo walked up the hill to Don Caprano's house. A dozen *bravi* lounged outside cleaning their weapons, waxing the insides of the barrels of their shotguns so the shot would ignite fires when they struck a target, oiling their long knives with garlic to create infection. They all stood up, everybody watching the two Americans suspiciously.

Parnell paused. "I want to see Don Caprano," he said.

No one moved. Finally, an older man went up the step and

knocked softly on the door. Another mafioso opened it. He had a terrible scar across his forehead. The older man said something and Scar disappeared inside. A moment later, Don Vino came to the doorway. He was still dressed in his funeral suit. He looked down at Parnell, his thick face as blank as a fresh sheet of paper.

"I have come to offer my sympathies, Don Caprano," Red said slowly in the best Italian he could muster. "To you and your family and to the families of those who were killed."

The Sicilian nodded.

"I have also come to offer my assistance in your efforts against your enemy."

For a tiny, fleeting moment the Sicilian's eyes went smaller. Then he said brusquely, "Is no necessary."

"I believe that is a mistake." From the corner of his vision, he saw all the men stiffen. He heard Cappacelli shift nervously beside him. Don Vino's face showed nothing. Parnell went on: "Your enemy possesses stronger weapons than you. My men and I possess such weapons. We can render great assistance."

The don said nothing.

Arrogant son of a bitch, Parnell thought. He said, "May I know when you intend to strike your enemy?"

The answer was quicker than he expected. "Before sunrise," Don Vino said.

"I intend to accompany you."

"Come if you desire, stay if you desire." With that, Don Caprano turned and shut the door.

Going back down the hill, Angelo said, "Jesus, Lieutenant, you almost said too—"

"Lock it up," Red snarled.

Six

A young Sicilian named Placido Scuzzulato came to waken the team. He spoke some English and had brought their horses. It was several minutes before 4:00 in the morning. They assembled in front of their stable and loaded their gear: weapons, field rations, explosives, grenades, and spare ammunition, Laguna packing Parnell's MCR 300 radio.

The dark sky was filled with stars, the moon gone now. The air had gone absolutely still. They could smell cooking fires and men were gathering in the town square, their horses restless and clattering on the cobblestones.

Soon everyone mounted up, waiting for Don Vino to come out of his house. Parnell counted forty-eight riders besides his own men. At 4:00 sharp, the don came out. They all moved slowly down the hill past the cemetery and cut across the rolling hills headed due east, directly toward the distant glow of Mount Etna. Far to the southwest and west were ships' lights out in the ocean and now and then came the very faint sounds of gunfire.

Blue Team and Placido rode slightly behind the others, the clot of *bravi* cantering ahead steadily but without haste, Don Caprano in the lead with the other, lesser capo mafia directly behind him. No one spoke, everybody wearing head bandannas and goat vests with bandoleers and *luparas* slung across their chests and the horses' harnesses tinkling in the darkness.

Bird pulled abreast of Parnell. "Them ole boys look like Pancho Villa's *banditos* headin' for the border."

Red chuckled. "Yeah. Well, I think we best put out our own flankers. Two on each side, two in the rear. I don't want any surprises."

Wyatt dropped back, snapping orders. A moment later, the flankers rode past Parnell and Scuzzulato, veering to the side while Wyatt and Smoker lay back.

Red looked over at Placido. "Where you learn how to speak English?"

"One time I *live* in Boston, A-mer-ica," the Sicilian answered. He looked to be about twenty. He had a withered right arm that swung unnaturally as he rode. His eyes were dark and hidden under a protruding brow. "Upstairs in tenten houses in North End." He grinned. "Very close by is the house of Paul Revere. You know Paul Revere?"

"Yes." Red let his eyes slide over to the man's shrunken arm, slid away.

"Oh, *this?*" Placido said, catching the look. "My papa, he beat me, break my arm. From then she no going to grow okay. He was Italian, from Milano. Someday I return America. I find him, I kill him." Matter-of-fact.

The dawn came on swiftly, as if yellow-gray light were fuming up out of the earth. Sparrows and starlings twittered in the maquis brush. In the southeast, high columns of dust rose into the air, which Parnell took to be armor on the move. They crossed through lemon orchards and then fields of corn, the stalks and leaves thin and dry, planted without rows. Now and then they saw small clusters of fieldworkers' huts made of straw like Zulu kraals.

"How does Don Caprano intend to fight this battle?" Parnell asked.

The young Sicilian shrugged. "Is simple. We fight his men, we kill them, we cut off their heads and arms. *Bam! Bam!* Then we take *their patrona* and we come back."

Parnell shook his head sadly.

Angelo Cappacelli felt good. He inhaled the dawn, cast his eyes across this wide, empty land, and felt an invigoration capture him. He and Fountain were on the right flank of the mounted men. He glanced over at them. They looked dark and grim and vengeful, his fellow mafiosi hunting for blood demanded by a woman's curse and passions as old as this land.

Cowboy rode up past him, cutting off his view for a moment. Angelo felt a sting of irritation at the disturbance to the picture of Don Vino's men on the move. He pushed it back. Ever since that moment in the granary guardhouse, he had had to keep reminding himself that he was an *American* in an *American* unit, only here to do a job.

Then he thought, *No, it's more than that.* Something about this particular place. He let his mind drift, form a picture of after the war. Maybe he'd come back here, find himself a woman, earthy and born of this land, settle down, and create a family. Maybe become a wise guy, a *Sicilian* wise guy. Maybe even someday a full *capofamilia*. After all, this was where it began, like the foundation, the *Noble Madre di Mafia*, the Nobel Mother of the Mafia. Even in the States everybody spoke in hushed reverence of *this* place.

He inhaled again. The fantasy drew from his memory an old saying his mother had often used when he was a boy: *When the stars talk in the night sky, the wind is silent.* He had never understood its meaning, nor did he now. Yet it was so Sicilian and seemed to carry a stirring knowledge and from that a dream that infused in him a sweet, hot pride.

* * *

Tino Borgo couldn't wait to show off his new acquisition, two German Model 34 Maschinengewehrs, 7.92mm machine guns with Solothurn-type breeches and sights set for two thousand meters. They were gifts from Major Keppler, one still in its wooden crate, the other set up on the beach where Tino had already cut loose into the surf, howling with delight as he nearly emptied the fifty-round drum until the German soldier Keppler sent along to show him how to use it told him to only throw out short bursts or the barrel would distort with heat.

He and Erice had met Keppler outside the north coast town of Cefalù ten miles east of Palermo. He and his *bravi* had brought in four members of the CVF and turned them over to the German major, three men and a woman. The guns were a gift for his efforts. Now he waited for his father, who was on his way to their hometown.

The beach was deserted, a line of cypress trees above high water, and the day hot, the Tyrrhenian Sea sparkling with sun diamonds. He couldn't keep his hands off the machine gun. He caressed it, smelled the still-warm barrel grease, the oil of the cartridges. Even Erice had fired the weapon, moaning with excitement as the rounds made hard, dull collisions in the surf, hurling spray. Afterward, they stripped and went swimming and Tino took her in the water while his men lounged back in the trees and the Germans watched.

Don Gio came with his *conciliaro,* a thick-bodied man named Michelangelo Drago, the two men coming down trying not to get sand in their shoes. Tino showed them the machine guns, grinning, saying, "Go on, Papa, try it out. See what power it has," and the don squinting at it in the sunshine, then nodding his head toward the trees.

They walked up to them. In their shade, he told his son, "Don Caprano is coming."

"Good," Tino said. "We are ready."

"No. I have changed my mind. We will not fight this way. It is without honor."

Tino's grin snapped off. "Honor is for shit. With these we can kill them all."

"No. When wolves fight they use only their teeth."

"These are bigger teeth."

Don Gio's whole face went stiff. His white hair fluttered in the shore breeze. "I say *no!* My *conciliari* agree. We fight Don Caprano in the old way, in the mountains."

Tino shot a narrow-eyed look at Drago, came back. "We must meet him in the *open*. You cannot *see? There* we have advantage. These *cannoni* can reach out two, three thousand meters. Caprano and his men will never close."

"Enough talk," Don Borgo shouted. "You and your men will be in Vinzzini by sundown." He turned and he and Drago walked out from under the trees and up onto the coast road, Tino watching them go with eyes gone hard.

The hotel was called the Targa Florio, named for the famous road race that had been run here since 1906. Now the building served as the headquarters for the German 3rd Grenadier Panzer Division. One of its third-floor rooms, originally an ornate bedchamber with gold embroidered walls, was now an interrogation cell.

It contained a single long table and several chairs. A heavy iron bar had been set up between the walls. Several sets of straps and handcuffs dangled from the bar. The four CVF prisoners were now cuffed under the bar, their arms behind them, their feet on wire crates. All were naked. Two German soldiers stood guard at the door.

Major Keppler sat at the table quietly smoking a long, brandy-dipped cigarette. He held it between the little and ring fingers of his left hand. Sunshine streamed into the room through a large window, glistened off his hairless head. The effect gave his deep-set eyes a stark intensity. Beyond the Via Porpora, which ran along the side of the hotel, was a huge, fortresslike cathedral, the Duomo di Cefalu built in the twelfth century.

Keppler inhaled, released the smoke into the air. From somewhere came the grumble of artillery fire. He said, "I will ask again. Where is your headquarters?"

Silence.

The three men stood with their heads down. All were sweating profusely. After a moment, the major rose, walked around the table. He stopped before the first man. He, like the others, was young, in his early twenties. He was thin without hair on his chest. Keppler studied his face. The man would not look directly at him. After a long moment, he moved to the next.

He reached the woman. She was pretty with auburn hair that was sun-streaked. Her body was very white save for her tanned arms and face, her breasts heavy with small, dainty nipples. He reached up, turned her face to profile, examined it.

"What is your name?"

"Anna," the woman said. Her voice trembled.

"You are a Jewess."

No answer.

His gaze drifted down her body, paused at the dark triangle of her pubic hair. It was black with a reddish tone. "You are a Communist," he said.

Again she refused to respond but her eyelids blinked rapidly.

"Ah." Keppler took another drag from his cigarette, then held the tip against the woman's pubic hair. Anna sucked in her breath and jerked back her hips. For a second some of the hair sizzled, releasing a tiny wisp of smoke. Chuckling, the major walked to the window, stood looking out at the huge tile mural of *Christ Pantokrator* on the facade of the cathedral. The Christ figure held an open Bible in one hand. It bore a Greek inscription.

At last he returned to the first man. He could smell the musk of his fear. Moving his leg with lightning speed, Keppler kicked the wire box out from under his feet. The man dropped, forcing the straps to jerk his arms up behind him. He screamed as his shoulder joints cracked. The others looked away. The man, gagging with pain, swung there, his face contorted.

To each Keppler did the same. The woman fainted. He stood before them. "One last time," he shouted. "Where is your headquarters?" The men groaned, the woman hung limply. Shaking his head, Keppler returned to the window, once again appraised the *Christ Pantokrator*. "Do any of you understand Greek?" he asked casually. "No? Then let me translate what it says on that Bible. *'I am the light of the world; he who follows me shall not walk in darkness.'* " He turned. "Do you believe that? Mm?"

One man cried out, "Please!"

"Of course you do not believe it. You are atheistic Communists." He disinterestedly turned to the guards. "Shoot them."

They killed the four in an alley behind the hotel. Six German soldiers were lounging near a personnel carrier. They all straightened as the prisoners came out, one of the guards carrying the naked woman under his arm like a sack of grain, the three men walking stiffly, their arms hanging disjointedly. Two were sobbing.

They were lined against a stone wall, facing it. The woman had come out of her faint but could not stand. The guard propped her against the wall on her knees, her forehead to the stone. Her buttocks looked as pale as the meat of a fresh apple.

The second guard walked behind the prisoners and shot each in the head with his Luger pistol. Their heads snapped forward against the stones and blood spewed. The gun's reports echoed back up the alley. He had to lift the woman's head by the hair to hit the base of her skull. When he shot her, blood splattered all over his hand. Cursing, he walked away, flipping it off his fingers.

On the morning of 18 July, at the precise moment when a U.S. task force was taking a beating off the Island of Kolombagara in the Solomons, and Hitler and Mussolini were meeting in Feltre near Verona, Italy, to discuss desperate tactics to save Fascist Italy. Major General L.K. Truscott Jr., commander of the U.S. 3rd Infantry Division, told his senior officers, "I want to be in Palermo in five days." They were now nearly a hundred miles from it.

The American thrusts toward the north coast of Sicily had become a competition between the 3rd and the 45th Divisions, both now attached to Lieutenant General Omar Bradley's II Corps, despite the fact that the 45th was at a disadvantage since it had been ordered from its original route of advance by General Sir Harold Alexander, Eisenhower's deputy commander, so as to allow Montgomery's Eighth Army wider movement in the western Catánia Plain once he began his offensive.

Still, while Monty remained bogged down and waiting for reinforcements from Africa, the Americans continued driving deeper and deeper into the interior of the island with unparalleled speed, investing town after town.

They were camped in a grove of jacaranda trees on the southern slope of an eight-hundred-foot-high hill called Serre a few miles outside the town of Ciminna. The ground was littered with the pink cotton of the tree's blossoms. It was nearly nine o'clock at night and the moon was out, glistening on the surface of the Macaluso River, which wound through the valley below them.

Parnell and his men were off by themselves, the rest of the mafiosi sixty yards away huddled around three cooking fires having supper. Roasted snails and flat bread and wine from leather bags. The Americans ate K-rations, cold tins of frankfurters-and-bean stew, Saltines, and chocolate bars. Red preferred no fires, no giveaway silhouettes, wary of night attack.

Scuzzulato was with them as he had been for most of the day. The area was full of outcroppings of limestone rock white as milk and clumps of maquis brush and tare grass. He warned them to watch for vipers. "When hot time comes they always angry, you know? Especially at night. They like your body stink. But when you sleep make rope around you. Like this?" He imitated the making of a circle with his hands. "Then they no cross."

Through the scorching heat of the day they had continued slowly, steadily across country, first east and then southeast. When they reached Highway 121 to Palermo, there was a long column of Italian soldiers, trucks, and supply vans, ambulances, personnel carriers, and a few tanks with men clustered like flies on them and horse-drawn field guns, everything heading north. The soldiers were dirty and sluggish and many were wounded. It was the remnants of an entire division in full retreat.

A little after noon a flight of six American Lockheed Lightnings strafed the column, the sleek, twin-engine aircraft coming in low from the south, their shadows flashing up and down over the grassy hills and their .50s and 20mm nose cannons tearing hell out of the scattering Italians. It wasn't until late in the afternoon that the column thinned enough for Don Vino's force to cross the highway.

Now Wyatt tossed away his empty stew tin and looked over at Parnell. The tin tinkled on a rock, causing their browsing horses to lift their heads. He, Kaamanui, Red, and Placido were sitting with their backs against twin jacarandas. Their bark smelled like dirty feet. "You want double security out, Lieutenant?" he asked.

"No, one man'll do. Two-hour watches. Remind 'em about the snakes."

"Right." Bird moved off.

Red lit one of the ration cigarettes, his Zippo lighter snapping shut with a sharp, metallic click. "Where exactly are we headed?" he asked Scuzzulato.

"Don Gio's *paese*. His village? Is Vinzzini, in the mountains."

"How far is it?"

"Maybe hundred kilometers now."

"What does he think will be there?"

Placido looked at him quizzically. "Don Gio, *tenente*. What else?"

Parnell drew smoke, exhaled. Twice during the day he had attempted to speak with Caprano but was totally ignored, the man as remote as usual. Like the heat, Red's anger and frustration had been steadily increasing. "What about those German automatic weapons and grenades? He ready to go up against *them?* "

The Sicilian shrugged. "Is no difference. Is *omerta*, Mafia law. You understand? Is *punto d'onore*, point of honor. No, Don Gio, he *must* fight with honor."

Red and Sol exchanged glances. Red said, "And the attack on your village? Was that *omerta*, too?"

"Oh, *sí*. Except for when Don Gio *bravi* steal our *patrona*. No, that no is *right*." He shrugged. "But maybe he don't *know* his men do this thing. So now he know and he must fight correct."

"Or else what?"

Placido sucked saliva nosily through his lips, made to bite the back of his hand. "Then is *infamita*. Don Gio no longer can be *pezzo di novanta*. People will spit when they say his name."

Sol snorted, shook his head. "Man, we got some fucked-up thinking going on here, Lieutenant," he said.

The young Sicilian laughed. "You are Americans, you cannot understand. You watch, you see."

"Yeah," Parnell said grimly.

Now he noticed some of the Sicilians downslope coming suddenly to their feet, squinting out into the moon's half darkness. There was the faint drumming of a single horse approaching rapidly. The three Americans picked up their weapons.

A moment later a horseman flashed up into the light of the don's cooking fires. He drew rein, slipped from his mount. The mafiosi gathered around him. The Americans and Placido moved closer. The rider was talking to Don Vino, breathless, Caprano stolidly listening.

"What the hell's going on?" Red asked Scuzzulato.

"Is Don Gio's *bravo.*" He tilted his head, listened, then said excitedly, *"Sí, sí."*

"What?"

"Is formal challenge from Don Gio. He will fight us at the Tempio di Giove by Montemaggiore." The Temple of Jupiter near the town of Montemaggiore.

Down near the fires the man stopped talking finally. Don Vino nodded. His own men moved back slightly. Caprano extended his hand to the rider. The man hesitated for a few seconds, then took it. Instantly, Don Vino's other hand came up and across. In it was a long-bladed sickle. The rider did not move, appearing paralyzed. The sickle sliced through his throat, bringing a spray of blood. It looked black in the fire-light. He fell to his knees. His nearly severed head lolled, still pumping blood.

All three men jumped, Sol crying out, "Good *Christ!"*

The Tempio di Giove site was a perfect defensive posi-tion, the German sergeant said in pidgin Italian, the man all cold Nordic gruff and built like an Alpine wrestler making motions so they would understand. His name was Habstreise. He and five of his troopers from the 3rd Grenadier Panzer Division had been assigned by Keppler to help these mafiosi shit dogs kill those other shit dogs.

Tino and Erice followed him around as he pointed out the site's military advantages, the don's son nodding and saying, *"Sí, sí."* Both Sicilians were dressed in their peasant raider clothes again, the bloodstains still showing on the goat vests, Erice in a bright yellow bandanna. The sergeant didn't like it, too bright. He pointed at it, then made like a bullet strik-ing her chest, its bright color making her a good target. She understood. In elegant Italian she told him to go fuck himself. He waited, uncomprehending, then shrugged and moved on.

The temple had been built in the fourth century B.C., a graceful peristyle structure with an inner court and a surrounding portico of Ionic columns. It was roofless and all its exquisite tiles, murals, and statuary were long gone. Even its pediment friezes of *Korai Maidens* had nearly disappeared and its once pure white stone was now a rich honey golden in the midday sun.

The temple hill sloped away on all three facing sides, down into rolling grass hills. Anything attacking the position frontally across a 180-degree arc would be fully exposed to plunging fire from the top. Directly below the temple was a large grove of ancient olive trees, their trunks gnarled. It afforded excellent defilade.

But the primary defensive character of the site was the cliff at its back, a nearly sheer limestone face about seventy feet high that then sloped down to a branch of the Torto River far below. Clumps of grass and cacti and random stands of eucalyptus trees covered the lower ridges. About a mile upriver was the tiny village of Santo di Causo.

Sergeant Habstreise had already deployed his weapons, the two machine guns on either side of the olive grove to give interlocking fields of fire downslope, his three mortars to the side of the temple behind fallen blocks of marble. His men had instructed the *bravi,* about fifty men with Tino, on how to operate all the weaponry. They themselves would only observe unless the Sicilians proved ineffective.

Now the sergeant ordered that the guns be test-fired for range, the short bursts of the machine guns rapping in the stillness, throwing out tracer rounds that looked like tiny, streaking pellets from the sun, the firing azimuths interlocking six hundred yards out. Then the mortars, four light 50mm Leichter Granatenwerfer 36s, which cast a 2.2-pound shell that left the barrel with a hollow, ringing *thrump.* Six hundred yards away they impacted with a jolting crack, throwing up dust clouds that hung listlessly in the windless air, one to the left, one to the right, one straight ahead. The Grenadiers then set their traversing arc pins to twenty degrees, the widest setting to allow the inexperienced Sicilian gunners a coarse ranging.

As the last dust slowly settled, Habstreise spotted a lone horseman suddenly appearing from out of a rift in the grassy slope, coming on hard. He adjusted his binoculars and watched him, the rider a Sicilian peasant with a red bandanna. He carried a long pole. At the end was a human head.

Tino had spotted him, too. He said something. The German handed over the glasses. The young Borgo studied the figure for a long moment. The rider had stopped now, just beyond where the mortar rounds had come down. He held up his pole, then jammed it into the ground, twisted his mount, and rode away.

Tino lowered the binoculars. He looked at Erice. There was a grin on his face. "They accept," he said. He gave her the glasses. She looked and looked, finally taking the binoculars from her eyes. They flashed excitedly while her lovely face remained cool with deadly serenity. "Good," she said. "Now there is no quarter."

Habstreise snapped an order and one of his men fired a long burst from his machine gun. It stitched a hedge of dust a few yards behind the rider. The gunner lifted slightly, was about to fire again.

Tino shouted in Sicilian, *"No! No!* Let him go."

The German looked at him, then turned and snapped another order. The gunner eased back. He turned to Borgo once more, appraised him with narrowed eyes. *Dumm scheisskerl italienisch!* he thought contemptuously. The stupid bastard had just let an enemy escape who knew his weapon strength and the positions of his firebase.

Scuzz, everybody calling Placido that now and him liking it, pointed to the east. *"Il tempio* is that way."

"Exactly that way?" Panell said.

"Sí."

"Hold it." Red took a compass bearing of the direction the young Sicilian indicated. "How far away is it?"

"Twenty-five, thirty kilometers."

"What does it look like?"

"Il tempio?"

"No, the surrounding ground."

Scuzzalato thought a moment. "Is on a hill with all around grass. On the backside is a *scogliera* that go down to the Fiume Torto. Then is Santo di Causo."

"A cliff to the river?"

"Sí."

"How high?"

"Fifty meters. Maybe."

It was now the evening of the twenty-first, the sun gone and the land all golden as the distant mountains slowly turned blue. All through the day Parnell had fretted restlessly, wanting to talk to the don although he knew it would be useless. Then Caprano and several of his men left before dawn. To gather more *bravi,* Scuzz said, the young Sicilian starting to work himself into an excited giddiness over the coming battle: "Oh, *baa-by,"* he crowed, "This gonna be one *sweet* fight."

In contrast, the Americans sat around in the heat, sweating and looking sullen and watching more dust clouds and grass-fire smoke to the west along Highway 121, obviously advance units of the American 3rd Division dogging the retreating Italians. Later they saw thick black smoke rising to the northwest as units of the U.S. Destroyer *Squadron 8* shelled Palermo Harbor and military installations along the base of Mount Pellegrino on the cape. They also watched Parnell and waited.

All except Cappacelli. He seemed as excited as Scuzzulato, acting as if he were actually one of the mafiosi. Yet even *he* had been shocked by the sudden, brutal murder of Borgo's emissary last night, the man's blood still staining the earth

where he fell. Afterward, the Sicilians had dumped the head-
less corpse into a limestone hole where, by midday, the vul-
tures had found it, coming from nowhere, their black shadows
drifting lazily over the grassland.

It wasn't the killing that had so sobered everyone, but the
method and circumstance of it. The horseman had come in
with a white flag, at least figuratively. So what the hell kind
of uncivilized people slaughtered a man under a flag of
truce?

Around noon, Don Vino's own emissary returned, his horse
lathered white with sweat. Parnell sent Scuzz down to find
out what he said. He returned to tell them that Borgo's *bravi*
had fired at the guy, from a mile away, many bullets coming
at once. And before that he had seen explosions among the
grassy hills but without cannon booms. Hearing that, the
Americans looked at each other, knowing exactly what that
meant: mortars and machine gun emplacements.

Parnell grilled Scuzzalato: "How do you people fight this
kind of battle?"

"Che?"

"What tactics?"

"Oh, this is *special.*"

"How, for Christ's sake?"

Squatting like a Japanese fishmonger, Scuzz spread his
good arm, made dramatic movements. "When comes the
sun—"

"You hit at daybreak?"

"Oh, *sí.* Must be in sunlight. You know? We make a line,
all the riders spread out. Below the *tempio.* When comes first
light, everybody all at once race up the *hill.* We fire guns and
then we fight *mano a mano.* You know? Knives, sticks, *teeth,*
too." He grinned broadly. His own teeth were crooked and
yellow. "Just like *Airrol* Flynn. You know? When the cow-
boys kill them fuckin' Indians?"

Wyatt expelled air, turned his head, and spat. "Errol Flynn,
my ass."

Don Vino returned with twenty more men, everybody and

their animals covered with dust. He immediately huddled with his capos, the Sicilians in a circle with the don and his Buddah face nodding.

Bird said to Parnell, "Yo'all gonna talk to that spaghetti-eatin' sumbitch again, Lieutenant?"

Red shook his head. "No."

Wyatt spat, nodded. "Like bangin' your face against a fence, ain't it?"

Parnell had already figured out what he was going to do. Being ordered to protect an uncivilized son of a bitch in a private vendetta was one thing. Sending himself and his men frontally against mortar and machine-gun fire like the goddamned Light Brigade was something else.

He said, "Get 'em ready, Wyatt. Only spare ammo and grenades. We're pulling the hell out of here as soon as it's dark."

Wyatt looked at him, his eyes smiling. "Yes, sir," he said and moved off.

Seven

Weesay Laguna hated horses. Goddamned things smelled bad, drooled, and made his ass and inner thighs hurt like hell. He never seemed able to get his stupid animal to move in a smooth way, not like Cowboy Fountain, the goddamn New Mexican John Wayne sitting up there on his mount like he was part of it. No matter what gait Wessay's horse got into, it still tossed him up and down, his Thompson and eight-magazine bag pounding him on the back.

At eight o'clock that evening Parnell had huddled them, his topo map laid out in the dust to show where they were going. Someplace with a temple and a river and a small town named Santo di Causo, Red saying, "These dumb shits don't know what they're up against. We gotta even things out." And old Scuzz, not a bad *companero,* shaking his head, disappointed his new American friends were deserting. None of the other Sicilians seemed bothered at all, just silently watched them ride off.

Now they moved steadily through the darkness, the night still hot, powder-dry dust two inches deep fuming up off the horses' hooves. They were in a line with Parnell in the lead. Always a friggin' line, Weesay thought with disgust. The army operated in lines. And it was even worse here, *every-*

body in line for *anything*. So where was *he* in this line? Where else but in the back, him and Cappacelli riding drag and sucking up Sicilian dust.

He turned and looked back at Angelo, wondering about him again, the guy getting all juiced up over this mafiosi rumble as if it were *his* turf they were fighting over. Laguna understood the gang concept, all right, knew that it was pure loyalty that kept a *cuadrilla* tightly together. Hell, that attitude was and always had been his *own* guiding principle. Many's the time back home it was what had fueled his rage and determination whenever he and his *pachuco* boys took on another *caudrilla* over either territorial rights or pussy.

He chuckled, remembering one fight in particular, the last one with those *lambiosos,* the *Caballeros Negros,* from Thirtieth Street and Maple Avenue in west L.A. *Ay, caramba!* was beautiful: chains and baseball bats and spiked knuckles working hard, kicking Black Knight ass. It was after that one that he got sent to the army.

His thoughts returned to Cappacelli. It wasn't right, man, the guy's thinking, his *priorities*. He was a Mohawker now, a Blue Teamer. *Hermanos,* baby, brothers in arms. So his loyalty should be to them and *only* them. Not split, one side a soldier, the other side a goddamn Wop hood. He hissed a curse. Betrayal infuriated him. And also this Frisco guinea had a smart mouth on him, even when he spoke to the lieutenant, for Christ's sake.

Bouncing and cursing sullenly, Weesay decided he'd keep a close eye on old Ange-*lee*-no. And in thinking this he suddenly realized that they were about to go into combat again and felt that first gentle, almost pleasurable tightening in his groin. Like when he led his *pachucos,* swaggering and don't-give-a-shit tough, up some half-dark Los Angeles alley to do battle, bodies charged up with that nervous but sweet sense of machismo.

Then, like the turning of a coin in a beam of light, he glimpsed the darker side of that moment. Ever since North Africa, Laguna had experienced deep changes in himself, a tempering of those memories of old street glories. The horrendous reality and savagery he had come to know on *this* side of the world had somehow dissolved those bright reminiscences into diminished illusion.

Countessa Erice Salici liked being watched having sex. It gave her a sense of tremendous power, all those hot hungry eyes out there in the darkness like animals in a forest, looking and looking and wanting to hurtle forward to ravage her.

It brought memories of other sexual encounters, in those harlequin-and-gladiator sex cabarets on the Boi de Boulogne in Paris before the Fall, or the Begger's Lane finishes of old London town where the cities' beau monde libertines went to indulge their fantasies in late night orgies, men and women writhing in licentious abandon on small platforms, their entangled bodies glistening in blue and red and green light while other patrons lasciviously observed from screened balconies and awaited *their* turns on the miniscule stages.

Now it was Tino's *bravi* and those grim-faced Panzer soldiers who watched, she and Tino completely naked in the temple courtyard on marble that was twenty-four hundred years old, twin flashlights mounted on columns shining down on them like stage spots and the night perfectly still except for her own moans and frantic urgings.

The thrill of it impelled her orgasm, exploding now, up through her legs and body and head. She closed her eyes, went drifting ecstatically into space. Vaguely, she heard engines, the dusty skid of tires. When she opened them again automobile headlights were shining luminously into the courtyard, casting the temple column shadows like huge bars.

Beneath her, Tino's head came up. He swore and abruptly shoved her off. She rolled onto the cool marble, felt their piled clothing bunched under her legs and the sharp coldness of Tino's MP-40 machine pistol and belt knife.

Violent Sicilian cursing erupted from the darkness behind the lights and then Don Gio and his *conciliaro,* Drago, came bursting up into the light and stormed through the shadowed columns, both men in dark suits and overcoats and fedoras, their white shirts buttoned at the throat, looking like a pair of outraged Chicago priests.

Tino rose to his feet. His father, grunting with fury, slammed a fist across his face. He fell back, came up, and was struck twice more. *"Brutto cafone!"* the don bellowed, standing over his son. "You betray me. You come this place, challenge in *my* name?" His jowls worked. He spat viciously at Tino. *"Maledetto l'incubazione diavolo!* From now, I have *no* son *no* more."

The spittle had struck Tino's shoulder. He reached up, touched it disbelievingly. Then his beautiful dark eyes went wild. Erice felt his hand slap her thigh, move on, slapping, searching. He found what he wanted, his knife. Lunging up beneath his father, he shoved the blade into the older man's stomach, through overcoat, jacket, Egyptian cotton undershirt. Again and again he stabbed him, the don arching backward in agonized surprise. His fedora fell off. In the headlights, his hair shone like filaments of white silk.

Drago instantly charged forward with a roar. He caught Don Gio falling back, cradled him, gentled him to the ground, and then came on again. Erice lifted the machine pistol, aimed it at him, and pulled the trigger. Nothing. The safety was on.

Tino had scrambled to his feet, his bloody knife down low, circling. Drago lunged at him, missed, whirled, lunged again. Erice found the weapon's safety, clicked it off. Her heart pounded with excitement.

The two men merged for a moment, stark shadows. Then Tino fell back, recovered. They separated. Erice pointed the weapon at Drago's massive bulk again and fired. The rounds went out with a furious rapidity. Empty shells flew, the blasts bouncing and rebounding off the ancient columns as the sharp stink of cordite fumed back into her face. She emptied the clip, every bullet hitting, hurling Drago back and down.

There was a sudden thick, vacuumed silence, the only

sounds the soft idling of the car engines and the fading echoes of the gunfire.

Tino dropped to one knee, stunned, croaking repeatedly, *"Madre di Dio!"*

Erice skittered to him, bent close. "Get up, you fool! They'll kill us now." She dragged at his hair. "Get *up*. *You* are don now. Tell them, *tell* them!"

Tino turned, looked at her. His face was anguished. At last, he rose slowly and moved through the columns, stood in the full glare of the car headlights. He held up his knife like a sword. *"I* am capo di capi now. By blood right. Pledge to me or kill me."

Nothing moved out in the darkness. There were the sharp metallic clicks of receivers. Erice's breath paused in her lungs. Seconds dragged past as sluggishly as ants in molasses. Figures appeared through the lights. One by one, Don Gio's bodyguards came up to Tino and laid their weapons at his feet. They bowed and took his bloody hand to kiss.

0403 hours

Keying off his topographical map, Parnell had brought them straight as an arrow to the Torto River, or actually a branch of it, down in a cut through igneous rock massifs. The water was a mere stream but very cold and clear as gin. Stands of beech and eucalyptus and maquis brush lined it. In the distance, they could see the dim lights of Santo di Causo Village and to the southeast the intermittent flashes of ar-tillerylike heat lightning.

The cliff at the back of the Tempio di Giove had a steep, slanting pitch filled with narrow shelves and creases. In the starlight and the faint glow from the moon now waned to a crescent sliver, the rock looked white. On examining it, Parnell had warned them to be extremely careful going up. Igneous rock was solidified magma, he said, and would crumble easily with weight. He sent Smoker and Cowboy, the two most agile, up first to test the climb and secure the top.

Now they were nearly there, ten feet apart. A wind had sprung up as they came up the stream. It was stronger now, hot and lifting the odor of the rock, which smelled like sun-dried sheets. Passing through a small cluster of eucalyptus saplings, their trunks twisted like Js, Smoker braced his boots and reached for another, higher rock hold. A few feet above him, he saw the top edge of the cliff silhouetted against the stars.

The rock crumbled in his hand, the chips bouncing off the face as they fell. He swore, tried for another handhold, got it, continued up. That tiny moment flashed a memory: Nashville, Tennessee, in '38 when he was still an itinerant boxer and on the bum. Flat broke, he'd drifted into town hoping to get a fight, maybe take the place of an undercard no-show, get banged around for a few bucks. Instead, he went on a four-day wine binge in the train yard with an old man who had a wooden leg and ended up at the Salvation Army mission on Eighth and Broadway with one helluva hangover.

The mission super got him a day's work putting in yard sprinklers at a big two-story white house with columns out front in the exclusive Franklin Heights district. Another guy went with him, a wino Cherokee Indian called Calypso. He told him the house belonged to a big-shot heart specialist who was also a world-class mountain climber.

The doctor stood around in a silk bathrobe and leather slippers and watched them work, calling them "boy": "Make sure that line's in straight, boy," and "Goddammit, boy, I said *two* feet down." Smoker finally had enough. He said to the man, "Y'all call me 'boy' one more time, asshole, I'm gon' take your goddamned head off." The physician saying, "Oh? You think you can do it?" And Smoker saying, "I don't think you want to find out." And the doc smiling, answering, "All right, then, let's get to it."

They fought bare-knuckled for nearly forty-five minutes

in the backyard, the man's wife watching out through a so-
larium window. The doctor turned out to be fast and as strong
and wiry as a coal miner with the strongest legs Wineberg
had ever seen. Eventually they both got too exhausted to continue, just stood there all bloody with their hands on their
knees, gasping.

"What the hell's your name, fella?" the doctor croaked.
Smoker told him. "Damn, Wineberg," he said. "You're pretty
good."

"Y'all ain't so bad yourself," Smoker answered.

The doctor invited him into the house and they had lunch,
thick ham sandwiches and French cognac, and he told him
all about his mountaineering exploits, ending with, "By
God, you'd make one *hell* of a climber. . . ."

A flashlight beam suddenly shot out over the top of the
cliff, three feet above him, and he shoved his body against
the cliff face. He heard the scuff of boots. The light beam
went out and down, moving casually across the eucalyptus
tops. It began to probe to Smoker's left, toward Cowboy.

Wineberg braced his legs, his heart singing with adrenaline. He reached down and took his trench knife from his
boot. The light beam swung wide, then jerked back. A man's
voice cried, *"Ach! Wer ist?"*

Smoker propelled himself up over the cliff's edge. He
collided with the man's calves, climbed up them, the German
shoving back with a stifled cry. He began to pummel Wineberg's back, Smoker hanging on, climbing, and then his
trench knife came up and over in a roundhouse and the blade
went deep into the man's left eye.

The German started a gasping scream, clawed at the knife
blade. Wineberg slammed his other hand against the man's
mouth, stifling it. They struggled. He felt teeth clamp down
on his palm with a sharp stab of pain. He finally got his knife
free and plunged it back in again, this time into the German's
neck. Dropping to his knees, he pulled the soldier's weight
over him. For a moment, they both hung on the edge. Then

the German went headfirst over the cliff and slid, tumbling, down the face.

Smoker went to ground, laid himself out flat, listening over his panting. Nothing. A few yards away rose the temple, a triangular shape against the stars, its columns faintly glowing. He glanced back, saw Cowboy coming over the cliff edge, rolling, swinging his Thompson off his back. They remained stark-still. Smoker pointed at the temple. Cowboy nodded. Together, they rose and dashed for the edifice, running low, and went up between the columns.

Inside, it seemed dark but stars still filled the wide opening where the roof had once been. They were sharp and glittery, yet beyond them the sky was already lightening with a faint infusion of gray. The two men moved forward.

Smoker stumbled over something. He jerked back, bringing up his weapon. There was a dark object on the floor. He reached out, touched it. Clothing. Something harder, a body, already stiff in rigor mortis. In moving it, he had released that peculiar smell of death, a cloying dense odor that could be nothing else. He discovered a second body a few feet away, this one on its back with blood all over the place, sticky as half-dried glue.

Cowboy had crossed to the other line of columns. Now he came back. Smoker pointed at the body, held up his fingers, indicating two. Then he motioned for Fountain to return to his side of the temple and scooted to the opposite side. He squatted with his shoulder against the stone. It felt pockmarked, ridged with wear, its pedestal all rounded corners.

Nearby he saw the dark shapes of two automobiles and caught the smell of horses, heard a chuffing whinny. The animals were among olive trees downslope and to the left. Looking out the sides of his eyes so as to create better definition in the dark, he scanned, right to left and back.

For the last hour there had been distant artillery going from the lower the slopes of Etna. Now in the light of two quick flashes, he saw shadowy figures at the edge of the trees on the right and the momentary gleam of a gun barrel. Then, from the other side of the temple, came the clear, hollow sound of something striking a mortar tube.

There was a movement behind him. He whirled around as a whispery voice challenged, "Straw." He relaxed. Parnell had assigned the word *strawberry* as a recognition signal. Smoker gave the countersign: "berry."

Red came up. They leaned close. "Mortar on the left," Smoker said. "I think an MG in them trees yonder." He flicked his thumb. "They's also two dead civilians inside."

Parnell turned and looked at him, started to say something. Kaamanui crept over, squatted, his Thompson's butt-plate on the temple stones. Red leaned around the column, studied it and the others for a moment, then pulled back. He leaned closer to Sol.

"This is the best cover," he said softly. "Set up interior positions." He pointed toward the olive grove on the right. "Possible machine gun." Next, he pointed across to the other stand of trees. "If they've got more, they'll be there. At least one mortar on the east side. Two men on security. We'll hit the bastards at the first solid light. Machine guns first, then the mortars."

Kaamanui nodded, turned, and faded back into the lightening darkness.

Don Vino Caprano and his men halted, their horses blowing and stamping. As if by silent command, the riders began to spread out into a single line in a shallow rift of the grass plain, all facing toward the Tempio di Giove, which wasn't yet visible a mile uphill. On the southern side of the great dark bulk of Mount Etna with its orange crown shimmering with heat distortion, the horizon now held a rapidly emerging line of grayish yellow light.

The men were silent, seventy mounted riders with the don out front. Only the occasional snort and nicker of a horse or the tinkling jingle of a harness sounded. Then came the sharp metallic clicks of rifle bolts, the snap of shotgun breeches. Men bowed their heads, made the sign of the cross, and kissed their thumbnails. They adjusted their buttocks in their makeshift saddles, tightened their head bandannas.

Then everyone went still, waiting.

Sergeant Habstreise knew they were out there although it was still too dark to pick out objects on the plain below. Even in the random flashes of artillery he had been unable to detect any movement. But he knew, *sensed* the enemy there with that honed instinct of a combat soldier.

He walked farther down the slope and emerged from the lower side of the olive grove. Birds were beginning to twitter in the branches and the air had the dense coolness of predawn. The sky was quickly expanding with light, the horizon now crayoning softly with streaks of pastel red.

Such *Sicilienischen Scheiskerl* down there, he thought contemptuously. *They've already wasted their best advantage for attack, in the dark, instead of charging up in broad daylight. Unzivilisiert.* Just too ignorant to comprehend the exquisite beauty and effect of a well-executed tactical assault.

He turned and looked toward the other olive grove. In the increasing light, he could see Tino Borgo and his woman sitting together at the edge of the trees. Now *there* was a pair, all right. Fucking for everybody to see and then the man killing his own father, the woman like a whore-witch with more steel in her than him. *Scheisse!* He shook his head, made one last sweep with his binoculars, and went back up the hill.

One of his men was with four Sicilians at the first machine gun position. "Everything ready here?" he asked his comrade in German.

"*Ya, Feldwebel,*" the soldier answered. "As ready as monkeys *can* be."

The two Germans laughed.

"It won't be long," Habstreise said.

"Ya. I think I can smell them out there. Or perhaps it is just *these* fellows, eh?"

The sergeant grunted, looked around. "Where is Gunter?"

"I thought he was with you, *Feldwebel.*"

Habstreise had sent his squad leader, Gunter Kittel, to circuit the position's perimeter twenty minutes before. Frowning, he hurried to the other machine gun crew. Kittel wasn't there, either. Going farther upslope, he checked with the two men positioned with the Sicilian mortar crew. Still no Gunter.

The hair on the back of his neck lifted and his instincts clicked up several notches. "Weissen," he snapped. "Alert the others. Double-check the lower perimeter. Kittel is missing."

The soldier darted away. The dozen or so *bravi* sitting beside their mortars watched, puzzled.

He took hold of the other soldier's tunic, lifted him. "Come with me. Watch yourself." Clicking off the safeties of their MP-40 machine pistols, they moved cautiously up the hill and then turned to work their way around behind the temple.

Bird watched them coming, the two Germans crouched, picking their way slowly toward the rear of the building. He was on the upper right side of it, Cappacelli down on the left so his field of fire could cover anyone approaching from where the automobiles were parked. Wyatt had instantly recognized the "splinter and water" camouflage pattern of the Germans' uniforms, Panzer Grenadiers, one a sergeant. Good soldiers, these.

The Germans paused. The sergeant said something to his companion and the two separated, the other soldier advancing to and up the pedestal steps. Bird pressed back against the last column, the thirteen others on his side lined away into perspective in the increasing light. It was creeping steadily upward, fusing like the houselights in a theater, causing objects to emerge out of the shadows. The soldier on the pedestal cautiously peered between two columns near the middle and then stepped between them.

Wyatt eased out his belt knife, the soft whisper of steel on leather. With his other hand, he gently rested his Thompson, butt down, against the column. Straightening, he listened intently for the miniscule sound of boot to ground. He was calm but tightly alert, always the soldier's soldier, his entire body coalescing down into a single, ready-to-move entity.

Time was like a sound, a hum in the stillness. He turned, looked into the temple. Empty. When he swung back, there was the German sergeant fifteen feet away, his head turned to look over his right shoulder, his machine pistol waist high, pointing in that direction. Wyatt's mind flashed through possible options, his eyes measuring the distance between him and the Kraut. Too far, too much ground to cover. Swiftly, he bent and swung up his Thompson, the weapon's momentum bringing it to his other hand as he dropped the knife from it to take the trigger. It clattered noisily onto the stone floor.

At that same instant there was the short, sharp sound of a man gagging, the scuffle of boots deeper in the temple. Someone taking out the other German. The Grenadier sergeant's head instantly snapped around. He saw Bird. Each looked into the other's eyes, the German's widening, Bird's unconsciously doing the same. For one long deathly moment that seemed composed of a thousand moments, the two men stared motionlessly at each other.

Then they moved. Wyatt brought up his Thompson and the German pivoted his body, swinging around but having to come nearly 180 degrees. He fired too soon. His rounds slammed into the two columns to Bird's left, sent stone chips flying. As the muzzle of his machine pistol completed its arc, the hole seeping a faint feathering of smoke, Wyatt fired a full burst, the Thompson climbing in his hands. Eight bullets stitched up the sergeant's body, blew his face apart, their impacts hurling the man off his feet.

An utter silence folded in as the cracks of the guns were

quickly absorbed by the open sky. Bird's heart pounded in his head and his ears rang. Yet his hearing was so acute now he actually detected the faint drone of bees, which had been wakened by the approach of dawn and were now hovering over the two dead civilians. Several more seconds ticked past. Then the two downslope machine guns opened on the temple.

A half minute before, the faces of every man in Don Caprano's force had been riveted on the eastern horizon, each man bent forward on his mount as the animals, sensing what was coming, stamped and sidestepped. In the sky, the reds and strong yellows that had enriched it earlier were gone now, leaving only the dull, gray pewter of dawn. A sudden, faint rainbow formed along the rim of the sea and then vanished as the brilliant white-yellow arc of the sun flared into view.

Don Vino raised his right arm, holding a shotgun. From up the hill came the sudden muffled chatter of machine guns. The distance isolated each bullet's ignition and their bursts came down slow and spaced. The men looked at each other, then back at the don. His arm came down. In one wild, screaming surge, the riders lunged forward, the thunder of their mounts picking up in volume as they poured out of their rift and began the long charge toward the Tempio di Giove.

Erice and Tino were still down below the olive grove, both of them lying with their arms over their eyes, dozing. At the first crashing blast of the machine guns, they jerked upright, Tino cursing with surprise. Erice looked out at the plain below, thinking it was Caprano and his men. Far away she saw the dark shapes of riders emerging from behind a low rise and come pounding toward them, their line losing straightness as the faster horses surged ahead. Dust rose be-

hind them, coiling and twisting up into the increasing daylight.

"They're coming!" she cried excitedly. Her eyes sparkled
and danced, so wide their whites gleamed. "Give me a gun.
Give me a fucking *gun!*"

Tino stared up at the first machine gun emplacement. The
German soldier had pushed his Sicilian crew aside and was
now handling the weapon. Shouting, Borgo leapt to his feet
and sprinted up toward the trees with Erice right behind him.

Parnell was on the left side of the temple, behind the third
column from the front, Cowboy and Sol farther down and
Smoker across. He'd watched the two German soldiers approach the building and then the one had come up and entered it. He heard the gagging scuffle as Fountain killed him
and a fraction of a second later the twin bursts of automatic
fire from the back of the temple, one weapon a German MP-40,
the other a Thompson.

Now the machine gun rounds were tearing up the temple
columns, ricochets screaming off, chunks of stone blowing
everywhere as the gunners rapidly traversed to lay in a wide
arc. He heard bullets slamming into the two automobiles.
There was a powerful, *whooshing* detonation as tracers hit a
fuel tank and exploded. Metal pieces hurtled out, striking
the columns with the metal crunch of a car accident. A large
piece of hood went skidding and smoking across the floor.

Down near the mortars, four small 50mm Leichters in a
line beside a rock outcropping, he saw the Sicilians hunkered down, their heads popping up now and then in confu-
sion. As he watched, they suddenly jumped up and scattered
in panic downslope toward the trees.

The German machine guns stopped to let them come in.
Instantly, Blue Team's Thompsons opened up, sending a volley of rounds snapping down through the trees. Two Sicilians
stumbled and fell, lay still.

Red saw a German soldier break out of the olive grove and head uphill toward the mortars, running headlong through the fleeing *bravi*. "Son-of-a-*bitch!*" he hollered. He knew what the Kraut intended to do, get a mortar going, lower its elevating arm to zero deflection, and shoot the damned thing at them like a rifle. Those 2.2-pound high-explosive shells would tear hell out of them and the temple. He fired a quick burst at him, missed just as the man launched himself through the air and disappeared behind the rocks.

One of the machine guns started again. When it stopped, the other picked up the fusillade, the gunners alternating bursts now to lay in continuous fire without overheating their barrels. During that momentary pause as they transferred, Blue Team responded, racking the trees with more plunging fire. They rolled grenades down the slope. Unfortunately, one exploded far short of the trees.

Parnell bellowed, "Mortar! On the left!"

As the Kraut guns transferred again, Red lunged to his feet and headed down toward the mortar position, sprinting, moving automatically without conscious thought. Behind him, he heard the full rushing volley of Thompsons as they covered him.

Rounds began striking the ground behind him, coming on. *Oh, Jesus,* his brain kept repeating. He neared the rocks and jumped toward them, landing behind one just as a fan of bullets went whipping above him, sizzling with the sounds of water droplets striking a hot griddle.

The German soldier was on one knee, working on a mortar. His head jerked up. Before he could react, Parnell was on him. The momentum of his 230-pound body carried them both beyond cover. The man struggled, trying to get to his bayonet. Red bulldogged him around, grabbed a handful of hair, and yanked his head back. In the same movement, he jammed his elbow under the man's chin, locked his other arm around the back of his head and twisted. He felt the soldier's neck snap, his cheek against the man's vertebrae. The

Kraut went limp. Red let him drop away and hurled himself backward to cover again.

The machine guns and Thompsons continued their alternating firing. And finally there were scattered shots from the Sicilians, Italian rifles, and MP-40s and the big booms of *luparas*. Smoke from the burning car and a grass fire it had started had begun pouring through the temple, its sparks and ashes drifting daintily up into the new morning sky.

There was another pause in the shooting. A few seconds later, Kaamanui came vaulting in over the rocks. Quickly he and Parnell shifted the mortar around and braced its baseplate against a rock, its tube so deflected it nearly rested directly onto the ground. They aimed it toward the closest machine gun position, which had begun firing again. Its tracers exploded out of the trees like white-hot baseballs.

With Parnell anchoring the mortar's baseplate with his boots, Sol scooped up a shell. It was black, shaped like a reversed hourglass with fins on the rear. He yanked the point-detonating fuse pin and rammed the shell down into the barrel, hard enough so it wouldn't hang up inside the tube. There was a sharp crack and a hollow, ringing *pa-wrumpp* as the missile went out in a blur. It exploded down among the trees with a bright burst of light and brown smoke filled with tree branches and bits of trunk.

They fired two more times, the baseplate getting too hot to touch. The third shell took out the machine gun and sent a Sicilian flying crookedly through the air. The body caught in tree branches and dangled, head down. The firing from the trees stopped abruptly. It was only then that they became aware of the shouts and thunder of Don Vino's incoming horsemen. They watched as they came flowing up over a rise just below the trees and charged forward in full gallop.

It didn't take long. Tino Borgo's *bravi* had been completely terrified and disoriented by the double attack. With all the German soldiers dead, Caprano's men went savagely about their killing. Parnell and his team immediately backed off, taking no part in the hand-to-hand fighting going on down there in the trees. Riderless horses screamed and bolted in all directions and were soon joined by Tino's mounts, the frightened animals fleeing wildly down the slope in a bunch. The automobile continued to burn. Now the grass fire reached the fuel tank of the other vehicle and it went up, dimming out the new sun with a pall of greasy brown smoke.

There were fourteen Borgo survivors. Caprano's *bravi,* still charged with bloodlust, kicked and dragged them to the edge of the olive grove. Back under the trees, others began slitting the throats of the wounded. The survivors came slowly, their hands on top of their heads, staring at the ground.

Cowboy cried out, "Goddamn! Lookit! Them sons a' bitches're killin' the wounded."

The entire team rose and moved forward, Parnell growling curses. Ten yards down, he turned his head, shouted, "Form a skirmish line. Stand ready." The men quickly fanned out, their weapons coming up. All except Cappacelli. He hesitated for a moment, then fell into line. But his Thompson was still lowered.

The survivors were kneeling now, some having been knocked down with rifle butts. Most continued staring numbly at the ground, silent, looking like penitents before an altar. Don Vino came up out of the trees, his clothes and hands covered with blood, carrying a long-bladed machete in one hand and his *lupara* in the other.

Red hollered at him, pointing at the kneeling prisoners. "You can't do this. I won't let you do this."

All the Sicilians paused, turned toward Blue Team coming down. There were nearly fifty of them. Parnell drew up about twenty yards away. The two groups faced each other, the *bravi* hot-eyed, blood-smeared.

With a shock Parnell realized one of the Borgo survivors was a *woman.* Beautiful dark hair, disheveled, framing exquisite features and eyes that were fierce and wild. She was kneeling beside a young, extremely handsome man. Unlike the others, however, she screamed at the Caprano mafiosi, hissing curses at them, shrieking that she would see them all in hell. The handsome young man beside her looked straight ahead, his own beautiful eyes darting, his face pale in the smoky sunlight.

Don Vino turned and stared at Lieutenant Parnell with his dead snake's eyes.

Parnell shouted again, "This is *murder*, goddammit."

Caprano snapped back, "Is no your saying now. You can leave."

"Bullshit," Red shouted back. "We ain't going anywhere. We're American soldiers, not *butchers*."

The don tilted his head, studied him. "You want to fight us?"

"Yes, if necessary."

"Then you will die. Maybe even *I* die. What your government is saying then?"

That stopped Parnell. *Shit!* But he continued staring balefully back at the Sicilian. From the corners of his eyes, he saw his men watching, even noted that Cappacelli had finally lifted his weapon. In frustration, he drew his lips back over his teeth, then he inhaled deeply and lowered his Thompson. "Stand down," he said quietly.

For the first time, a tiny smile touched Caprano's thick lips. He nodded. "You are very brave, *americano*. And also you free me and my brother. Then you fight my enemies. I admit respect for you. But now is your leaving."

He turned his head, growled an order. Immediately, Scuzzulato stepped forward. He had a bleeding wound on his cheek. The don instructed him to guide the Americans to the coast. The don swung back to face Parnell again. He was no longer smiling. He said, "Hear this, *tenente*. We meet again, I will kill you."

"And I'll kill *you*, you dago son of a bitch," Parnell snapped. They locked eyes again, the Sicilian's dark and dead, Red's smoldering At last he turned and headed back toward the temple and the cliff edge beyond, the team members following, moving swiftly, their minds and ears closing off to what was happening behind them.

Sergeant Bird came abreast of Cappacelli, slowed, keeping pace with him for a moment. He stared at him, then said, "The nex' time y'all balk when the lieutenant gives you a direct order, cousin, it'll be the *last* fuckin' thing you do." Without turning his head, Angelo nodded. Wyatt moved by. As the others also moved past, each gave Cappacelli a long, foreboding look of disgust.

Late on the afternoon of 22 July, forward elements of the 15th Regiment of General Truscott's 3rd Infantry Division entered Palermo. Although Patton had ordered him to hold his troops out so that he himself could triumphantly enter the historical port city with the 2nd Armored, a municipal delegation had pleaded so desperately with Truscott for troops to restore order in the city that he chose not to wait and sent units in immediately.

Nevertheless, General Patton had his glorious entry the following morning, Palermo citizens waving hastily drawn U.S. flags and cursing the Fascists. He set up his Seventh Army headquarters in the ancient palace of the Norman kings and immediately ordered his forces to race along the north coast toward Messina. He was more determined than ever to beat Montgomery, who by now had returned to the offensive and was moving up the eastern coast of the island.

Three days later, Italian King Victor Emmanual III, spurred by the imminent collapse of his country and the first devastating Allied air raid on Rome, which had destroyed the Holy City's Corso railroad station, its university city, and the Littorio marshaling yards on the nineteenth, deposed Mussolini and turned the government over to Marshal Pietro Badoglio, who had made secret peace overtures to Eisenhower's chief of staff, General Bedell Smith, in Lisbon and Sicily. On hearing this, Hitler instantly ordered more fresh German divisions south into Italy to stop the Allied invasion of the mainland, which he was certain was coming.

Meanwhile, it took Parnell and his men fourteen days to cross the Nébrodi Mountains and reach the tiny north coast fishing village of Santo Zappulla, four miles southwest of Cape d'Orlando. Constantly dodging German patrols, they were nevertheless able to destroy a small rail line near Mount Zimmara and a highway bridge between Cesaro and Femmina Morta using the last of their grenades.

Scuzzulato left them among the steep ocean cliffs outside the fishing village, the Sicilian actually getting teary-eyed, promising to visit them in America. For the next five days they remained in hiding, living off stolen German rations and trying fruitlessly to raise their OSS liaison in Palermo. On the morning of 11 July they helplessly had to watch as a small American amphibious landing force got driven off its beachhead at Brolo, six miles away on the other side of the cape.

Forty-eight hours after that they finally linked up with units of the 3rd Infantry Division and the 36th Engineers, who were furiously rebuilding trestles and ravine bridges along the coast road, which the Germans had destroyed as they withdrew.

At last, in the early morning hours of 17 August, Blue Team was with advance elements from Combat Force A of the 2nd Armored Division when they entered the badly bomb-damaged port of Messina. The Germans and Italians had already abandoned the city four days earlier in a brilliantly executed evacuation of troops, weapons, and armored vehicles across the Strait of Messina. Only two hours later the lead tanks of Montgomery's Eighth Army rumbled into the city from the south. Patton had won his race. Now his GIs good-naturedly taunted Monty's troops with, "Hey, where in hell you been, tourists?" while the Brits, smiling grimly, yelled back, "Hello, you bloody bastards."

* * *

Parnell knocked lightly on the mahogany door. Someone shouted, "Enter." He stepped into a large, ornately paneled room. It was on the third floor of what had been Messina's post office. Now it housed the field headquarters of the U.S. II Corps. He strode forward and braced before a cluttered bivouac table sitting in the center of the room.

An officer in shirtsleeves stood at the window with a pair of binoculars. Down below was the vast Plazza di Duomo. It was now filled with jagged bomb craters and blast debris, the ruins of a huge twelfth-century cathedral and massive fountain called the Fontana di Orione. Here and there lay the truncated, nâked marble bodies of Greek ocean gods turned to mere chunks of stone. The officer was General Bradley's adjutant, Lieutenant Colonel Chet Hanson.

"Lieutenant John Parnell reporting, sir," Red barked. An hour earlier, he had hitched a ride with a messenger from the 2nd Armored and was still in his filthy battle dress, his face covered with a month's growth of beard.

Without removing the binoculars from his eyes, Hanson said, "I've been expecting you, Lieutenant." He continued peering out for a few more seconds, then turned back, shaking his head. "Can't understand it. We've bombed hell out of this place and those damned pigeons are still here."

He smiled and extended his hand. They shook. He was a chunky man with sun-reddened skin and short white hair. The room was humid, heavy with the smell of bomb dust and expended explosives and harbor water. "How's the team?" he asked.

"Fine, sir."

"I understand you were successful in helping save some goomba ass?"

Parnell's eyes went hard. "Yes, sir."

"Well, I'm afraid I've got some bad news for you. Sticks has asked that I personally inform you." "Sticks" was Colonel Dunmore's nickname from college. "He's been sent back to England. He tried to get word to you through your Palermo contact, but OSS put the quietus to that. I'm afraid your team's no longer under his command."

Parnell drew back. "Sir?"

"You're now officially an operational unit of OSS."

"Damn it."

"Yes, I'm sorry. Sticks nearly had a fit when he was told. Your new CO will be a Major Max Nunn. He's scheduled to arrive here tomorrow."

"Yes, sir."

"Is there anything you need?"

"No, sir."

"Well, good luck."

"Thank you, sir." Parnell braced again, spun, and strode out.

SALERNO/NAPLES
Operation Avalanche

Eight

The sub's escape chamber was an iron barrel, the floor corrugated, the bulkheads of tempered steel. There was a hatch wheel on the top with a ladder leading to it. A thick window framed in bolts gave out into the forward torpedo room. It was cool inside, unlike the oppressive heat of the other compartments of the submarine, and stank of Bunker-C diesel fuel and the foundry odor of raw metal.

All of Blue Team was in there, standing in a circle and bracing themselves along a small railing. Each wore a Momsen lung, a black rubber bag strapped around their necks and waists. It had two hoses connected to a mouthpiece, one hose for inhaling, the other for expelling used breath, which returned to the bag for cleaning and reoxygenating.

Besides the Momsens, each man carried a standard paratrooper M1936 musette field bag on a harness. It contained his disassembled Thompson and spare clips and grenades along with his jump boots and trousers, dyed black cotton ODs.

All the bags were encased in oilcloth envelopes that had been heat-sealed. Around this outer covering was a rolled-up truck tire tube that had a CO_2 cartridge in its stem for instant inflation. The men were barefooted and dressed in tight black T-shirts, black swimming trunks, and belt knives. Their faces, arms, and legs had been smeared with Bunker-C to hide the sheen of their skin.

They had practised this escape procedure twice before in the waters off Palermo aboard this same vessel, the USS *Manta,* SS-185, a fleet submarine on detached duty with Vice Admiral M. Kent Hewitt's Western Naval Task Force 80. Now she drifted stationary fifty feet below the surface, just beyond the fifteen-fathom curve off the southern rim of Salerno Beach, Italy.

Parnell gave each man a last check, a tap, a nod, then he turned to the round window and gave the sailors outside the thumbs-up sign. There was a rumble of water blowing through piping, then the sharp hiss as it began pouring into the chamber through vents in the deck. The chamber was completely filled within a minute. The rush of the water jostled the men against each other. It was pleasantly cold, everyone breathing through their hoses now, heads down, eyes closed, feeling an ache in their ears from the increasing water pressure.

The venting ceased, the sounds of it echoing back through piping. Parnell felt the buoyancy in his body lifting him slightly. There was a solid knocking on the bulkhead, the metallic rapping exaggerated by the confined water. Quickly, he went up the ladder and felt for the safety dogs along the rim of the hatch. He held his eyes open, the oil in the water making them sting. Everything was blurry and the light through the window made a shaft of fuzzy gold. It suddenly disappeared, the sailors shutting it off so as not to show a gleam when they opened the outer hatch, instantly plunging the chamber into a solid blackness, the only sound the soft, rubbery inhalations of the Momsens.

There were six safety dogs. Red released each one and then spun the hatch wheel. He heard the suck of seals, braced himself, and pushed against the hatch. It was heavy. But once he got it moving, its counterweight quickly pulled it open and back onto its hinges. He climbed through and drifted into open ocean.

It held the soft, filmy glow of moonlight, faintly blue white. Aft of the escape hatch, he could see the huge, blurry shape of the sub's conning tower and the long black expanse of its upper deck. Somersaulting, he signaled for the others to follow. One by one they exited and headed for the surface. Just below it, they would inflate their tires and ease them through it.

Kaamanui was the last one out. He and Parnell closed the hatch and Sol swung the wheel until it locked. Using the handle of his belt knife, Red tapped on the deck. An answering tap came. They pushed off and stroked for the surface.

They were only five hundred yards from shore since the bottom off this coastline dropped quickly into depth. The shore itself formed a white ribbon, no lights visible at all. Inland, mountains arose on the right and far left covered with forest that was interspersed with exposed rock outcroppings that gleamed in the moonlight. Between the mountains was flat sea plain with occasional hilly undulations. There was no wind, the water flat as a mirror on which the moon cast a perfectly straight line.

Forming abreast and towing their tire rafts, they swam toward the right where an ancient rock jetty poked out into the gulf. At the end of it was a squat, round stone tower that had been a lighthouse in Roman times. The air was sea-fresh, tinged with the sweetness of pines and still-sun-warmed sand.

The rocks along the foundation of the jetty were thick with seaweed, slimy as river mud. Using little shelves worn out by the sea, the men hurriedly unwrapped and assembled their weapons, deflated the tires, folded them, and stuffed them and the rest of their gear into the field packs. Harnessed up once more, they returned to the water and stealthily moved closer to the shore, remaining in the shadows of the jetty.

The beach dune line lay about a hundred yards from the water. On the ocean side there was a double-apron barbed-wire fence. Occasionally there was a pathway through the wire. Each had what the Germans called Spanish riders, sturdy wooden frames that could easily be wheeled into place to cut off access from the water. A second line of barbed wire, this one composed of three rolls of concertina wire, lay inland another fifty yards. Between them were four rows of antitank dragon's teeth, three-foot-high tetrahedral-shaped concrete blocks.

Squatting side by side in the moon shadows of the jetty head, Parnell and Bird surveyed the German obstacle defenses. Earlier air reconnaissance photos of the landing area had been correct. Intelligence reports stated that the Germans were expecting an invasion but did not know precisely where it would come in. As a result, they had constructed similar beach barriers from Naples thirty miles to the north all the way down to the Gulf of San Eufimia 120 miles southward.

The first phase of Blue Team's Tactical Mission Order was to quickly verify the air-recon photos of these obstacles along with possible gun emplacements and fire lines. Parnell would also test the beach sand to see if it would carry the weight of assault vehicles. During the coming invasion, which was less than twenty-seven hours away, this stretch of shoreline, designated Yellow Beach, would be the center of the American landing force.

Once this information was collected, the team was to head inland and rendezvous with a small band of partisans who had been operating in the area for three weeks gathering intelligence. Their combined information would then be relayed to the USS *Manta* holding on picket duty offshore.

Parnell would then divide the team, sending Bird and a crew northeast to blow a key bridge on the Sele River, which would hopefully delay German armor from moving south into the Salerno Plain. Meanwhile he and Kaamanui would set up forward observation positions south of Paestum from which they could call in naval fire missions against German reinforcements. Their fire requests would be fielded by the USS *Jeremy Jacobs,* a reconstructed destroyer that would act as a monitor ship off the American beaches during the invasion.

Now he scooped up a handful of wet beach sand, pinched it between his fingers, then ground it between his palms. It was good quartzone sand with feldspar and plates of white mica mixed in. It immediately compacted into a solid layer. Good, the beach would carry assault vehicles well enough. He checked his watch: 12:43 A.M. Giving the moonlit dunes one last scan, he turned and signaled the wire probers out.

Two men moved out of the shadows and back into the water, drifting slowly along in the small shore wavelets.

Cappacelli knew he'd screwed up back there at the temple fight. Yeah, he thought, the goomba had hesitated. It was all that coming-back-home nostalgia, getting back and close to the deep traditions of Mafia that had thrown him off his stride. Okay, so he'd fucked up, but he'd made up his mind he'd never do it again.

Certainly not over *here.* This wasn't fun and games, all for show, like back in Boston or San Francisco with the would-be wise guys sitting around the social club bullshitting each other, everybody trying to out-tough one another. No, over here things got hot *real* fast, down and dirty-vicious and deadly. He knew that even though he hadn't bonded with these particular men, they needed him and he needed them.

It had been a whole lot easier in Yellow Team establishing necessary comradeship and unit loyalty. With men like Lieutenant Choo-Choo Cooper, a good head, and Joey Allioto and Franco Gambarri, both out of Chicago and nearly made guys. They talked his talk, came from the same background with the same ancestral blood. But with Blue Team, what did you have? Hayrackers, a spic-a-rooney, a Kanak, and an ex-pro head-knocker commanding officer, all tight because they'd seen heavy killing together.

Still, when he considered it, he couldn't blame them for their animosity. He wondered if old Sergeant Bird would really take him out if he screwed up again. And thought, *Hell yes, why not?* He *should* have been shot back there at the temple. Instantaneous obedience was what kept people alive in war. Actually, it wasn't much different in Mother Sicily or in the Families in the States. Your capo told you to shit, man, you shit, you didn't ask into what hole.

Since the fight at the temple, Angelo had kept to himself, as much as that was possible in such a small unit. Otherwise, he literally jumped at orders, keeping right up there with the others. Once or twice, he'd attempted to draw one of them into conversation, maybe explain why he'd done what he'd done. They always cut him off.

Although he'd fully expected Parnell to jump him, maybe even transfer him back into the Mohawker reserve pool, the lieutenant never mentioned the incident. Still, it was obvious they were all watching him closely, checking for the first sign of another momentary betrayal. Well, they didn't have to worry. He'd carry his part of the load just like the rest of them.

He shoved all of that into the back of his mind and instead focused on the ground directly in front of him and on the soft, delicate penetrations of his knife blade. He and Wineberg were slowly probing the outer double-apron fence, him in the lead. They were already several feet into it, the thing constructed like a wire tarp over a stack of timbers.

The Germans were known to lay antipersonnel mines in these fences, placing them in the intervals between the layers with trip wires fastened to the diagonals. As he inched his way forward, he sweated profusely. This goddamn probing for mines made his throat constrict as if a chunk of dry ice had lodged in it. The sand was very white in the moonlight and kept getting sucked up into his nostrils, his face so close to the ground.

There! He stopped dead. A tiny thread of light glistened directly ahead of him. Trip wire. He followed it to the right where it disappeared into the sand, then signaled Smoker with a soft hiss. Very gently, he began probing into the sand, almost immediately felt the upper edge of the mine casing. He ran his blade half around it, recognized its contour, an S-Mine fitted with twin ZZ-35 pull igniters.

He paused. His hands trembled. He blew on them, rubbed their tips across the rough handle of his knife. Then, he meticulously began displacing sand until the mine's two pull igniters were exposed. First checking for antihandling devices, he quickly neutralized them by snapping their lock pins back into place. He twisted the knife in his hand and prepared to cut the trip wire.

"No!" Smoker croaked in a harsh whisper. "Check the other side first."

Angelo froze. Then, still holding the wire, he followed it to the left. Sure enough, there was another mine on the other end. The pull of his cutting would have triggered it. He put his forehead onto the sand, inhaled. *God, God.* Steadying himself, he dug away sand to expose the igniters, neutralized them, and then severed the wire.

He and Smoker moved ahead again. At the inner edge of the fence, he found a third mine. This one had its wire hooked to a diagonal. Once more he ran through the defusing procedure, cut the wire, and slid out into open ground. Wineberg followed quickly. Back under the fence, two more Mohawkers were already coming through.

The team moved through the dragon's teeth, staying low, darting, and holding, covering each other, going quickly. They knew the Germans wouldn't waste antipersonnel mines on this ground, and any antitank mines would never trigger off from their light body weight. In the brilliant moonlight, the cement blocks looked like miniature pyramids.

They'd covered about two hundred yards when Bird on point stopped abruptly, waved. Everybody went flat. Parnell waited a moment, then crawled up beside Wyatt. The dragon's teeth and wire continued on for another hundred yards. Then there was an open sandy area that fronted a little collection of stone huts with driftwood and straw roofs, a fisherman's permanent camp. There were racks used to dry fish and the long, narrow skeletons of fishing boats turned upside down.

Bird leaned in. "Observation post, Lieutenant. Second shack. I caught static."

Red studied the position. Beyond the shacks a stream emptied into the ocean. On both sides of it was thick maquis brush above the high-water mark and low oak trees farther inland. He squinted, scanning the trees. "Probably another one up in them trees. What do you think, two-man post?"

"Yeah. I seen only one muzzle."

Parnell cursed. "All right, we'll have to take them out."

Bird nodded. He turned and signaled the two men directly behind, Wineberg and Fountain. He explained the objective. Quickly, the three crawled deeper into the dragon's teeth, headed east. Parnell immediately set out the remaining men so they could lay in cover fire if things got hot.

It was very quick, the two German soldiers half asleep inside the stone room, its rocks simply laid one on top of the other with no back door and the ground sandy. It contained only a Model 34 Maschinengewehr on a bipod mount, several ammo cans, rations, and a Telefunken 15Z *feldtelefon* set on one of the cans.

The three Mohawkers rushed right in. There was a German obscenity and then only the sounds of grunting, fighting men, the moonlight streaming through the gun port. Cowboy got his knife blade into the right ear of one of the soldiers. A needle-thin stream of blood shot right out of it as he withdrew and the man fell so quickly and so heavily that they could hear his knees cracking. The other died murmuring a German obscenity.

While Bird and Cowboy dismantled the machine gun's breech, Smoker returned to the dragon's teeth to inform

Parnell. Once again grouped, the team moved to the streambed and headed inland. There was only a trickle of water in the bottom. The silt stank of rotten fish, and crabs skittered in the moonlight like huge spiders. A half mile inland, they came up into marshland, long stretches of saw grass and clumps of balsam willow with little open ponds, each with its own reflected moon like a pupil.

Double-timing, they moved in a line along narrow fishermen's paths, hearing now the distant growl of machinery too far off to identify. Soon they reached a broad, two-lane coastal highway, the road made of cement blocks. A road marker said AGROPOLI with an arrow pointing south. Once beyond the road, Parnell took another compass reading and they continued on. Two miles due east were the ancient ruins of Paestum.

The ruins stood on a low hill, a collection of partial walls and foundations surrounded by a high wall. It was dominated by three large buildings, a temple to Ceres, a basilica, and a smaller temple to Neptune. Built in the fourth century B.C. outside the ancient city of Lucania, the buildings were surprisingly intact although their Doric columns, pediments, and foundation stones were fractured and rounded with age. In the lowering moon, they created a dark, brooding presence from which the men could almost conjure the eerie voices of ancient maidens.

The partisan leader was Augustin Friedl-Real. He and another man were casually waiting on the top step of the temple to Ceres. Parnell flashed a recognition light. It was instantly countersigned by Real, using a mirror to capture the moon.

He turned out to be a tall, slender man in his late twenties dressed in tight black trousers, black turtleneck sweater, and beret, which made him look like a French Apache dancer. The other man was silent, with a sullen, lean face. Parnell and Real shook hands.

Augustin's English was very good, spoken with a soft,

lisping Castilian accent. He introduced the other man, Milovan Yildirim, a Yugoslavian Communist connected to Tito's Resistance Partisans. While they talked, Bird posted security guards around the ruins.

Freidl-Real watched the men move off into the darkness. "I thought you would have a larger force," he said.

"We'll be enough."

The partisan's teeth gleamed as he smiled. "Yes, of course."

According to OSS briefings, the Resistance movement in Italy was composed of a hodgepodge of different political entities: Communists, Socialists, Labor Democrats, Actionists, *Autonomi,* Italian soldiers who had deserted and managed to evade *Waffen SS* hunter squads, and even members of the Camorra, the Neopolitan Mafia.

Freidl-Real's own little band belonged to a particularly militant Trotskyite unit of the Italian Communist Party called the Red Flags but now associated with the CVF. Most had been students before joining the Resistance. Augustin himself was a native of Barcelona and had fought with the Loyalists in the Spanish Civil War while attending Madrid University. After his parents, both famous writers, were murdered by Franco thugs, he had fled across the Alps to Slovenia where he created an anti-Fascist student cell that put out an underground newspaper called the *Red Orchestra.*

He eventually crossed into Italy and linked up with the Italian Communists and finally with the Volunteers. At the time, they were involved in violent labor strikes in Turin and Milan in early 1943. British intelligence reports described Real as brilliant, intellectual, and courageous, although condescending to the point of contempt toward anyone he did not consider his equal.

For the last six months, both OSS and British intelligence had been supplying the Communist bands with equipment, weapons, and money, bringing them in to pickup points along the western coast or dropping them by parachute. In return, they supplied the Allies with updated intelligence transcribed by clandestine radio or on microfilm smuggled out in bundles called "butter packs." They also conducted hit-and-flee raids against rail lines and Nazi supply convoys south of the Liri Valley.

Although the CVF didn't know the specifics of the coming invasion, Augustin and his small team had been dispatched to collect data on German military concentrations and units along the Gulf of Salerno and the Sorrento Peninsula six weeks earlier. When it was decided that Blue Team would effect their own prelanding mission, Freidl-Real had been chosen to act as their liaison and guide.

He now led Red deeper into the temple, where they pried up a section of the marble floor where Real had hidden a cache of weapons, ammunition, explosives, and two short-wave radio transceivers that had been air-dropped four days earlier. Meanwhile, Yildirim quietly disappeared into the darkness. A few minutes later, he returned driving a German Mercedes-Benz Type-170 light personnel carrier the band had stolen from a depot outside Battipáglia.

The gear was loaded and everyone climbed aboard. With Real driving, they sped off into the night, the vehicle's headlights merely dim blue slits. Soon, they passed down into rolling farm country with orchards of orange trees and quince and pomegranate and open stretches of harvested tomato fields where the rotting leftover fruit made the air smell like catsup.

The camp sat beside the Fiumarello River in a grove of scrub oak, a sordid collection of lean-tos, and tattered tents in a circle. Beyond the tents was a small corral made of oak boughs containing scrawny sheep and goats and several ponies. A soft breeze sifted through the scrub oak and patches of broom grass.

Freidl-Real hurled the German personnel carrier into the center of the encampment and skidded to a stop beside one of the tents, dark-colored with tassels hanging from its corners. He climbed out, leaving the engine running. "Come,

Lieutenant," he said. "I'll show you my maps and intelligence notes."

Red got out, stood for a moment looking the place over. The air smelled of corkwood and olive-pit smoke and animal dung. In the vehicle, Yildrim immediately slid into the driver's seat. A pony whinnied somewhere in the darkness and a man coughed, the sound of it phlegm-filled, harsh.

Cowboy said, "What the hell *is* this place?"

"Looks like a Gypsy camp," Red answered.

"That's exactly what she is, Lieutenant," Wineberg said. "I used to live in one. When I was on the bottle in Missouri? They all smell the same."

Parnell glanced at Wyatt. "Set up a security perimeter." The men immediately dismounted and moved back up the road, their weapons unshouldered. Yildirim drove out between two tents and killed the engine.

The tent was stuffy and hot. Red waited inside the entrance while Real lit a lantern. It had a red glass chimney that gave everything a battle-lantern sheen of red. Intricately designed woolen blankets were spread on the dirt ground, the cloth exuding the musky scent of unclean bodies and sexual activity. The tent also contained a table fashioned of wooden fruit boxes, an old leather valise, bundles of clothes, and a case of expensive Bordeau wine.

A young, black-haired woman was asleep on the blankets. She lifted her head and then sat up, sleepily brushing hair from her eyes, which were deep-set and downward slanted. She was completely naked. Her breasts were heavy and dark-nippled and her pubic hair was very black but fine as down, her skin dusky. She studied Parnell without any hint of embarassment.

Freidl-Real said something to her in French. She rose, smoothed down the blankets, then retrieved the valise. Red watched her. She wasn't a particularly pretty woman yet her body was ripe and sensual and she seemed to possess a certain little-girl innocence in the way she moved and the way she stood watching, her fingers clasped together.

Augustin knelt on the blankets and opened the valise. He took out several maps and a leather-bound notebook. Pausing, he glanced at Parnell, who had remained near the tent flap. In the light, Freidl-Real was clean-shaven and smooth-skinned with a shock of unruly black hair. His features were well balanced and he had penetrating eyes that, even in the scarlet glow, carried a look of mocking insolence.

"Let me introduce you to my second-in-command," he said. "This is Cesara Arance. Cesara, Lieutenant Parnell." He smiled amusedly. "You needn't be embarrassed by her nakedness, Lieutenant. *She* isn't. After all, she's a whore. Fortunately, she's also part Corsican Gypsy, which is why the camp *voivode* has permitted us to remain while we conduct our business."

Parnell's gaze moved between the two. Then he stepped forward and lowered himself onto the blankets. Real's data turned out to be quite astounding in depth. He had detailed information on German army positions, specific units, and even their equipment and strengths. He had also pinpointed supply depots and heavily used roads and rail lines, particularly those through the mountains to the east and southeast. One ominous bit of data had just come in over the last thirty hours. It claimed that forward elements of the 16th Grenadier Division had been seen entering the Salerno Plain from the north.

Red grunted. "I'm impressed. You got all this in three weeks?"

Augustin shrugged. "A lot of our people are here. I was able to draw from many sources. And, of course, there was Cesara." Again he gave Red his little, off-center smirk. "Wonderfully surprising how much information a woman can get from a German soldier who has just fucked her."

The sound of a night bird suddenly drifted out of the stillness, a series of trilling notes as fragile as smoke. Quickly it faded. Augustin growled, "Germans." He instantly began gathering up his maps as Cesara leapt to the lantern and blew it out. Red came to his feet and headed for the tent flap. As he reached for it, it was snapped back and a large shadow loomed in the entrance.

It was Kaamanui. "Krauts, Lieutenant," he said quietly.

Parnell stepped outside. "How many?"

"Can't tell. Two small officers' vehicles."

"Don't engage them," Augustin said quickly from behind him. "They're not in force. Probably looking for a piece of ass. I'll handle it."

Red thought a moment, then touched Sol's arm. "Let 'em in. But heads up." Kaamanui darted away.

Real had gone back inside the tent. Parnell moved between it and the one beside it. The moon was low in the west now, the night entering that darker dark just before dawn. He could now sense the river nearby, hear its soft burbling whisper, and feel the coolness of its passing. He swung the Thompson from his shoulder, clicked off the safety.

The whine of small engines came, suddenly, as if the vehicles had been in a hollow and had just come over a rise. He spotted two pairs of blackout headlights approaching rapidly along the entrance road.

The cars came into the camp and stopped, sliding, sitting side by side, open four-man Schwimmwagen officers' cars. Dust fumed up over their lights, dimming them for a moment, then clearing to cast little pools of blue onto the ground. Red could make out two men in each vehicle. They all wore the high-crowned Einheitsmutze field cap of officers in a Grenadier Division. They were arguing and sounded inebriated.

Finally, one man climbed out and flicked on a flashlight. He played it over the tents and lean-tos. The officers in the other vehicle seemed to be trying to persuade him to leave. He waved them away and walked to the closest tent, whipped back the flap, and shone his light inside. After a moment, he moved to the next and did the same.

Parnell saw Freidl-Real step from his tent and move to the side of one of the cars. He said something in German to the lone officer. The man swung around, startled. *"Was ist los, Arschloch?"* he barked. *"Fur wen haltst du dich eigentlich?"*

One of the others said scoffingly, *"Ach, hat un einzig Scheisskerl Gipsy."*

Real spoke again, his voice warm and friendly. He turned slightly, indicated his tent, coaxing the German to use Cesara. *"Kommen sie, mein Herr. Ist sie Jungfrau. Die titten und Muschi einer Jungfrau."*

The German said, *"Ah? Es ist Schon?"*

"Ja, Leutnant," Augustin said. *"Ja erste Sahne."*

One of the officers in the other car said, *"Nein, nein, Kurt. Dis est dumm."* He shouted to the one with the flashlight who had just disappeared into the fourth tent in the circle. *"Helmuth, kommen—"*

From the tent came the sudden, high-pitched scream of a woman. There was a violent German curse and another man shouted several words in Romany, the Gypsy language. There was a tiny pause and then two revolver shots cracked through the darkness.

Parnell jerked up, thinking, *Oh, shit, this is all we need.*

The other German officers had instantly leaped out of their vehicles. Grabbing for their own sidearms, they headed in the direction of the shots, their boots slapping on the hard earth. Augustin had pulled a handgun from behind his back. As the last officer crossed through the car's headlights, he shot him, the man reeling off to the left and going down into shadow.

The other two stopped and whirled around. In the reflected glow, they both lifted their right arms, weapons extended, growling obscenities. Parnell shot the first, a double tap of his Thompson, two rounds blowing out in a single burst. From two other points around the circle of tents came two other Thompson bursts, which threw the second officer off his feet and down.

The one with the flashlight dashed from the tent where the firing had begun. He cast his light onto his two downed comrades. One was clawing at the ground, his uniform tunic soaked in blood. The German put his arms up, surrendering. Augustin shot him twice. He fell back onto his buttocks. A dark shadow leaped onto him viciously and began stabbing him repeatedly.

Parnell lunged out from between the tents. Cesara was standing just outside her tent, still naked. He shouted at her in Italian, "Get your gear. We're leaving."

Freidl-Real was going through the pockets of one of the Germans. There was a long, still moment. And then Gypsies began pouring out of their enclosures. Nothing was said, not a word. Three men carried the body of the shot Gypsy out of the tent and laid him on a small wooden horse cart. Others began hurriedly dismantling the tents and lean-tos. Several of the older children opened the corral and started bringing out the animals, the goats bleating skittishly and the ponies snorting and tossing their heads.

Red whistled his men in just as Yildirim came swinging back into the circle with the German personnel car. Two more of Freidl-Real's small band were with him, both young men. A moment later, Cesara emerged dressed in men's trousers and a dark sweater. She had the leather valise and some clothing. An Italian bolt-action rifle was slung over her shoulder.

Using the personnel carrier and one of the Schwimm-wagens, they raced out of the encampment, Augustin driving the heavier vehicle, Cowboy the other. Busy at their work, the Gypsies didn't even watch them go. It was 4:07 A.M.

A mile north of the camp, they crossed the river on an old stone bridge where the water ran over the roadbed. Then they turned onto a narrow, dirt road that led up into the foothills of 2,500-foot Monte Sottane. The air was chilly now, heady with the smell of the sea as they climbed higher. The surrounding ground was covered with thickets of scrubby broom and tall rock outcroppings and then there were scattered stands of scrub oak and the road swung back and forth in steep switchbacks.

As the light of dawn began to silhouette the huge bulk of

four-thousand-foot Monte Soprano farther east and the ring of mountains to the north, the oak stands faded into ilex and pine forest. Some of the ilex trees were forty feet high with spreading branches that made a thick canopy that held the darkness. Their gray-white trunks snapped into and out of the soft blue glow of the headlights.

Parnell sat beside Fountain, thinking about the poor Gypsies back there. How silent and patiently efficient they had been in their sudden flight. Something eons-learned. He remembered Gypsies back in Colorado, seeing them even in the high country around Leadville and Fairplay, the colorful round-roofed wagon caravans that suddenly appeared, the women in long dresses and ringlets and the men in sheepskin coats looking as if they had just stepped out of a Franken-stein movie.

While they stayed, the men mended cooking ware or treated sick animals and the women read palms and made potions and the young men of the town whispered that they also whored. Then one day they'd be gone, vanished in the night like some itinerant circus folk.

He wondered how many of them the Germans would find and kill. Then he looked at his watch and thought, *Maybe none.* He grinned. In less than twenty-three hours, the Krauts would certainly have something much more *important* on their minds.

Nine

On 12 May a conference of the Allied Combined Chiefs of Staff was convened in Washington, D.C. Pushed by Churchill's continued insistence on maintaining operations in the Mediterranean, the British senior commanders wanted to mount another combined invasion of mainland Italy as soon as Sicily was occupied. Keep the momentum going, they said.

The Americans were suspicious of British motives. They didn't want to bog down in another Mediterranean campaign. Instead, they wanted Operation Roundup, the landings in France tentatively scheduled for May 1944 and later called Overlord, to be the main priority for ship, men, and matériel. The meetings were heated. A compromise was finally worked out and the planning for the invasion of mainland Italy was okayed. With one proviso: Rome, the invasion target, would have to be occupied by April 1944. At that time, troops and material would be pulled from the Italian theater and sent to England for Overlord.

On 26 July, when Mussolini was deposed and the occupation of Sicily was almost complete, a full green light for the landings was given. Ike was again appointed Allied Supreme Commander: Mediterranean. The invasion itself was assigned to the U.S. Fifth Army under Lieutenant General Mark Clark and to Montgomery's Eighth Army. The Gulf of Salerno was chosen as the major assault point since Naples, a more important target thirty miles to the north, had powerful German coastal batteries. The operation was given the code name Avalanche.

The first landings were made on 3 September when British forces crossed the Strait of Messina and struck at Villa San Giovanni and Réggio di Cálabria on the Italian toe. Both were quickly taken. Montgomery immediately consolidated his units and began the long push northward to link up with Fifth Army, which would push east and south after the main Salerno landings scheduled for 0330 hours of 9 September.

The Salerno assault force boarded the ships of Task Forces 81 and 85 in North Africa on 6 September. Two days later they reached assembly points off the Sicilian coast north of Palermo and shaped a course for Italy.

The landings would be conducted in two assault groups. A Northern Group, composed of the British X Corps with its 46th and 56th Infantry Divisions along with the 7th Armored, Second Commando and three U.S. Ranger battalions, would go in just north of the city of Salerno and at selected points along the Amalfi coast. A Southern Group, made up primarily of the 36th and 45th Infantry Divisions of the U.S. VI Corps, would land ten miles down the coast from the town of Salerno at the beach just west of the ancient ruins of Paestum.

The day before the landings, the Italian government officially signed an armistice with the Allies, pledging to use their military forces in the fight against the Nazis. Although Ike would not announce this until 6:30 that evening, rumors quickly swept through the assault ships. The troopers were elated. With the Italians completely out now, they felt this would be a walk-in.

It would prove much bloodier than they thought.

Sitting on a rock outcropping at the two-thousand-foot level of Monte Sottane, the stone warmed by the late-morning sun, Parnell slowly glassed the Salerno Plain far below him. Beside him was his radio in a field-green canvas pack. The plain was half-moon shaped and enclosed on three sides by mountains. Several fair-sized rivers and numerous streams threaded their way through it and there were also large sections of marshland. The rest of the country was cultivated into wheat fields and olive and orange orchards and the darker, stoop-labor fields of tobacco and tomatoes. For the last two years, much of southern Italy had been under drought conditions, and even from this height, Red could see how withered and dry the fields and orchards were.

Earlier, as full dawn came in, Real and the Americans had set up their command post in sandstone caves in the higher forests of the mountain, leaving the two vehicles camouflaged in a deep, brush-covered draw downslope. During the morning, they had spotted German patrols moving through the lower foothills, but none ventured up into the higher ground.

At 0630 hours, he had dispatched Bird's crew to head across the plain to their first demolition objective, the bridge at the junction of the Sele and Salone Rivers seven miles to the north. Accompanying Wyatt was Fountain, Wineberg, Cappacelli, Yildirim, and another member of Freidl-Real's little band, Carlo Cucinotta, a tall, bony man with wild hair and wilder eyes who seemed always to be smiling crazily.

Augustin told Red about him, a onetime juggler and acrobat who had been an assassin for the Camorra and a morphine addict. He'd been captured twice by the Germans, who brutally tortured him. Both times Carlo had escaped by crawling through sewers and scaling sheer walls. Now he was addicted to wine spiced with cocaine, which he made periodic runs to Naples to obtain.

Parnell shook his head. "This guy sounds unstable as hell. Isn't he a risk?"

"No, he's merely a weapon," Freidl-Real answered. "A very lethal one. And like any weapon, he's only dangerous when you point him at something. Besides, he knows this country extremely well."

Before Bird and his men trooped off down the mountain trail carrying their weapons and Combat Demo Kits, Red warned Wyatt about Cucinotta. "Watch out for him. That crazy Wop son of a bitch's liable to go off on you." He held Bird's gaze for a long moment, the look telegraphing something: *If he jeopardizes the team, don't hesitate to kill him.*

Bird nodded acknowledgment and wordlessly moved off.

Red returned to his binoculars and notebook. It was obvious the Germans were expecting something big along this strip of coast. Even though much of it was camouflaged, he could easily pick out the strong defensive positions. Forward checkered-section areas undoubtedly covered by medium and heavy machine guns and mortars set up with interlocking fields of fire. Crawl trenches and bunker quarters two hundred yards back from the beach dunes. Intervening spaces laid with wire and mines.

A mile farther back were artillery quads of 20mm antiaircraft and 75mm howitzers that formed battalion-strength picket lines, their positions under camo netting and devoid of earthworks that would make shadows visible in air-recon photos. Added to these were scattered batteries of mobile 88mm dual-purpose guns and what looked to be at least two tank battalions, scattered out there in three-vehicle squads of Mark IV Panzers.

Parnell lowered the glasses, hissing. "Jesus," he said aloud, "those poor bastards're gonna be up against some heavy shit." Disgustedly he sat back against the rock. A mountain breeze shifted through the trees, freighted with the cool, Christmas scent of pinecones. There was the sound of a shoe sole on rock. He snapped around, his hand automatically reaching for his weapon.

It was a member of Freidl-Real's band, Evan Couprier. "Oh, forgive me, Lieutenant," he said, his words tinged with a French accent. He smiled shyly, a slender, pretty-faced young man with long, dark eyelashes and open, guileless eyes. "I did not mean to startle you. . . . May I sit with you?"

Red relaxed. "Be my guest."

The young man settled himself on a rock, drew up his legs. He lifted his face, closed his eyes, seemed to be tasting the air. Parnell watched him. He looked too fragile to be a Resistance fighter.

"What's your name, partner?" he asked.

"Evan. Evan Couprier."

"French."

"Oui. I was born in Brittany."

"How'd you get here?"

"I was at the university in Madrid when the Nazis occupied France. They killed my family. So when Augustin left Spain, I went with him." He tilted his head, pleasantly studied Parnell. "When your men speak of you, they call you Red. It is your hair?"

"Yeah."

"They said you played American football. Is that like soccer?"

"Not quite."

"When I was little, my father would take me to the soccer matches in Le Mans and Paris. He loved them so much."

Red glanced at his watch. It was ten minutes to 11:00. He quickly reviewed his notes, checking a plastic encryption card and then making three-letter code references in the margins. His first contact with the *Manta* was to be at 1101 hours, precisely. He would make a second transmission at 1801 hours. Both times the submarine would be at antenna depth and he would have exactly sixty seconds to send his message before the vessel returned to deeper water.

His radio was a Morse-code-adapted SCR-511-CN portable marine transceiver. His transmissions to the *Manta* would be sent on specific in-between frequencies so as to make it harder for the Germans to jam his signal or fix his position with their radio detection gear. He'd be using a three-letter encryption system in which each grouping stood for specific things or numbers. Before leaving the sub, he'd been given the code list, which he had stapled to his waterproof notebook.

His coded message written out, he pulled the radio over and opened the front flap, extended the antenna, and hooked up the Morse key wires. Then he swung the frequency dial to the first setting, which he had memorized, idly asking Evan, "What's the story on the hooker?"

"Pardon?"

"The hooker, the prostitute."

"Cesara?"

"Mm."

Evan smiled. It lit up his face. "Oh, she is not a regular prostitute. She only does such things for the Cause. She is really an art student from the University of Bologna."

"I thought she was a Gypsy."

"Yes, from her mother. A Corsican. Cesara was born at La Spezia where her father was mayor. She is very passionate against the Nazis. They killed him." He turned and looked out over the plain, pensive for a moment. "But sometimes I think she is very sad inside at what she must do."

Red checked his watch again. It was eleven o'clock sharp. He said, "Go tell Real I'll be transmitting in one minute. Get ready to move."

"Yes, of course." Couprier pushed himself from the rock and hurried down to where Augustin and Cesara were waiting.

Parnell kept his eyes on the watch's second hand. At three seconds before 11:01, he flicked on the radio. A wash of static whispered from the speaker. From upslope, a bird chirped in the brush. He flipped the transmit button and began sending his message, first tapping out his call sign, two groupings of three Bs each, *da-dit-dit-dit,* followed by a short pause so the radioman on the *Manta* could fine-tune his signal. Then quickly he ran down his listed code groupings, his finger working the key, the sets snapping out with double-click-long pauses between each one.

The seconds ticked away: 20 . . . 25 . . . 30 . . .

A wild screeching erupted from the speaker, made him jump. It climbed up through octaves, up into a thin needle of sound, and then back down again into a rushing, static-heavy burst. The Krauts were jamming his signal.

He stopped transmitting, leaned in, listening. The rush of sound went up again. Deep in it he could hear a different, wavering acoustic that swept in and out like waves rising and receding. "Oh, yeah," he snapped. He knew somewhere a German radio operator was ranging through frequencies, trying to reacquire his signal and pinpoint his location. He instantly shut down the radio, scooped it and his weapon up, and headed down the slope.

Sergeant Wyatt Bird lay with half his body in water and slushy mud among saw grass. The water was tepid, filled with algae that made it stink like a cesspool. The others were scattered behind him in the grass. It was now 2:30 in the afternoon, the sun hot coming down through the reeds. He could hear furtive movements in the grass, snakes or rats. But mostly he could hear the two German antitank gun crews talking and laughing two hundred yards away.

All through the morning, the team with Yildirim and Cucinotta had moved across the Salerno Plain, down out of the foothills, and among orchards and wheat fields. Despite the heavy farming on the land, Cucinotta told Wyatt, the area was sparsely populated, most of the farmers living back in the hills since early times because the area was known to be malarial.

They had encountered a few peasants, mostly women in black shapeless dresses and scarves carrying baskets made of sticks as they gleaned rotted tomatoes left by the harvesters, the tomato plants brown and trampled. Occasionally dust rose from roads on the rim of the plain as German convoys and platoons of armor moved about.

The team traveled in single file rather than in regular overwatch patrol formation, which would have appeared suspicious. Instead, they looked simply like a group of farmers in their peasant clothes, which Real had supplied, their weapons under bulky smocks and the explosive packs hidden in canvas tool bags as they passed through orchards and fields and wove their way over narrow berm trails in the marshlands.

Bird and Cucinotta were in the lead, Wyatt giving the Italian steady, studied looks. The guy was a real loco, all right, a goddamned Section 8 if there ever was one. He hummed and giggled to himself, bounced when he walked, jigged, and dipped and dodged for no apparent reason, his bright-crazy eyes alight with cocaine energy.

Except when two Messerschmidt 190s crossed high overhead. Then the man's eyes went stone-cold dark. Still, Bird had to admit he knew his way around this country, keeping them in concealment most of the time and guiding them across the least open areas of the marsh.

At one o'clock, they spotted the German gun crew's dust a mile off, coming their way swiftly. Bird immediately put the binoculars to them, saw they were two 7.5cm Pak-40 assault guns mounted on Pz-Kpfw IV tractor chassis, each vehicle crewed by four soldiers. He immediately ordered everyone into the marsh reeds and they watched the Germans take up a position close by on a landing above the marshland where several trail berms converged. It had obviously once been a truck loading point during the harvesting of marsh reeds, which the peasants used to fashion their roofs.

The enemy artillerymen set their vehicles so as to have a wide traversing field of fire that would include a dense group of olive orchards a mile to the west. Then they began covering the tractors with camo netting and bunch grass and set out their shell cases, getting ready to fire.

Bird kept looking at his watch and cursing silently as the hot afternoon moved past. They were now bogged down and losing precious time. He wiped sweat from his brow. Periodically huge mosquitoes came floating through the reeds and stung like fire cinders when they landed. His anger peaked.

We're going past them Kraut sons a bitches, he thought angrily, *come hell or high water. And we ain't waiting until dark to do it.*

They *couldn't* wait. That would put them at the bridge way too late. Then when they tried to recross the plain, they could end up getting caught in the middle of the landings with every goddamned German gun in the area opening up.

Okay, he considered, *how do we do it? An ambush firefight?* No, he dismissed that. Automatic fire would carry across this open ground like a siren, bring Kraut patrols down on them within minutes. A knife attack? He lifted his head, took a quick look to measure distances from the edge of the landing to the gun tractors. There was good concealment to the edge, but then they'd have to come up out of the water and rush the Krauts across thirty or forty yards of open ground. Tricky.

He settled back into the mud to consider. A moment later, Carlo Cucinotta crawled up beside him, grinning his mad grin. "We have a problem," he said.

Wyatt looked at him, turned, jetted spittal through his teeth. "Yeah," he said.

Carlo studied the reeds, bobbing his head as if keeping time to some inner song. Then he lifted slightly and looked back the way they had come, to orange orchards a half mile back. He twisted around, checked out the Germans, and then dropped down again.

"Senz'altro, amico," he whispered happily. "We will rush them. Kill them easy with blades."

Bird shook his head. "We can't risk a firefight."

Carlo turned to him. *"Che cosa hai detto?"*

"A firefight, a battle. Too much noise. *Ka-peesh?"*

"No, no," Cucinotta said merrily. "I go over there first. You know? I make them look at *me.* Then you come behind and . . ." He drew his hand quickly across his throat. "You see?"

"Y'all jes' gonna walk up big as shit, eh?"

"No, no. You will see. Be ready." Before Wyatt could say anything, the Italian turned and slid away among the reeds.

Cowboy came wriggling over. "Where in hell's that crazy bastard goin'?"

Wyatt didn't answer, thinking about what Cucinotta had said. He decided, *What the hell, why not give her a shot?* He quickly explained what Carlo intended to do and told Fountain to tell the others that they'd be moving up as close to the landing as they could get. On the chance Carlo could actually distract the Krauts long enough, they'd take them with knives. Cowboy moved off to pass the word.

It seemed excruciatingly slow, advancing along the edge of the marsh road, crawling and sliding on the mud, pausing to listen for any sign of detection, then moving on. To their own ears, they made too much noise in the humming, hot silence with only the sounds of coots squabbling out in the deeper part of the marsh.

When they were still fifty yards from the landing, they heard a man singing and there came Carlo, striding bouncingly up the road with a long pole on his shoulder. Such poles were used to shake ripe oranges from the trees. This one had a flat iron bar on one end. He came right on, singing heartily, his voice strong and surprisingly rich.

The German soldiers had completed their preparations and were taking a ration break, sitting under their camo nets eating sausage and black bread. They watched him approach, nudging each other, laughing, figuring this stupid *Italienisch* was drunk.

Cucinotta hauled to a stop in front of the two vehicles. He said hello to them in cheery Italian and, nodding at their food, asked if he might have some. One of the soldiers angrily shouted back, *"Verpise dich, du alter Sauskoph."*

Taking advantage, Wyatt and the others slipped closer to the edge of the landing.

Out on the road, Carlo made a deep bow, holding his pole like a lance, and then moved inconspicuously nearer to the

Germans. When he was about ten feet from them, he spun the pole around and poked one end into the ground, slanted slightly. Quick as a cat, he climbed it, pulling it back toward himself until it was upright with him at the top, balancing.

Slowly, with delicate movements, he raised his legs until he was standing on his hands on the pole's metal bar. The German soldiers laughed and clapped and then rose and gathered around him to watch. For the next six minutes, he performed for them, doing handstands and push-ups and scissoring his legs rapidly, the muscles in his bare forearms and shoulders quivering with strain.

On the other side of the landing, the Americans and Yildirim came up out of the marsh and crept unseen to the back of the gun tractors. Silently, Bird signaled them into attack positions: three to one side, himself and the other two opposite. They inched even closer, the camo nets fluttering in the slight breeze with only the cackle and throaty grunts of the coots and Carlo's labored breathing filling the hot afternoon air.

Their rush was in almost dead silence, just the quick, flicking shuffle of their shoes, and then they were on the enemy soldiers, the Germans unaware of their presence until they felt knives being buried into livers, down through breastbones, sliced across carotids.

Carlo instantly dropped to his feet and swung his pole like a two-handed sword. The metal bar crushed the skull of one of the soldiers, flicking his eye out of his head like a tiddlywink. It rolled along the ground. He then whirled to attack a second man, his knife suddenly there in his hand, slashing.

All the Germans were down now, screaming and gagging, rolling wildly, trying to fend off their attackers' knives. Within a minute, all were dead, the ground saturated with their blood, some of it flung forth in droplets by aortal force, looking like bright red coins in the dust.

The team quickly stripped the soldiers of their weapons. With Cucinotta gleefully driving one of the gun tractors, they headed north again, the vehicle's tracks clanking and thundering on the hardpack, driving a pure white heron up out of the road ditch. It lifted sluggishly, its wings working in slow motion as it headed into the sky.

The two little Gypsy girls, each no more than six, did not make a sound as the Nazi soldiers beat their father with rifles and machine pistols. Yet their tiny, round, brown faces were engorged as if with blood, as if they were deliberately holding their breaths against some unfair command.

Major Witt Keppler and his six-man squad of *Waffen SS* troopers had discovered a Gypsy family cowering in a small cement ferry house four miles downriver of the camp: one man, two women, and the little girls. With them was a pony carrying their belongings and a half-grown female goat.

It was nearly evening. The soldiers would pause in their beating and demand that the man tell them where the other partisan assassins were. But he wouldn't say anything. He simply glared at them and spat blood into the river. They finally beat him into unconsciousness and then started on the women. One was very old and fell back into the river the first time she was struck with a rifle butt. The other woman tried to recover her, but the Germans dragged her back and beat her with their fists.

During the final days in Sicily, Keppler and his men had been ordered to link up with a unit of General Hans Hube's XIV Panzer Corps. Then on the night of 12 August, they were evacuated across the Strait of Messina aboard a naval MFP or F-Lighter, a fast patrol boat similar to an American PT.

Earlier, the Gestapo and *Abwehr* agents had been reporting a rapid buildup of partisans along the western coast of Italy, particularly around such ports as Naples, Salerno, and Basilicata. Kesselring's intelligence staff rightly assumed this indicated that Allied landings somewhere along a four-hundred-mile arc of the coast were imminent. So as soon as Keppler and his hunter unit reached the mainland, they were immediately ordered to Naples to track down partisan bands to learn intelligence about enemy intentions.

He'd been informed about the murder of four German officers near a Gypsy camp southeast of Paestum at 9:00 that morning, obviously by partisans. Their bodies had been found tied to their staff car and then shoved into the Trentinara River. A field autopsy had showed that two of the bodies contained .45-caliber slugs, bullets almost exclusively used by Americans or the partisans whom they supplied.

By noon, the *Waffen SS* hunters had thoroughly examined the deserted camp. Infantry search parties had already been dispatched to track down the Gypsies, but so far none had been found. Keppler split his force into three squads and sent them out to double-check the same countryside.

Now he paced back and forth in his pale sandy yellow tropical uniform with its high-peaked death's-head cap and glistening black mountain boots and watched his men work, a cold, dark anger showing in his eyes. At last, he paused and called out, *"Stoppen.* We waste our time. Kill them."

His troopers turned and looked back at him, hesitating.

"I said *kill* them," he bellowed.

One of the men, a sergeant, asked, "The children too, *Herr Hauptfach?"*

"Of course, you fool. And the animals."

The machine pistols cracked open the evening's silence. Their rounds punctured the body of the unconscious man as if going into a pile of clothing, merely jerking his jacket. The younger woman was hurled back into the river by the force. Then they turned their weapons on the older woman, who had floated downstream, and shot her in the head. When the bullets struck the little girls, they sundered them like watermelons.

Then, killing the animals, they kicked all the corpses into deeper water. The Gypsies' blood momentarily turned the surface crimson gold in the slanting light. The soldiers came back up the bank, their faces stark. Keppler formed them up once more and they moved off farther downriver, fanning out, searching for more game.

* * *

The water of the Calore River was cold with the feel of mountains in it, but not nut-busting cold, something they could adjust to.

Bird's crew had remained with the gun tractor until they reached the road to the foothill town of Albanella, which bisected the Salerno Plain. There they hid the vehicle in an orchard and continued on foot to the river, the evening coming on slowly and the distant windows of Albanella and Altavilla in the eastern hills glinting in the last orange-tinted rays of the sun.

They struck the Calore a half mile from its junction bridge. Wyatt had chosen Cowboy to accompany him as demo team. The others immediately moved off along the river to set up security positions near the bridge's southern ramp. Meanwhile, he and Cowboy rechecked their demo packs and waited, giving the others time enough to reach the bridge, recon it, and achieve positions.

They had three packs. Two contained ten two-pound bricks of Du Pont Hi-Drive gelatin dynamite, a water-resistant, high-velocity/high-pressure explosive often used for deep-hole seismograph shots and underwater salvage. Besides that, they had tape, spools of wire, and cutting tools. The other pack held Nitromon primer caps, a fifteen-pound silver-chloride, rapid-discharge battery, and two twelve-hour timers. At exactly eight o'clock, with the countryside dark since the moon had not yet risen, they slipped into the river.

The water moved them along at a moderate pace. Bird pushed the explosive packs ahead of him. The air bubbles entrapped inside the dynamite gel made the packs lighter than water. But Cowboy was having to fight the weight of the battery. It kept trying to pull him to the bottom. He finally got into a rhythm of kicking his legs to keep afloat yet not letting them break the surface.

The bridge turned out to be all steel girders, full of angles. It looked like a kid's Erector Set. There were dim red lights on both sides. In their faint glow, the two could make out the silhouette of the gun turret of a German four-wheel Panserspahwagen armored car on the right and the tiny, firefly dots of the bridge guards' cigarettes.

A searchlight suddenly flicked on, throwing a shaft of bright white light upriver. Cowboy's heart jerked in his chest. He glanced at Wyatt, a dark shape beside him, both of them angling slightly, trying to time it so they'd reach the bank directly under the bridge. It drew nearer with frustrating slowness.

The light darted and jabbed at the river, then slid along the bank through thickets of pussy willows and cattails. It returned to the river. The light bounced off the surface, casting little curlicues of shadow from the eddies onto the brushy bank. The beam swept past ten feet behind Cowboy. Then abruptly it lifted and swung to the other side of the bridge.

Fifteen seconds later, Bird and Fountain slid beneath the structure. As they pulled themselves up out of the water and onto the base of the piling, several swallows burst from beneath the span and went squealing and sailing downriver, crossing through the spotlight beam. The two men froze. The spot lifted slightly, following the birds. Someone laughed, said something in German. Wyatt and Cowboy relaxed, the guards obviously assuming their light had frightened the swallows.

The bridge was thirty feet across with decking fashioned of thick wooden beams. The support pilings were made of concrete and granite stone, their upriver sides showing drifts of sticks and brush jammed between them and the bank. The span stringers were all heavy I-beam girders, each at least eighteen inches high with two-inch-thick I-sections. Everything was coated with bird guano, which mingled with the sour stink of old steel and wood tar.

They quickly studied the beam plan, picking out the main weight-bearing stringers. There were four. If they could take these out, the entire north side of the span would fall down into the river. Their demolition plan specified that the charge timers would be set for 0400 hours, thirty minutes *after* the landings actually began. By then, the Germans would undoubtedly be moving men and armor across this river and into the Salerno Plain. If by some chance the explosions didn't completely shear the stringers, the added weight of the traffic on the weakened girders would definitely bring the structure down.

Wyatt signaled Cowboy to take the two downriver I-beams and passed him several primer caps. Crab-walking, Fountain moved to the second piling, strung his demo pack around his neck, and began crawling out along the stringer, hanging upside down, pulling with his hands, and then bringing up his feet.

It was a bitch, the bird shit making the steel slippery and the weight of the pack pulling against his throat. Forty feet out, he chose a spot on the outer stringer. Bracing himself between the bottom of the beam and the wooden deck, he coiled down tight and began placing the first charge, this one on the outer beam.

He set the charge packs in opposition, taping one on either side of the beam. This would create a shearing effect. He then taped another pack to the outer side of the stringer since these always had strengthening flanges welded or bolted to the bridge uprights.

His hands worked quickly, his back and leg muscles burning from the tight position. He now inserted the primer caps and hooked all five wires to a single run-out wire. Working his way around to the second stringer, he repeated the procedure. When all the charges were taped and capped, he connected the two run-out wires to a main spool lead, then gripped the spool with his teeth and crawled back to the bank, unwinding wire as he went.

Wyatt had already finished placing his charges and was readying the battery when Cowboy reached the bank. Working by feel, Bird spliced the two lead-in wires together, taped the splice, and connected them to the timers that he had linked just in case one malfunctioned. Setting both timers to 0400 hours, he switched on the battery. Both the pinhead-tiny red timer check lights clicked on. All the charges were ready.

Wyatt paused suddenly, his head tilted, listening. A moment later, Cowboy heard something, too, the faraway sound of trucks approaching from the north. Both men moved back against the bank. Ten minutes later two motorcycles roared up and crossed the bridge. Behind them came eight Opel 3-ton trucks carrying troops. The tires rumbled on the wooden decking and the smell of exhaust fumes drifted down through the cracks.

Quickly the convoy moved off deeper into the plain, the sounds of their engines fading to a distant, surging whine. Bird gave the timers one last check, then he and Cowboy silently slipped into the water and drifted away. Two hundred yards downriver, they made the bank and went up into brush. The moon had just risen and the Salerno Plain was beginning to emerge all silvery blue out of the darkness.

Slowly, in pairs, the rest of the crew came down, whispering their countersigns. Forming into line again, they moved away from the river and back into the flat country, going quickly, double-timing, no one speaking.

A little after eleven o'clock, flares began going off in the sky just beyond the beach five miles away. At least a dozen and a half, balls of bright white light slowly floating toward the sea. The team stopped, fearing the invasion convoys, still way offshore, had somehow been discovered. But nothing happened. Even long afterward, there never was an explanation as to why the Germans had set off flares. One by one the lights reached the water and went out. No others were fired and the team moved ahead again.

It was nearly midnight when they finally relinked with Parnell and the others at the prearranged rendezvous point, an abandoned stone sheepherder's shed in the Monte Sottane foothills. It sat at the edge of a moon-washed meadow fringed with stands of scrub oak and cypress trees beyond which Freidl-Real had parked the German personnel carrier. They hurried across the meadow, the grass dry and crispy against their legs, boarded the vehicle, and headed higher into the hills to take up their observation positions for the invasion, now only three hours away.

Ten

The Tyrrhenian Sea lay in brilliant, moonlit splendor, flat as a Kansas cornfield. To the east, the shore and the Salerno Plain were in blue-white darkness. Only a few lights from tiny mountain villages twinkled against the backdrop of the mountain massifs that ringed the plain.

Fifteen minutes earlier, the ships of Task Force 81, carrying the assault units of the Southern Attack Group, had just reached their release points ten miles off the Gulf of Salerno. Now they sat dead in the water, the cruisers *Philadelphia, Savannah, Boise, Brooklyn,* and HMS *Abercrombie,* fourteen destroyers from DesRons 7, 8, 13, and 60, eight minesweepers, assorted troopships, LSTs, and LCIs in addition to salvage, picket, and diversion vessels, all waiting for the signal lights from the two beacon submarines, HMS *Shakespeare* and USS *Manta,* to guide the assault waves to their assigned beach sectors.

At precisely 2400 hours they came, bursts of white light flashing in rapid pairs. One minute later ships' loudspeakers blared all through the task force, followed by the shrill keening of boatswains' whistles and the rumble and clatter of davits as landing craft were lowered into the sea.

The first put down were four small, high-speed boats using

muffled gasoline engines. The men aboard were all volunteer navy Scouts. They were to race to within five hundred yards of the shoreline, locate each of the four color-designated beaches, and then lead those landing craft assigned to that beach in by flashing lights coordinated to that beach's color: red, green, yellow, and blue. Directly behind the Scout boats came the eight minesweepers, moving in from the flanks of the task force to sweep channels through the German mine-fields.

Meanwhile, eight miles away, the same procedure was being executed by the Northern Attack Group. It consisted of elements of the British X Corps who would strike at the cities of Salerno and Vietri. With them were British Commandos and three battalions of U.S. Rangers assigned to take the town of Maiori on the Almafi coast that was the key to the passes through the Sorrento Mountains to the Bay of Naples.

By 0100 hours, the first wave of the Southern Attack Group was headed toward shore, troopers of the 141st and 142nd Regimental Combat Teams of the U.S. 36th Infantry Division. This was to be their first blooding. Remaining back in temporary reserve were two other RCTs, both from the U.S. 45th Division, which had already seen combat in Sicily.

At 0330 hours the first Americans to step onto mainland Italy hit Yellow Beach. Within seven minutes, the other beaches were also stormed. But then a fatal decision made during the planning of the operation exploded in their faces. In order to achieve surprise, the planners had opted not to stage a preinvasion naval barrage. Now the assault units ran head-on into a hurricane of waiting German fire while Kraut loudspeakers blared, "Come on in and give up. We have you covered."

Commander of the German Tenth Army, General Heinrich von Vietinghoff, had strongly suspected Salerno would be the principle target of the Allied invasion. As a result, he'd been reinforcing his units and constructing defensive positions east of Naples and in the Salerno Plain for over two weeks. Now proven right, he pleaded with Field Marshal Kesselring to send him help, especially asking for the 26th

Panzer Division, which was fighting a delaying action against Montgomery south in Calábria.

Quickly, the second and third assault waves began getting jammed up on the beaches. The heavy fire forced incoming LSTs to remain farther offshore so they couldn't unload cargoes of tanks and field guns. Only a few of the smaller CCVPs reached the beach and deposited some light field howitzers and equipment.

A shuttle was immediately started using the new DUKW amphibious trucks called "ducks" to haul small cargo from the ships to the beach. Then another problem swiftly developed. With the stevedore shore parties pinned down and unable to shift the arriving gear away from the waterline, the stacks of it began blocking landing craft from reaching sand, forcing them to off-load troopers into chest-high water and deadly fire.

Unlike the American sector, most of the Northern Attack Group had initially gone ashore against only moderate opposition. But as dawn turned to day, enemy resistance stiffened until both sectors were locked in a bloody slugfest of attack and counterattack.

Parnell had heard the engines, first the minesweepers and then the incoming landing craft, a wavering sound that surged and withdrew, coming toward him from the sea. Slowly, the black shapes of the ships and the landing craft began emerging into view, stretched across the calm moonlit gulf. He looked at his watch. It was almost precisely 0330 hours.

Then, in what seemed one, continuous deafening, cracking roar, it started. The night turned into a wild, seething matrix of crisscrossing fire trains as German machine guns and mortars, 155mm field pieces, antitank 75s, and mobile 88s with their peculiar hollow snaps opened up on the invaders. Explosions hurled sand and water upward along the shore, out among the approaching assault craft, the blasts appearing with eye-blink swiftness, red and orange and white plumes.

Phosphorus shells rained down, going off in fiery eruptions like fountains of white-hot snowflakes.

Flares lit up the sky, casting the ocean into a plain of slate gray across which crept the assault craft slowly, sluggishly, trailing their ribbons of prop wash. Nebelwerfer rockets began firing off with their vicious, teeth-hurting hisses followed by long, moaning sounds before they struck targets.

German night fighters arrived, twin-engine Junker 88s, sweeping low over the mountains to strafe the beach. Their tracers and 20mm rounds went so slowly, bouncing like Roman candles. The aircraft made several passes and then turned east again to rearm, screaming close over the mountain ridges, their exhausts flaming red.

Parnell watched it all happen and thought, *There are a helluva lot of men dying down there.* Yet he was surprised at his sense of disconnect to that stunning reality. He swung his glasses eastward, over the Salerno Plain. It was nearly impossible to see specific objects in the darkness, things coming to him in quick flashes of light, blurry images of soldiers and guns and vehicles caught in stop-action against the drape of the night.

But whenever he lowered the glasses, he felt the full impact of the battle. Its vast panorama of bursting light and discordant, thundering sound rolled over him like a series of waves, up into the cool, turpentine sweetness of the mountain, carrying with it the stink of cordite smoke and explosive residue.

Earlier that night, after linking with Wyatt and his bridge crew, they had returned to the caves, sat around drinking grappa-spiced coffee heated by stolen Kraut heat pills, which gave no flame. They cleaned weapons, made up fresh demo packs, and listened to the BBC on Augustin's small Fleming-Hawke shortwave radio the British SOE had issued him. The BBC always began their broadcasts with the first four notes of Beethoven's Fifth Symphony. Between musical selections, they sent out coded messages to the Resistance bands in Europe.

Afterward, Parnell huddled with his two sergeants and Freidl-Real to go over their plans once more. For the first time, Red informed Augustin of the precise timing of the invasion, watched as Real grinned his white, sardonic smile. The plan called for Real, Red, and Sol Kaamanui to set up a spotter position in the lower foothills, one that would give them a complete overview of the plain. From it, Parnell would call in naval fire missions against enemy movements and strongpoints once daylight came.

Meanwhile, Wyatt and the others were to move down to the road that led to the mountain towns of Vesule and Trentinara and seed it with trip-wire demo charges to block German spotter patrols from reaching the higher ridges of the Sottane range.

At fifteen minutes after 2:00, the two crews split up and headed downslope.

Now Kaamanui said, "Those boys are getting everything but the kitchen sink thrown at them." His big Samoan face looking calmly grim kept jumping in and out of view, his nose and thick brow casting grotesque shadows in the intermittent flashes of artillery.

Around them, the air was cool, yet Red felt sweat on his own face, his blood rising now, caught up in that ringing adrenaline surge that always came with the imminence of personal combat. As always, his senses were tuned to a superlevel. He saw things with astounding clarity, smelled the tiniest odors in the air, could actually pick out the rapid muzzle spacings of a single 88mm Flieagerabwehrkanonen firing antitank rounds, or the isolated poppings of rifle fire like steel bearings striking an empty gasoline drum.

They watched and waited for the daylight.

Bird heard the horses' hooves a full minute before he saw the German patrol. He instantly signaled a halt and hit the ground. Slowly the riders came into view, six soldiers all mounted on dark horses, coming up through a stand of oak.

They trailed two packhorses. Wyatt squinted at those. One was carrying an MG-34 machine gun with its belt ammo boxes and a tripod mount. The other had canvas field packs.

He had been point man, the rest of the crew strung out in patrol formation behind him. In the first, faint gray of the coming dawn, he could now just barely see them lying flat on the ground. Directly behind him was Cesara, the hooker, and the French kid, Couprier. Both were armed with British Sten submachine guns.

They were now about a mile southwest of Parnell's position, on the western slope of the Sottane at about two thousand feet. It was an area of sharp switchbacks and steep cliff faces. The Salerno Plain and beachhead were hidden behind a secondary ridge, but the constant battle flashes silhouetted the ridge as the thunder of guns echoed up through narrow canyons.

He swiveled his head again. Fifteen yards to his left was his slot man, Laguna. Cappacelli was to his right. They were both already moving, taking the downslope, while Smoker and Cowboy shifted to his left, the team knowing what to do, setting up an ambush fire line.

The Germans were now about seventy yards away. In the dim light, they and their mounts blended into the trees. Gently, Bird cupped his left hand over the breech of his Thompson to muffle the click of its safety and flicked it off. The movement made him aware of a stiffness in his face, his skin pulled tightly against cheekbones. It was an unconscious reaction that always came just before a firefight.

The patrol drew closer amid the soft tinkle of harnesses. Sixty yards . . . fifty. His eyes slid to the right, caught a glimpse of either Weesay or Angelo, crawling now. He tensed, rising slightly, his breathing calm and steady.

The Sten went off right beside him with the crack of shotgun blasts. *"Gawddamn!"* he growled. *Too soon, too soon!* But he immediately opened with his own weapon. He heard the others firing too, their rounds slashing down through the oak trees.

A horse screamed and fell down. The others lifted their forelegs, rearing back, twisting with fright as the Germans soldiers instantly dropped out of their saddles, already returning fire. The *raps* of their machine pistols were so fast and tight they formed single *burrings*.

The firing continued for several seconds, then abruptly everything got very quiet, a pocket of silence with the air smoky and feeling compacted with soundless sound like the pressure in a storm front.

Bird's mind ordered him to move. *Rush the sumbitches before they form a fire base.* He leaped up and started forward, darting, firing. To his right he saw Laguna and Cappacelli rising up, charging, too. Bullets sizzled past him like racing wasps.

Amid the harsh din of weaponry, he heard the snap of a grenade's safety arm, saw it go sailing through the air for a second. A German shouted. The grenade exploded with an orange-white flash. The ground trembled. He watched a chunk of earth fly up into the air, reach its apex, and start down again. He realized it was a man's foot. He waited two heartbeats and started forward again, firing until his clip was empty.

There was another sudden bubble of silence with only the insect tick of heated gun barrels. All the Germans were lying on the ground. He took cover behind a tree. Its trunk had been splintered by gunfire, the underwood a creamy yellow and swarming with ants. Thicker smoke drifted in the air. In his nose it felt gritty like processed sugar.

Fifteen feet from him one of the German soldiers suddenly thrust himself to his knees. He tried to stand but couldn't. He began searching the ground for a weapon, dazedly falling off to his left. Lying directly behind him were two others. One had taken the full blast of the grenade on his hand and face, probably while trying to throw it back. His features were a mass of blood and raw tissue. Already the blood was beginning to draw up in that peculiar pattern of clotting.

The kneeling German kept cursing furiously and trying to

get up. Then he started clawing at his sidearm holster. Wyatt sprang up and held his Thompson on him. The German stopped and stared at him, swaying back and forth slightly like a drunk. Cowboy came up, hot-eyed. "Fetch that god-damn horse with the MG," Bird yelled at him. Fountain turned and sprinted down the slope.

Bird studied the German. He bounced the muzzle of the Thompson, indicating for the man to raise his arms. The soldier didn't move. He looked angry, unafraid. His uniform was dusty, a reed-green coat, gray trousers tucked into black calf boots. He wore a web harness loaded with cartridge pouches, entrenching tools, and a canvas backpack. At last, he slowly raised his arms. In the increasing light, his eyes were very blue.

Wyatt started to say something. There was a quick movement beside him. A muzzle shoved forward and a woman's voice shouted an Italian obscenity. A second later, Cesara blew the German off his feet. The Sten's spent rounds flicked across Bird's face, the blasts bounding and rebounding through the trees. The soldier went into a crazy backward somersault and then tumbled loose-jointedly down the incline and finally came to rest against a flat granite stone.

Wyatt whirled. *"Gawddamn* you, you fuckin' bitch," he bellowed at her.

In combat, Wyatt Bird always remained slightly outside himself in that emotionlessness of a veteran, simply going about his business. He neither hated nor particularly thought of his enemy. He sought to kill him as swiftly as possible merely to preserve his own life. But *this,* the outright slaughter of a man who had just surrendered, was gravely improper to him.

He turned his head, spat contemptuously, turned back. "It was *you* opened too early, wasn't it?" he growled.

Cesara lowered the Sten and started to turn away. Wyatt grabbed her arm roughly. "Y'all hold it there, girlie. *This* here unit don't shoot no prisoners." He shook her. "You god-damn *kapeesh?"*

Cesara looked steadily back at him. Her eyes were full of black light. Her cheeks quivered. Then, for a split second, her gaze flicked away. She nodded, a perfunctory dip of the head. *"Sí,"* she said. She jerked her arm free, turned, and walked down to the other dead Germans and began going through their pockets.

They took the Germans' weapons. Cowboy couldn't retrieve the machine gun horse, which had already disappeared far down the hill with the others. Fortunately the one that had been wounded had radio gear, a Feldfernsprecher FU-8 set with nickel batteries and a coil antenna. The horse was lying brokenly against a tree, its breaths coming in surging heaves. Fountain shot it and they loaded up and quickly moved out, leaving the dead in the gunmetal light under the trees.

By the time the sun finally broke over the main ridgeline of Monte Soprano, they were laying out trip charges on the Trentinarra road.

At 0457 hours, General von Vietinghoff again personally spoke with Kesselring by landline telephone. He updated the field marshal on the Salerno situation and again appealed for more reinforcements. To his relief, Kesselring told him that units from all over Italy were already being rushed to his aid. The 15th Panzer Grenadier Division was coming from Frosinone, the 3rd and 26th Panzer Grenadiers from Rome, and the entire LXXVI Corps from Calábria.

Kesselring's final words were to the point, "Destroy them on the plain, Heinrich. Then shove their goddamned remains back into the sea."

"Yes, *Herr Feldmarschall,*" von Vietinghoff said. "I will do precisely that."

The spotter position Parnell had chosen was on the upper side of a small amphitheater of rock. Now, at 7:00 in the morning, the stone faces looked stark white in the early sunlight. All three men were intently glassing the plain, Red's transceiver already flicked on, its speaker alive with bursts of cross talk, both German and American.

Below, the Salerno Plain was a confused melange of fighting. Yet, from their height, it seemed to possess some absurd symmetry, its movements almost set-piece as tank platoons and mobile armor shifted positions in tight formations and infantry columns double-timed out of assembly areas and artillery batteries dueled with interchanging barrages like the thrusts and ripostes of saber fencers.

The Americans had still made little penetration inland of the Paestum assault zone. Along a ragged perimeter, firefights and skirmishes were taking place, some as small as squad on squad. Now a dozen aircraft burst low over the ocean, Seafire fighters coming in from British escort carriers far offshore. They immediately climbed, their underbellies a pastel blue, and began crisscrossing at mountaintop level, setting up an air cover umbrella over the slender Allied beachhead.

Ships were scattered all over the gulf, the German shelling heaving water geysers among them. Some of the LCTs and LCIs had been hit and were burning. The smoke looked brown and greasy, like creosote smeared on glass.

Parnell, slowly scanning the ocean now, noticed three American destroyers suddenly pick up steam and begin a frantic dash toward the shore. In echelon formation with wakes boiling white, they recklessly weaved their way through the minefields. They closed the beach to within five hundred yards, swung into perfectly synchronized turns, and cut loose with their five-inch batteries, Oerlikon 20mm AA cannons, and .50-caliber machine guns. German counterfire immediately straddled the ships, tearing up the surface of the ocean. Three times the destroyers ran broadside to the beach raking enemy positions. They were hit by gunfire several times but managed at last to turn and race back out to sea.

At 0913 hours, the bigger gunships began laying in fire missions, the rounds coming in with that distinctive whispering rustle like the tearing of cloth, as the cruisers *Philadelphia,*

Savannah, and *Boise* opened at fifteen thousand yards with 8-inch salvos, taking targets on the north side of the Salerno Plain near the Sele River.

Sol tapped Parnell's shoulder, pointed down into the plain toward the northeast. Red swung his glasses and picked up a single lead German Mark IV Panzer in his lens. He swung slightly to the right, left. Deployed behind the tank in an arrow-point formation were eight Mark IVs, all racing across a wheat field just beyond the toe of the Sottane foothills.

Here we go, he thought.

"Coordinates," he barked to Sol. "Give 'em a two-grid lead."

Kaamanui was already rapidly trying to pinpoint the tanks' positions on his battle chart. He had three of them, each with a different code reference. They were marked off in numbered coordinate grids, each grid loosely representing a ground area seventy yards across and 150 yards deep, which was the approximate size of a standard four-round sheath salvo impact pattern.

Once he defined the target's convergence grid, he would pass it to Parnell, who would then radio a request for a fire mission to the designated NGLIS, or Naval Gunfire Liaison Ship, assigned to this sector of the landing. In this case it was the LCT 624, code-named Fieldhouse. Its fire coordinators would quickly assess the request and assign it to any gunship that had the proper ordnance to destroy the called target and was momentarily free of missions.

Red swung his frequency dial to the designated fire mission range, then sat tapping his fingers against the mike. *Come on, come on.* He could hear other FOOs, Forward Observation Officers, calling in missions, a blur and crackle of cross talk. Kaamanui finally handed him the grid designation.

He keyed his mike: "Fieldhouse, Fieldhouse, this is Blue One. Request fire mission. Grid Q-set. LN eight-two-niner-niner. Tank column, niner, Mark Fours. Close AP fire. Commence fire immediately."

Pausing, he bent closer to the radio. From it came scattered static, voices drifting off, roaring back, drifting off again. Seconds ticked away. At last the assigned gunship's radioman came on: "Salvo, Blue One."

Down in the wheat field, the German tanks continued charging ahead. Their tracks left trampled pathways through the winter wheat. They looked unutterably lethal, bounding, their gun barrels glinting darkly in the morning sun.

More seconds disappeared into the air. He heard rounds coming. Suddenly the gunship radioman came back: "Splash, Blue One."

Red narrowed his eyes, fixed them on the three lead enemy tanks. Exactly three seconds later, four 8-inch rounds struck. Even from this distance, he felt the impacts. Earth exploded into the air in four rushing upheavals of smoke and fire, which immediately set the wheat aflame.

Parnell cursed. They were all short and slightly to the right.

He keyed. "Blue One, up four hundred, left two hundred." *Seconds ticked past.*

"Salvo, Blue One."

Again the wait. Then, "Splash, Blue One."

The lead Mark IV took a direct hit, which blew it apart, sending fiery debris whirling outward, spinning off trails of yellow smoke. A second tank was hit close aboard. The blast spun it completely around. For a moment, it stalled, then began moving ahead crookedly. The other tanks veered slightly but continued coming on.

"Down two hundred, no change," Parnell shouted into the mike. "Rapid fire for one minute."

Seventy-three seconds later, the enemy tanks ran head-on into a wall of exploding ordnance. Two were instantly destroyed. Smoke and fire surged into the sky. Another salvo came in, then another. Two acres of wheat were fully aflame now. The remaining Mark IVs instantly scattered, going off in separate directions.

One crossed into marshland, hurling reeds. It staggered forward for a few moments and then became entrapped in water up to its turret. The hatch cracked open and the German tankers began leaping out and swimming away from it. The other vehicles were rapidly moving toward cover back beyond the foothill ridge.

Parnell felt a rush of pure joy go through him like a clean, icy wind. He clicked his mike, shouted, "Fire effective. Armor withdrawing." He looked at Sol, both grinning.

Jesus Christ! How powerful he felt, all that explosive destruction at his singular command. He returned to his binoculars, glassed the entire fire zone. Chunks of things lay about among the wheat flames. Off to the right, the soldiers from the submerged tank had reached solid ground and were climbing out, running after their departing comrades. He swung back to the kill zone, saw a lone soldier thrashing around on the ground beside the burning hulk of a tank. His clothing was fully ablaze.

Parnell watched him without any disturbing emotion. Slowly the German stopped moving. Red kept his binoculars on him, the man seething smoke and flames. Just then, inexplicably, Parnell thought of his father. *What? Here, now?* He let the thought expand.

As a crack engineer, "Big Jack" Parnell had traveled all over the world, had seen many deaths. Red wondered whether he had ever seen such vast, regimented slaughter. What would *he* say if he were standing beside him? Through his flush of triumph, he felt a quick, sharp edge of sadness. But, again, why? For his father, already so long gone? Of course. But for something else, too, something elusive, down too deep, evading the light. Could it be the slow vanishing of that grounded essence that had been himself?

Or was it already gone . . . ?

Sol shouted, "Watch out!"

Parnell twisted in time to see a German Fi-156 Storch reconnaissance plane lift over one of the lower ridges and come drifting slowly toward them at a hundred feet. It looked like a green-brown dragonfly with its slender wings and spindly landing gear.

He grabbed the radio and his weapon and launched himself off his boulder, down into prickly straw brush and wild
bougainvillea, just as the Storch went skimming close overhead, its sewing machine single engine purring. He could
see the pilot and spotter in their black Luftwaffe jumpsuits.

"Shit," Colonel Dunmore said, studying the running teletype message. He glanced over at Lieutenant Colonel Chet
Hanson and shook his head grimly. Both Dunmore and
Hanson were on temporary loan from II Corps, over to assist
Seventh Army's intelligence staff during the invasion. Patton
and his senior G-2 were in England working on plans for a
secret operation connected with the scheduled Overlord invasion of western Europe.

Hanson and Dunmore were in a side room of the High
Court Chancellery for Palermo in the city's Palazzo dei
Normanni, the Palace of the Norman Kings, which Patton
had chosen for his headquarters. This particular room had
been set up for his intelligence section.

It was large with an intricately carved wooden stalactite
ceiling and Byzantine tile walls now completely covered
with battle charts. Radios and encryption-decryption units
were scattered everywhere with a dozen sitting operators
busily transcribing and decoding the constant stream of battle reports coming from General Mark Clark's Fifth Army
headquarters aboard USS *Ancon,* the flagship for Task Force
81.

The teletype stopped. Dunmore tore off the yellow paper,
reread the message, and then handed it to Hanson. It was an
intelligence memo listing German units that were believed
to be racing toward the Salerno area. He moved off and stood
in front of a large, lead-glassed window overlooking the
palace's western courtyard. It was filled with military command cars and half-tracks. Directly across from the courtyard was the Porta Nuova, its conical copper top gleaming in
the morning sun.

Hanson said, "Kesselring's pulling out all the stops, isn't he?" Chet had the athletic look of a gym instructor, his hair trimmed to the skull, his broad, thrusting jawline like Dick Tracy's. He sighed. "Well, at least Hewitt's finally ordered in his gunships." Vice Admiral H. Kent Hewitt was task force commander for the Western Assault Group.

"Too goddamned late," Dunmore said harshly. "I told you that decision to put troops ashore without a preassault bombardment was pure lunacy."

Hanson shrugged. "They wanted surprise. It was a reasonable conclusion, considering."

Most of the earlier Allied intelligence reports had shown that Kesselring and his senior staff officers were expecting the Allies to hit the *southern* coast of Italy, perhaps even somewhere along the Adriatic side of the Italian peninsula. Nobody suspected General von Vietinghoff thought differently and had taken it on his own to strengthen his defenses in the Naples/Salerno area. On top of that intelligence void, he'd managed to accomplish the whole thing in near secrecy. Even British air recon photos and ground intelligence had shown only a generalized buildup.

Dunmore snorted with disgust. "But *we're* the ones got surprised."

Hanson went back to the message, thoughtfully ticking his fingernail against the sheet. "From the number of units he's repositioning, I suspect old Kesselring's got his nuts to the fire about now."

"Of course he has. He's *got* to stop us here." He turned back to the window, distractedly watched a seagull tack into the sea wind over the Vittorio Emanuele Boulevard. His thoughts turned to Blue Team, his favorite. There was a good chance they were about to be abandoned out there, having to go pure guerrilla if the beachhead was eliminated. Well, that's what they were trained for. Yet he couldn't hold back the return of anger.

When he was first told that the Mohawkers were being taken from him and placed under OSS operational command, he'd gone livid. If he could have found Major Nunn at that moment, he'd have beaten the hell out of him on the spot. He had immediately appealed to Patton. The general listened impatiently, distracted by his own personal problems.

During the Sicilian campaign, he'd made two potentially career-ending blunders, physically slapping two soldiers suffering battle fatigue. When news of it got out, the army wanted his head. Fortunately, Eisenhower realized how valuable Patton's battlefield leadership would be in the coming invasion of western Europe. So, he ignored the army's demands, ordered Patton to make a formal and humiliating apology to both soldiers, and then safely tucked him away in England in command of a nonexistent army designed to fool the Germans.

The general yanked his cigar from his mouth and sharply cut Dunmore off. "Colonel," he growled, "you haven't got a goddamned snowball's chance in hell of getting that order rescinded. That gum-sucking son of a bitch Donovan's personally pushed it through. Roosevelt's fair-haired boy." He chortled with disgust. "My only advice to you is swallow your pride and bide your goddamned time."

He did. It was a bitter pill, particularly when OSS deliberately kept him out of the loop concerning Blue Team. Still, he had the power of Bradley's II Corps behind him and had managed to at least keep track of Parnell and his men. Now they were somewhere inland of the Salerno beachhead, smack dab in the middle of where every goddamned German unit in southern Italy was headed.

A young lieutenant approached. "Excuse me, sir. You might want to see this." He handed him a radio intersection memo from one of Fifth Army's G-2 section liaison officers attached to Clark's intelligence unit.

He scanned it, then looked up, shocked. "I don't believe this! Clark's just instructed his people to work up a contingency OP to shift the Paestum force and consolidate it with Tenth Corps."

"What? He's going to pivot north *now?* He can't, he hasn't gained enough room to maneuver yet."

Dunmore shook his head, his eyes tundric. "He's not going to pivot. He intends to shift by sea."

Hanson sat up. "You mean a full beachhead withdrawal and repositioning under this kind of fire?" Hanson sucked air through his lips. "Oh, Jesus, this is bad."

They couldn't hear the first mortar rounds coming in, only the sharp double clicks of their arming fuses just before they struck. Both Parnell and Kaamanui instantly hit the ground, bellowing, "Mortar! Mortar!"

The three rounds exploded with a ground-shuddering impact, their concussion waves sweeping past filled with metal fragments, stone chips, rock chunks. Red felt his eardrums' pain as he lay flat, sucking the ground into his body, thinking wildly, *The bastards saw us!*

They'd been moving up out of the rock amphitheater in single file, going uphill toward a dense stand of oak and white pine. The German recon plane had made only one pass over them before it turned south and disappeared beyond a lower hogback. It looked as if they hadn't been spotted. Still, Parnell had decided to move a few hundred yards upslope just in case.

Now he lifted his head slightly, ears ringing, debris thudding down all round him. His mind raced through thoughts, images. A crazy identifying: *55mm Granatenwerfer 36, muzzle-loaded, high-angle fire, range 1,500 to 2,500 yards* . . . He looked up the hill. The rounds had left three in-line shell holes fifty yards above his position. His heart gripped up. He knew the German gunners would lay in their next sheath a click lower, working their way downslope.

Click-click.

The second sheath lifted him two feet off the ground. Their concussion waves savaged him. Things tore past. His hearing went, came, went. He glanced to his left. One round had struck less than twenty feet from him. *Move, move!* his mind screamed. He came to his feet, stumbled, searched for his radio. Shrapnel had torn it apart. His Thompson. *There.* He scooped it up, ran.

Sol appeared beside him. Just ahead Freidl-Real lay on his side. He didn't look injured but his eyes were crossed, wide and large, and his face was stark white. They grabbed him and dragged him along.

Click-click.

This time the explosions cast debris high over their heads, the impacts far down the slope. Instantly they were up again, running, Augustin finally getting his legs back. One more sheath came in as they reached the lip of the amphitheater. Before the echoes of the strikes riffled off, they were racing across a small grassy meadow, knowing the Kraut gunners would soon be laying ordnance back up the slope once more. Four minutes later, they made the cover of the trees and disappeared into the denser stands of white pine.

Eleven

For the next forty-eight hours, the Allied beachheads hung on tenaciously against constant pounding by the Germans, who were increasing their forces by the hour. Some American units were actually pinned down on sand for a day and a half, unable to even move to the dune line. Still, the troopers of the U.S. 36th Infantry Division, who landed at Paestum and were now undergoing what would prove to be one of the bloodiest baptisms of fire throughout the European campaign, simply refused to give in.

In the north, the British X Corps was also struggling. Its two main objectives, the Montecorvino Airfield and the Ponte Sele, both situated at the apex of the entire beachhead, were not taken on schedule. Only along the Amalfi coast had there been success as the U.S. Ranger and Commando battalions quickly reached the summits of the Chiunzi and Nocera passes, which led directly down into the Bay of Naples. But then, at daylight of the tenth, the Germans hit their firebases with five vicious counterattacks and they were forced to retire from the high ground.

Besides the dogged determination of the assault troops throughout these critical hours, one other factor helped maintain the fragile beachhead: naval gunfire. Both British and

American gunships were answering hundreds of fire missions, including sixteen-inch salvos from the British battleships *Abacrombie* and *Muritius,* which lay fifteen miles offshore.

The battle continued without letup. Then, by midmorning of the eleventh, Clark began shoving in his floating reserves, primarily the Regimental Combat Teams of the 45th Infantry Division. Concentrating on Red Beach, these fresh troopers managed to extend the Paestum salient nearly a mile inland.

For Blue Team these forty-eight hours were a time of constant motion and activity as they hustled all over the Sottane and Soprano hills, dodging German patrols, sleeping in snatches, living off K-rations and oranges. In order to make their operations more efficient and to lessen the chance of losing all his men, Parnell had split the team and then split it again, using crews of as few as two men.

He and Kaamanui continued calling in naval fire using their backup radio and continually transmitting from different positions. During the afternoon of the tenth they had broken up another armored column, four Mark IVs and three half-tracks speeding north on Highway 18 outside the coast town of Agropoli, along with two mobile 88 batteries on the road to Altavilla.

On the eleventh they put a machine gun company under 6-inch fire as it tried crossing the Trentinara River a mile from the old Gypsy camp. That afternoon, they requested and got three more fire missions, one against a fixed howitzer position and two against convoys of supply trucks.

Meanwhile, the rest of the men went out on recon patrols or small opportunity hit-and-flee strikes on isolated German outposts in the Soprano/Sottane foothills, maintaining contact with Parnell through walkie-talkies using only their transmitter switches. To retain cover, they often traveled with groups of refugees fleeing the fighting

Periodically Parnell also sent updated observation reports to his OSS liaison man, who had set up a monitoring station on Pointe del Faro, Sicily. He always sent them in thirty-second transmissions using a code system based on a chessboard with its white king placed directly on the foothill town of Mantinella. Each starting chess piece then represented a specific grid position on an accompanying overlay topo map. By using set letters and numbers, he could relay data on enemy positions and force movements. To increase security of his messages since he was transmitting in the open, he changed letter/number sets and frequencies after each transmission.

Freidl-Real continued monitoring the BBC, which was now broadcasting continuously. He was listening for messages specifically intended for the Resistance in the Naples/Salerno sector. The messages were always hidden within inane bits of information, for instance, "The sheep farmers in Wessex have experienced a slight reduction in wool prices over last month," or, "Dr. Jeremy Fall-Smith will speak on the theological aspects of Chapter sixty-one of *Moby Dick* this eve at the rectory lecture hall of Saint James on the Swann." Both Parnell and Augustin carried codebooks that deciphered key phrases.

Late on the afternoon of the eleventh, Smoker, Cowboy, and Couprier, on their way back to the base cave after a dawn raid on a small enemy vehicle-repair facility near Vesole, ran into a German search patrol. The Krauts had two huge Airedales with them and had detained several Catholic nuns near the tiny river village of Torre Osala.

Something about the nuns had apparently infuriated the animals. They were attacking them viciously, tearing at their habits, the women screaming and begging the soldiers to pull them away. At first, the Germans tried to haul the animals off. But finally they stopped and merely stood there, watching. One of the nuns was already unconscious and badly bleeding.

Wineberg and Fountain, who had instantly gone to brush, now glanced at each other, then at Evan. Nothing was said. Almost as if with one thought, all three rose, stepped out onto the narrow dirt road, and opened on the Germans soldiers. They killed all nine within twenty seconds. Then they shot the dogs.

They roused the unconscious nun and helped bandage the women's wounds. When they left, the sisters were praying over the bodies of the dead Germans and begging for their forgiveness.

Later on that same afternoon, a BBC message finally came through containing the word *Cornfield,* which was Blue Team's OSS code name: "Farmers in the cornfield country of Spalding have experienced a renewed interest in synthetic fertilizer fashioned from ancient coastal carbon deposits. . . ."

Hurriedly deciphering the completed message, Parnell learned he was to dispatch a small raiding force south to sabotage two high-speed enemy E-boats that had begun operating from an abandoned fish-processing plant south of Agropoli. The raiders were to rendezvous with another partisan agent code-named Sand at a river crossing on the Alento at 2300 hours that night.

Red chose Kaamanui as leader since he was the best underwater demo man in the team. Cappacelli quickly volunteered to go with him and so did Cesara, saying that she knew the Agropoli area and Sand. The three headed out just after dark, carrying prepared limpet bombs that would be placed on the hulls of the patrol boats.

Naples, Italy
1745 hours

Major Keppler had been waiting for nearly an hour, sitting on the veranda of the Castel Nuovo, the fourteenth century annex to the older palace of Charles I of Anjou. Both buildings sat on the edge of the city's waterfront beside the summer-brown lawns of the Parco Costello. The *castel* was now a forward field headquarters for General von Vietinghoff's Tenth Army.

Earlier, he was ordered in from Nocera five miles east of Naples where he and his *Waffen SS* troopers had been temporarily attached to a regiment of the 26th Panzer to conduct hunts for Resistance fighters. It angered him to leave. So far, his men had caught and executed over forty partisans and obtained solid intelligence on a hundred others.

Now the distant, sporadic thunder and chatter of battle drifted in from the other side of the Sorrento Mountains. He looked seaward. In the long, slanting evening light, the gulf islands of Capri, Ischia, and Procida seemed to float on a placid prairie of blue-black sapphire. He dismissed the image. Merely an illusion of beauty. Keppler hated everything about Naples, the place even filthier and shabbier than Palermo, its past glories gone.

Eventually a sprightly corporal came for him. He led the major through the building and down into what had once been dungeons. The walls were of chiseled gray stone coated with moisture and sour-smelling fungus where the trapped air reeked of rat dung. He was ushered into a large room filled with radio gear, a field intelligence office.

An *Oberstderzahlmeister*, a G-2 administrative colonel, seated at a beautifully tiled desk flicked his finger at him. Keppler strode forward and braced the prescribed two feet in front of the desk's edge.

"SS Major Witt Keppler reporting as instructed, sir," he snapped curtly.

The colonel's name was Ernst Wurlitz, a small man, well known for his crudeness of speech and a propensity for pre-teen girls. He was also first cousin to *Grosadmiral* Doenitz, commander in chief of the German Navy. "So," he barked in a deep bass voice, "how is your hunt progressing?"

"We are making headway, Colonel."

"My ass!"

Keppler showed no sign of disturbance. "Sir, we have killed forty partisans and have information on many others."

Wurlitz snorted. "I'm told you're an expert in prying out partisan maggots. How true is this?"

"I have been very successful in the past, sir."

The colonel thrust himself forward. His eyes were like black nail points. "But you're falling on your cock *this* time. These Resistance *cunts* are operating freely. All over the Salerno

Plain. *Untouched!* They blow up railcars, bridges. They demolish ammunition depots. Now they even call in Allied naval fire missions." He stared challengingly at Keppler. He had a curious way of widening, then narrowing his eyes. It gave his stare the look of pulsing energy. "What do you say to *that*, Major?"

"Sir," Keppler answered calmly, "may I remind the colonel that my men and I have been operating east of Naples, not in the Salerno Plain?"

"Then you've been *operating* in the wrong *place*." He hissed and closed his nail-hard eyes for a moment. They were still closed when he commenced speaking again, as if he were picturing what he was saying. "We've intercepted many Resistance radio dispatches. Unfortunately these faggots move too swiftly. All *over* the damned landscape." His eyes shot open. "I want them *stopped*. Do you *hear* me?"

"Perfectly, sir."

"*Generalfeldmarshall* Kesselring has assured the Führer we will make a stand here. That assurance *will* be carried out. Abandon all civility toward the populace, Keppler. Kill anyone who protects these partisan scum. Slaughter the whole *population* if you have to. But"—he slammed down his fist—"find and *destroy* them."

"Yes, *Herr Oberst.*" A tiny smile of pleasure touched at the corner of Keppler's mouth.

Wurlitz instantly jumped on it. "You find my instructions *amusing*, Major?"

"No, sir. Forgive me. I consider them a splendid challenge. One I will thoroughly enjoy carrying out."

"I don't give a monkey's ass if you enjoy it or not. Just *do* it. Now get out."

"Yes, sir," Keppler said, gave a sharp salute, whirled, and hurried from the room.

Sol never did get a good look at Sand's face. A thin overcast had moved across the moon, thinning its light. In the dimness, he appeared to be a tall, lanky man dressed in fisher-man's garb. His actual name was Anthony Santamaria.

He had been the keeper of a small lighthouse on a tiny rock island off Pointe Licosa eight miles south of the town of Agropoli. As such, he kept a constant watch on the coast in his area and reported his findings to the SOE. They had smuggled him a collapsible kayak to conduct his nightly runs. Then, two months earlier, the Germans had shut down his lighthouse and replaced it with an automatic radio bea-con.

The two Americans and Cesara reached the rendezvous point at 9:30. The river crossing was merely a fifty-gallon steel drum hanging on a cable strung across the river. Cesara whistled the identifying signal, an old Gypsy song, which was instantly countersigned by Santamaria from across the river.

In very bad English, he quickly explained their mission. Soon after the Allied invasion began, the Germans had sent two *Schnellboots,* or E-boats, from the naval detachment at Sapri on the Gulf of Policastro thirty miles south. From their abandoned fishing shed, they were now attacking Allied shipping off Salerno each night and seeding the area with dozens of Type-E GS acoustic mines.

Santamaria slapped his hands together, sliding one quickly over the other. "Very fast, dis-a boats," he said. "Your radar, no, no good. Too many ships, too much noise. She's-a gonna shoot guns, drop mines, then quick she's-a run away."

"How close can we get to the pier?" Sol asked.

"Most close. I have dis-a kayak. Dynamite, too. Pier easy. With boats, we gonna dive under. You see?"

"Are both boats in right now?"

"No. Dis-a time only one she's-a go out. The other is-a engine no working. But pier she's-a got plenty mines. We blow up her, *everyting* go."

Santamaria led them due west across marshland. When they reached the coastal highway, they had to wait for nearly forty minutes before crossing it, it being full of German convoys and armored units moving north. Beyond the highway was a flat coastal plain filled with sand dunes and stands of sea pine. The agent had stashed his kayak and explosives in a reedy cove. It was nearly midnight when they reached it.

While he set up his kayak, Sol huddled with Cappacelli, Cesara listening. "Set your timers for 3:30," he told Angelo. "Then get back here fast. We don't show up by 0200, get your asses out."

"Right. Which one goes with me?"

Sol dipped his head at Cesara. "Her."

A sudden German barrage started far to the north, lighting up the underside of the overcast with yellow-white flashes, the sound of it like combers. Almost immediately Allied gunships, keying on the enemy's muzzle bursts, opened with counterfire. The big gun salvos made huge holes in the night far out at sea, their smoke and orange-red barrel flashes visible for a second, the cherry-red rounds arching in.

Cesara lightly touched Sol's arm. "I wish to go with *you*," she said. "I am good swimmer and I know where the fish house is."

He looked at her for a moment, doubtful, not liking the idea of handling explosives with an amateur. Then again, what the hell? The hooker could sure as hell kill efficiently enough. He shrugged. "Okay."

He and Cappacelli synchronized their watches. He explained to Santamaria that the woman would go with him. The agent nodded without comment. They loaded the limpet bombs into the kayak while Angelo and Santamaria shouldered their explosive packs and the walkie-talkie and wordlessly moved off, quickly disappearing among the sea pines.

Sol and Cesara eased the kayak down the small cove beach and slid it into the water. It was a dark brown, canvas, with wooden rib struts and narrow wooden seats. The limpet bombs were stacked at the bow and stern, four in all, along with two small waterproof flashlights.

Kaamanui had jury-rigged cartridges of Torvex-Extra 500 explosive gel using cores of number 6 blasting caps hooked to acid-activated timers. This particular gel was of medium water resistant explosive, used mostly to destroy shallow underwater installations. He knew it to be touchy and easily degraded when immersed in water too long. He had used the same stuff back when he was with the Corps of Engineers, blowing pillar boreholes in static water down to 250 feet. But those had been quick firings. Here these charges would be in water for four, maybe five hours before detonating. Dicey.

He looked out at the entrance of the cove, scanned south to where the fish-packing shed would be. Crabs clicked softly and tiny wavelets rippled against his calves. He glanced down at the water. Even in the dimmed moonlight, he could see rocks on the bottom, the water crystal clear. He didn't like that.

Poking the butt of his Thompson into the sand, he swiftly pulled off his sweater, tossed it up near some pines. "Take off your clothes," he said quietly. "Easier to swim. Bring only your belt."

Without a word, Cesara began to undress, Sol watching her nicely compact and curvy body emerge out of the clothing. He noticed how she openly stared for a moment at his large, pendulous penis. Finally, her eyes lifted to his face, watching him as she slung her Sten over her shoulder, turned, climbed into the kayak, and settled her soft round buttocks onto the front seat.

They went swiftly, the woman handling her double-headed paddle expertly, synching perfectly with his stroke, feathering on the forward sweeps. The bow of the little boat hissed through the water. They turned at the cove entrance and headed south, hugging the shore. It was mostly beach now, yet here and there were rock outcroppings covered with seaweed. Night seabirds were feeding at the edge of the waterline, their squeaks like rusty hinges.

Ten minutes later, Cesara stopped paddling and turned around. "The fish house is half kilometer," she whispered.

Sol studied the shore. There were thicker stands of sea pines here. He steered closer to the beach and they continued slowly forward. The barrage up north had died down now, but they could see what appeared like a low bank of clouds up there. Allied destroyers were laying smoke to throw off enemy gunners. Germans never fired on targets they couldn't clearly see. Occasionally, a flare would pop into life beyond the smoke, farther north near Salerno, looking look fuzzy stars.

A faint blue glow gradually emerged out of the night. It was directly ahead three hundred yards, dim, the color of an acetylene torch. Sol could make out the loading pier, a dark shadow going out into the water for about fifty yards. He hissed a warning to Cesara and turned the kayak toward the beach. They slid quietly up onto the sand and quickly unloaded their gear, then hauled the kayak up into a cluster of small trees.

For a moment, Sol went over the attack plan with Cesara, showing her how to place the magnetic disks of the limpet charges directly onto the boat's hull and then setting the timers. "These E-boats don't have riveting," he whispered. "The hull plates are welded so you can't feel any seams. You'll have to estimate where a transverse is and place the bomb directly under it."

She touched his arm. "What is transverse?"

He pointed to his side. "The boat's rib frame. You blow it there, it causes more damage."

"*Sí, sí.*"

Each bomb was wrapped tightly in the oil-paper packing that had come with the weapons and explosives Freidl-Real had stashed at the Paestum ruins. Kaamanui had sealed all the seams with candle wax, but he knew the they would begin leaking soon after they were immersed. That could foul up the entire detonation sequence. It couldn't be helped, they'd just have to keep fingers crossed, wait, and see.

Each carrying two bombs strapped around the waist, they moved up through the trees, the sandy ground covered with pine needles soft on their bare feet. Land crabs scurried ahead. The air smelled like green turpentine.

Soon, they were able to make out the complete shape of the main packing shed and pier. The shed was three stories high, made of stone, and sat at the pier head. The pier itself had a wide roof that extended half its length. Beside the packing shed was a repair way with its keel poppets and shoring boots still standing. Beyond it, the Germans had brought in three mobile fuel tanks for the E-boats. They sat under netting with pine branches adding to the camouflage.

The single German *Schnellboot* was berthed just under the north side overhang. It was 115 feet long, a sleek craft narrow of beam. Sol knew it ran triple two-stroke diesel engines for quick acceleration and prolonged-speed runs. It was painted a zigzag camo pattern and its up structures included a swept-back control cabin, twin quads of 20mm guns and six twenty-one-inch torpedo tubes, everything now bathed in that soft blue glow. A dozen crewmen were busy loading mines onto two stern release racks, looking like huge basketballs with spikes, their metal housings gleaming lethally in blue. The sailors laughed and joked as they worked.

Kaamanui studied the layout for several minutes, then touched Cesara's shoulder and pointed to the water. They moved to the edge of the trees, then crawled across the beach and into the water. It felt soft and caressingly warm, the two floating on the gentle shore current, their bombs buoyant. At last, they leveled out and began breaststroking toward the German attack boat, their heads low in the water, arms never breaking the surface.

They came right up to the hull amidships, touched it, pressed tightly against it, it feeling cold as iced steel. Kaamanui indicated for Cesara to stay, took three deep breaths, and went under.

Using his hands, he followed the hull down to the keel. The bottom was V-shaped. He flicked on his light. The high-tensile steel plating was discolored to a copper tinge by heat tempering and the oxidation layer from marine microorganisms.

On the starboard side was the black wall of the rock pier. Only a thin line of blue light came down there. On the port side, the light created faint shimmering shafts that dissolved out about ten feet down. He could see Cesara's hazy silhouette against the light, her legs gently sculling. As he moved toward the stern, he heard machinery start up, felt the hull tremble.

The three propeller shaft housings and their rudder posts were all painted in red lead. The props themselves were huge, their smooth, glistening brassy curves looking deadly even in repose. Sol's lungs were beginning to ache with oxygen need. Moving faster now, he quickly chose a transverse point and attached one of his limpets.

Turning his face away, he shone his light directly onto the timer's face for a few seconds, letting the phosphorous coating on the dials absorb it. He turned off the light. The dials made two tiny glowing lines in the darkness as he set the timer. He kicked back to where Cesara hung in the water, came up beside her, slowly releasing his breath and sucking in fresh air soundlessly.

Reaching down, he took one of her bombs. Using hand signals, he told her to place her remaining one directly inboard of their position, then pointed forward, indicating he intended to put the others nearer the bow. They quietly oxygenated their lungs, then went under, pulling side by side for a few feet, their little lights coming on, and then Sol veered to the left and disappeared.

As he set the timer on the last bomb, he noticed a delicate stream of bubbles seeping from the seal. He shook his head disgustedly and started back. Apparently, Cesara had completed her placement and gone out for air, but was back again, waiting. In the little oval of his flashlight, she grinned at him, her face looking pale, her dark hair coiling and drifting like black snakes. Rising slowly, they started for the port side.

A brilliant white beam of light shafted down through the

water, probing, its brightness diffusing deeper down yet power-fully silhouetting the angular junction of the hull. Sol instantly drew back. His head lightly banged against the boat's bottom. He reached back, felt Cesara's breasts, turned her, and shoved her toward the starboard side.

Hurrying deeper, they cleared the keel and then surfaced between the boat's hull and the rock pier. They could hear voices calling quietly above the tiny clicking of crustaceans on the rocks and the lazy rasp of mooring lines.

Another beam of white light played for a moment along the pier a few feet away. Instantly, they both went down and under the bottom of the hull again. The second light came down into the water on the starboard side. For a few seconds, both beams continued to explore. Sol felt Cesara's hand grip his biceps, felt her fear in it. He put his own hand on hers, gentled her. Seconds like hours floated past.

Finally the port light went out, then the starboard. But suddenly there was a deep grinding sound and the rumble of machinery came. The two outboard props began spinning, going slowly at first, then faster as the engine roar increased, the blades creating cavitation bubbles in the water and a throaty popping as the hull began to shake overhead. It continued for a few moments, then abruptly stopped, leaving only the turbulence in the water and the cavitation bubbles hissing and fading back into silence.

Fifteen minutes later, they retrieved their kayak and headed back to the cove rendezvous.

The Isola Licosa lighthouse stood twenty feet high, a truncated cylinder of granite stones built during Roman times. The top of it still had the fire pit in which ancient coast watchers had lit bonfires. There were also the rusted remnants of metal reflectors from the 1800s and the empty housing of the spring-driven motor that had rotated the old fish-oil lamp signals, everything thick with seagull guano. The Germans had installed a tall antenna and in the room directly below was a automatic, battery-powered, Rundfroid 1500 WSA radio beacon transmitter.

Santamaria's quarters had been on the bottom floor, a small cell with rock walls that still had the ancient Roman sand coating called *pazalan* that made it waterproof. His straw cot and kerosene stove were the only things the Krauts had left, discarding everything else to make room for radio cables and spare batteries.

It was now 3:01. Sol, Angelo, and Cesara were sitting on top of the little lighthouse while Kaamanui used Santamaria's binoculars to glass the old coast road and Highway 18 farther inland. The rumble and growl of armor and machinery came clearly off the land, heavy enemy reinforcements moving north to the battle zone. Something big was coming, Sol knew. He had already clicked a warning to Parnell with the walkie-talkie. Now they waited.

Earlier, they had tried to get back across the highway to the Alento River and the Sottane foothills. But the German convoys and armored units were too numerous, at least an entire division shifting position. Knowing their E-boat charges would soon go off and bring German hunter parties into the area, Kaamanui decided to take temporary refuge in the lighthouse until they could return to the mountains. If they weren't able to get across at all, he intended that they drift out to sea and go aboard one of the ships in the assault fleet.

Once they reached the lighthouse, Santamaria had informed Sol he intended to take the kayak and follow the coastline south to spot out the strength of the German movement north. He promised to be back the following night with food.

Sol agreed and flicked his thumb at Cesara. "Take her with you. It'll be safer."

"No," she instantly cried. "I will remain with *you*." He started to argue but she shook her head, saying, "No, no," and walked away.

They watched as Santamaria headed south and then swam the quarter mile to the tiny lighthouse rock, angling toward it against a slight current, the water glowing with phosphorescence.

At precisely 0330 hours, the fishing shed charges exploded. First the muffled jolt of the limpets and then the louder crashes from Angelo's and Santamaria's charges, two solid bursts of fiery light followed immediately by a series of violent explosions as the German mines, triggered by the sudden pressure waves, went off, hurling smoke and incandescent debris. The pier roof was quickly engulfed in fire and soon the three fuel tanks ignited, black smoke roiling above the flames.

The three grinned at each other and watched as vehicle lights immediately came off the highway to race toward the inferno. After a few moments, Sol told Angelo, "I'll take first watch. You and the broad go get some sleep."

"I ain't tired, Sarge. Let me take the first."

Sol shrugged and he and the girl climbed down to Santamaria's old quarters.

The room held an ancient chill and the granite odor of centuries mixed with the plastic essence of cable grease, the faint ammonia of battery packing. Cesara lay on Santamaria's straw cot in her man's clothing, Sol on the floor with a wiring box for a pillow.

He felt the exhaustion come up through his body, his heavy muscles relaxing quickly in the way of a soldier at last allowed to rest. His mind drifted. He thought about the E-boat, pictured it skimming the sea, rooster tail astern, water hurling off her chines. He chuckled lazily. *Not tonight, assholes.* Sleep hovered close.

Cesara said, "Are you of *Rom* blood?"

Her quiet voice drew him from an emerging dream. He opened his eyes. "What?"

"I ask if you are *Rom*. That is what Gypsies call each other."

"No, I ain't no Gypsy."

"Your skin is dark. I thought perhaps you were Indian. All Gypsy ancestors came from India a thousand years ago."

He laughed. "No, honey, I'm a *kanaka*. A Polynesian."

"Ah, yes," she said. "Where Gauguin painted his famous nudes. Tha-hee-tay." She gave the word the soft tongue sound of Castillian Spanish.

"Not Tahiti. Samoa."

"Ah." She was quiet for a few moments. The sound of war filtered through the stones so faintly it may have been only the hum of ocean distance. "Where in A-mer-ica you are from?"

"San Francisco."

"As a boy?"

"Yeah."

"Among the *gadje?*"

"The what?"

"The Gypsy call anyone not of the blood a *gadje*. It means barbarian."

Again he laughed. "I guess I did live with some *gad-jee* in the city."

"Did they mock your skin?"

That brought him up sharp, the woman touching something way down deep. Memories, not thought of for a long time . . . schoolmates calling him a Pacific nigger until he got big enough to kick the crap out of anyone daring to say it . . . his father telling him, "We're Hawaiians, goddammit, not *coons*." Yet it had hurt all the same, even with the explanations, and now, suddenly, out of nowhere, all of it remembered in a flash.

Shit.

"Why'd you ask me that?" he said.

"They mock-ed me, too."

He grunted.

She was quiet again. Then, very softly, she asked, "Do you want to fuck me?"

He twisted his head, looked up at her. He could not see her in the dense darkness. "I don't fuck whores who fuck Germans," he said.

"This will not be like the other."

He sat up. What the hell was *this*?

Over his adult years, many women had offered themselves to Solomon Kaamanui, mostly in those beer-smelly honky-tonks where the "good" people never went, the women intrigued by his size, his skin color, some perhaps sensing his horse-sized cock and thinking, *Oh, I can handle you, big boy.* But there were also "good" women, too, married ones, encountering in him the sudden urge for the forbidden, the crossing of boundaries.

Yet this one now seemed unlike the rest. Something about her open, frank honesty. He felt the sudden ache of lust come warmly up out of his groin, felt blood engorging in that automatic, eternal male response to a woman offering her body.

"Why me?"

"You are willing to give your life for my freedom."

Ah, yeah, payback. "Everything for the war effort, eh?"

There was a sudden sharpness in her voice: "I said it is different." Silence. When she spoke again, it was softer, huskier, the timbre of it coming at him from out of the blackness. He heard her shift on the straw. "I have great desire for you," she whispered. "I want badly to feel you inside my body."

He reached out, exploring the darkness like a blind man. He touched her face, her throat. Her breasts were bare, his fingers brushing a stiffened nipple, feeling, sensing, the swelling heat below the tissue. She brought his fingers to her mouth, licked them.

Urgent gropings in the blackness, the fumbling shedding of clothing. When he first entered her, she growled deep in her throat and then clung hungrily to him as his massive body thrust back and forth above her. She whimpered and murmured breathless words he didn't understand, in Romany and Italian and French, and cried muffled screams as she came. Soon he felt his own shuddering and then held her and took her again and still again until they both lay panting, satiated, the straw beneath them squeaking and the air ripe with the odors of sweat and pudenda.

They fell asleep.

Fourteen minutes later, at precisely 0415 hours, *General-feldmarschall* Kesseling hurled his entire Salerno force at the Allied beachhead line.

All through the twelfth, the fighting had been vicious but sporadic. Objectives were taken, lost, and retaken. Still, the beachhead line, particularly in the American sector, had slowly, doggedly advanced. By evening, some forward units had actually penetrated as much as seven miles into the plain. But as night came, the entire battle line remained extremely unstable.

The first enemy thrust of Kesselring's counterattack came against the British X Corps near the town of Battipáglia on the northern edge of the plain. The Brits were quickly shoved back nearly a mile before they could regroup and set up a new defensive line. But the main attack was focused on the thin left flank of the U.S. VI Corps west of the town of Ebola along the conjunction of the Sele and Calore Rivers.

The bridge Blue Team had destroyed had been quickly rebuilt after the start of the invasion. Now German armored units, towed fieldpieces, and dismounted infantry from the 26th and 29th Panzer Grenadier Divisions raced across it and along the banks of the two rivers to attack scattered positions of the U.S. 45th Infantry Division. Farther east, the 16th Panzer hurtled into the heart of the plain along the base of the mountain range east of the Soprano/Sottane hills, nearly wiping out an entire American unit called the Martin Force near the foothill town of Altavilla.

Meanwhile, also heading toward Salerno was the XIV Panzer Corps from Gaeta and the 3rd Panzer Grenadiers from Rome. South of the Paestum beachhead line, the leading units of the LXXVI Panzer Corps drove north across the Trentinara River and into the bottom of the Salerno Plain.

By noon of that day, the German counterattack had driven the Allied beachhead back toward the sea nearly four miles.

Twelve

Commander of the Fifth Army, Lieutenant General Mark Clark, was concerned. In fact, the usually taciturn, rawboned man with the countrified style of a Down East lawyer was deeply worried. He nervously paced his small quarters aboard the Task Force 81 flagship USS *Ancon* while his adjutant, Major Gerald Allison, watched in silence.

It was 12:30 in the early afternoon of the thirteenth. All morning he and his staff had been monitoring battle reports pouring into the Fifth Army's Operations Control Center, which was located directly above him on the command deck. Within hours of the opening of the German counteroffensive, it was evident to everybody that Kesselring was going full-out on this one. And he was succeeding. The entire beachhead was on the verge of collapse.

Clark also felt deeply frustrated. He firmly believed that he had the tactical answer to the situation, the complete evacuation of his Paestum force and its consolidation with the British X Corps farther north. A single, solid front. Unfortunately for him, nobody else agreed. General McCreery, commander of X Corps, and Admiral Cunningham, head of all Allied naval forces in the Mediterranean, had both vehemently opposed the idea right from the beginning.

Now they'd finally convinced Eisenhower and his deputy, General Sir Harold Alexander, to their way of thinking. At 9:00 that morning Clark had received a cable from Alexander's HQ at Cassibile, Sicily. He was absolutely to refrain from executing such a "dangerous, almost suicidal" maneuver.

He paused for a moment, shook his head. "They're wrong, Jerry," he snapped. "Goddammit, they're *wrong*. Blast their Limey hides. They're all like Monty, never willing to take a risk without overwhelming force."

Allison was silent for a moment, then asked, "May I be frank, General?"

"Of course."

"I believe you *have* to commit Ridgeway's force now, sir." Major General Matthew Ridgeway was commander of the 82nd Airborne Division. "It's the only thing that could stall Kesselring."

Clark shook his head. "It's too late. I'd be ordering those men into a slaughterhouse for nothing!" Earlier, he had discussed this option with his senior staff officers. They, like him, felt certain Ridgeway couldn't get his men prepared in time to make a difference.

At the moment the 82nd Division was in Sicily in inactive reserve. As part of the original Avalanche plan, it had been scheduled to jump directly into Rome just before the assault on Salerno began. Even Ike okayed the operation. But General Ridgeway and his senior artillery commander, Brigadier General Maxwell Taylor, had reservations. He felt that the Germans were too densely concentrated in and around the Holy City. He was also highly skeptical about Rome's Italian troops supporting the Americans once they were on the ground.

He convinced Eisenhower to allow Taylor to make a personal inspection of the city. Late on the evening of 7 September, he and an air surveillance officer were smuggled into Rome. There they met the Italian commander, General Carboni, and studied German dispositions. He was back the next day with dire news. There were over fifty thousand Germans on both sides of the Tiber. As for the Italians, they didn't even have ammunition or gasoline. The Krauts had stripped them of both. Ike canceled the drop, even while some of the troop-laden C-47s were already in the air.

"But, sir, what else can you do?" Allison protested. "We've lost most of our naval fire support and our lines are falling back too quickly to get reinforcements here in time. There's the key, time."

The truth of that statement hung in the air like a foul odor. General Clark began pacing again. His adjutant sat forward earnestly, a tall, lean man with a youthful shock of brown hair and a perpetual tan. "I think Matthew *can* do it, General. My God, if there's anyone who can, it's him."

He continued: "I believe we'd catch Kesselring and Vieting-hoff completely off guard. You know they don't consider para-chute infantry in their strategic planning anymore. Not since Hitler's fiasco with them in Greece. So they won't be expect-ing *us* to use them, either. One paratrooper regiment landing right in von Vietinghoff's face could throw his entire front into disarray."

Clark lowered his head for a moment, gradually stopped moving. He stood there staring at the deck, then lifted his eyes abruptly. "Give him the go-ahead."

"Yes, sir," Allison said. He bounded to his feet and hur-ried away.

At 1330 hours of that day, Clark personally spoke to the commander of the 82nd by SIGSALY, the new cipher phone developed by Bell Labs. He quickly laid out the tactical plan. He ended with a single, pointed question. *"Can you get your men operational and over here by 1800 hours today?"*

Ridgeway's answer consisted of four words: "Consider it done, sir."

It had been a vicious eight hours since sunup, Parnell and Wyatt still working fire missions up there on their shifting perches as they watched the madness unfold down on the plain. German armor and infantry units seemed to come from everywhere, all of it covered by heavy artillery barrages. Slowly but certainly, the entire Allied beachhead line was being driven back toward the gulf.

Red had had a surplus of targets. But most of them were too closely engaged with Allied units, making it impossible to bring in naval fire. The few times he did request fire, he had to wait too long before being assigned a gunship. By then, his targets had deployed out of concentration.

Over half the smaller Allied gunships had been forced to return to Palermo to replenish their magazines. Of those still in the gulf, many had been hit by the German shelling and guided bombs. Several were still burning close to shore, unable to withdraw.

Despite that, Parnell did manage to shell a column of ten Mark IVs that were moving north along the coast highway. He knocked out two tanks along with a half-track before his gunship was shifted to another forward observer. In the late morning he brought fire to bear on a company of infantry near the Sattone foothills. These he sent scurrying back beyond the ridgeline in total disorder.

Yet even with those successes, Red was angry at himself. He should have seen the German buildup and attack coming. Even though they'd done most of their tactical shifting at night and had brought units in from the north and northwest, too far out for him to define dispositions. Still, he should have *sensed* it, that's what a seasoned combat soldier did, for Christ's sake. At the very least, he should have sent recon crews *into* the plain instead of holding everybody back in the high country.

By noon, it was obvious to him and Wyatt that unless the Americans stopped the German momentum long enough to reform a defensive line within the next twenty-four hours, it would be over. If that possibility developed, he knew what he'd do, take the team deeper into the mountains and go to pure guerrilla fighting.

The rest of the men were now out on two separate missions. Laguna, Fountain, Wineberg, and Cucinotta were observing enemy movements around the plain towns of Albanella and Altavilla northeast of Monte Saprano, the second highest summit in this part of the Apennines.

Freidl-Real, Comprier, and Yildirim were on the hunt for a wounded German officer who refugees claimed was hiding in the small mountain town of Roccadaspide. If they could capture him, they might extract valuable intelligence about the German counteroffensive. The same refugees had also given him dire information, that deadly typhus had begun showing up in some of the smaller upland villages.

As soon as Parnell realized the strength of the German counterattack, he ordered the crews in immediately. Once the Krauts again dominated the entire area in strength, their patrols would be swarming these hills. It was necessary he maintain his full force against sudden attack. Cowboy came back quickly, *click-click,* acknowledging. But he'd heard nothing from Kaamanui or Freidl-Real.

At precisely 4:22 that afternoon, his radio suddenly blared with the dits and dots of his fire mission code call sign, Blue One, in Morse code. It came in on his emergency frequency from the monitor ship.

The vessel's radioman had a rapid thumb, his entire message lasting only fourteen seconds. Four minutes later, he repeated it, and three minutes after that repeated it again.

Red tapped his transmit key to signify receipt. He then quickly deciphered. It was an order directly from Fifth Army headquarters directed through his navy liaison. He was instructed to pick out a suitable landing zone within the Knight's field of his OSS number-three topo overlay map. He was then to transmit every ten minutes a thirty-second homing signal, starting at exactly 1900 hours that evening. Once radio contact was made with the incoming aircraft, code-named Papa Brown, he was to mark out the drop zone with a large, lighted T.

He handed the decipher to Wyatt. "What do you think? Supplies or paratroopers?"

"It's gotta be troopers, Lieutenant. That's the only thing makes sense."

"Let me see the number-three overlay."

Bird retrieved it, laid it on the ground. Parnell focused on the Knight's field zone. It was located at the toe of the Sattone foothills, four miles due east of the Paestum ruins. "That's where we linked after the bridge." He drew up a mental picture of the area: a small sheepherder's hut, a wide meadow full of deep bunch grass surrounded by stands of pine and cork oak, good flat ground with a slight slant to the south and a quick upsloping toward the foothills. He poked his forefinger into the map. "There, we'll bring them in right there."

He settled back on his haunches, thinking, *How do we set it up? First off, what can we use for the T marker? Fire, of course. Gasoline? Pour out a pattern and put a lighter to it?* No, that meadow was end-of-summer dry. Fire would spread too rapidly. By the time the aircraft got to the drop zone, there'd be no discernible T marker. *Okay, then we'll just use canisters of gasoline lit off like torches.*

"How much fuel we got in those two Kraut vehicles?" he asked. Both were still stashed near their base cave.

Wyatt shrugged. "I'd say they're about half-full, including spare jerry cans."

Red checked his watch. It was 4:38. Far down and away a sudden fusillade began, a rifle battle, the shots scattered pops in the late afternoon, just like in the movies about the Civil War, Yankees and Rebs skirmishing from cover.

"We've got two and a half hours to set up."

They headed up the slope. All around them the air was drowsy hot and filled with the hum of bees drifting through the brush. With this was also the acrid stench of war, which came up on the wind.

They had been on a forced march up into the forests of Monte Cofano, which rose north of the Trápani-Milo Airfield in Sicily, troopers of the 504th Parachute Infantry Regiment of the 82nd Airborne Division, Colonel Reuben Tucker commanding. Ever since the canceled Rome jump, the entire division had been trying to maintain its razor's edge, exercising, running maneuvers and forced marches.

At 2:30 that afternoon, just as they reached the top of the cone-shaped mountain that Rudyard Kipling called the "City in the Sky," a half-ton ammo carrier with an officer from divisional headquarters came barreling up the narrow dirt road. It hauled to a stop and the officer leaped out, shouting for Tucker.

The colonel came striding down the hill, his battle jumper black with sweat. The two officers spoke for a few moments. Tucker immediately sent a runner for the rest of his staff and senior noncoms. The officers piled into the ammo carrier, which spun a U and went tearing off as the noncoms started bellowing for platoons to form up. Within minutes, the regiment was headed back down the mountain to their company areas.

While the men descended, their officers were being briefed by General Ridgeway. "Gentlemen," he began in his booming voice, "you're about to get another chance at kicking some Kraut ass. And pulling Fifth Army's balls out of the fire at the same time."

He turned to a wall map. "You'll be going in here, three miles east of the Thirty-sixth's front, at 1900 hours tonight. I repeat, to*night*. Once you've assembled on ground, you are to deploy immediately. South to set up defensive positions against Panzer Grenadiers already across the Trentinara River. And northeast to the outskirts of Albanella. Have your men and their gear at the field at 1730 hours. Questions?"

There were none.

"All right, let's get this show on the road."

At 5;15, trucks arrived in the company areas to take the men to the airfield aprons where eighty-seven C-47s and C-53s were already completing refueling. As soon as they got there, an officer in a jeep came swinging along the line of aircraft, shouting out tail numbers to each unit. The troopers dismounted and laid out their gear and cargo bundles on the ground beside their assigned aircraft while their platoon leaders were briefed by their company commanders.

Everybody was in high spirits, charged up, catcalling to each other. Soon the trucks carrying the riggers arrived. They began handing out chutes. Hurriedly, the men loaded their cargo bundles onto the para-racks inside the bellies of each plane, then chuted up and climbed aboard, struggling with their heavy gear through the cargo loading doors.

The playful joshing disappeared as the troopers stepped aboard, inhaling that familiar smell of Cosmoline and cargo webbing, aware fully now that soon they would be in combat. Each man shuffled quietly to his position on the long bulk-head bench, double-checked his gear, and sat down, staring at his hands or the deck, going down into himself, into his own thoughts and deeper silence.

At one minute after 6;00, the transport planes began lifting off the runway, those aloft circling until the entire flight was up. Then, in staggered jump formation, they flew over the high slopes of Monte Cofano, still lit by the last rays of the sun. Beyond it, the planes dropped altitude, crossed the Gulf of Castellamarre, and turned northeast toward Salerno, holding at a thousand feet over an ocean that was gradually deepening to an inky blue as evening swiftly approached.

They were laying out the gas canisters, Parnell and Cucinotta, not really canisters, just containers: ammo boxes, cut-off canteens, even strips from the thin side paneling of the Kraut officer's car hammered into receptacles. There were twenty, most of them small. Parnell knew the planes would come in low, slow enough to see the small flares. Once he received a signal from the formation leader, he and one other man would light off the canisters using torches made of oak branches and strips of shirt dipped in engine oil.

They'd driven the bigger personnel carrier right down

into the meadow, leaving deep tracks through the grass. It was nearly night now, the land full of twilight. A few of the brighter stars had emerged out of the eastern sky like distant watchtowers seen from way out at sea. But the plain and surrounding mountaintops still held a soft glow in which appeared occasional bursts of gunfire and explosions like sudden, quickly disappearing rips in the land that showed a fiery place beyond.

Half the gasoline containers were placed now, the crossbar of the T a hundred yards long facing due east, the stem seventy-five yards due west. The two men moved along, stepping out the pattern carrying jerry cans of gasoline and filling the canisters, then stomping down the long grass around each container so its flames could show clearly.

Cowboy and his crew had returned to the operations cave earlier that afternoon and were waiting for Parnell and Bird when they got there. Fountain reported to Parnell that they had heard a lot of enemy movement the previous night. Mostly in the hills to the northeast. But they were never able to clearly see anything.

Once daylight came, however, they spotted two squads of *Waffen SS* in the foothills, obviously search-and-destroy teams hunting for partisans. Around noon, they'd seen something disturbing, down on the plain where a big fight had taken place earlier in the day. Kraut mortuary teams were out collecting both German and American bodies, piling them into shell holes for later disposal. But when they left, starving packs of wild dogs crept in and dug up the corpses to feed on.

Four minutes to 7:00.

They waited. The sky was like velvet, lots of stars now, so distant, so untouchable. The usual gentle onshore breeze was steadily picking up, gusts sweeping up through the trees. It carried the saltiness of ocean and the rust stench of ship steel and explosion smoke, both a sharp overlay like the acrylic scent of nail polish.

Red glanced toward Cucinotta, fifty yards away. He was

squatted at the head of his line of canisters, the stem of the T. He began to sing softly to himself, a humming mostly as if he didn't know all the words to his song. Parnell listened. The man certainly had a nice voice for such a crazy son of a bitch. But still, he was exposing their position.

Parnell drew up, about to give a whistle to quiet him. Then he paused, cocked his head to hear the tune more clearly. Its tone was filled with a sweet melancholy, not like Carlo's usually ribald songs. It sounded familiar. Where had he heard it before? With a sudden jolt of memory it came to him, one of his mother's favorite operatic arias, the death scene from *Madame Butterfly.*

For a sharp, aching moment, the song evoked a powerful image, his mother playing their old black upright piano in the two-story on Fullerton Avenue in Leadville, Colorado, when he was seven. He saw again her long auburn hair trailing down her back, entangled in a shaft of sun glow, Simmy Parnell, the beautiful daughter of a preacher's son and a half-Lakota schoolgirl, full of laughter and sorrow, who had followed her husband across the world and then suddenly, stunningly, had died, leaving him and . . .

Seven o'clock.

He sent out his first transmission, holding down the microphone key for thirty seconds, then off, the crackle of white sound issuing from the loudspeaker along with voices extremely faint, like the ghosts of voices. He gave a low whistle and Cucinotta stopped humming.

He listened intently, straining to catch the faint roar of approaching aircraft engines. Ten minutes passed. He transmitted again. The grass around him seemed alive with soft clicks, rustlings. Another ten minutes, another transmission.

A sudden German rocket barrage let go from somewhere near the Sele River, the earsplitting banshee screams of Nebelwerfers emptying their racks, the rocket casings full of holes to make an ungodly sound in flight. When they struck their targets, even from this distance, he felt the ground tremble gently, the wild noises lingering in his ears.

Seven-fifty.

He lifted the microphone, depressed the button. At that precise instant came the sudden blast of two grenades from the far rim of the meadow, followed by the throaty rap of Thompsons.

Cowboy was the first to see the small German patrol, steel helmets catching flecks of light from the explosions down on the plain, the men descending through the scrub oak, one man on point, seven, maybe eight in all, fanned back behind him. Fountain glanced to his right, Weesay over there in the dimness. Bird and Smoker were farther back, down near the sheepherder's hut. His heart jumped into speed as he flicked off his weapon's safety.

They were good, these Krauts, he thought, moving silently, just shadows, shifting darknesses on the lighter darkness of night. No clink of gear, no strong boot steps. He slipped a grenade from his harness. It was not hung by the handle, but taped. He laid it in front of him. Took another off, placed it beside the other.

He watched the point man approach, moving gingerly but apparently not expecting anything, a little too upright, coming too rapidly. The adrenaline made his fingertips tingle. His thumb on the back of the trigger guard tapped lightly. He turned and looked down toward Laguna again, saw no movement but knew, instinctively, Weesay was down there getting ready.

Okay.

He picked up one of the grenades. For utterly no apparent reason a kid-time jingle came into his head from across the years, from Estacado Navajo Junior High School at Caprock, New Mexico, the Navaho kids playfully teasing him, the only white boy in the place: *Ole Jim-mee Foun-ten was a paleface soul. . . .*

He pulled the grenade pin, lifted slightly, rising up, and let it go, its arm snapping up with a loud click. He ducked.

With a buckskin bel-lee and a paper ass-hole . . . The grenade
went off with a loud crack. Right behind came another explosion, Weesay's grenade. The Krauts instantly hit the ground,
one yelling something out and then moaning. Cowboy and
Laguna opened with their Thompsons, the weapons held sideways sending bullets slicing through brush, fanning, cordite
fumes rolling back, spent cartridges bouncing hot off his knee.

As the gunfire sounds went *whomping* off into the upper
slopes, Cowboy was already moving, shifting firing position.
A rock loomed. He went down behind it as the Germans cut
loose with counterfire, the night suddenly full of noise. He
hugged the rock, counting their weapons. He recognized the
individual sounds of them, the *burring* rip of two MP-40
machine pistols, the spaced cracking pops of rifles, 33/40
Gewehrs, short-stock paratrooper weapons, at least four of
them. That made six men.

The firing stopped; everybody hunkered down, squinting
into the darkness. He started to lift his head for a peek. There
was a click, sounding like the flick of a cigarette lighter. He
heard something tumbling on the ground. *Oh, shit!* He
slammed himself to the ground just as a German potato-
masher grenade went off several yards to his right and down,
near where he had been. Shrapnel went sizzling overhead.

His head buzzed and whistled as another enemy grenade,
then another, went off. Slowly his hearing came back. He
heard a German talking, low, the words running together, then
the sharp static of a radio and a metallic voice coming back.
Two other Thompsons began banging away from his left, up
the slope. Bird and Wineberg.

Jesus, they came up fast.

The Germans answered. Cowboy lifted up, let go a burst,
another, going for muzzle blasts. Instantly he was down,
rolling away, down over rock scree and brush.

Silence.

He licked his lips. His mouth felt like cotton. He heard the
air sighing through his nostrils, the ground still day-warm,
dust like talc. Now for the cat and mouse. He unsheathed his

belt knife, stuck it into the ground beside his face, eased out a fresh clip, held it in his left hand.

He waited, his mind repeating over and over, *buckskin belly and paper asshole.* . . .

Just beyond the ridge two miles away, Major Keppler roared orders. He and twenty of his *Waffen SS* had been working their way deeper into the Sottane foothills from the coast highway, hunting. The rest of his company, working in small patrols, was also searching farther north and east.

A radio van with direction-finding equipment accompanied his patrol, its operators constantly monitoring radio calls, swinging through frequencies. Most of the intercepted transmissions were merely chaotic battle gibberish. But once they *had* picked up something interesting, an American voice code-named Blue One. Sounded like a forward artillery spotter, the signal very strong, indicating he was close. Unfortunately, they'd only gotten the tail end of his transmission, not enough to get a location fix.

Now one of his squad sergeants had just radioed in that he was under attack by what appeared to be a small enemy unit, due north, near the edge of the foothills. The attackers were firing American Thompson submachine guns. Keppler instantly ordered him to hold until he could come up in support.

Moving in a double line, his men in column started down a narrow mountain road, running in the dark, the men silencing the jingle of their bayonet and canteens and "bread bag" cans until there was little sound save the steady striking of their boots and the soft rumble of the radio van following.

"Blue One, Blue One, this is Papa Brown," Parnell's radio barked abruptly. Papa Brown had a slight southern accent, casual, homey. The transmission was as clear and loud as the signal from a commercial radio station just up the road. "I have your signal on vector. Approaching Knight's field. Open the gate. I say again, open the gate. Do you copy?"

Parnell hauled up his mike, keyed, "Papa Brown, Blue One. I roger that. Lighting off now. Over." As his transmitter key clicked off, there was a moment of scattered static, then, "Blue One, roger that and out." And he was gone.

Here they come.

The firing and grenade explosions back up in the trees had tapered off. Red had been following the engagement with his ears, unable to see anything up there yet knowing that his men had ambushed somebody and now the four of them were flanking whoever it was. He had counted the enemy weapons, figured six, possibly seven, a small patrol. Off to his right, Cucinotta was cursing loudly in Italian, wanting to get up there, get into the fight.

Then he heard them. A soft droning like heat on a summer day, then gradually louder, growing into a distant humming roar that intensified until he could distinguish individual aircraft in it. He saw them, dark lines in the sky, their engine exhausts like tiny flickering candles in the dark.

He hollered to Carlo and quickly fired up his torch with his Zippo lighter. It wouldn't catch. "Come on, goddammit!" It finally did, smoking for a moment and then blossoming into a triangle of bright orange flame. Then he was up and sprinting along the line of gasoline containers, pausing just long enough at each to ignite its fumes with a popping blue *whoosh.*

When he reached the third canister, the Germans up on the hill had started throwing everything they had down at him and Cucinotta, realizing what they were doing. Bullets *zinged* and *hissed* past him, slammed into the grass. He heard the Thompsons blasting away again, stop for a count of three, then start once more.

The light from the gasoline flares threw dancing orange shadows through the grass. He passed the conjunction of bar and stem, saw Cucinotta going down his line of containers, lighting off. He ran on, dodging this way, that, lighting off, moving on, the smell of the fumes powerful in the night air. Overhead the roar of the incoming aircraft was loud, sounding as if there were engines all over the sky.

There, it was done. He hurled himself to the ground and looked back down along the line of his flares. Perfect. But something was wrong. Where the hell was Carlo? He couldn't see his torch and only five of his gasoline canisters were lit. He pushed to his feet and sprinted toward them.

Cucinotta was lying on his side, his body lengthened out as if he were sprinting sideways. Two bullets had struck him in the left temple. His eyes were open, bright in the flame of his fallen torch. A patch of grass had ignited where it fell. Red knelt, turned Carlo's head. It moved limply on his neck, dead weight, surprisingly heavy. The right side of it, exit wounds, had been blown out. Brain matter dripped, smelling like hot mucus.

Goddammit.

The leading aircraft were nearly directly above now, moving steadily, no more than six hundred feet high. Their engines made a deep, steady roaring. Red stamped out the flames around Cucinotta's torch, scooped it up, and ran along the line of unlit gasoline torches, lighting them. At the last one, he shoved the torchhead into it with a flaring of flame, ran back for his radio, and then sprinted up the slope toward the trees, panting from the running, one-handedly swinging his weapon off his shoulder.

Behind him, the gasoline flares made a slightly crooked T. Thin smoke drifted up and out of the flame light. He looked back and up in time to see the C-47s silhouetted against the stars and then the first sticks of paratroopers jumping out, the men coming one right behind the other, twisting, falling, trailing their static lines. Then came the sudden sound of opening chutes, surprisingly close, silk panels popping, risers snapping taut as hundreds of dark blossoms were suddenly there and the first out now close above him, dropping fast and hitting, tumbling, instantly up and running, shadows all across the meadow.

* * *

Far up the hill, Keppler had watched through binoculars as the fleet of Allied transport planes came roaring in low over the gulf, saw the lopsided T slowly forming up down in a meadow and then the hundreds of chutes and dangling figures dropping down. He cursed. Paratroopers! There seemed to be thousands of them, their chutes underlit by the small flames on the ground.

He turned and ran toward the radio van, shouting for his men to pull back up the mountain road. Hauling himself onto the vehicle, he shouted to one of the operators to immediately notify General Vietinghoff's headquarters at Sant Angelo di Lombardi high in the Appennini Mountains about the Allied paratroop drop and give them the drop zone's coordinates.

The other operator cut in, *"Mein Herr,* I just intercepted another Blue One transmission. His approximate position is there where the Americans have just landed."

Verdammt! That Blue One again. He looked out the rear of the van as the driver swung it around on the narrow dirt road. A spotter team? Maybe something more. They gathered speed, racing after the rest of his men already down beyond a low hogback ridge.

Captain Joseph Steinbeck, CO of D company, Second Battalion, 504th Airborne Infantry, had a slight Maine accent, the faint aura of a whaling port about his vowels. He shook Parnell's hand, his grip viselike. "Outstanding job of marking out the DZ, Lieutenant," he said.

Around them paratroopers dashed through the darkness forming up into squads and platoons, their leaders whistling them to assembly points. Each man was heavily laden with equipment yet moved with a sharp, snapping efficiency. In the dying light from the gasoline canisters, their greased faces and white-rimmed eyes gave them a cold, spooky appearance.

"How many in the drop, sir?" Red asked.

"Thirteen hundred. Another three thousand will be in by dawn." For a moment, he studied Parnell's dirty peasant clothing, grinned. "You look like you've been busy around here."

"A bit, sir." He shook his head. "The situation's not good. To tell you the truth, we're getting our asses whipped."

"All right, what can you tell me?"

"I've pinpointed several enemy strong points and artillery positions. But the Krauts're moving their armor and self-propelled guns all over hell very rapidly. Mounted infantry, too, plugging gaps. Particularly along the north sector of the plain and out on the coast road south of Paestum."

Steinbeck unzipped his map case, laid a tactical section map on the ground. He shone a flashlight onto it. "Show me where exactly."

Parnell quickly went over his observations of the last twelve hours. Steinbeck made Xs and notations on the map with a red pencil. As the red markings began forming a pattern, he shook his head but made no comment.

A runner approached out of the darkness. "Sir, Colonel Tucker's sent out officers' call. He's set up his CP at a small hut right up the slope."

The captain nodded, turned to Parnell. "You'd best come along, Lieutenant. I suspect Major Garby'll want a word with you." Garby was Tucker's intelligence officer, he explained.

They started up through the grass. "Sir," Red said, "my men and I could use some fresh ammo. If you can spare any?"

"Sure. What do you need?"

"Thompson rounds and frag grenades."

Steinbeck turned to his radioman, who was following a few steps behind. "Tell Sergeant Noakes to bring up eight five-by-twenty pouches of .45 ammo. And a couple boxes of M-20s." He turned to Parnell. "Weapons?"

"No, sir, we've got all we need."

"How about smokes?"

"Yes, sir, thanks."

"And stick in some issue," he called after the departing radioman.

Before they reached the sheepherder's hut, German artillery began shelling the area, the first rounds striking north of the meadow, 105mm field howitzers and 88mm carriage guns firing high-explosive stuff and star shells, everything coming in with that peculiar cloth-ripping sibilance before they hit. The ground shook violently, the explosions lighting up the landscape. Soon grass fires were burning as the German gunners began walking their rounds farther south.

A few minutes later, Allied gunships opened up with counterfire, their six-inch salvos making scattered eruptions of light along the north side of the plain. The German barrage began to thin out and finally stopped except for occasional harassing rounds every minute or so. By now, the paratroopers had vacated the drop zone, some elements already moving south and northeast, everybody double-timing it.

The officers' call briefing was very short, the men hunkered down in a circle around Colonel Tucker beside the stone hut. Meanwhile, Major Josh Garby listened to Parnell as he repeated his intelligence data, shouting over the thunder of the barrage. Garby didn't say a word, just stood with his head down, listening, absorbing. When Red finished, he said simply, "You and your men will come with us."

"Sir," Parnell said, "my TMO specifies we are to continue operating in this sector as a recon and spotter unit until further orders from OSS."

Garby looked up. He had bushy eyebrows and particularly wide shoulders. "Who did you say you were attached to?"

"OSS, sir."

The major grunted. "Well, good luck, then," he said and moved away.

Wyatt and the others had come down and were standing nearby with one of Steinbeck's sergeants handing out the ammo pouches and wooden grenade boxes. To the east, the moon had risen just over the higher ridges of Monte Soprano. It resembled a huge, deformed grapefruit made greasy brown by the explosion smoke and dust riding on the sea wind.

Carrying their new supplies, Parnell and the others returned to the trees and began working their way back into the mountains. Bird told Red they had killed six of the German soldiers in the patrol and wounded two. All had been in camo smocks with helmets bearing the runes and black-and-red swastika of the *Waffen SS*. They had field-dressed the two wounded Krauts and left them under cover. Bird didn't think they'd live very long.

By the time they reached the upper foothills, they could hear American weapons firing to the southwest as the forward elements of the 82nd made first contact.

Keppler watched as the artillery-created fires continued to burn northeast of the Allied drop zone, irregular orange lines that sent up a pall of underlit smoke. It was now nearly midnight with a crooked moon almost directly overhead but almost hidden by a thick overcast that had moved in during the past three hours.

An hour earlier, he'd set his men into night defensive positions on the reverse slope of one of the higher ridges of Monte Sottane, among a stand of cypress pine. Above him, the trees heeled in the wind. He felt comparatively safe here. He was sure the Allied paratroopers would strike either south or northeast, challenging strongpoints in Vietinghoff's frontal line in an attempt to destabilize it. They wouldn't waste men immediately up into these foothills.

He snorted softly. How useless it would be. These ignorant Americans had come too late, their generals acting too timidly. The German counteroffensive still had too much momentum to be halted by such a small force. No, Vietinghoff would triumph. Within hours these American and British *Schiesse* would be fleeing back to sea.

He put his binoculars down but continued watching the far-off fire lines. They looked like the last remnants of a burned-out city. The image immediately drew a memory into his mind, one that had marked a particularly satisfying moment in his military life, the destruction of the Czech village of Lidice in June 1942 when he and his *SS Einsatzgruppen* detachment had burned it to the ground in retaliation for the murder of SS leader Reinhard Heydrich. . . .

They herded all the inhabitants into the village square. A woman and young boy tried to run away. They were shot. When the others saw this, they cowed against each other as the SS officers went through the crowd, separating all the males over the age of fourteen, 119 in all. These were marched off to the local church and locked inside.

The women and children were ordered to remain in the square. During the night, the soldiers went among them and sodomized the prettiest, taking them in the anuses because they were inferior beings whose vaginas were unfit to enfold such splendid Aryan penises. Just before dawn, the women were loaded onto trucks and driven to the Theresienstadt concentration camp. Three who were pregnant had their babies cut from their wombs and stomped to death. Then they, too, were killed.

As the first rays of the sun appeared, the village church was set afire. When the walls and windows began to fall down, some of the screaming men tried to escape. They were machine-gunned and their bodies thrown back into the inferno. Then the entire village was set ablaze. It was still burning by that night, casting a foul pall of underlit smoke into the air. . . .

A corporal approached. *"Mein Herr,* there is a message from Sergeant Eicke."

"Yes?"

"He has captured a partisan in the town of Roccadaspide. There were three of them, all armed with American weapons. They were attempting to capture a sick German officer."

"Ah?"

"One was killed, another escaped. Two of our men were lost. Sergeant Eicke has interrogated the prisoner. He refuses to speak but he carries letters that mention an Augustin Freidl-Real."

Keppler sat bolt upright. "Is Eicke certain of that name?"

"That's what he said, sir."

"Order him to bring that prisoner to me immediately. And I want the one who escaped hunted down. Move!"

"Yes, sir," The noncom hurried away.

The major sat back, smiling. He took a cigarette from a silver case, lit it. The sweet scent of brandy mingled with the odor of the pines. Freidl-Real with American weapons. He looked off in the direction of Roccadaspide.

So perhaps at last we begin to close in.

Thirteen

They tortured him for nearly two hours, Evan Couprier tried to hold the pain inside himself, make no sound. *Don't give them the satisfaction, these filthy Nazi pigs.* They beat him, forced water into his belly, and then slammed it with sticks until he puked and lost his bladder. They burned the tips of his hands over a cigarette lighter, these *Waffen SS* soldiers in their dusty camo battle dress. All the time, Evan holding his mind together, focusing on memories, things, whispers, *anything* that allowed him to hold himself within his *own* mind. Only once did he lose control, crying out in French for God to help him.

They had him in a radio van that was parked in a small stand of cork oaks. Between the bouts of torture, a German major talked to him, sat directly in front of him. The light in the van was a soft red. The officer had a perfectly round bald head and in the crimson glow his eyes would open wide and then narrow to slits as he smoked a cigarette scented with something.

Evan could smell it strongly although his nostrils were clogged with his own blood. He focused on the odor. Brandy. Just like the scent of brandy and tobacco and leather that his father always carried with him. Like the way their house on the river Sarthe had smelled when their cook Clarisse made brandy cakes in the autumn with the frost forming pretty patterns on the windowpanes of his bedroom.

The major was saying, "Augustin Freidl-Real is a Jew." The German spoke adequate French. Lifting his head, Evan looked directly at him and a crazy thought materialized. Was this what the devil looked like, a *bald* devil in red light? His thinking that seemed utterly ridiculous. He wanted to laugh but his stomach tightened, hurting.

"Yes, a Jew," the major went on soothingly. "Did you know that?" His voice was so quiet. Yet there was something terrifying about it, too. It was like when Evan's father had been angry at him, speaking gently at first, questioning, then losing his patience and shouting, his face livid as he beat him with a strap made of goatskin. The terrible part had been the knowing that it was coming, dreading it and trembling with its knowledge. Now he shook again.

"One of the very *slime* who betrayed *your* country," the German officer went on. "One of the very slime who has infected *all* of Europe." Smoke drifted about the major's face as if his tissues were hot enough to give off vapor. "Do you love France? Yes, of course you do. Yet you protect the ones who raped her?" The major seemed distressed. "I find this hard to understand."

It had started raining about an hour before, a downpour. Now the van was stuffy and hot and thick with the cigarette smoke. The rain pounded against the top of the vehicle, everybody packed in there among radios and panels of detection gear. Evan ran his tongue over his lips. Even that hurt. He closed his eyes, drifted away, going back to his capture. . . .

He, Augustin, and Yildirim had remained hidden outside Roccodespide all through the day. Though they couldn't contact Parnell, they knew the Germans had launched a massive counteroffensive. They could hear the heavy battle sounds and see the dust clouds of enemy units on the move.

Just before evening, they finally went down into the village. It was deserted, rows of dark stone hovels and a tiny whitewashed church. Several dead bodies lay in the road, others in the front of doorways. The road was rutted with the tracks from trucks and armored vehicles. Two of the bodies had been run over. The weight had burst their stomachs and maggots fed on their entrails, making a soft, wet sound in the evening stillness.

Eventually, they found an old man sitting beside a dry creek bed. The bed stones were white and resembled the tops of human skulls partially buried in dust. The old man was very ill, his skin red and raw with large welts on his throat like insects beneath the skin. *Typhus!* They asked him about the German officer. He spat and pointed toward the church.

The Nazi captain lay in front of a small stone altar with its crudely carved crucifix. He was dressed in the full *Einheitsfeldmutze* uniform of a Panzer *Sturmartillerie*. A young, beautiful Italian woman was with him. She tried to kill them with the officer's Luger. Yildirim shot her with his Thompson. The soldier watched, his eyes glazed and hot, like an animal in a savage fight. Yildirim killed him, too.

The sound of the American weapon had drawn other Germans, a small patrol of *Waffen SS*. They came at them from out of the darkness. In the short firefight, the Yugoslavian was killed instantly. Evan and Augustin were separated. He had run through a stand of brush pine and tried to hide in a hole but they found him. . . .

The sting of the major's riding crop across his face jolted Evan from his thoughts. He blinked. The German major said, "Once more we try this, eh?" He remained silent. After a while two soldiers came into the van. They were soaking wet. They carried him outside into the rain. It had released the smell of turpentine from the trees and he saw the drops falling against the red light when the door was opened.

In that light, they cut off his right forefinger. The knife blade was as sharp as a razor. One soldier held his hand down while the other cut the finger off, the man not slicing but pressing the blade through. When it hit his bones, the pain went up into his head like a cracking flash of blue lightning. He heard himself sobbing.

They wrapped the stump with a white cloth and the German major squatted down and said, "Enough?"

"Please."

"Of course. Where is Freidl-Real?"

"Please."

"Where is Freidl-Real?"

Evan held his eyes tightly shut. The pain had begun to subside into a wild throbbing. He pushed it out of his mind. *Imagine, imagine.* In memory, he found himself in his tiny bedroom again. Yes, there was the window with the frost patterns and far down was the bank of the river and the water so frighteningly dark in the twilight. *Remember, remember. . . .*

They cut off two more fingers. Then Major Keppler lost patience and shot him in the forehead.

Bird came up the narrow footpath in the rain. The ground was slippery, brush whipping in the wind. It smelled of ocean, warm and sticky, tropical rain. As he neared the ridgeline, he paused, knelt. A moment later, Cowboy challenged him, barking out, "Yankee." He called back, "Clipper," rose, and continued up.

Fountain was huddled under a small, wind-bent pine, his peasant collar up and woolen watch cap pulled down over his forehead. Wyatt slid down beside him.

"Damned if I ain't half drowned up here, Sarge," Cowboy said.

"Anything working?"

"Them Eighty-second boys come in about a half hour ago. Dropped yonder up near Albanella, looks like."

"Yeah, we heard the planes."

"They run into some heavy shit, though. There was a helluva fight for a while. . . .What time you got?"

"O four hunnert."

The pine tree's branches jerked and snapped in the wind,

its trunk squeaking. In the pauses, they could hear water runoff hissing over rocks. They were about fifty yards up the slope from the base cave. Smoker was down in the other direction, Parnell wanting two-man security out while the others slept.

They had gotten back to the cave around one o'clock to find Kaamanui, Cappacelli, and Cesara finally back from the raid on the E-boats. Sol quickly briefed Parnell about the hit on the fish processing pier, told him they'd gotten one of the boats but then had to hide in a lighthouse until they could get across the coast highway and back into the foothills.

He said they had witnessed an entire Panzer division moving north on Highway 18, told Red he'd sent him a message about it, which Parnell somehow never received, the walkie-talkie undoubtedly beyond its range. When they at last were able to cross the road and go up the Trentinara River, they had to dodge German patrols all over the low ground.

Now Bird said to Cowboy, "Y'all best get some sack time. Lieutenant says we gon' be headin' east come full light."

"Right." Cowboy rose, stretched, and went back down the trail, muttering, "Fuckin' rain."

Wyatt looked out over the plain. Their present position was approximately midway between Capaccio and San Lorenzo where Monte Soprano made its full thrust to the east. Beyond were the even higher ridges of Monte Alburni that formed the barrier at the eastern end of the Salerno Plain. All these endless mountains were part of the Great Appennine Range, which ran from far in the north to the mountains of Sicily.

The rain blotted out all moonlight and the entire plain was now in darkness save for scattered fires and the flashes from artillery barrages, their distant thunder rolling up to Bird like the sound of empty barrels tumbling on wooden floors.

He hunkered down, crossed his arms. The wind came in powerful gusts, slammed fans of rain into him. It reminded him of being on storm maneuvers up Kolekole Pass at Schofield Barracks, Hawaii, when he was with the old 25th Infantry Division before the war. This storm had the same soggy, warm-ocean feel to it, not yet hurricane strong but still powerful enough to make life miserable.

He knew what a real hurricane was, through. Back when he was a kid in Beauregard Parish, Louisiana, those big black slammers used to come in off the Gulf of Mexico still packing oceans of rain and boiling with tornadoes. Floods ran off the fields of hardpack scrabble as if the ground had been steel plate.

But only once had he seen a full-blown hurricane head-on, that time in New Orleans while he was with the Advanced Infantry School at Fort Bliss, Texas, three months before Pearl. He'd watched it come ashore, the wind terrible, as if a great hole had been punctured through the earth's crust and the escaping air was rushing out sideways, while he sat on the balcony of a whorehouse on Iperville Street drinking beer backs, shots of Jack Daniel's, with a prostitute named JoAnn, who was too cooled-out on morphine and plain don't-give-a-shit to be afraid. When the tidal surge came, it jammed twelve feet of water up through the narrow streets and alleyways of the city, sending burial cases from the St. Louis Number One cemetery floating down Basin Street like abandoned boats. . . .

He hunkered down deeper under the whipping pine and lit a cigarette, hiding it under his coat. Another barrage started. It was quickly answered by a gunship, a cruiser from the looks of the muzzle flashes, blurry in the rain as if he were seeing them through frosted glass. There were three ships burning out there, too.

Clark's adjutant had been right about his appraisal of Ridgeway's ability to get his men ready with astounding speed. He'd also been correct about the effect the 82nd troopers would have on the German line. Within hours of their drop, the southern elements of the 504th Regiment had stopped the flow of enemy reinforcements from the south with a solid defensive line from the Sottane foothills to Highway 18.

Then, in the early hours of the fourteenth, another 2,200 paratroopers of the 82nd came down behind the Kraut offensive front, just outside the town of Albanella, these sticks guided in by Pathfinders using homing radios. After a short but fierce fight, the German positions were overrun and the town invested.

This sudden and successful counterattack by the Allies, aided by the drenching rains that quickly turned parts of the plain into a quagmire, disoriented German field units. When word of it flashed through both the American and British divisions on the line, it was like a shot in the arm. Despite being totally exhausted after days of intense combat, the Allies were able to regroup, each front line unit determined not to give up another inch of ground.

The Kraut soldiers were also weary. Worse, they were rapidly depleting both their force integrity and their supplies from the north. Just as in Africa, this was due to an ego clash, this time between Kesselring and Rommel. Hitler had placed the Desert Fox in command of all German forces in northern Italy while Kesselring remained overall commander in the central and southern part of the country.

Badly needing reinforcements at the Salerno front, Kesselring had asked Rommel to dispatch two of his panzer divisions southward. He flatly refused. As far as Rommel was concerned, the rest of Italy was already a lost cause. He firmly believed the only way to stop the Allied thrust into the heart of Europe was by setting up an unbreakable defensive line across the Italian Alps. Why waste men and time by defending the useless south?

By midnight of the thirteenth, more good news had arrived at Fifth Army headquarters. Admiral Cunningham, finally aware of Clark's desperate situation, had ordered a flying column of six heavy cruisers and two battleships north through the Straits of Messina to bolster the gunship armada already there. They were scheduled to arrive in the Gulf of Salerno by noon of the fourteenth.

That day would still see savage, head-on battles on the plain, particularly in and around the Sele River sector. This was the weakest point in the entire Allied line, where the British X Corps and U.S. VI Corps merged. A singularly bloody encounter there would later be known as the famous Fight for the Tobacco Factory, located less than a mile from the bridge that Blue Team had blown earlier.

Now, as the troopers of the 82nd moved through the streets of Albanella, Clark's intelligence unit, hounded by lack of sleep but fighting it with coffee and cigarettes, were frantically trying to work out an option report for the general's morning staff briefing. They optimistically based it on the contingency that the Allied line *would* restabilize and that the German thrust had begun to run out of steam.

What they didn't know was how Kesselring would react to such a development. To make the mix even murkier, another factor had recently been added. According to underground reports out of Naples, German demo teams were actually blowing up critical waterfront facilities. What did *that* mean? Were they intending to abandon the entire Naples/Salerno area? Or was this simply false information leaked out to make the Allies assume that while Vietinghoff actually regrouped his forces to hit them again with another massive counteroffensive?

To get a truer perspective on this situation, they desperately needed some good, dense intelligence from behind the enemy lines.

"Lieutenant," the voice said.

Parnell had been way down, somewhere in a Colorado wood, running water, a stream. His father was with him and he was five years old. They were fishing, the stream bright in a shaft of light down through the trees, the water rippling and polished with illumination and the stones all rounded and feathered with moss. And then came the sudden, deadly buzz of a timber rattler, somewhere in the brush, his father holding up his hand for him not to move a muscle. . . .

Instinct was too strong. Despite the dream, his hand reached out for his weapon. He opened his eyes, keeping his body motionless. Kaamanui was kneeling beside him. Sol handed him a canteen cup of coffee, K-ration Nescafe powdered, and said, "It's coming on first light, Lieutenant."

Red sat up, the tiredness still inside him, under the outer tissues like a heavy weight glued to his organs. His head ached, his mouth felt sour, gummy. He rubbed his eyes. He could hear the rain outside the cave entrance.

Inside it was dark except for a tiny flickering light from a lamp made of woolen strips wound around a wire and stuck into a can of citronella oil and gasoline. The citronella smelled strong, like concentrated lemon juice. But it was insufficient to blot out the deeper stench of bat guano, a sharp odor that reminded Parnell of dried chicken shit. The cave floor bore the signs of transitory habitation, human and animal bones, white as chalk, fragile, as if formed of ash, a handmade sandal like a medieval peasant's, the remnants of old campfires.

He looked at his watch. Ten minutes to 5:00. He glanced across the cave at the dark shadows of the others still asleep on the rock floor. The cave formed an L. A stolen German-issue purple woolen blanket had been hung up at the angle of the L to keep light from showing outside. He dimly saw Cesara leaning over one of the prone shadows.

"We just got an emergency call," Sol went on. "Direct from Fifth Army. They want a hard recon on a Kraut divisional headquarters in sector 166."

"You check **that** position yet?"

"It's just outside the hill town of Castelcivita. They want updated tactical maps. Maybe a German senior officer if we can grab one. All within twenty-four hours. They've assigned the code reference Orange Grove so we get immediate clearance."

Red grunted, took a drink. The coffee was oily and tasteless.

Sol jerked his thumb over his shoulder. "Augustin come back about thirty minutes ago. He said him and his buddies got hit in Roccodaspide. Yildirim's dead and he thinks they captured the little Frenchie, Couprier. He himself's got a through-and-through in the upper right thigh."

"Shit." Parnell took another drink, thinking about that. He pictured Evan, a decent, gentle kid. *Too* gentle. He was sure the young man wouldn't have enough staying power once the Krauts got to working him over. He'd tell them where they were for sure.

He rose and went over to squat beside Real and Cesara. "What happened?" he asked.

Real's face was filmed with sweat, his skin tight. He explained.

"Was it a single patrol or a larger force?" Red asked when he finished.

"A small patrol. *Waffen SS* scum. I'm sure they came when they heard Milovan's weapon as he shot the girl and her officer."

"How are you doing?"

"He's lost a lot of blood," Cesara said, interrupting. "He's very weak."

"No, don't worry," Augustin said. "I can walk." He gave a strained smile. "I got here, didn't I?"

Red said, "We've got to leave here fast, move deeper into the mountains. The kid'll talk."

"No, he won't," Cesara snapped sharply.

Red looked at her as Freidl-Real said, "Yes, Cesara, he will. Evan won't be able to withstand their torture."

"We'll find someplace where you and the girl can hole up till we can get back to you."

Augustin swiveled his head. "What do you intend?"

"We just received orders to reconnoiter the area around Castelcivita. A German divisional headquarters."

"Yes, one is there. Unless they've recently evacuated it. It's in an old Bourbon citadel outside of town." He sat up, grunting with effort. "It has lots of artillery and a marshaling yard for armor coming over the mountains from the Basilicata area."

"You know anything about its interior?"

"No. I think it was built in the seventeenth century. So we must think old in its architecture." He started to rise. "I must go there with you."

"Yes," Cesara said. "We both go." In the flickering light, her dark face looked primitive, like a woman who had been discovered living in dark woods.

"No," Parnell snapped. "We'll be moving too fast."

"But I am familiar with—" Real protested.

"No. Now get ready, we'll be leaving in five minutes."

They emerged into a solid downpour, the rain cold now from the night. Wyatt took the point with Sol as rear security, everyone moving hastily along the narrow paths. Cesara had rebandaged Augustin's wounds and given him a second morphine shot from one of their medical pouches. At first he seemed able to keep up, but then he began to lag and his face grew very pale.

The dawn light was increasing, at first making the rain appear like fog. Then its color brightened and objects began merging into view. Far off, lightning strikes lit up the higher ridges, sounding like distant artillery.

Parnell finally whistled a halt and went back to Real. "We're moving too slowly. We'll have to carry you." He motioned Cowboy over to take his weapon, then fashioned a gun-belt carry rig and hiked Augustin up onto his shoulders.

They started off again, Red adjusting the man's weight so he wouldn't be off balance. But the incline was steep, the ground covered with stones that made his boots shift and slide. His chest began to burn, his legs ache with strain. He focused his mind against the pain, continued on.

Twenty minutes later, Sol moved up to spell him.

Soon they began seeing more refugees moving in the higher hills, as if a second stream were now afoot, old men and women mostly, some with young children, carrying their possessions and prodding goats and ponies loaded with more possessions ahead of them. The animals slipped in the mud and complained while everyone, even the children, bore that closed-down, patient, staring look of enduring, all of them headed upward, to cross the spine of the Apennines and drop into the hilly Basilicata country beyond where they hoped to find sanctuary in towns like Moliterno and Ratondella and Lake Colobraro, as yet untouched by the war.

The land was changing, the long meadows of grass getting smaller while the stands of oak and taratura trees and pines thickened. It was raining heavily again, the air moist and chilly. Freidl-Real grew steadily worse. He was feverish and rambled on incoherently.

At last, Parnell called a full break, the rain pounding down on them. He checked his watch. It was nearly 10:00 in the morning. He and Wyatt conferred, going over their topo map. They were still eight miles from Castelcivita.

"We've gotta leave them right here," Red said. "We're losing too much time." He signaled the next man in line, Cappacelli. "Go up into those woods, see if you can find a cave or someplace we can stash Real and the girl."

Angelo nodded and moved off.

Parnell checked Augustin. The man's face seemed to shine from the fever. His eyes could not hold steady. Red looked at Cesara but said nothing. Cappacelli returned a few minutes later.

"There's a small hut up there, Lieutenant," he said. "An old woman and couple kids."

They crossed up into the woods. The hut was no larger than a shed, stone, windowless. It sat among the trees like a weathered outhouse. Thin smoke seeped from beneath its pole rafters. Wyatt and Cappacelli approached it first, went in. A moment later, Bird signaled the others to come down.

The door sagged on leather hinges and the floor was dirt. There was no furniture, only blankets spread on the floor and piles of meadow grass. Along one wall were several rolls of grass tied together into bundles. A small fire burned in one corner. An old woman sat beside it with two children, a boy and girl of six or seven, on either side of her. All of them were twisting strands of grass, forming the bundles that they were using to keep the fire going. They stared dully at the men but didn't stop working.

When they carried in Augustin, the old woman's head lifted alertly. Her face was dirty and webbed with wrinkles. As they laid him down, she rose and went to kneel beside him. She touched his face, then said something to Cesara. They covered him with a ragged blanket the color of slate.

The children watched, still twisting grass. Their features were gaunt and their bloated bellies showed under their rough cotton shirts. The soldiers brought out some K-ration boxes, opened them, and offered the contents, smiling, coaxing gently. The children were not afraid but their eyes had a sadness, a sweet look of resignation like the eyes of puppies kept too long in a cage. Only when they saw the rations' Hershey's candy packets did they react, smiling, reaching out.

Parnell left all their rations and a handful of extra .45-caliber rounds with Cesara. "Fire only if you have to," he cautioned. "They hear that Thompson, they'll be right on you. Then get the hell out fast. I don't think they'll hurt these people." He could see she didn't believe him. "If we're not back in two days, don't wait." He nodded toward Real. "And if he's not out of the fever by then, leave him. He won't ever be. Try to lose yourself among the refugees until you can link up with another partisan group."

She nodded. Red noticed her eyes slide to the right, hold on Kaamanui for a long, wordless moment, then slide away. Sol's face remained impassive.

"Good luck," Red said to her.

They went back out into the rain. It came down through the trees sounding like the rush of a stream, the higher branches slashing back and forth in the wind. He formed the men into normal forest patrol formation and they headed northeast.

About a half mile away they cached their packs and rations, leaving everything unnecessary below a rock face that had the profile of a Trojan warrior. Down in the plain, isolated battles were going, scattered but short artillery duels.

Parnell took a compass heading and, carrying only their weapons, spare ammo clips, grenades, and the radio, they started out again, moving at a fast trot.

All through the early afternoon they traveled, beside steep ravines filled with storm runoff, through ever-thickening pine forests where spring water gushed from rock seams and sudden meadows where the ground was mushy and shifting. The rain continued intermittently, often very heavy. The sky was a thick, dull gray like old film footage and the wind remained constant, oddly always blowing uphill. Now and then they saw human movement disturb the landscape, more refugees trudging along in their stolid flight.

At a little after 4:00 in the afternoon, they reached the first of a series of sharp ridges, the tops wind-scoured. And there, a mile below them, was the town of Castlecivita. Leaving the others down among the trees, Parnell and Bird crept to the ridgeline and lay on the reverse slope to glass it.

The town sat in a wide sloping meadow surrounded by terraced fields of slender poplar trees and orange and lemon orchards. Thick grapevines encased the trunks of the poplars and spread from branch to branch. Beneath the trees the ground had been plowed for winter wheat, the stalks now only half grown.

A main road ran directly through the town and up into the mountains. Many of the buildings were in ruins, piles of rubble and rain-filled bomb craters from Allied air strikes. Its rail line had obviously been hit several times. There were twisted rails beside it and fresh fills in the embankment.

The old Bourbon fortress was a quarter mile up the meadow's rise, a huge star-shaped building of gray stone. It had barrel-vaulted spires and thick outer walls with archer slits and odd-looking barricades mounted on top that resembled upside-down steel clothespins. Much of the building had also been destroyed by bombs and strafing.

To the left of the citadel a tank company was scattered

through an orange orchard, some of the trees knocked down, Mark IVs, Schwerer half-tracks, mobile 75mm assault vehicles, and trucks. The rest of the area was swarming with troops. Throughout the downslope were numerous artillery nests, sand-bagged and camo-netted, 105mm mountain howitzers and 150mm fieldpieces. Gun crews were in the process of disman-tling the netting, shifting ordnance from the powder pits. Beyond the citadel, the mountain road climbed constant switch-backs where several more tanks were spaced along the road.

"Looks like this outfit's fixin' to pull out, Lieutenant," Bird said.

"Sure as hell does, don't it? But where're they headed? Could be to assembly points down on the plain for another offensive."

They continued studying the ground for a few more min-utes, found areas that had the tiny yellow flags that marked out minefields. Once there had been a moat around the fortress, but now it was only a shallow ditch filled with rainwater.

They returned to the others. Everybody was soaking wet, holding the muzzles of their weapons under their coats. Parnell described the fortress, then said, "It appears they're moving out. It's a toss-up as to where. What we gotta do is try and find out *where.*" He paused, wiped water from his face, and snapped it off his fingers.

"Come dark, we'll go in. There're seven guard posts with wire and mine corridors. Lucky for us, the rain's exposed many of the mines. But watch it. Don't anybody get careless. Also, keep a sharp eye out for anything Fifth Army can use. Vehicle symbols, uniform insignia, the type of armor, *anything.*"

He looked around, fixed on Wineberg. "Smoker, you and me'll take first security watch. Wyatt, spell us in an hour." The rain came in a sudden surge. The drops, sundered by the higher pine branches, drifted down in a mist. "Double-check your weapons and ammo. Try to get some rest."

He shoved the butt of his Thompson against the ground, rising, then turned and headed back to the ridge as Smoker went off in the other direction.

Fourteen

Parnell said, "Three men in. Me, Wyatt, and Smoker. Sol, you and Cappacelli set up opposite the up guard post on the south side. You keep the radio with you. Laguna, Cowboy, on the down post. We'll go through the wire between them."

It was dark now, a few minutes before eight o'clock. From downslope came the rumble of engines, metal clashing. The German work crews were still working, carting gear from the citadel and moving some of the artillery pieces, their flashlights jabbing about in the dark.

Just before evening, the sun had broken through for a few minutes, the light slanted, giving everything a soft glow, dripping and saturated. It allowed Red to study the citadel thoroughly. In doing so, he saw several interesting items. First, the old moat that circled the entire fortress was now merely a shallow rain-filled ditch. Yet it would afford a good defilade when they moved laterally along the outer wall.

Next, much of the Kraut spool wire had been knocked down by tanks and vehicles as the unit prepared to vacate the position. There were now pathways through the wire. That meant any alarm lines would no longer be functioning. The final thing he noticed was that there were peculiar slide channels from many of the windows in the outer wall. It took him a while to figure out what they were: garbage spouts for dumping refuse down into the old moat.

He chuckled. *That's how we'll get in.*

"If a major firefight starts before we exit," he continued, "hit those two guard posts and then scatter. If we make it out, we'll rendezvous at the gear cache. Wait till 0700. We don't show up by then, get out. In that case, Sol, you raise the monitor ship for orders." He looked around at dark faces. "Anybody got any other suggestions?"

"I think we'd best wait for the rain to come back, Lieutenant," Bird said. "She looks like she's fixin' to start up again. We'd have better cover crossin' that open ground."

"I agree. We'll give it a half hour."

They waited.

First came a misty drizzle and lightning far off in the upper Apennines, bowling balls coming down the valleys. Then it got heavier. Soon it was a drenching rain again, big drops pouring down through the trees and slamming into the ground.

Parnell rose. "Okay, security teams out," he said quietly. "You got ten minutes to set up." Wordlessly, the four men rose and disappeared into the wet darkness. He hunched back down, his watch close to his face, the tiny luminous dials blurred slightly by the water on the crystal.

The minutes ticked off: 8:11. He tapped Bird's shoulder. "You take point. As soon as you're through, head straight for the moat. Smoker, hold one minute spacing." He took a deep breath, felt the raindrops tremble on his lips. "Okay, let's do her."

Wyatt crossed the road on his belly, the ground soaking, tire tracks rounded by the rain. He hit the first wire coil forty yards in, the stuff looming up, silhouetted on his left by the working crew hand-lights. He could see the closer guard post, piled sandbags, the sheen of a machine gun muzzle and helmets. Their radio antenna made a thin line of reflected light.

He moved into the wire, feeling it with his hands, feeling the ground, probing for the least indentation or wash hole, the edge of a mine, a trip wire. There, a sharp corner. He touched it. Wood. Recently, the German sapper teams had started placing their antipersonnel S and T mines in small boxes that Allied detectors couldn't pick up. A few feet from him was a yellow marker flag, the cloth thrumming in the wind. He stretched toward it, pulled it out, rolled the cloth, and put the slender shaft of wood between his teeth.

He squinted, trying to see the sheen from collected water in other wash holes. He found several to his right that formed a line across his front. *Okay,* he said to himself, *they usin' an echelon pattern, pointed to the left.*

He returned his attention to the barbed wire, checked and double-checked for alarm trip lines just to be sure. None. Quickly, he took out his pliers and began snipping until he had a narrow hole through the coils. Just then, he felt Parnell come up against this foot. He turned slightly, held up his hand, palm facing the lieutenant, the signal for mines. Then he chopped it diagonally to the left. Parnell tapped his boot, acknowledging.

Wyatt cut a diagonal path through the wire. The jaws of the pliers made a loud snap each time they cut. Slowly, meticulously he went forward. At last he was through. He came to his feet, holding low, going cautiously. The ground was spongy and pooled with water. He continually swiveled his head back and forth, searching for objects in the dark. He spotted another line of mines, these in echelon to the right, a zigzag. When he reached the end of the second line, he planted the yellow flag to mark the point where they'd cross back through the wire.

Once beyond the mines, he moved rapidly, crossed the free ground, and slid into the old moat. The water was cold, oily, two feet deep, and smelled of disinfectant, the Krauts obviously spraying the grounds against typhus fleas. He saw Parnell coming, precisely following his pathway, then Smoker farther back, almost invisible in the rain.

He glanced toward the west, beyond one of the star tips of the fortress wall. Just beyond it, an artillery crew was busy hauling one of their fieldpieces from its position, their voices echoing, flashlights and combat lanterns forming a misty tableau. Directly above him was the end of one of the garbage chutes, about twenty feet up. The rain slid off the foot-wide channel in a thin waterfall that landed right beside him, burbling and frothing. Parnell slid down into the moat, then a few seconds later Wineberg came in. They all huddled together, studying the chute and stone face of the wall.

Two minutes later came the whistling, slurring *shush* of an incoming American 105mm round.

Cappacelli tried to get as close to the ground as the shape of his body would allow. Fucking bumps and humps in the earth made his body hump and bump. He was scared, good, solid, deep-down terrorized. He'd heard about going through a barrage, this his first, and they'd always told him it was the one thing that could make a man shit his pants. He hugged the earth and focused his mind hard that he wouldn't do that, *oh, sweet Jesus, not that.* And, son of a bitch, it was *American* gunners who were trying to blow his poor guinea ass all to hell.

He and Kaamanui had taken up their security position sixty yards from the upside German guard post, across the road, a low silhouette of sandbags braced by coil wire on either side. Now and then, he spotted the Kraut machine gunners, their helmets shiny from the rain. Back down toward the town, there were lots of small lights and trucks and half-tracks hauling field guns around.

He allowed himself a slight lift of the head. The artillery strikes were moving back down the slope, their impacts hitting with sharp, ear-jarring explosions accompanied by rushing sounds as the ambient air was hurled out and then instantly sucked right back into the burst vacuum. Concussion waves

rocketed through the ground and the air stank of spent powder and was quickly heated by the explosions.

He watched the hits move away from him, felt a rush of
salvation, realizing the American artillerymen were walking
their rounds back down and across the citadel. His mind settled. Apparently the Allied lines had advanced back into their
earlier positions, which were now close enough to use their
75s and 105s in a saturation bombardment, not ranging off
specific coordinates from spotters.

He turned, looked toward Sol but couldn't see him clearly.
The rain surged hard, fuming off the ground, making everything misty, even the orange-and-white explosions that lifted
through the darkness with stunning suddeness, sending shrapnel skewering through the air. His heart still raced so fast he
was certain it would leave impressions in the mud.

It suddenly picked up again. The incoming round impacts
were returning, back toward him. *Oh, Jesus,* those stinking
asshole Yank gunners making a reverse sweep back into the
higher ground. He shoved his face into the water and mud
and prayed, *Dear God, don't let one find me, please, please,
Christ Almighty,* and listened to the deadly whistling rush of
the ordnance drawing ever nearer.

Parnell had a hellish time getting up the garbage chute. It
was a foot and a half wide and slick as goose shit. It had
been bad enough just getting to the bottom of it, going from
stone crack to stone crack, his boots holding by quarter inches.
Now, goddammit, chunks of shrapnel and tree bark and rock
were slicing the air and slamming into the citadel wall all
around him.

He fought the chute for about six feet of its length, then
figured out that by climbing sideways, with his boots braced
against one side of the small channel, he was able to grab
stone holds enough to inch ahead. By the time he got to the
small window at the top, he was panting.

He squeezed through into a dark room with its front open to the outside. He felt Wyatt squatted right beside him and could sense the room's closeness overhead. He flicked on his vest light, which showed that the enclosure was formed of neatly set red firebrick. It was an old gun gallery, part of the original fortress's barrage battery.

A naval forty-pound siege cannon was still there, mounted on huge wooden wheels, the muzzle pointed through the arched opening. It had a hoist loop on its top and its bronze breech was two feet thick, corroded and etched with metal rupture. In a back corner, they found two stacks of cannonballs and the remnants of black-powder boxes bearing French writing and the year 1785 stamped into the wood.

Smoker came lunging through the chute window and dropped to the floor. At that moment, two rapid explosions cracked through the building, their flashes close by outside. The floor heaved, knocking all three down, and continued trembling as the explosion sounds echoed off through long corridors. Dust drifted off the ceiling.

They found a door that led out the rear of the gun gallery. It was steel, totally rusted, with a sliding bar and double rings on the wall. Parnell tried the bar. It was stiff with rust but he finally got it moving and pulled the door open. It broached onto a narrow, curving corridor. On the opposite walls were slit windows. He moved to one, peered down into a small courtyard filled with the dark, shapeless shadows of stone rubble.

Spaced five feet apart, they advanced along the corridor, going to the right. It was cold and the air was damp and smelled like the monastery catacombs of Isole Marettimo. They reached a stairwell that went down a half story to a large chamber. In it were brick-lined holes, four of them, about six feet square and four feet deep. In each were thick metal gratings on the bottoms. From the holes ran shallow stone channels in the floor that disappeared into the walls of the room at various points.

Beside each hole was a brick structure resembling a large

barrel with a beehive dome, the bricks of it laid in ascending ovals. On the tops of the domes were steel turning wheels like the hatch locks on an old sailing ship. Just below the domes were metal spigots that hung out over holes in the floor.

Parnell played his light over the peculiar fixtures and knew immediately what they were. He'd seen pictures of such apparatus in his engineering texts back at Colorado. He turned and grinned at Wyatt. "We just hit the goddamned jackpot, baby."

He explained. "This is a water heating room. In the old days, those big floor holes would have had copper liners and fire grills." He put the light on small round holes in the ceiling. "And the smoke from the grills would have left through pipes up there. You see, they'd heat the water and then channel it down into the main rooms in this part of the fortress using gravity feed. It'd flow out either under the floors or along troughs that rimmed the individual rooms to keep them warm in the winter. Then they'd pump it back up here to be reheated. Those dome things? They're displacement plunger pumps."

He grinned at the two of them. "You understand what I'm saying here?"

Wyatt, who had been closely studying the floor channels, nodded. "If'n we crawl through them channels, we could get anywhere in this section of the fortress without being seen."

"*Bingo*. Hell, there *must* be command staff offices in this part of the building. They would have deliberately put them in big rooms, the kind with heating conduits. If we can find one, we'd be able to check out all their tactical wall maps and the bastards wouldn't even know we were there."

Looking at the floor channels, Smoker chuckled. "Hey, them little things're gonna be tight, Lieutenant. 'Specially for y'all."

"I'll squeeze it." He put his head down, tried to pinpoint potential difficulties, came up with two. "Okay, listen up. Don't go getting lost down there. If you have to go into a branch channel, mark the junction with a bullet so you can find your way out again. If you *do* get confused, just keep going forward. The thing's gotta come out somewhere. But remember, sounds will be magnified in these things. Like you're in a barrel. Use that to home in on where they are. But stay quiet. None of us speaks Kraut but try and pick out the names of towns and units."

He checked the time. It was 9:03. Outside, the barrage was still going on, the sounds farther out now, muffled, directionless.

"Take only your handguns," he added and laid his Thompson on the floor. The others did the same, pulling their pistols and cupping them and their vest lights in a single hand. "Ready?"

Wyatt and Smoker nodded.

"Let's go."

Each took a channel, lying out flat and then pulling himself forward. Within seconds, they were gone.

Parnell went like a snake, using his shoulders and hips to move himself along the narrow water channel. It was dusty, cobwebbed. Bugs skittered away from him, one a seven-inch-long centipede, orange plates scurrying along, its legs a blur. It kept ahead of him, leaving tracks in the dust layer. Each time he caught up with it, he'd blow air through his lips and the insect would dash off again. He called it Willie.

Caves and tunnels and drill holes had always been pleasant places for Red, dark recesses of the earth, explorations. He'd never had any feelings of claustrophobia. But now, down here in this channel, his shoulders squeezed together as if he were in the barrel of a cannon, he felt the first flutterings of disquiet begin edging the peripheries of his mind. Snorting at such foolishness, he pushed them away. Two feet ahead, Willie the Centipede paused again, its forked tail up straight, its head like a round, orange marble. He blew air, it ran.

He reached a T in the channel, ninety-degree drifts to either side. *Shit.* It was too tight, he'd never be able to get around the

corner. He inhaled, held his breath, listened. Sounds came
through the stone, one like water running through a tap somewhere, crazy, and now and then the shudder of a barrage
round, its crack drifting past him, as if its energy were progressing by like a wave of molecules.

He started back, everything in reverse. He'd have to explore a different channel. The crystal of his watch and the
black metal of his Colt .45 made tiny shafts of reflected
light. The centipede had disappeared up one of the drifts.

In contrast, Wineberg scooted along like a mouse, raw sinew
shifting and pulling, moving fast. He ignored the bugs, swat-
ted a couple of big spiders, *squish,* against the wall, their flu-
ids yellow in the light. Occasionally, he'd stop to listen, nothing
coming back at him except the sound of stone and faraway
artillery rounds hitting.

Close quarters never bothered him. He'd been down too
many mine shafts for that, even places where the goddamned
transporter cages were as narrow as this thing, carrying two
men at a time, dropping them down into coal drifts a thousand feet under ground. Oh, yeah, mines in Harlan County,
Kentucky, and Wayne and Lincoln in West Virginia, back-
woods country of hollow-eyed hillbillies and cousin-fuckers
coming out of the pits. No, he'd actually enjoyed those dark
recesses with walls that glowed like black diamonds in his
hat light.

He reached a T, got his wiry body around the corner, leaving a bullet mark in the gray stone. Thirty feet farther on, he
heard German voices. Faint, hollow. He sped up, the voices
getting louder and louder, and then he heard the clack of tele-
types and the soft buzz of phones and bursts of radio talk, the
German like men with mouthfuls of marbles, all the volume
coming from their throats.

He came to a slight slant in the floor. The sounds were
loud now. The slant opened suddenly into a wide space, like
the foundations of a house except here the bottom was rock,

not dirt. There were metal pipes bracing the ceiling, all in lines. He realized he was under the floor of a big room, a staff office by the sounds in it.

He lay there silently, his chin resting on his curled hands like a cat. There were thumps and bangs along with all the other noises and lots of boots crossing inches over his head. He was able to catch a few phrases, the names of two towns, Potenza and Melfi. He remembered seeing those on Parnell's maps, somewhere east of them in the middle of the Italian peninsula. He also recognized word *panzers—pahn-zers,* the voices pronounced them—and something about the XVI and XXII Divisions, *Sechzehnt* and *Zweiundwansigste,* the fucking burr-heads and their block-long words.

Time slipped past. He began to think this was a waste of time, down here under their boots. He wanted to *see* something. He retreated to the slant and returned to the drift, then continued on along it.

Suddenly, he saw light ahead, lots of it. He slowed, turned off his vest light. The sounds were nearly normal now, unobstructed by barriers. A minute later, he emerged into a two-foot-wide trough as deep as the space under the floors. It ran the full length of the closest wall, then turned and ran along a connecting wall for as far as he could see over the top of the trough. This one had a huge carpet hanging from it, intricate with the woven images of knights in full armor astride horses also armored and pennants flying.

Keeping in the shadows, he surveyed the room. It had a high, cantelivered ceiling and ornately carved pillars. It was painted a pastel green, newly sprayed. At least two dozen soldiers and officers in gray uniforms moved about. Radio consoles lined one of the walls. He could see that several had been removed, their power and antenna wires hanging loosely out of metal conduits that led up through the ceiling.

Some of the soldiers were packing papers into metal footlockers, documents and folders. He lifted his body higher, saw a huge fireplace on the opposite side of the room. Its pedestals and mantel bore stone gargoyles and winged dragons. Two soldiers were burning papers and booklets in it. The entire room had a sense of hectic removal.

He twisted his head, spotted several large maps on the far wall. They were covered with acetate overlays that had numerous colored markings, indicating time references and unit dispositions. Streams of red arrows showed tactical field movements. He quickly saw that the accompanying time references were all for the next two days, from the fifteenth to the seventeenth of September.

He studied each map, trying as hard as he could to absorb the whole of it, its red lines, their directions and convergences, unit symbols. Someone in the room suddenly cursed loudly and shouted something. Wineberg dropped down and hurriedly slid back into the channel, his finger easing off the safety of his Browning Hi-Power and then moving to the trigger.

Several people were talking rapidly, angrily. There was the sound of boxes sliding across the floor. Another officer shouted, something about "coffee." Several seconds passed and the room began to fall back into that clicking, murmuring hum of men at work.

Smoker relaxed, put the safety back on his weapon.

It was almost ten o'clock now. Smoker and Wyatt had both already returned to the heating room, Bird telling Wineberg how he had gotten into some sort of bathing room, turned up a secondary channel, and ended up in what might have once been a bedroom but was now filled with artworks, paintings wrapped in paper, and statuary. He'd found no command centers, no soldiers even, and had come back.

As Smoker started to recount what he had seen, Parnell came sliding out of a channel, backward, cursing under his breath. Once completely free, he turned and gave them a disgusted look. "I found shit."

"I scored, Lieutenant." Wineberg grinned. "Big."

He went over what he'd seen and heard in the staff room,

the maps and red arrows and the names of towns and units. Parnell and Bird listened intently. Outside, the Allied barrage had stopped. Now the only thing filtering into the heating room was that peculiar stone sound like the sensation of running water.

When Smoker finished, Red said, "Looks like they're moving east and northwest. It's a full disengagement. Fifth Army's gotta know right quick. Maybe they can intercept the bastards in transit. And lay in some concentrated fire right here. Take out some of those tank units and mobile guns before they leave." He picked up his weapon. "Let's get the hell out of here."

They headed up the steps to the gun gallery. Then stopped short. A man's voice had just echoed along the corridor, a bitter laugh and a German curse. Then: *"Er liegt mir schon seit Tagen mit dieser Sache auf den Ohren."*

A second voice: *"Ach, Rolfe, pass auf, dass du ihn nicht sauer machst."*

The first man gave a snort. *"Das is mir scheissegal."*

Two German soldiers rounded the far bend of the corridor. One had a heavy hand lamp and both carried shovels and shoulder-slung machine pistols. Red pressed back against the wall of the stairway, his hand going straight for his boot knife, pulling it out smoothly with a tiny whisper of leather. He heard the others doing the same.

Abruptly the German soldiers stopped and Parnell thought, *Uh-oh!* The one with the light held it higher, saying with surprise, *"Was ist das? Fussabdrucken. Noch et mehr!"* They stared at the wet footprints and scuff marks the Blue Teamers had left.

Red moved, lunging forward, already running, his boots making tight, sharp slaps on the stone floor. Right behind him came Bird and Smoker, all three rushing, bumping into each other, moving straight for the Germans. Both Krauts snapped their heads up, their faces opening with a look of stunned shock. The lamp hit the floor. In unison, both men swung around, clawing for their weapons as they ran.

Parnell caught the man who had the lamp by the collar, hauled him back, letting his own full momentum crash into his back. They went toward the floor, his knife coming up and across. It went into the German's neck just forward of the spine. He shoved in and raked forward. The soldier screamed, not a sound, more like a bursting of flesh. Blood flew.

Wyatt flashed past him and leaped onto the back of the other German. The man yelled a wordless bellow of terror. They tumbled to the floor, Bird's legs wrapped around the man's thighs. The machine pistol clattered to the floor as Wyatt proceeded to swiftly, methodically stab the soldier, in the liver, twice, three times. The man vomited and then let out an odd moaning sound as if he were saying, "What? What?" deep in his throat.

Both soldiers died quickly.

"Grab their weapons," Parnell growled, rolling to his feet. He slipped the one from his kill as Wyatt got the other. Smoker returned to the stairway for their Thompsons. They hurried back down the corridor and darted back through the gun gallery.

The flare hurtled up toward the gray overcast, leaving streaks, and then popped into a brilliant, unearthly light like a new sun, worse than a new sun, too damned close. It swung up there in wide arcs, buffeted by the wind, and sizzled and sparked. Its little parachute fluffed and the rain looked like a curtain of plastic beads all around it.

A few seconds later, another flare went up, on the other side of the citadel. Cowboy watched, knowing this was a common German trick, checking out the ground after a barrage to see if they could catch infiltrators crossing, using the big guns as cover. A third flare went up.

These last two sharply silhouetted the citadel towers and the upside-down "clothespins." Beyond the buildings, they flooded the decimated orchards from which the tanks had scattered at the start of the bombardment. All but a few disabled ones were gone now, out there in the darkness somewhere. German troops emerged from their holes and slit trenches like zombies stepping from the earth. He caught the sharp voices of Kraut sergeants calling roll, trying to pinpoint casualties.

Cowboy ducked back, his face again into the slimy mud and pooled water. Six feet away, Laguna's head showed, round black watch cap, the triangle of his jacket collar, him and everything around him in this ghostly, phosphorus light. They were lying in an indentation in the slope, scattered brush around them, the tops fluttering in the wind.

After a moment, he lifted his head again, moving it ever so slowly. Down the slope and across the mountain road, he saw the German guard post clearly now, a sandbagged Tobruk pit, its three gunners all hunkered down and sharp light reflecting off their Model 34 light infantry machine guns and also a Panzerbuchse 39 antitank rifle with its telescoping barrel and that ungodly large front sight.

He caught a sudden movement on his right, down near the road. Instantly the guard post opened fire, the suddeness of the blasts making Cowboy jump. *Jesus!* The rounds slammed into the road, climbed the slope beyond, came back before the burst stopped, the bullets coming so fast they made one long, stunning explosion. Another burst went off and gun smoke whipped up into the rain, wispy against the flare light.

Two other machine guns began firing, guard posts on the far side of the fortress, Cowboy thinking, *My God, have they spotted Parnell and the others?* He listened. No Thompsons. He made another quick scan, saw what had moved. He ducked back, grinning, and looked over at Laguna. The little Chihuahua's face was all frowny, silently asking, *What?* Fountain waved his hand: *Nothing.* It had just been jumpy gunners firing at a small tree branch that the wind had skidded across the road.

It seemed to take forever for the flare to reach the ground, crackling and popping as it hit rainwater pools. It burned brightly for a minute or so, then finally went out. The others dropped behind the fortress, making it look like the backlit cutout of a castle on a huge stage.

Cowboy turned his head, couldn't see Laguna anymore, his retinas still holding the receding image of the flares.

The flares filled the entire gun gallery with light. The three men back at the far wall squatted down behind the cannon-ball piles. Parnell knew what the Germans were doing, looking for infiltrators. "Hide your eyes," he snapped. "The minute those goddamned things go out, those sentries'll be blinded for about forty seconds. That's when we go."

When the firing first started, Parnell's heart had gone stiff. *They've located the security teams.* He heard Smoker growl softly, "Bastards!" He listened intently. More firing, German weapons, but nothing opposing, no Thompson counterfire. *Good, good, Krauts jumping on shadows.*

The rain slapped against the edges of the gallery port and the wind threw gusts of spray over them. Above these subtler sounds, he heard the approaching sizzle of the flare, growing louder. He said, "Smoker, you out first, then Wyatt. Roll out of the way when you hit the ditch. Then run like hell for the wire. Watch for the yellow flag."

They waited, heads down, eyes jammed shut.

The sizzle was very loud now, as if it were right out there beyond the gun port, and then there was a loud sputtering and popping as it hit the ground. He lifted his head, opened one eye a narrow slit. Light was still coming into the gallery. He shut his eye again, waited, the lit square of the gallery port fading from his retinas. The popping stopped. Again he looked.

Blackness.

"Go!"

He saw Wineberg dart across the gallery, crouch, and was gone. Then Bird. He followed, feeling for the sides of the chute window. He lifted his feet and launched himself through, on his back, hitting the chute and instantly going down, sliding, the sides of it scraping along his arms, buttocks, the thing slick, a roller-coaster ride. Then it was no longer under him and he was in air, falling. A second, another, and his legs jolted as he hit water and mushy ground.

Instantly, he was up, his body already in momentum, running hunched over, Bird's shadow right ahead of him and somewhere behind him the glow of the other flares beyond the citadel like some sort of false dawn, yet faint. He saw the remnants of their flare off to his right, tiny embers flickering. The stench of burning cloth and phosphorus, an ashy odor that reminded him of crematoriums. Beneath it was another smell, very familiar, the sweetness of crushed orange blossoms from the orchards, so tropical-heady it seemed incongruous among these deadly hills.

In the darkness, part of his mind was counting off seconds, had started the moment he went out the garbage chute window, now on *one-thousand-twenty-eight, one-thousand-twenty-nine.* The other part of his mind fixed the remembered positions of things in relation to himself: the guard post, the road, the wire coils. A jolting thought crept in: *What if . . . ?* He shoved *that* out instantly. A thick deluge of rain came sweeping into his face. He was terribly aware of the squishy thuds his boots made.

One-thousand-thirty-two . . .

He saw the tiny yellow flag, fluttering like a fallen insect. He dropped to his stomach beside it, holding both weapons in one hand as he crawled wildly forward along the zig, then left into the zag.

One thousand-thirty-nine . . .

He was into the coils. The muzzle of his Thompson caught a wire with a tiny *thwang.* He freed it, hurried on. He was through, at the edge of the road, Wyatt directly ahead crawling across, so close his boots threw mud into Red's face.

One-thousand-forty-one . . .

At last, he lunged over the far edge of the road and down into the water-filled ditch, the others already moving away from the crossing as the rain pounded down. He reached the small ridge down which they had come earlier. There was brush on both sides. As Red came up, he saw Wyatt's shadow move into it. He followed, still belly-crawling, panting heavily now, sucking in rainwater, but just flat *going*.

Ten minutes later, all three were two hundred yards up the main slope, resting for a moment behind a low hogback. They didn't say anything, just sat there with their heads down pulling in air. After a moment, Smoker moved slightly to his left, lifted his weapon, securing the position. On the other side, Wyatt did the same.

Abruptly from the trees came a whispered "Blue?"

Wineberg called softly back, "One." Cowboy and Weesay materialized out of the rain.

Wordlessly, they waited. From the citadel the throbbing whine of engines continued, shouts as faint as those from a company picnic in the next grove. But they were clean sounds, working sounds, no alert siren or gunfire. Another challenge call came whispering. It was quickly countersigned and Sol and Cappacelli came in, looming, silent, Kaamanui carrying the radio pack.

Thirty minutes later, they were a half mile away, set up in a tight defensive position, watching their back trail.

"Fieldhouse, Fieldhouse, this is Blue One. Come back." Parnell hunkered down with his radio pack, the extended antenna nodding in the wind. Static came like dry brush being dragged along an asphalt road. He tried again: "Fieldhouse, this is Blue One. Come back, please."

"Blue One, go ahead."

"Riding Orange Grove clearance. Request immediate relay. Over."

"Stand by." He put his head down. *Come on, come on.* Then: "You are cleared, Blue One. What is your CD reference?"

"CD is Oscar Sally Sally Cornfield. Using code Green. Stand by."

He pulled out his acetate notebook on which he had prepared his message. He would be using the OSS three-letter cipher system, the particular one designated code Green. Wyatt leaned in, held his vest light onto the notebook.

Parnell keyed, "Fieldhouse, message follows." He immediately began reading off the three-letter combinations, pronouncing each letter slowly, pausing a double-click at each break. When deciphered, the message would read: *OBT 1123 hours . . . HQ enemy division, triangular . . . Designated Sixth Panzer . . . 40N/45E . . . Imminent general withdrawal Salerno forces . . . Northwest and east . . . Potenza and Melfi significant.* He finished with, "Message complete. Do you copy?"

"Affirmative."

"Also request for heavy ship fire mission. Will contact again plus forty. Over."

"Stand by." Almost two minutes passed before Fieldhouse came back. "Blue One, you have priority. Come in on Baker frequency. Over."

"Roger that. Out."

At precisely 0101 hours of 16 September, the naval barrage against the German VI Panzer Division headquarters at the citadel began. Although Parnell didn't know it, this time Fifth Army had specifically chosen the USS *Boise* to bring her sixteen-inch batteries to bear.

The rounds came hurtling in sounding like trains in the sky. Up the slope, Red and Wyatt called them in as German tanks and infantry scattered like ants out of a disturbed nest. Both Americans were stunned by the destructive force of what they were seeing. Parnell felt that exhilaration again, only this time stronger, full of shock, this time the sense of utter power, *God Almighty,* all of it right there at his thumb tip.

They felt the tremendous shaking of the ground each time a round struck, heaving up instant volcanoes of fire, and the concussion waves rushing away, actually visible, riding the expanding energy of pure high explosive. Parts of bodies and vehicles and artillery, trees and ground and great stone sections of the old Bourbon fortress of Castelcivita all went spinning and plunging up and through the rainy night air.

They looked down at this chaos of bursting light and roaring sound, smelled the stench of burnt powder, felt the heat of exploding ordnance sweep over them, and then looked at each other. Neither man was smiling.

At noon of 16 September, General von Vietinghoff, at his headquarters at San Angelo di Lombardi high in the Apennines, launched one final strike against the Allied forces in a desperate attempt to regain the momentum of his earlier counteroffensive. It was futile. His Tenth Army had spent its stamina.

In contrast, the Allies were strengthening every hour as massive amounts of supplies and reinforcements poured onto the Salerno beaches. All the gunships that had left for Palermo were now back with full magazines. They immediately went into action, sending their deadly salvos against German positions. Then at two o'clock that afternoon more good news came in. The first elements of Montgomery's Eighth Army had finally made contact with American units outside the coastal town of Agropoli immediately south of Paestum.

Field Marshal Kesselring, knowing the fight for Salerno was now completely lost, ordered his full withdrawal plan be put into effect. By that evening, all German units had wheeled northwest in a fighting retreat. As they pulled out, they blew bridges and rail lines and destroyed every town they vacated. Even Naples was being abandoned. There the Nazi demolition teams that had already begun their work suddenly increased the destruction, demolishing the entire waterfront, all docking and train facilities, along with the city's water and power systems. They also left behind thousands of mines and booby traps amid the shattered buildings and the rubble in the streets that towered three stories high.

As the German retreat began its final phase, Parnell and

his men were ordered to immediately cross back into the American lines near Altavilla and report to the 504th Parachute Infantry Regiment headquarters there. The order came directly from Fifth Army.

On the night of the seventeenth, another regiment of the 82nd Division, the 509th, had been dropped into the town of Avellino on the eastern side of the plain, three miles behind German lines. The operation turned out to be a near-massacre. Now surviving paratroopers were scattered all over hell out there and being methodically hunted down by German patrols. Blue Team was dispatched to help locate some of these lost units and guide them back to the American lines.

Then, in the last quarter of the month, they were temporarily attached to the intelligence section of the 141st Regimental Combat Team of the U.S. 45th Infantry Division, which was trailing the Germans in the northwest. Each night they crossed into enemy lines to gather intelligence and then crossed back again before dawn.

By the end of September, the bulk of the German Tenth Army had successfully crossed the Volturno River, thirty miles north of Naples. There, Kesselring halted the retreat and set out a new, powerful defensive line that stretched completely across the entire waist of the Italian boot to the Adriatic Sea. This was to be the first of several such defensive lines destined to be the sites of some of the bloodiest fighting of the entire European war.

But for now, on the bright, sun-drenched morning of 1 October, Blue Team, operating with D Company, Second Battalion, 141st RCT, linked up with patrol elements of the British Dragoon Guards on the outskirts of Naples. They were right on the heels of the last departing Nazi demo teams, could even hear their explosions still going off along the roads leading out of town.

Then, at precisely 0932 hours, they entered Naples, the first Allied troops to invest this ancient city.

MONTE CASSINO
Hill 516

Fifteen

Parnell flexed his hands, cupping the fingers inward. They were stiff, felt slightly numb. *Getting goddamned old,* he thought. The night wind came slamming in through the side of the British Manchester JZ-14 aircraft, the door frame removed so the men could exit quickly. It was full of frigid rain and sleet needles. The aircraft jostled and dipped roughly. Below them, right down there almost near enough to touch, was the dark earth. Contested ground, *enemy* ground. Some of it the bloodiest in Italy.

He turned around, glanced at Bird directly behind him. In the thin glow from the flight instruments, Wyatt had his head back, eyes closed, the quintessential combat vet grabbing rest while he could. Beyond in the darkness of the cabin was the rest of Blue Team and Freidl-Real, everybody squeezed together with their chest chutes, weapons, demo packs in the limited space.

He studied them for a moment. They no longer looked like soldiers, all scraggly bearded and grimy, like refugee scavengers in their peasant clothes mixed with yoke harnesses holding grenades and demo and clip pouches and carrying three-day patrol packs. They fumed that heady, sometimes unbearable stench of combat, of unwashed skin coated with accumulated dirt and sweat and all the other malodorous effluences of the human body; exhausted men, lead-in-the-bones, red-eyed tired from too many sleepless nights, too much constant tension, too many images of the obscenities of war forever imprinted on their minds.

He turned back, looked out at the night. The JZ-14's engine droned steadily, loudly, a straining sound, the chunky patrol craft not built to carry this much weight. To his right he could feel the stretch of the wing jerking up and down in the wind gusts, the whistling rush of the airstream slipping over its surfaces. Below was pitch-blackness.

The pilot was a young RAF lieutenant named Nigel Berkhart. He reached over and tapped Red's leg, silently indicated that he would hold his flashlight for him so he could study his aero map. It was clipped to a kneeboard. In the light, he checked points, did a few quick calculations with a slide rule, finally nodded. He held up two fingers: *two minutes.*

Parnell leaned back and nudged Wyatt with his elbow. "Get 'em ready," he called over the engine noise. "In two." Bird nodded, the others hearing, sitting up.

Berkhart seemed to be listening to the rebound of his engine off the ground, giving tiny adjustments to his stick. As an experienced patrol pilot who flew photo missions low and slow over this area, he had learned to sense the earth close under him. Now he lifted the aircraft slightly and they banked, going into a wide, climbing turn.

He leaned over, shouted: "We just passed over flat ground. I'm coming around for another pass. When I tell you to go, make it bloody quick. One minute."

Red glanced at the altimeter dial. It showed a slow climb: 400 feet . . . 450 . . . 500. Berkhart stopped it there, leveled.

The men were on their feet, hunkered down, Wyatt moving up to hunch over Parnell, the others doing the same behind him. A slash of sleet slammed into the side of the plane, made it sideslip sharply. Berkhart instantly brought it back, releveled.

Red placed his boots right at the edge of the opening and looked down into the darkness. They would be jumping into hill country, right on the edge of mountains. For a moment, he imagined what might be down there, German gun positions, steep rocks, forest. His tiredness had vanished, his hands were no longer numb. Instead, he felt the surge and pump of adrenaline. He waited.

Berkhart bellowed, "Go!"

He lunged forward, shoving with his feet, feeling the full force of the wind come into him as his body turned, vaguely aware of the aircraft's rear wheel passing off his left shoulder and then gone and the feeling of falling, the sensation of floating as his hand yanked the chute ring, snapping, and then the pop and slap of the chute pack as he hurtled toward the black ground.

Salerno and Naples were only the beginning.

General Kesselring had long believed that the only way to stop the Allied advance in Italy was by setting up a series of strong defensive barriers across the entire boot. Hitler agreed. As soon as the Salerno units had retreated across the Volturno River thirty miles north of Naples in October, he ordered his divisions to turn and form a defensive line that would extend from the Gulf of Gaeta on the Tyrrhenian Sea, across the Apennines, the spine of the Italian peninsula, to Fossacesia on the Adriatic. It was called the Gustav Line and into it he immediately began pouring reinforcements from northern Italy.

The American Fifth Army, flushed with its Salerno victory, had also crossed the Volturno and was rapidly sweeping along both sides of the ancient highway to Rome called the

Via Casilina. But on the twentieth, its forward patrols ran head on into the Gustav Line and the U.S. advance was stopped dead in its tracks.

Meanwhile in the east, Montgomery's Eighth Army had also moved swiftly up the Adriatic coast. The initial plan to take the Italian center called for him to take the two coastal towns of Térmoli and Vasto, then wheel to the northwest, cross the Abruzzi Range of the Apennines and link with the Americans near Venafro, the entrance to the great Liri Valley and the Via Casalina. In coordinated movement, they would then roll directly toward Rome, 110 miles west-northwest.

Unfortunately, the Italian rains had started. This year would develop into the worst winter in thirty years, storm after storm turning the low ground into impassable seas of mud and the upper ridges of the Abruzzi into snowy killing fields. Day after day both Allied armies hurled themselves against the Gustav Line and day after day they were repelled. Casualties skyrocketed, some units actually losing 60 percent of their men. The situation slowly, grindingly deteriorated down into one endless, slogging, bloody stalemate through November and into December.

It was obvious to the Allied Chiefs of Staff a new plan of attack had to be effected. Driven by Churchill's constant insistence for a second front, they came up with Operation Shingle. In an end run around Kesselring's right flank, the U.S.3rd Infantry Division with two Ranger Battalions would make a landing at the twin towns of Anzio and Nettuno 140 miles up the coast from Naples. It was scheduled for 22 January.

The prime purpose was to draw German forces from the Gustav Line. The American Fifth and British Eighth Armies would then drive through the Liri Valley to link up with the invasion units coming inland at the town of Frosinone on the Via Casilina. In concert, they would then mount a massive drive directly to Rome, just forty miles away.

As it would turn out, however, the ACS planners had made two major blunders. The first was their underestimate of the strength of German opposition to the Anzio-Nettuno landings. The second was the great Benedictine monastery on top of Monte Cassino, which dominated the southern Liri Valley.

For Blue Team the intervening months since their triumphal entrance into Naples had been anything but routine. Once again under the complete command of the OSS, they existed totally beyond the now static Allied lines, operating in the Liri Valley and the high rugged ridges of the Abruzzi Mountains, more like guerrillas than soldiers. They raided enemy supply dumps, destroyed communications facilities and rail lines, and sent continuous surveillance data back to the OSS liaisons in Naples and Benevento.

Nearly always on the move, they lived off the land except when air-dropped fresh supplies. They learned the interlinking networks of the partisans, became more adept at the Italian language, slept in caves or shell holes, forever deep in mud and fog, holding off trench foot and malaria, and twice, out of ammo, had had to fight the enemy with knives and stones.

Their lives now consisted solely of destroying and killing and staying alive. As the days sloshed frigidly past, that shell that had begun to seal off all their civilian moralities and injunctions starting in Africa now steadily thickened. They became ever more cold, evermore the efficient professionals.

Except for Freidl-Real and Cesara Arance, they worked with shifting bands of partisans, mostly young students and Communist hardliners from the prewar Italian unions. And in those rare moments of relaxation, they would get knee-walking drunk on Molesian grappa and plundered schnapps and lie with stiff partisan girls who afterward mouthed Marxist slogans at them.

Then in early January, Cesara was killed during an Allied air strike against a German armored column outside the valley town of Atina five miles north of Monte Cassino. The P-51 Mustangs had come out of a rare morning sun loaded with two-hundred-pound high-explosive wing bombs. Several had fallen short and into the stand of trees where Blue Team had set up its observation point.

One landed within a few yards of the Gypsy girl. Shrapnel decapitated her and the concussion blew her ribs and heart through her back. All that afternoon, they had to remain motionless while enemy patrols moved through the area. After nightfall, Kaamanui carried what was left of Cesara and buried her down among the roots of a cork oak tree. He wouldn't let anyone help him. Afterward, he cut a deep X into the tree trunk and left a .45-caliber bullet in its center to mark her grave.

Then late on the afternoon of 11 February, Parnell received an emergency coded message from the OSS agent in Benevento. Word had just been received that one of the two senior partisan leaders, Dr. Constantine Fratoni, had been captured and was being held prisoner at the small hill town of San Vittore di Lazio, eight miles southeast of the Liri Valley.

Blue Team was ordered to make a forced march to a small combat fighter field outside Venafro on the Allied perimeter. There they'd be met by a British recon pilot with fresh ordnance, rations, and maps who would fly them to a drop zone four miles from San Vittore. Once down, they were to go rapidly cross-country and rescue Dr. Fratoni from his captors.

Lieutenant Berkhart had been dead-on. They came down onto a slanting meadow, the ground grass-covered and spongy, rain-soaked, the darkness no longer complete, with objects standing out and the rain pounding on Parnell's head as his chute collapsed in the wind, dragging him several feet before he got it under control.

They had been so close to the ground leaving the aircraft, the entire team landed only yards apart. Rolling his chute, Red quickly hid it under soggy grass, the others emerging out of the rain. They gathered around him, down on one knee like football players just off the field, gathering beside their coach.

"Call out," he said. Each man shouted his name. Everyone was there. "Anybody hurt?" No. He flicked on his vest light and took a compass reading, quickly switched it off. "Smoker, you got point. Weesay and Cowboy on security."

They formed up and headed off at double time. To the north, artillery was going, flashes in the mountains and the sporadic chatter of gunfire, the night full of distant warfare. They went up into a rim of forest. The wind and rain made the trees hum and shift.

After a half hour, Parnell whistled a halt so he could check his map. There had been a bitter fight all through this area earlier in the month. It started as a small skirmish between German and Allied patrols but then grew into a sizable engagement with armor going head-to-head for two hours. Equipment littered the forest floor and there were water-filled shell holes everywhere, trees cropped from air bursts. It still stank of expended explosives and soaked ash mingling with the sweetness of pine.

Parnell's TMO had been precise. He had to "extricate" Dr. Fratoni before he could be moved to Gestapo headquarters at Rome. Unknown to everyone except Bird, it also carried an XOX addenda, the code indicating that if a rescue were not possible, Parnell was to personally kill the partisan leader.

Fixing an azimuth, he whistled the team forward again and they melted off into the night.

Major Keppler was losing patience. He paced around the small basement room in the San Vittore jail. It was small, cold, and wet-feeling, with white stone walls and a barred door beside a wooden one. There was a small desk made of boxwood with a framed snapshot on it, a small wedding group, country folk in tight black suits grinning dramatically at the camera. In the corner was a copper washing bowl, the metal tarnished green like sewer piping.

He paused to look at Dr. Fratoni again. The prisoner sat on a bench with his ankles tied to it and his hands handcuffed behind his back, his spine arched backward as if he were howling, and Keppler thought, *The man can certainly stand pain.*

For the last six hours, they had been torturing him, whipping him with lengths of cable from one of the military trucks. Then they poured salt and battery acid onto the raw wounds the cables had left on his body, but the doctor seemed to close himself down against the pain, his face bulging, red as if he might explode if he relaxed his mind.

He didn't look like a doctor. He was large and barrel-chested with thick black hair across his pectorals, all of it now bloody, his flesh ruptured into strips of puckered, black-and-blue cuts. One of his nipples had been ripped away by the cable end. He had a heavy, gross face formed of thick, pockmarked skin. His eyes were black and large and filled with defiance each time they opened. He exuded a musky odor like a dog in a fight.

Keppler said, "I compliment you, Herr Doctor. You possess a high tolerance for pain. We Germans can appreciate such gifts. Tell me, how do you manage it?"

Fratoni stared at him. Sweat dripped from an eyelash.

"It has been difficult, hasn't it?"

Silence.

Keppler turned away, stared at the low ceiling. "It will get worse, I'm afraid." He came back. "First here and then in Rome. Ah, yes, the Gestapo will offer exquisite pain for you to test your magnificent reserves. And they will be here by morning. Does that prospect entice you?"

Fratoni spat at him. Keppler's entire head slowly turned red, his cheeks quivered. He flicked the glob of saliva from his tunic. Then, with obvious effort, he finally quieted his rage, turned, flicked his finger. Two soldiers stepped through the door carrying the cables. They beat him again.

This time, the major did not watch. Instead, he sat turned to the side. He smoked. He picked at his fingers. He stared at the ceiling. All the time asking the same questions, over and over. What are the names of your key men? Where are they?

How many are in your group? What do they intend to do? Who
helps you? Who supplies you? What are your codes? On and
on, endless questions asked in a low, monotonic voice.

The doctor screamed inside his throat each time the cables struck. Yet no sound escaped from his mouth, only a
contorted grunting, as if his big body were absorbing bullets
or he was fornicating and plunging on in wild abandon toward the orgasm that hung right there, just out of touch. They
continued beating him. He continued to grunt and stink and
finally lost his bladder, drenching the front of his bloody
trousers.

Keppler sighed. "Enough of this," he snapped. "Bring in
the girl." The doctor's head snapped up. His eyes flared like
a sudden burst of flame on gasoline.

Her name was Gabriella Fratoni. She was the doctor's
daughter, twenty-two years old, dressed in men's clothing,
brown hair cut short like a boy's, her body chunky like her
father's and big-breasted with thick thighs and eyes as dark
and defiant as his. The soldiers held her arms. When she saw
her father, those eyes for a single moment went soft with shock
and pity and fear. Then they immediately hardened again.

"Strip her," Keppler ordered.

They did so. She did not fight them, just stood there as
they pulled off her coat, then her boots and trousers, the men
bending and twisting, working expressionlessly. Quickly,
she was naked. Her hips were wide and her nipples dark as
brown quarters stuck to the whiteness of her breasts.

Keppler intently watched the doctor, the man's body now
straining with rage instead of pain, his peasant's face con-
torting. "Rape her," the major said evenly. "Bring in every
man of the platoon, one at a time."

For the first time, Fratoni's voice burst forth, a bellow, a
scream: "You filthy Nazi pig!" Then he began to weep.

It was tragiccomical, the men coming in embarrassed, their
battle dress covered with mud and rain, pulling down their
pants. Gabriella was bent forward on the desk, her face against
the wood, motionless, as the men tried to get their penises

up, aware that their major was watching, and then fondling her, her buttocks and neck and hair, and at last being able to do it and entering her swiftly, her body lifting slightly, silently, the muscles of her back tightening as they thrust in and out, the men finally responding and getting with it, closing their eyes, their heads back until they shuddered in orgasm and the final spastic jabs and then the embarrassment again.

Three men . . . four . . . six . . .

Fratoni exploded. With a roar, he lunged to his feet, the bench swinging around his ankles. He went straight for Major Keppler, the German rearing back. Soldiers leaped forward to intercept him. They went down in a mass of tangled, flailing arms. The bench crashed into the desk.

Keppler, on his feet now, watched stiffly. The doctor managed to get to his feet again, once more came at him, bellowing incoherently. At that moment, Gabriella rolled off the desk and also went for Keppler, her scream like a screech of insanity, pawing for his sidearm.

She got it, pulled it free of its holster, then lost it as it tumbled to the floor. A soldier moved past Keppler, who had ducked back just as Fratoni and the bench slammed into him, knocking him back against the wall. There was the resounding crash of an automatic weapon. The bullets nearly cut the doctor's arm off just below the shoulder. Blood blew out of the wound as he crumbled to the floor.

Gabriella had again retrieved Keppler's Luger. Several soldiers came through the door now, went for her. She shot one in the face. Arms grabbed at her, clawed at breast and leg and hair. She tried to shoot another. One hauled her up, his arm around her throat. She let out a gagged scream, put the Luger's muzzle into her mouth and fired. The bullet went through her skull and into the forehead of the soldier holding her. They both reeled backward into the wall and then to the floor, leaving blood and brain tissue smeared on the white wall.

* * *

Blue Team's progress was slowed twice by German picket patrols, small units isolated out there in the woods in the rainy night. Each time, they'd have to go into squad defensive flanking movement, the men shifting security positions, moving laterally and then coming back onto the compass heading to San Vittore di Lazio.

The night was filled with continual noise. Always artillery, once a sudden, crackling firefight from somewhere in the direction of the town of Cassino, the stony hills magnifying and funneling the racket. Still, here in the woods the predominant noise was the whistling of the wind and the constant dripping of water down through the trees with the ground matted with soggy pine needles and the air freezing cold.

It was nearly 2;00 A.M. when Smoker came running back, suddenly appearing out of the dark. "Lieutenant, I think there's armor up ahead," he whispered. "About fifty yards out. I can hear rain on hollow metal."

"You and Cowboy check it out."

At least eight Mark IVs were scattered tightly among the trees, just sitting there, immense and silent and lethal-looking like huge animals gone to night rest. They were painted a dark green camouflage pattern with their 75mm long guns bearing colored unit stripes, which the men couldn't distinguish in the dark. The heavy raindrops from the trees made a discordant drumming on their hulls and once there was a burst of muffled radio static.

The men went right through them, sometimes moving close enough to touch the huge vehicles, smelling of transmission oil and leaking gasoline and suspension grease. *What the hell are they doing here?* Parnell wondered. Figured they were possibly being held in reserve to guard against expected enemy flanking thrusts up from the lower foothills.

Once beyond the tanks, they crossed a road and went down into a small meadow and then a thick stand of oak trees, everyone moving rapidly, holding tight formation. They skirted a narrow ridge and went down into a glen, then over another ridge and again into a long, slanting valley.

At 3:21, they reached the outskirts of San Vittore di Lazio.

Now there was another sound in the night, a pleasant sound, the rush and hiss of a small stream swollen from the rains. The surface fumed in the cold, the current going down and then paralleling the road that went into the town. The town itself was about a quarter mile down the incline. A small wooden waterwheel spanned the stream, its hub bearing squeaking as it spun in the water's flow. A small abandoned stone hut was to the right along a narrow trail.

San Vittore was completely dark and gave off no sounds, no animal bawl, no thud or murmur of human habitation. Now and then the flicker of sheet lightning illuminated it for a fraction of a second. In the blue-white light it looked completely bombed out, a few standing buildings, partial walls, the remnants of chimneys poking up, but mostly piles of rubble and burned-out debris in the narrow streets.

The team was lined along the stream. Parnell, Wyatt, and Real squatted down near the waterwheel to talk. Red disgustedly hissed air through his teeth. "It don't look like anything's down there. OSS must have been wrong."

"Maybe they've already moved Fratoni," Real suggested.

"Maybe." Red squinted into the darkness, thoughtfully rubbed his thumbnail with his forefinger.

Wyatt said, "I don' like this, Lieutenant. It don' feel right."

"Yeah, I'm picking that up, too." He continued studying the demolished town, then nodded. "All right, send in a couple scouts, see what the hell is there." He consulted his watch. "We still got a few hours of darkness. Tell them to make it fast but to watch out."

Wyatt moved off.

He and Augustin waited. He kept distractedly tapping his finger against the trigger guard of his Thompson. The situation was sending red pulses through his instincts. *Could* the Krauts still be down there with the doctor, somewhere inside a ruined building? Still, why hadn't they moved him already if he was so important? Fratoni was the biggest man in the Resistance movement.

Parnell waited expectantly for each flash of lightning, the landscape glowing blue white in its miniscule burst. Each time he would quick-scan the ruins, searching for a silhouette of a military vehicle or maybe the glisten off a muzzle or helmet, anything that might indicate there really *was* enemy down there. He spotted nothing.

Twenty minutes went by. The rain continued coming in waves. With the men stationary now, the cold went through their winter jackets and the sleety rain needled their faces and hands. Thirty-five minutes passed. Beside them, the water-wheel hummed woodenly. Forty minutes.

Smoker was the first back, coming in swiftly to kneel beside Parnell. "They're there, all right," he said. "One gun position on the side of the road that comes up here."

"Just one?"

"I didn't spot no others. But I can *feel* the bastards, Lieutenant. They's scattered all over hell among the rubble." He snorted. "That little old town got the shit barraged out of it."

"Minefield markers?"

"None."

"This doesn't make sense. What the hell kind of night perimeter is that?"

"Maybe these boys ain't infantry," Wyatt said.

Red nodded. "Yeah, that's so. Probably a small intelligence unit, *Abwehr* or even Gestapo." He turned back to Wineberg. "You see any *lights?"*

"Onct, jes' a flicker. From one a' the buildings 'bout near the center a' town."

Parnell grunted.

Laguna came in a few minutes later. He told Red he'd spotted another single gun position on the eastern outskirts of the town, guarding a small road that went out into meadow-land. But he'd heard German voices deeper in the town. He also saw light from the same building Smoker had seen, a stone structure only half demolished with bars on its remaining windows. He figured it was a jailhouse.

"How about infiltration points?" Parnell asked.

Smoker said, "Yeah, the one I went in on. It's this side of the gun, maybe twenty yards. Through some animal pens."

"Weesay?"

"If we take out that gun on the east road, we could have good cover in and out."

Parnell nodded, considering, figuring deployments, approaches.

Outside the circle of soldiers, Freidl-Real listened without comment. Over the months operating with Blue Team, he'd changed, become more somber, inward, no longer the contemptuous, aristocratic wiseass. The loss of Evan Couprier and Cesara had affected him deeply and had thrust him into the real and immediate horrors of combat.

Now it was no longer a thing of exquisite vengeance, or the intellectual excitement of collegiate debates on the issues of clashing ideologies, or even the once-perceived glamour of being a resistance fighter against tyranny. It was all about simply surviving and his introduction to an ageless truth, that war is dirty and violent and random and, in the end, meaningless. So now he simply sat and silently let the professionals work out the details.

"What kind of numbers you figure we lookin' at here?" Parnell asked Smoker. Wineberg had always exhibited a keen sense for terrain and opposing force parameters.

"I'd say thirty, thirty-five men," Smoker answered after a moment of thought. "Maybe a full platoon."

Red turned to Laguna.

"Yeah, I agree with that, Lieutenant."

"All right," Parnell said, his mental considerations completed. "We'll go in in three teams. First two men on each gun position. Take 'em out fast and quiet. Main Action Unit hits the jailhouse. That's the only likely place they'd have Fratoni. After we extract, I'll fire three rounds, one-second spacing. Everybody withdraw. Right here's primary rally point."

He paused, mentally going over his topo map. "If something goes haywire, secondary RP is a rail crossing a mile due south. One thing, don't use your demolitions unless it's absolutely essential. We might need 'em down the road. The word *Stormfront* will be challenge." He looked around at the faces in the rainy darkness. "If we can't link at all, everybody go to ground and stay there until you get a chance to return to our lines."

He glanced over at Bird. "You, me, Angelo, and Real are MAU. You got anything to add?"

Wyatt shook his head. "No, Lieutenant." He, Smoker, Weesay, and Kaamanui rose and moved off along the stream bank.

Red tapped the back of his fingers against Augustin's shoulder. "Check your gear for anything that makes noise."

"I have."

"When we breach that jail, you follow me. Right on my ass."

"Yes."

Parnell settled onto his haunches, his mind probing one last time, checking for anything left out. He was satisfied. He felt the tingling of adrenaline seeping into his body, the so-familiar sensation only now no longer a wild rush but rather a directed, controlled, cold preparing for combat. He automatically checked his weapon and grenade slings. Then he and Real followed the others down the slope.

The two security teams left first, simply dissolving off into the rain. Red again looked at his watch: 4:07. He waited five minutes, the four of them motionless, heads down in the rain. Sounds, their presence suddenly made more apparent by the waiting, riffled in from far away and flashes of sheet lightning trembled over the higher ridges, casting everything into a ghostly burst of phosphorescence that was instantly sucked back into the night.

At last, Parnell shoved to his feet. "Okay, let's go," he snapped.

Sixteen

The smell was everywhere, close to the ground from the pressure of the rain. It came from four dead mules near what had been a stone stable on the downside of the road, the bodies bloated, two popped open, the others with the rain tapping hollowly on their distended abdomens.

Smoker crawled forward, elbows, hips swiveling, as if the stink weren't there. Pervading foul odors had been a part of his entire life and he'd learned to override his sense of smell. Unless a specific odor compelled significance, similar to the way the hurt cry of a child amid play shouts drew his mother's immediate attention.

He and Kaamanui were on the downside of the main road leading into the high mountains. They were retracing the same route he'd taken earlier, among shattered tree trunks and explosion rubble and down into what had been some sort of communal animal enclosure. The ground was layered in deep mud that clung thickly to his body, like crawling through icy, partially solidified honey.

He reached the same low wall he'd used before. Next to it was a deep shell hole half filled with water. The rain pecked and splashed against the surface, sounding like someone taking a shower. He squinted to his right. There, the German machine gun position, thirty yards away. It was formed of stones piled into a semicircle back against a half-blown-out wall.

Sol came up and Smoker pointed. Kaamanui nodded. Someone laughed, to the left, very close. Both men froze. Then came a specific smell, floating through the dead-mule stench. Cigarette smoke. Wineberg slowly turned his head, saw the darker dark of Sol's body. Another gun position was over *there,* in a stone shed.

Damn, how'd I miss that the first time around?

He settled back against the wall. Moving slowly, he shifted his Thompson to his left hand and unhooked two grenades from his utility belt. Their flip-up arms were taped. He gently pulled the tape free, laid one on the top of the wall, and held the other with his right hand. He knew Sol was doing the same thing, no words needed.

He waited, feeling suddenly energized, a fight coming, right around the corner. He looked up at the sky. The cold rain peppered his face, stung his eyelids. He nestled his body in under his clothing, slowly shifted his feet until they were beneath him.

A Nebelwerfer rocket barrage started down on the low ground, the missiles screeching as they left the launch tubes and the rounds making that long, drawn-out moaning as they raced across the sky, the sounds bouncing off the overcast, echoing and reechoing like wolf packs challenging in the hills.

Weesay Laguna sometimes was certain he could *smell* Krauts. Not their clothes or soap or tobacco. No, this was a deeper odor, a skin scent. It was from all that canned meat and sausages they ate, fucking horse shit, a sour tang. They smelled like white men, but more gringo than gringo. Not like the cool chili sweetness of his own Chicano body.

This time he was wrong.

He had been crawling along, sniffing at the rainy air like

a rat seeking out hidden cheese, he and Fountain following his first entry path, right down into the town from the east, among stone and brick rubble and rain pools and chunks of shrapnel. They'd already skirted the jailhouse and were now angling to the right, to set up on the gun position he'd spotted before.

Suddenly his hand touched cloth, thick, rough material. He stopped. A second later, something loomed up in front of him. A soldier under a blanket, the man sleeping beneath a boulder of shell-sundered wall. For one miniscule fraction of a second, Weesay's surprise immobilized him. Then he was bringing the butt of his Thompson around off his forearm to slam into the top of the blanket. He felt a solidity, heard a muffled grunt, the German fumbling under the cloth.

Laguna hurled himself onto him, his boot knife already out and coming up straight forward, plunging it through the cloth, into softer solidity, the German under him now, the two tumbling silently under the stone overhead like kids wrestling in a bed. Again and again Weesay blindly drove his blade through the blanket, feeling it go in, feeling it ricochet off metal. The man groaned loudly, snuffled, slumped.

God, oh, God, I done it now.

He froze on top of the inert form, listening with all the intensity he could bring to his ears. Rain pattered on the rubble stone, the distant cry of German rockets. Then a quiet shuffle and another shadow loomed. He swung to it, knife ready.

It was Cowboy, half lying a few feet away looking in at him, his head tilted. He held his hand up. Neither moved. Seconds drifted past. At last, Cowboy made a circle with his thumb and forefinger and pointed ahead. Weesay slid off the dead German and lay out on the ground, his weapon again resting on his forearms.

They crawled forward.

Major Witt Keppler had been experiencing a case of *Dunnschisse*, diarrhea, over the last two days. It would sometimes come at him like a whip to his bowels. Damned *Italienisch* country. Ruined one's digestion, a wonder they all didn't have dysentery.

He was seated on a porcelain commode in a tiny room off the main hall of the jail, holding his buttocks up off the filthy ring, pants down around his ankles and his thigh muscles straining to hold the uncomfortable position. His stool had just shot out of him, messy and liquefied. The toilet had no seat, cockroaches skittering down inside when he first looked, his flashlight scaring them. Part of the wall had been blown out. Now the rain sent a mist of icy air into his face.

His rage over the death of Fratoni still roiled through him like a cold wind. Now the Gestapo would come and turn their dark eyes on him, negating all the splendid work he had accomplished over the intervening months hunting down and executing hundreds of Resistance fighters. And now doing it with only a handful of men, those not his best. These had been stolen from him by line regiments to bolster the German defenses along the Garigliano and Rapido Rivers. They left him with replacements, useless, behind-the-lines service troops.

Dr. Fratoni would have been such a magnificent coup, the man right at the heart of the Movement. Surely he would have garnered his *Obersleutantcy* from such a capture. No one would know it had been mere accident, the doctor and his daughter and two Red priests caught hiding in a church in the tiny hill town of Croce di Trevino a mile to the east. Only the result would have been primary in his after-action report.

Using the last of his field toilet tissues, he cleaned himself and redressed. For a moment, he paused to examine his face in a small stained mirror on the wall. The flashlight cast his features into dark hollows, a smooth-headed gargoyle in a dirty uniform. He sighed, felt again the painful sting of disappointment.

A fresh deluge of rain came roaring down, sending in a thick wave of mist. And suddenly with it, shattering the night's stillness, came the slamming *thwruuuuup* of a Schmeiser MP-40 machine pistol. Inside the building! Three seconds later it was answered by the deeper, slower rap of an American weapon. Then the hollow blast of a grenade from somewhere outside, followed immediately by three others.

Keppler whirled, his hand pulling at his sidearm. His holster was empty. *Ach du Scheisse,* he'd left it on the table in the basement. Growling at his own carelessness, he lunged through the partially destroyed doorway.

Their attack had come swiftly, no fanfare, four men going up the steps of the jailhouse and right at the two guards standing with their heads down, coat collars up at the old wooden doorway.

The first was dead with Parnell's long-bladed boot knife straight down through his collarbone into the aorta. The other let out a cry of terror-shock, turned, fumbled for the door handle, got it open, and started through as the full momentum of all four men hit him. He went down, rolling, groaning as two knives plunged into his neck and liver.

Red was the first into the outer hall. Pitch-blackness. He felt his way along the wall of blocked stones, rough to the touch. The thick odor of explosion dust and withered wood like old barns, the floor slippery with a film of water and scattered with ceiling rubble.

He reached a door. It was part metal, part wood. The wood portion had curlicues carved into its surface. Another door. No light was visible anywhere. He heard something clank below, like the closing of a cell door.

Someone came up beside him, Wyatt, only a dark shape in the bigger darkness. Red pushed his palm forward. Wyatt moved away. He heard Real directly behind him, breathing hard. A glimmer of light flickered at the end of the corridor. It went out. Again silence save for the soft whisper of the rain blowing through the main doorway.

A male voice called out, whispery, *"Hauptfach Keppler? Ist das Ihnen?"*

More silence.

Then a shout of warning. Red dropped to the floor, felt the sharp edge of a stone jab him in the throat. Immediately, the corridor was filled with sound and muzzle flashes. Bullets *whanged* against the shattered ceiling, richocheting off. Parnell saw Wyatt's silhouette lying flat ten feet ahead, saw the back-flashes of his Thompson as the sergeant opened up.

The Germans retreated back downstairs. In a moment, he was beside Bird. Real came up, as did Cappacelli. Grenades were going off outside, his two security teams engaging the German gun positions. Quickly a full firefight developed out there.

"Two," Wyatt growled. "In the basement."

Red twisted, leaned toward Augustin. "Stay here. Watch for anything coming down from above us."

"Yes, yes."

Cappacelli moved up. Wyatt was squatted beside the stairs, Parnell right up against him, Angelo a foot away. Both men unhitched grenades from their utility belts, slipped off the safety tapes. German voices shouted from the basement, the crack of boots.

"High and low," Red said. "Now!"

The grenades arched through the air for a few feet, hit a wall, and tumbled along the lower steps, fuses clicking and hissing. Someone yelled, *"Stielhandgranate!"* Then something struck the same wall the others had hit. It made a hollow wooden sound.

"Stick grenade!" Wyatt shouted. All three men hit the floor.

They heard the German grenade friction igniter sizzling. Then there were two resounding explosions that came nearly together, then a deeper, heavier blast as the half-pound bursting charge of the Kraut grenade went off. Heat and flash blew back up the stairwell, the concussions overlapping each other, tearing dust and small chunks of stone from the ceiling and walls that showered down.

As the sounds echoed off down the corridor, Bird lunged up and darted down the stairs, firing twin bursts. Parnell went right after him, down into blackness and the thick fume of explosive smoke, dodging to his right. He went down on one knee and opened up, one-handed, felt the Thompson jump against the webbing of his thumb, and caught the familiar acetylene stench of confined cordite smoke. Directly behind and above him Cappacelli's weapon began hammering, Red hearing the rounds going hot and supersonic out of the muzzle.

There was no answering fire. They stopped. The air seemed to ring with the memory of the gun bursts and grenades. Parnell listened, his head forward, ears whistling as if clogged. Yet he was still able to hear something bang in the darkness, muffled, from another room.

He moved forward cautiously. The floor was littered with stone blast debris. He felt something soft, tested it with the sole of his boot. A hand, an arm, torn off at the shoulder. He moved on, feeling along the wall. Ahead a sliver of light shone near the floor. The bottom of a door.

It had bars across the sills, then the wooden door itself. He ran his fingers along the bars, rusted, an inch thick. The sliver of light disappeared. He heard the metallic *chunk* of a machine gun receiver slamming forward. He turned, Wyatt and Angelo looming through the settling explosion dust.

From somewhere above them, Freidl-Real let out a choking scream.

Oh, shit, Parnell thought, *we're vertically bracketed.* He twisted his head. "Cover it," he barked.

Amid the explosions and gunfire, Major Keppler had crept along the hall of the upper floor of the jail like an assassin, stealthy with uncertainty. His mind told him exactly what was happening, partisans come to rescue their beloved doctor.

He was aware of a peculiar tightness in his chest. This was the first time an enemy had actually targeted *him*. In *close combat*. In the past, he'd always been the aggressor or the observer. Now these bullets and grenades were meant to steal *his* life. For a moment, it was a disconcerting realization. Still, he told himself, these were mere partisans, undisciplined, vile dwarfs. He was a German *Waffen SS* officer leading *Waffen* troopers. The outcome was inevitable.

He again cursed his foolishness in leaving his Luger in the basement. Now the only weapon he had was his dress dagger, silver-edged and worn on an internal clasp beneath his tunic. He withdrew it and proceeded along the shattered hall. This part of the upper floor had been blown away. Rain pounded down through skeletal beams. Rats skittered and squeaked in the darkness.

The firing inside the building had stopped. Cautiously, he peered around a tumbled wall, its edge serrated with split bricks, and scanned the town. He could see scattered muzzle flashes, tracers slicing white threads through the darkness, could hear his platoon sergeants shouting position changes, engaging fully. *Good, good.* Soon they would storm the building.

He retraced his steps till he reached the stairwell at the commode end of the hall. He paused, listening. There was a tiny scraping sound on the steps. He shoved back against the wall, his heart kicking up instantly. He brought up his dagger, held it in thrusting position.

The sound of breathing came, then the sudden stink of foul body odor. Someone edged around the top of the stairwell. He could not actually see the person, only *feel* him there in the dark. The odor became stronger, the breathing holding and releasing, strained. A form appeared fully. He held to the wall, holding his own breath, the tightness in his chest like a ring across his upper ribs.

It crossed in front of him. There, two feet away. A grenade abruptly went off outside, made him wince. The flash flared at the end of the hall. In its dim reflections, Keppler saw a man's silhouette, his eyes catching the reflection and a head turning to look at him.

He drove his arm straight out, immediately felt the dagger blade go into cloth, flesh, felt it strike bone, veer. The man screamed, turned slightly away, shying from the knife. Blindly, Keppler thrust again and again, the blade hitting vertebrae now, the man's voice sucking up sharply as if he had just jumped into freezing water. Then his weight came fully onto the blade, pulling Keppler off balance as he dropped heavily, disjointedly, his weapon clattering against the stone floor. The knife finally pulled free of the body and Keppler pressed himself back against the wall, his own breath hissing through his teeth.

He remained motionless for several seconds. Something warm ran down the blade onto his hand. He distractedly wiped it away, listened. A compacted, congealed silence, the firing outside disconnected from it, here a cocoon of non-sound.

At last, he lowered himself, felt along the floor for the dead man's weapon. Touched flesh, a face, warm. He found the butt of the weapon, swung it up. Unfamiliar feel, heavier than an MP-40. He brought it in close against his chest.

A voice called out softly, "Real?"

Keppler froze. It had come from the bottom of the stairs. A surge of panic splintered up through his head. He swung the muzzle around and pulled the trigger. The blasting thunder of the weapon filled the hall. The gun fired deeper, slower than his own weaponry. Bullets hit the stairwell wall, ricocheting downward. He stopped, cut loose again. Then he turned and raced back along the hall to the sundered front of the building.

Behind him, he heard a snap, the safety arm of a grenade flipping up, heard it go rolling across the floor. Once again the panic struck him like a gust of chest-chilling wind. He threw himself to the floor. The grenade went off with a hollow, directed blast. Stone slivers flew over him and smoke and dust rushed up the hall. He felt something strike his left buttock. It felt as if someone had punched him.

At the stairwell, twin automatics opened up. The smoky air seemed alive with hurtling missiles. *They're coming!* Despite the sizzle of the bullets, his panic drove him to his feet. He lunged through the shell-torn wall, stumbling, frantically grabbing for a handhold, the weapon forgotten.

He gripped a brick. It broke away. Another, holding. He hung there. The rain lashed at him. Below was darkness. He let go, dropped along the lower portion of the wall, and landed in mud, his left leg hitting first, a jolt up through his calf. He rolled over and came to a crouch. His buttock began to throb.

From his left, an MG-34 was firing, short, probing bursts. He headed for it, hit a large piece of blasted rock, and fell down. Quickly he was back up, throwing himself forward. A man yelled close by. He stopped instantly, dropped. Two MP-40s began hammering away from where the voice had come.

Another yell, frantic, *"Hier! Komm hier, Herr Hauptfach!"*

He pushed to his feet, headed that way, went over a low wall of broken stone, hands grabbing at his tunic, down into more mud filled with spent cartridges. He shook off the hands, shouting, "Flares, you imbeciles. Put up flares."

One second after Sol heard the firing inside the jail, both his grenades had gone sailing through the air, him dropping instantly to the ground. A few seconds later, one went off, then the other, bright flashes and the ripple of ground movement beneath him. Smoker's grenades exploded then, sent another blow of light and a shivering in the earth.

Kamaanui was up now, moving forward at a crouch. He let go an eight-round burst, heard the bullets slam into rock, slap into flesh. A man sighed, as if he were lying down after a long day. Sol went over rocks and into the gun nest, his weapon traversing. Wineberg continued hammering away too. From the other side of the town, two more Thompsons were also firing.

Another groaning sigh. Sol fired at it, caught the unmistakable thick, wet sound of a bursting skull. Then everything broke loose as firing erupted from all over the town, wild, undirected bursts. He dropped, banging into the bottom of a machine gun mount leg and the corner of a cartridge box. Bullets cracked overhead, *whanged* off flat rock surfaces.

With his face in mud, he listened to the counterfire, picking out specific bursts, analyzing them: MP-40s, a single machine gun, lots of the sharper single barks of Karabiner 98s. He grunted, thinking, *Too many carbines . . . not an infantry unit . . . fire overly scattered without a primary fire base . . . must be a service unit.* He tried to pinpoint individual positions but couldn't. The heaviness of the rain and the thousands of flat stone surfaces distorted their direction.

He lifted his head slightly, looked toward the town's exit road. No fire from there. Good, they still had a withdrawal route. Gradually the German fire thinned out, the first shock of adrenaline settling as the gunners began searching out specific targets. He could hear their platoon leaders shouting, the voices throaty, sounding lethal out there in the darkness.

The muffled rap of an automatic weapon from inside the jail came. A Thompson. It immediately set off another blaze of gunfire, most of it centered on the building, rounds stitching across its white rock face. The racket was so loud he just barely heard the second burst and then a grenade going off inside.

Parnell and the others converging.

Again the firing eased off, then stopped completely. A thick silence. He shifted around and felt for the German machine gun. It was on its side. He righted it and, working by feel, quickly dismantled the receiver and took out the bolt and breech lock, disabling the weapon. He hurled both parts off to the right. They made two soft metallic chinks when they landed.

Instantly, an MP-40 threw a short burst at them, the muzzle's back-blast stitching tiny etchings in the dark. Sol fixed his barrel point on them and fired till his clip was empty. With his finger still on the trigger, he rolled over the gun nest stones and far to his left. Behind him, bullets came crashing into the gun nest, rounds pinging off the Kraut machine gun.

Another heady quiet. Minutes slipped past. Another round of scattered firing. Once more it petered out, quicker this time, nobody wanting to waste ammo, disclose positions.

"Storm." A soft hiss.

"Front."

Wineberg came slithering in, snapping a fresh clip into his Thompson as he moved. Sol also slipped in a fresh one, holding his weapon against his body to absorb the click. He came to one knee and cautiously peered around the edge of a block of masonry. Squinting, he tried to pick out the face of the jail building. It was too far away.

A moment later he heard someone calling. Then silence again. He leaned his head back and looked straight up. Rain slashed across his vision, pecked at his eyes. Was there a change in the light up there? He couldn't be certain, it was too subtle, an illusion. He checked his watch. Ten minutes to 5:00.

Easing himself gently around, he found a rock protrusion, rested the back of his head on it, closed his lids. He inhaled, let it out slowly, thinking, *We're about to get into some serious shit here.*

He realized that if the extraction wasn't completed by first light, the initiative would immediately switch to the enemy. No more boldness or rapidity of movement; they'd be pinned down, separated, each team suddenly into house-to-house fighting, always so bloody and time-consuming.

He opened his eyes, slid them around until he could pick

out Wineberg's shadow, a dark oval, shoulders a few feet away. He was looking at him, Sol knowing old Smoker was thinking the same thing.

There was a pop, another, and the twin slurring hisses of flares. Side by side, they arched upward, leaving trails of or-ange sparks shining through the rain. As they reached their apogee, they hung motionless for a moment, gravity and flight held in suspension, then they burst into stunning brilliance, flooding the wreckage and rubble and sundered buildings of San Vittore di Lazio into white daylight.

Wyatt and Angelo were back, Bird in close to Parnell's side, whispering, "Augustin's dead. One man. He went out through a shell hole. We cleared the upper level but they've just put up flares."

Red had seen the flare light coming down the stairwell, dim in the lingering grenade smoke. Freidl-Real gone, damn it, the only man who could ID Fratoni. Time to mourn later. He said, "All right, let's get this fucking thing done."

As if on cue, a machine gun opened up from inside the room, the reports slightly muffled but still thunderous. Bullets blew through the wooden door, crashed and bored into stone, flew off steel bars, everyone instantly flat on the lit-tered floor. It stopped for a few seconds, then let loose an-other burst.

They waited, motionless. Ten . . . twenty seconds. Parnell came to one knee. "Who's carrying the 39ers?"

Angelo fumbled with his belt, handed up a small round object, green with a white stripe, the size of a small grape-fruit. It was a German Nebelhandgranate 39, a smoke grenade containing hexachlorethane. This particular model also had benzene and creosote oil mixed in, which would give the blast an incendiary burn.

They leaned close, Parnell saying, "We blow the bar hinges first, then use the smoker. When we go in, I'm one, Wyatt two, Angelo on cleanup. Stay tight. Check your clips."

A German yelled something inside the room. It was heard clearly through the shattered door. The light from the flares had dimmed now. In a few moments, the basement was pitch-black again.

Parnell rolled the smoker grenade in his hand, ran his thumb along its lower beveled edge. His senses were vibrating with energy, almost making his skin quiver. The air in the room was frigid. He counted off to himself, priming, like a race: *Set . . . one . . . two . . . three.*

"Go."

Bird and Angelo moved forward to place their grenades, one on each hinge of the barred door, looping the igniter arms over the frame, easing them up so they wouldn't click and draw fire, then pulling the pins and lunging back and down.

Both grenades went off at the same second. The small outer basement room was enveloped in sound, the air shuddering from the blasts, going into vibration. The steel bar door was slammed against the opposite wall and rocks and chunks of wall and splinters of wood rocketed everywhere. Red felt things slicing into his neck, hot bites like wasp stings.

Before the echoes were gone, he rolled over, yanked the detonator ring on the 39er, and hurled it through the blown doorway. A shout and a single shot from a handgun. Then the inner room burst into bright orange-yellow light. Smoke fumed out through the doorway, glowing orange.

They went in commando style, Parnell the first through the doorway, then Wyatt and Angelo, each with their separate area of domination: Red the right wall and corner, Bird everything on the left, Angelo covering straight ahead. The smoke stung their eyes. There were dimly seen streaks of fire on the walls and floor where the creosote and benzene had been flung out.

With his eyes slitted, Red saw a figure emerge out of the smoke. A camo battle dress. He fired at it, saw it disappear. A Thompson to his left cut loose a long burst. The smoke was beginning to thin out, lifting. A pair of ankle boots appeared, black with webbing anklets, the legs also in camo gray, disembodied, moving to the side across the flames, a high-pitched voice yelling, *"Nien! Nien!"* He fired at where the German's stomach would be. The man dropped heavily to the floor.

"Clear!" Bird shouted.

Parnell moved forward along the wall. His hand brushed across some of the burning creosote. It sent a hot surge of pain through his palm. He slapped it against his pant leg as it bored in, hurting like hell. It faded. "Clear!" he called out. From directly behind him, Angelo said, "Clear!"

There were three German soldiers, all in *Waffen SS* light gray splinter-pattern camouflage battle dress, with them a model MG-34 machine gun. All were dead. A table had been blown across the room, was now burning. It lay on top of a naked girl. The back of her head had been blown out. Crumpled against the far wall was a shirtless man, his body as contorted as a stuffed doll's, his legs tied to a bench. He was barrel-chested and hairy and his eyes were open.

Parnell knelt beside him. The man's body was covered with stripe wounds, the blood congealed into scabby strings. Parnell tested his carotid, the skin stiff and cold. Nothing. Red cursed softly. *This must be Dr. Fratoni,* he thought. He shoved through the man's trouser pockets looking for something to identify him. They were empty. He turned, looked at the girl. He had no idea who she was.

The room was clearing of smoke but filling with the thicker stench of burning oil and the corrosive smell of benzene and chlorate like a bleaching plant. Two of the ceiling beams were starting to smoke. Red turned, pointed to the door. They left, moving swiftly, the outer basement flickering with flame light.

The firing from outside was still going but only in sporadic bursts. No Thompsons. Parnell held his wristwatch close to his face: 5;18. They moved to the main entrance, stealthily peered out. The rain had lessened. They could hear an artillery barrage going, very faint, the wet air seeming to carry it in off the faraway sea.

Parnell studied the sky, blackness up there, without seam. But then he noticed a difference in density, to the east, the overcast lighter, softer. *Dawn.* He turned around, looked back down the hall. Orange flame light flickered from the stairwell as the fire from the lower room began creping out into the main basement.

Keppler wrote very quickly, a corporal holding a flashlight on his notepad. They were scrunched down in a shell hole forty yards upslope from the jailhouse. His oil pencil dashed through raindrops on the plastic sheet.

Finished, he scanned the note. It said, *Must have reinforcements. Men and armor. Trapped partisans. San Vittore.* He signed it, tore off the sheet, and shoved it into the corporal's hand. "Find the nearest field unit," he snapped. "See the senior officer, no one else. You understand that? No one *else.* Give me your weapon."

"Yes, *Herr Hauptfach.*" The soldier handed over his machine pistol.

"Go! Go!"

The corporal climbed out of the shell hole and disappeared into the rain. Keppler checked the gun's load. He lay out on the muddy side of the hole and peered across at the jail. His buttocks were still throbbing but not badly now. One of his section sergeants suddenly came sliding down to him.

The major swung to him. "Well?"

"It is impossible to deploy, *mein Herr.* We have no idea where they are."

Keppler cursed. Amateur soldiers, fit only for *das Klo,* the shithouse. "Then concentrate fire on the jail, *Scheisskerl.* I want those men in there."

"Yes, *mein Herr.*" The sergeant crawled out and ran off.

Seventeen

At 5:30 that morning, *Artz-Hauptmann* Maximilian Sonne-mann, a captain attached to the *Standortarzl,* or garrison surgeon section of the Hermann Goering Division, had sped alone in his tiny Fiat convertible up the long, oak-lined Monastery Road to the Abbey of Monte Cassino, the road slick with rain and mud runoff.

Up close, the structure was massive with high somber walls and rows and rows of windows, which were now a dull silvery in the approaching dawn. It sat at the very tip of Monastery Ridge, a fifteen-hundred-foot-high promontory that extended out from the Abruzzi Mountains, the structure U-shaped with numerous wings, cloisters, and grand stairways. The main road from the valley wound up the relatively gradual western slope, circled the abbey grounds, and then entered through a huge gateway guarded by gigantic brass doors.

Because of its height and prominent position, the abbey had a completely unobstructed view of the entire southern and western floor of the Liri Valley. To its east were numerous barren, rocky ridgelines, and steep precipices that folded down to the valley floor and the higher peaks of the Abruzzi Mountains. A dirt road led northeast from the grounds to dense forestland.

Sonnemann reached the main gate. The single word PAX

was carved in its stone arch. All along the outside of the wall, he had seen refugee hovels made of rocks and brush, peasants fleeing the fighting in the valley below.

A monk in a black cowl swung one of the brass doors open and waved him through. Another monk on a bicycle, this one easily six and a half feet tall, led him to the entrance to the monastery's central cloister. The monk's name was Dom Matrinola, the Abbot's secretary. Sonnemann parked beside a water garden and followed the man into the cloister, which was filled with majestic stairs and statuary like a Roman forum. They passed through an even more elaborate basilica and then descended a spiral staircase to the basement.

There were dark, dank corridors with doorways into monks' cells and one on the west end that entered the Crypt chapel where Saint Benedict was buried. Many of the cells were now being used to house sick refugees, ragged women and children who silently watched the uniformed captain stride past through air that was freezing cold.

To Sonnemann, however, this enclave of magnificent buildings was sublime. Built in the sixth century by Saint Benedict, it was the mother abbey of the Benedictine order. But it wasn't religion that had brought this thirty-nine-year-old German officer here. It was instead the immense treasury of artworks and a magnificent archive that drew him. From childhood, Maximilian Sonnemann had possessed a deep passion for art and archeology.

The secretary-monk ushered him into a small, even colder room. At one time it had been part of the abbey's museum. There were shelves containing religious artifacts all over and the place had the feel of a dissecting station in a mortuary. Now it was the temporary office of Gregorio Diamare, the Abbot of Monte Cassino. He was seated behind a high, narrow desk the color of mold, a stooped, withered-faced eighty-year-old with a protruding lower lip and watery eyes.

The German captain braced before the desk and clicked his heels. The sound was like a .22-caliber rifle shot. "Thank you for seeing me," he said.

The abbot nodded and in perfect German said, "Please, sit." Matrinola withdrew.

The officer settled himself into an antique Arabesque chair and politely waited for the abbot to open the conversation. Diamare tented his skeletal fingertips. "You are a . . . captain?"

"Yes."

"And what can I do for you?"

"First, let me extend my regrets that this war has intruded into this peaceful place." His voice contained a slight hint of contempt.

Diamare nodded. "Indeed." Though the monastery and its grounds had not yet been physically touched by the conflict, the war had indeed affected it deeply. Its funicular, which hauled cargo and visitors to the top of the 2,500-foot mountain, had been destroyed by artillery that cut off its supply of necessary items from the towns of the Liri Valley. But the rush of refugees seeking sanctuary there had become a major problem. They were rapidly depleting its food supply.

Sonnemann said, "I have the unfortunate obligation to inform you that the fighting is about to intrude even more."

Diamare's old eyes narrowed. "In what way?"

"The abbey will soon become a battleground."

The abbot sat forward, shocked. "But why? Your own field marshal Kesselring gave the Vatican assurances it would remain untouched. He placed a three-hundred-meter boundary around it to keep your troops from entering."

"He is rescinding his order. Units of my own division are already preparing to enter the facility."

"Madre di Dio!" the diminutive monk cried out. He shoved himself to his feet, began agitatedly quartering the icy room, murmuring disbelief.

Sonnemann waited, impatiently tapping his fingers on the polished edge of his chair. Finally, he said, "If I may go on. I didn't come merely to tell you about the order. My real purpose is to save your art treasury and library." He nodded toward the shelves. "Even these sacred reliquaries."

Diamare glanced up. "What? What?"

"Your artworks and the archive. I wish to take them to a safer place."

"I don't understand."

"General Conrath has given me permission to remove them to your Abbot Primate in Rome."

"Oh, yes," the old man said vaguely. "Yes, of course."

Sonnemann's voice took on an even sharper brusqueness. "There's very little time. The moment the enemy realizes we have occupied the abbey, it will become a prime target. Their bombs and artillery will destroy it. *And* the priceless things it contains."

The abbot stared at him, then returned to his chair. "Will your troops occupy the monastery itself or only the grounds?"

"Both." He shrugged. "It would make little difference either way."

"What of the refugees?"

"They'll be trucked to work camps in the north."

"But surely not my *doms,* my monks?"

"Yes, they also."

"Impossible! We can never leave this place. We are forbidden by oath."

Sonnemann grunted. "A bit of advice. The Gestapo has been assigned to the removals. Your oaths will mean nothing to them."

"They would *physically* carry us out?"

The German nodded. "Or worse."

Diamare drew back, stunned. *"Kill* us?"

The officer nodded again. "If they want to."

Diamare eased back into his chair, his eyes defiant. "Then we'll *die* here."

"That's stupid," the captain snapped. He waved his hand dismissively. "But I have no control over what happens to you. My only interest is your treasury and archive. I want you to prepare it for shipment immediately."

"But I must consult with my—"

"Damn it, I've *told* you there isn't time for petty bureaucratics. As it is, it may be too late."

The abbot's face grimaced with a look of agony. He continued to hesitate.

Sonnemann came to his feet abruptly. "I can have these items removed *without* your approval. You understand this? But I would prefer to have your cooperation. . . . Well?"

Diamare finally nodded. "Yes. I will do as you say."

"Good. We will begin the removals tomorrow. Be ready."

"Yes."

Sonnemann braced again. A cold smile touched his eyes. "War is never a pleasant business, is it?" Then he dipped his head, snapped his heels, and withdrew.

The abbot sat motionless for a long time, staring at the closed door. Finally he began to weep and then openly sob. A little old man in a cold stone room shedding tears for the sundering of a way of life, a place, that had encapsulated his soul for a lifetime and that was now on the verge of vanishing.

They carried Augustin Freidl-Real's body down to the stairs that led to the basement. In the cold his corpse was already partially stiff. They sat him down on the middle step, facing the fire that had now begun crawling along the basement walls and floor, its heat funneling up through the stairwell, feeling good in the frigid air. Since they couldn't give him a proper burial, Parnell felt it would be better he burn, down into ashes, than have the Krauts mutilate his corpse, something they had recently started doing in furious contempt for the Resistance fighters.

They stood looking down at him, one of them yet not one, a young, arrogant man fighting against something in common. Finally, Wyatt and Angelo went back upstairs. The gunfire from outside had slowly diminished and finally stopped.

Red felt he should say something. What? Good-bye? A senseless phrase. Instead, he knelt beside the body and lifted Augustin's chin. He drew a sign of the cross with his thumb on Real's forehead, like the priests in Leadville used to do on Ash Wednesday when he was a boy. It seemed appropriate.

Light was beginning to seep into the ripped building, dim and gray-wet. He stood near a shell cavity near the front and peered out. Fog had moved in with the morning cold. It lay out there like a pulsing, drifting blanket of snow. At least *that* was a break, giving cover when they moved.

But they certainly couldn't go the way they'd come in, too many guns homed to it. They'd have to exit out the back somewhere, disappear before the Krauts started doing what normal frontline troops would have already been doing, coming after them in a concerted effort, probing out the different teams and eliminating them. These didn't even seem to have mortars or sapper teams.

Still, he knew they were in some trouble here. He had his three separate teams scattered in a decimated town full of similarly scattered Krauts. No specific lines to cross or defense perimeters to breach and withdraw from. For once the manuals on insertion-extraction technique had been off base, their always calling for the setting up of separated security fire teams. But that had broken his force unity. No, what he should have done was leave two men at the rally point, pick out primary and secondary exit routes, and then go in with the rest, maintaining close support, maximum firepower, and unit integrity during the withdrawal while still having a secure escape route.

A lesson for next time, Jackie Boy.

They quickly found a rear exit, a small, cold, somber room in the right rear of the building. It had no windows, no furniture, only a sixteen-by-sixteen-inch beam just below the ceiling. There were rope burns on the top side of the beam above the exact center of the room. The chamber had obviously been used for hangings.

A portion of the wide wall had been blown away, fog seeping in now. Across a small alley was the side of another building. They quickly crossed into it. It was a church. The entire roof had caved in, bricks and beams right down on the altar and front pews. Pools of rainwater had formed down under the debris and there was the soft chittering of rats.

On the other side of the church was its graveyard. Ancient statues and tilted headstones, gray black with moss, protruded above the fog layer amid leafless trees, their branches like jagged ink lines against the fog. They moved through it, stumbling over hidden tombstones and small wire enclosures, some with long-wilted flowers draped over the markers. Incongruously, a rooster suddenly crowed from some secluded niche.

The road they had come in on earlier ran in front of the graveyard. Outside the town it cut through deep meadow grass and then up into the line of trees. They paused for a moment beside the cemetery gate, its rusted wrought iron dripping with condensed fog.

"I'm gonna signal withdrawal," Parnell whispered to Bird. "We'll wait here till the others pull back this far and then make a break for the trees."

"Sol and Smoker can get out on the south side easy," Wyatt said. "But them other boys is pretty deep."

Red nodded. "If they're not out in ten minutes, we go get 'em."

He moved back into the graveyard and squatted beside a black angel. Lifting his Thompson, he fired three times, spacing the shots. Instantly gunfire erupted from all over, muzzle flashes in the fog like the grins of jack-o'-lanterns. Bullets clipped branches over his head, whined off headstones. *Son of a bitch.* He hit the ground, crawling. Bird emerged out of the fog, then Angelo.

Red looked back toward the road, the fog shifting slightly, drifting through buildings on the other side of it like water flowing upward. A single chimney stood out. A line of crows, perched along its edge, had scattered away, cawing.

* * *

For the past few minutes Kaamanui had been watching the landscape slowly emerge out of the darkness, overhead the rain clouds, low, beginning to turn a sullen gray black. Fog had formed. It settled into crevices and holes like soft cream and made the air dense and wet-cold, which went deep into his tissues.

Still, it had been almost pleasant sitting behind his huge chunk of bomb debris, Smoker over there about ten feet under the fog, and the Germans occasionally firing away, useless shots that simply disturbed the predawn stillness. They were greenhorns, Sol decided, jerk-off service troops who knew none of the intricate cohesions and movements involved in street fighting.

Then came Parnell's withdrawal signal, the three spaced shots cracking out there. It was instantly followed by a fusillade of German fire, jumpy gunners cutting loose. He saw Wineberg's crew-capped head lift out of the fog like a diver surfacing. He made a pistol of his fingers, pointed up the slope: *time to go.*

They had crossed less than fifty yards when they were taken under fire by what sounded like three riflemen, single shots from Gewehr 98 carbines, the sounds of the men slamming their bolts home clear after each shot.

Sol found defilade behind a wall. A moment later, Smoker came skittering over. Kaamanui pointed to the right, flashed his open hands three times: *thirty yards.* Smoker nodded. They separated and moved toward the enemy gun position, both crawling, belly in deep, frigid mud, the ground smelling of ammonia, sharp and cold in the nostrils.

There was a cow shed, wattle and mud. Inside were bundles of wet hay. Sol peered around the edge. The fog layer was in motion, movement down under it. A helmet appeared, dropped out of sight. Another. There was soft murmuring. The muzzle of a rifle poked up through the fog for a moment.

He moved to the side until he could see Smoker again,

signaled that it was a slit trench, and made a fist, extending his thumb and little finger, telling him they would use the standard squad trench-clearing maneuver. Again Wineberg nodded silently.

They used two grenades, cooking off two seconds of the four-second delay before heaving them. The things exploded almost immediately, sharp reports like two twelve-gauges going off right on the other side of the cowshed and mud and rock fragments whistling through the air.

They charged around the sides of the shed, Sol on the up-side, Smoker to the right, going fast but feeling their way over the hidden ground. Twenty yards out, Smoker disappeared under the fog, going to his belly and rolling, right over the lip of the slit trench and down into it, landing on fallen bodies that had that thick, heavy sound and feel of dead men. He rolled, coming up, his clothing covered with bloody tissue, just as Sol opened up at the other end of the trench, the rounds smacking into mud with a hollow sucking impact.

They heard a man whimpering. A gray *Waffen* SS tunic suddenly appeared, the soldier running away. Wineberg put his muzzle sight on him and fired. The soldier disappeared. Another round of firing came, this time concentrated on the grenade blasts and their Thompsons.

Both men lay in the slit trench. Something was directly in front of Sol's face, a section of bloody rib, shredded tissue, the bones white as new porcelain. Bullets tore the cowshed apart. The firing continued for several minutes, then slowly tapered off again. Voices called, echoing muffledly in the fog.

Ten minutes later, Kaamanui and Wineberg were moving up, deeper into the town toward the jail building.

Major Keppler raged, down in the little cavern of a gun nest into which he'd moved from the shell hole. He knew those three separated shots had been a signal. The scum were pulling out. He screamed at the gunners to continue their fire. Spent cartridges whirled, slapping against his winter jacket.

He sat there, like a pig in a wallow, feeling frustrated anger pound against his temples. *Imbeciles! These make-believe soldiers, clerks, and toilet detailers fit only for polishing the boots of real warriors.* In his frenzy he even questioned the thinking of his superiors for stripping him of his experienced men.

He had already dispatched two riflemen to order his non-coms to move forward with concerted fire, flush out the filthy partisans, and kill them one at a time. Gut them, hang their bodies up for the buzzards or the wolves.

Where was that damned runner and help?

Suddenly a fat, thick-glassed *Unteroffizier,* a corporal, came crawling through the fog. He was panting with anxiety and exertion. He had pale blue eyes. He rose, seeing the major. *"Mein Herr,"* he croaked. "Sergeant Luden says we must mass our weapons. He requests—"

Keppler slapped him with the back of his clenched fist, right across the jaw. The corporal recoiled. His glasses fell off. The major continued pummeling him, kicking him with his boots, growling. No one interfered, the soldiers staring, silent.

At last he stopped. The fat corporal cowered. "Get back to your position, you brainless *ox,*" Keppler bellowed. "Inform that *schwein,* Luden, I will personally shoot him between the goddamned eyes if those partisan apes escape. Do you hear me? Do you hear me?"

Murmuring, "Yes, sir, yes, sir," the corporal hastily crawled away, disappeared back into the fog. Two grenades went off, somewhere far over to the right, followed by the chatter of American automatic weapons.

The officer whirled about, stared at the two machine gunners, their heads bobbing up and down, trying to see. "Fire! Fire!" he yelled at them.

One turned, his face ashen. "I cannot see a target, Major."

Keppler picked up a chunk of bomb shrapnel and hurled

it at the man. It plinked off his helmet. "I say *fire,* you blithering coward. *Shoot!* And *keep* shooting!" The machine gun opened up.

Verdammte Scheisse! Where in God's name is that runner?

It had become like a child's game, but so much deadlier. Fountain and Laguna were playing peekaboo with two, maybe three Krauts on the other side of an automobile repair shop.

The little building had been completely untouched by the Allied artillery shells. It sat out there in the fog like the single lucky house missed by a tornado, surrounded by ruins. A chain hoist still hung from a lifting frame. There was a pile of spare parts, engine blocks, wheel hubs, chassis iron, poking above the fog like a little tropical mountain in a white sea.

Earlier, hearing the withdrawal signal, they had begun working their way to the east, back toward the entry road, squirming between boulders of shell debris and sundered walls. They had just skirted a small well, the wall stones polished and black-shiny from the fog, when they caught the sound of Kraut talk, back and forth, somewhere close behind the auto shop.

They tried to pass off its flank, but the Germans fired at them, drove them back to their defilade. They tried the other side with the same result. They were blocked. Listening intently, they tried to pinpoint the precise enemy position. The fog diffused sounds, distorted direction.

They hand-talked. It was necessary to take out the position so they could get past. They, too, agreed on the trench-clearing technique. They positioned themselves, checked their clips, untaped grenades, cooked off, and heaved them, both coming up, legs braced to charge.

At the precise moment their grenades went off, their legs already starting forward, a German stick grenade came tumbling through the air over the roof, its porcelain head black as a chunk of polished coal and its wooden handle serrated with antipersonnel grooves.

Weesay, the first to see it, bellowed, "Grenade! Grenade!" and hit the ground. When the *stielhandgranate* went off, it sent mud and wood and porcelain slivers out like bullets.

Goddammit.

Laguna quickly unhooked another grenade, cooked off, and threw it, angling its trajectory slightly to the right. Before it could go off, another stick grenade sailed over the shop roof. It landed behind a stack of oily wooden blocks, went off.

El pendejo!

A German voice abruptly called in badly accented Italian, "'*Ey, partisione, va a farti una fregata!*"

Cowboy glanced over at Weesay, the Mexican's mouth going, What the fuck did he say? Then he made a fist and moved it rapidly up and down in the motions of masturbation. Was *that* it? Cowboy nodded. The Krauts had just called them partisans and told them to go jerk off.

Cowboy touched his mouth, then pointed toward the Germans. Laguna bobbed his head up, down: *okay*. Fountain prepared another grenade, then cupped his hand around his mouth and shouted in his best New Mexico cowboy-border Wop, "Eat this, you fucking asshole!" He flung the grenade, twisted to the side, and dove behind the pile of spare parts.

A third German *stielhandgranate* came over the roof and landed exactly where he had been squatted.

Before the crack of its explosion had dissolved, he and Weesay were moving, around both ends of the auto shop. They found three German soldiers in their camo gray winter tunics slowly coming to their feet, looking upward. Cowboy cut the first one down. The man sank to his knees, looked at him, and then fell back into the fog.

Weesay's sideways spray stitched a bloody path across the chest of a second man, blew him right off his feet. The third soldier, farther back than the others, turned and dodged behind a partially dismembered wall. Laguna's bullets sheared off chunks of rock right behind him. The little Mexican started after him but abruptly pulled up as Fountain gave a sharp whistle. He glanced back at Cowboy, there in the fog holding up his hand, palm out: *listen, listen.*

There was nothing at first. Then, in a surging burst of sound, came the unmistakable metallic clanking and engine whine of an approaching tank.

It was a Mark III, black and gray, coming at full speed up the road to San Vittore di Lazio. In the gray dawn, through the mist of a fresh rain, it plowed through the fog layer like some mindless robot, the sound of its tracks clanking and wracking and the fog cleaving away and over its hull like drifting smoke.

It began to slow as it neared the outskirts of the town and finally stopped about 250 yards away. It sat there, the exhaust heat from its Maybach HL 120 TRM gasoline engine making a glassy shimmering that immediately condensed into a white plume. The gun turret pivoted slowly with a faint squeak of metal on metal. The vehicle had a black-and-white German cross on its Glacis plate, visible now as the 75mm cannon began traversing slowly, a tiny lateral arc, the gunner testing his ranging motors.

A loudspeaker blared. "Major Keppler, spot your prime targets with tracers."

Immediately two machine guns opened on the cemetery. After a prolonged burst, they both fell silent. The tank's turret swiveled back to straight ahead as the vehicle leaped forward again, coming directly up the main road, crushing debris, grinding and banging loudly in the sudden stillness.

It took up a position beside the jailhouse, skidding around into firing position. The first 75 round boomed, a *thrumphisss* as the projectile blew out, hurtling through the air and collapsing it with an earsplitting cracking. The round struck in the center of the graveyard. A brilliant geyser of flamed mud lifted through the fog, the fog itself parting at the explosion site, forming a ring in the concussion wave.

The second round hit a tree, blew it apart. Again and again, the tank fired, the impacts fanning across from entrance to rear. One of the rounds struck the corner of the church building, shattered it into a thousand chunks of brick and mortar.

Now it moved forward thirty yards and fired again, its MG-34 machine gun joining in, raking the cemetery. One of the cannon rounds had started a fire. It made the fog glow reddish like the bottom lights in a swimming pool filled with chalk dust.

From back in the ruins, German soldiers were slowly rising, moving toward the tank, fanning to the sides to exploit its barrage on the graveyard.

The first cannon round had filled the little alley with flying mud and rock slivers from the gravestones. Parnell and the others had been trying to work their way through the rubble on the opposite end of it, squirming through tunnels and shattered seams. Now they lay still, listening to the roar of the rounds slamming into the cemetery.

Red's eyes were ablaze. He couldn't tell the exact position of the tank, because it was back up the street and hidden by the church wall, its sound bouncing off stone surfaces. *Shit,* now they were in real trouble. That son of a bitch could hunt them out, team by team.

They had to destroy it, and very quickly.

He glanced over at Wyatt. He didn't give any order, didn't have to. He pulled a grenade from his harness just as the 75 stopped firing. They heard the tank moving. A moment later, it appeared beyond the edge of the church wall, huge out there, hull plates grimed with mud, the fog almost to its top treads. It stopped, began firing again, the barrel of the cannon canted down nearly to the top of the driver's plate.

Parnell lunged forward, Wyatt and Cappacelli right behind him. They ran hunched over to the upper road end of the alley. The tank's machine gun was still hammering away, raking the graveyard. He tossed his Thompson to Angelo and went to his hands and knees, down in the fog. Sharp rock chips lacerated him. He faintly heard German voices calling, farther back, somewhere near the front of the jail. He reached the edge of the road and was immediately into its muddy ruts.

The cannon fired again, its blast seeming directly over his head, filling the fog, the linked rapping of the machine gun going and going, seeming hollow by comparison. He abruptly ran headlong into the tank's fifth bogie wheel, its rubber tires and sprockets coated with chunks of mud, the hub hammer-marked. Once more the 75 went off, making the tank jerk back in recoil, the bogie wheels squeaking and the vehicle's suspension bouncing it forward, then backward, finally settling. He stared into the tread bay, solid with crusted mud, seeming so deep, smelling of hot iron and engine oil

He scooped off the grenade tape, pulled the pin. Reaching over the bogie tire, he slid it down between the hub and torsion bar, felt it jam. Quickly, he threw himself back, twisting his body, going down again, starting to crawl back toward the edge of the road.

The tank engine growled suddenly, climbed in pitch. He felt the monster move, shaking, gathering energy down through its driving wheels. They began to turn, the thud of treads so close to him, an arm's length away. The brakes screamed as the driver whirled the behemoth around.

The outer edge of the tread at the point where it climbed up to loop over the rear driver slammed him square in the ass, a horse kick that sent a shaft of pain up through his sphincter muscle, through his gut, and into his solar plexus, blowing the wind out of his mouth and throwing him four feet forward. The tank lurched off back up to the main road.

Gasping for breath, he sucked and sucked at the air, couldn't grab it, the thick, spent oil stink of exhaust fumes all around him. Yet his arms and legs continued working, crawling, pulling himself through the mud. He heard his grenade go off, a clear and sharp crack, unmuffled, lying out there in the road. *Godammit!* The Kraut tank had shaken it loose. Heavy balls of mud rained down onto him.

Then hands were hauling him forward, over the rutted edge of the road, up onto crumbled rock. He came to his feet, his lungs finally pulling in air. They moved together along the alleyway, voices still shouting, and dove back down into the rubble piles on the far end.

When Laguna heard those tank treads coming, he thought, *Now the big boys show up.* He and Cowboy looked at each other. Fountain put his hands out, palms open: *no more grenades.* Weesay himself only had one left.

They rolled away, squatted down behind a low wall, listening, finally getting the direction of the incoming armor. And there it was, highballing along the downside road, black and gray, plowing through fog in the early dawn light.

He watched it come, feeling his belly go tight. All foot soldiers felt instant terror whenever armor came at them. But for Weesay, behind the fear was a rush of challenge in going up against these steel monsters. As long as he had a decent antitank weapon in his hands, a bazooka or rifle grenade, slamming in a round with a high-explosive hollow charge and flash pellets, boring a red-hot hole through a tank's most vulnerable spot, and flat-out *frying* Kraut *cajones* inside. He'd taken out two tanks in the past and both times had felt this exhilarating feeling, man against machine, whipping ass.

But this one was going to be different. All he had were .45-caliber rounds and one frag grenade. Still, if he got in close enough, he could blow a bogie wheel or even ram the grenade down its cannon barrel.

The tank hauled to a stop fifty yards from their position, sat there big and solid, its engine grumbling. A loudspeaker blared from it, the tank commander talking rapidly. Immediately, Kraut guns began blasting away, marking targets. The tank waited a moment, then came on again. It rumbled right past them, thirty feet away.

He noticed it was a neatly designed thing, a Mark III, though he knew that this model was almost obsolete now, already pulled from the panzer regiments' Table of Equipment, this one probably just a platoon ammo runner. But its turret *was* sleekly shaped, square-edged with a huge counterweight on the stern, sitting up there on the hull like a stevedore's cap on top of a loaf of bread. The cannon and machine gun were swiveling slowly, the German cross and a number 7 painted on the turret coming around.

They both spotted the same thing at the same moment. As the tank had passed, it churned up the fog, lifted it eight or ten feet above the ground directly behind it. They exchanged quick glances and then took off, into its foggy wake, running, moving in close, and reaching out until their fingers touched the vehicle's rear plate, the gentle curve of it, the steel plating rough and the radiatorlike coils of its cooling vents over on the side scorching hot. Like two blind men holding on to a guide with the engine heat rolling out from under the tank and over their boots, they stayed attached to it, invisible, all the way across the town.

Suddenly, it stopped, snapped to the left, its brakes squealing. The big 75 opened fire, jacking the hull back sharply, a *whooshing* crack as the round went out. They hurriedly dashed to the left and were instantly out of the wake fog, their torsos in plain sight, running bent forward. They went to their bellies, crawling, the 75 going off again as they went down under the uprights of what looked like a partially demolished loading dock across from the side of the jailhouse, the stink of something dead under there and the collected mud and water pools like greasy paint.

Inadvertently what the tank's appearance had done was coalesce the scattered crews of Blue Team, drawing the three squads together like a pride of female lions homing to a rampaging rhinoceros in concentrated retaliation.

Kaamanui had watched and listened to the Mark III come clanking into the town, heard the loudspeaker, the *Waffen* Krauts telling the tank commander what they wanted him to shoot at, and then the paced slam of that big-bore 75 going at something behind the jailhouse. He could even hear the metallic, sliding clink of the 75's breach ejector working and the empty casings tumbling, clinking, onto the interior deck. He realized it *had* to be Parnell and his crew back there.

Sol hated tanks. The goddamned things coming at you could crush you like a peanut shell. And now the fucking Krauts were making them even bigger and more powerfully armed, Panthers and Tigers with long-barrel 88s and vertical and lateral armor plating a hundred millimeters thick against which bazookas and rifle grenade projectiles bounced off of as if they were .22-caliber rounds.

But not this little son of a bitch, he thought, a Mark III with its one vulnerable plating spot, right up there on the left side of the turret.

He twisted over, pulled up his mud-soaked demo pouch, whispering, "Hey, Smoker," Wineberg popped up out of the fog layer, it feeling colder now, thicker. The front of his jacket was filthy with blood and chunks of human tissue, black as pitch. He scooted over.

"We gonna take out that prick," Sol said to him. "Right now. I think they've homed on the lieutenant." All the time his hands were working, opening his demo pack to take out two of his kilo-sized packets of plastique charges, five pounds of crystal-blue ANFO-P dynamite. He put it between his big palms, kneading it, warming it. "I'll punch a hole through that turret plate. When it blows a hole, you hit 'em with a frag."

Smoker dipped his head. In his grimy face, his eyes were bright, his jaw working, his blood up.

Sol quickly completed making up the charge, the plastique flattened now. He reformed it into a ball and then molded a cone cavity in the bottom, two inches deep with a forty-five-degree angle on the cavity walls and a long slit in the bottom. Then on the upside, he inserted an M-61 nonelectric blasting cap and cut a two-foot-long piece of time-fuse wire from his small roll. It had a three-second-a-foot burn rate, six seconds after lighting off to clear away. He crimped the time fuse to the blasting cap, wound the lead-off portion around the charge, and tucked it into his jacket, against his skin to keep it warm.

He closed his demo pouch and picked up his weapon. "We'll have to draw the bastard in close first." He lifted slightly, scanned the town's shattered buildings, ducked back. "Take position about forty yards on the right. When you're set, we'll open on him. Give 'em enough of a burst to make him spot us. He'll come right at us, try to run us down, save his magazine. After you frag him, if we get separated, head for the back of the jail. That's where Parnell and his crew are."

"Right."

It took them five minutes to take position, all the time the tank shifting and firing, blowing walls and rubble piles as it methodically worked its way deeper into the town, the *Waffen* troopers, eight or ten of them firing intermittently, following behind it.

When it was fifty yards away, he and Smoker opened on it simultaneously. Their slugs ricocheted uselessly off the plating. The tank's machine gun cut to the right, blasted away, Sol flat down as the rounds went slamming close overhead, striking stone, tearing it apart, the air alive with hot metal. The tank continued coming in until it was thirty yards away.

The machine gun stopped. He could hear its swiveling motor whining again, the gunner traversing to the left to lay fire onto Smoker's position. He swung the Thompson onto his back and pulled a grenade off his harness in the same movement, ripping off the safety arm tape. The tank's 75 fired again, sounding horrendous. He saw the flash of the round's impact, over there where Wineberg was. *Jesus!* Then he was up and running, his boots hitting unstable ground, dodging what he was able to see.

Christ, don't let me trip.

He struck a large stone, a shock going up through his knee. He fell, rolled over jagged rock, but was instantly up, the adrenaline sucking any pain away. Behind the tank, the trailing German soldiers were turned toward him, snapping up their weapons. He dropped below the fog layer, rolled to his right over more jagged stones, paused to pull the grenade pin, hearing the arm snap up, the fuse sizzle lost in the sharp rifle shots as they fired at him. A slug creased along his shoulder, burning, another clipping through his watch cap, tearing it off his head.

One-one-thousand . . . two-one-thousand . . .

He rose, hurled the grenade. Two seconds after it left his hand, it exploded in the air almost over the Germans. Fragments whipped through the air, banged into the stern of the Mark III. Then Smoker was firing at the soldiers.

He's still alive.

Sol crossed the remaining ground to the tank in what seemed a sluggish passage of time, seconds drawn out like taffy, in slow motion, his body moving sluggishly, too. Bullets went by him, not many, like arrow shafts zipping past. At last he was there, leaping onto the second bogie wheel, hurling himself up. His knee struck a thick control cable conduit on the turret combing.

He stretched out, grabbing for a handhold, felt the 75's breech cup, the barrel, held on. It scorched his palm. The machine gun barrel was right there over him, the perforated barrel jacket fuming heat waves as it swiveled toward him. He slid under it, swung back, pulling the plastique from his jacket. He unwound the piece of time-fuse wire, slapped the charge against the turret, right between the foundation coaming and the gunner's hatch, the explosive malleable from his body heat, adhering to the mud-splattered steel.

He fumbled through his jacket pocket for his Zippo lighter.

Shit, it's not there! Desperately he tried the other pocket. Fire was coming at him again from farther off, the rounds pinging and slapping against the other side of the turret. He found the lighter, flipped the top up, and spun the flint wheel. It popped into a small, blue-yellow flame.

He held the flame to the tip of the fuse wire. It caught instantly, sizzling like a Fourth of July sparkler. He threw himself backward and rolled off the tank, hunkered down tight against the bogie wheel well, mentally counting off.

The Mark III lunged ahead, its SSG77 Maybach gearbox growling. Kaamanui spun away from the treads, the bottom sections grinding backward. The charge exploded, the force of it blowing through the thin turret plating, flashing a streak of back blast over the deck.

He saw Smoker dart in front of him, heard a grenade arm snap back, the fuse hissing, and then there was a second explosion, down inside the tank, the sound muffled. He came up out of the fog, Wineberg's face a foot away as the tank kept moving ahead.

They dashed to the left, went in behind a partially crumbled wall, bullets following them. A man screamed. Sol glanced back. The Mark III's hatch slammed open, the vehicle bobbing and swaying back and forth as it climbed over piles of rubble, still going aimlessly. The gunner crawled out. His clothing and leather snug cap were aflame. He tumbled onto the deck, slapping at the fire. Smoker shot him in the top of the head.

They moved and kept moving. Through shattered buildings, across an empty lot with a leafless tree and a decapitated goat's body caught in the branches where an explosion had flung it, the hide shredding off. Then they doubled back, scattered firing far to their left now.

Within minutes, they had reached the east side of the cemetery. They stopped to listen. The firing had nearly petered out. Then, clear as a bell, came Parnell's assembly call, three sharp whistles, a pause, and three more: *rally on me.*

Creeping cautiously among shell holes and splintered tree

trunks and shards of gravestones, they crossed the cemetery. A voice challenged: "Storm." They countersigned and moved in. It was Parnell, Bird, and Cappacelli emerging from cover. Three minutes later, Cowboy and Weesay came in.

Once more a complete, cohesive team, they quickly withdrew back up the entry road and went into the grass. It was soaking wet with fog dew. High overhead the sky was a bright pewter gray now and far to the west, shafts of sunlight were visible, deeply slanted and sharply defined like the rays in a holy picture. The constant rumble of artillery fire came from directionless directions and its flashes were like heat lightning over clouds at sea.

They reached the trees, crossed the small stream beside which they had paused coming in. It rushed and churned, nearly overflowing its narrow banks, the water dusky and edged with froth. They moved upward and were soon lost in the thick stands of pine.

At 2133 hours that night, in a light snowfall, they crossed back into the American lines.

Eighteen

On this day, central Italy was not the only place on earth where blood was flowing.

On the Eastern Front, the Soviets, aided by the ferocious Russian winter, were turning back the German advance, breaking the blockade of Leningrad, and wiping out the entire German Sixth Army in the Korsun Pocket. In Burma, the Japanese Fourteenth Army began hurling its troops against British forces at Imphal and Kohima, intending to drive directly into eastern India. Farther east, American and Australian units were taking on seasoned Japanese divisions in the dense, sodden jungles of the Huon Peninsula of New Guinea; while U.S Marines fought off repeated banzai attacks on Kwajalein and Namur in the Marshall Islands.

In Italy, the war had deteriorated into a deadly stalemate. By a combination of massive reinforcements and brilliant positioning and repositioning of his troops and armor, Field Marshal Kesselring had brought the Allied campaign to a compete halt, both along the Gustav Line as well as at Anzio and Nettuno.

The Operation Shingle invasion force was now solidly

bottled up on its beachhead by the entire German Fourteenth Army. Its troops and ships of the invasion fleet were under constant bombardment and division-sized counterattacks. Day after day casualties mounted with increasing speed.

Finally, on 30 January, the American ground commander, Major General John P. Lucas, ordered a breakout. He focused his main thrust at the Highway 7 junction town of Cisterno, two miles east of the Allied lines. He assigned it to the 7th Infantry Division, the 504th Parachute Infantry operating as dismounted troops, and three battalions of Darby's Rangers. It was a slaughter with American units outnumbered ten to one. Many companies actually suffered 60 percent losses. Ranger casualties were even worse. Of the 863 men of the First and Third Ranger battalions, only six returned to the American lines.

Farther east, the Allies were still battering themselves against the Gustav Line, primarily along the Garigliano River system that included the Liri and Rapido Rivers that flowed through the great Liri Valley. As the Anzio-Nettuno situation grew steadily worse, it became imperative that a whole new offensive be mounted in this area to draw off German units from the coast.

The Brits were given the lower Garigliano, where it emptied into the sea. The upriver sector and the Rapido were assigned to the U.S. 36th Division. On 20 January it attempted its first combat crossing of the Rapido near the town of Sant Angelo. Another bloody fiasco. But General Clark, determined to gain a victory at any cost, went against the advice of his own field commanders and ordered a renewal of the attack in daylight. In less than thirty hours, the Germans had completely stopped this second crossing with tremendous loss of American lives.

Meanwhile, at the entrance to the Liri Valley itself, the American 34th Division was completely pinned down by devastating German artillery fire from the many peaks and ridges of the western Abruzzi Mountains that rimmed the valley. The two deadliest enemy gun positions were located on the summits of Monte Cifalco on the western side and the fifteen-hundred-foot Monastery Ridge on the east. Atop the ridge was the magnificent Abbey of Monte Cassino. Nothing could move into the southern end of the valley without being brought under ferocious fire by the artillery batteries on these dominating peaks.

In late January, the 34th Division, bolstered by General Alphonse Juin's French Expeditionary Corps from Tunisia, executed its first assault against the western slope of Monastery Ridge. After ten days of intense fighting, the Allies were forced to withdraw with heavy casualties.

At dawn on 11 February, the Americans attacked the ridge again from the north. This time the 34th was so badly mauled it nearly ceased functioning as a division. The following day—at the same time Captain Sonnemann was meeting with Abbot Diamare and Blue Team was withdrawing from San Vittore di Lazio—General Alexander ordered the American II Corps relieved by Lieutenant General Freyberg's New Zealand Corps, tough African veterans of the 1st New Zealand and 4th Indian Divisions.

As his units moved up to occupy the American positions in preparation for a new assault on the Monte Cassino Ridge scheduled for 14 February, Freyberg personally conducted a meticulous reconnaissance of the target. The seeming impregnability of the abbey disturbed him, although earlier reports had indicated the Germans were not in the monastery. Then he got a look at the latest intelligence data. Enemy units *were* there, it stated, and daily were increasing their force capability within the abbey grounds. He immediately called General Clark's headquarters, which was now located at the small mountain town of Presenzano south of the Liri Valley

Clark wasn't there. Freyberg spoke instead to his chief of staff, General Alfred Gruenther, angrily insisting that the abbey be brought under heavy artillery barrage and saturation-bombing before his assault. Gruenther informed him that first of all Clark couldn't order such a bombing under theater-command parameters; and secondly he was also prohibited from destroying such a religious site by specific order from Eisenhower.

Freyberg's request was flatly denied.

The previous day at 8:05, Rome time, the American chargé d'affaires to the Vatican, Harold Tittmann, had left his quarters in the Papal Apartments beside the Holy City's St. Anne's Gate and started the long walk to the office of the papal secretary of state, Cardinal Maglione. He'd been summoned scarcely ten minutes earlier while at breakfast.

Tittmann was without direct link to Washington and literally a prisoner within the confines of the Holy City. As a result, all his coded communications to the U.S. had to be handled by a Vatican courier who flew to neutral Switzerland where he transmitted them to Washington. Still, Tittman remained an important intelligence link since he often was able to glean solid data about the Germans by his contact with religious visitors to the Vatican.

The day was overcast and bitingly cold. Crossing the vast, windy expanse of St. Peter's Piazza with ice crystals glistening in its fountains, he saw the familiar sight of German *fallschirmjagers,* paratroops, lounging along the white line that had been drawn just outside the entrance to the Vatican to designate where its boundaries ended and the rest of Rome's began.

He passed under the Arco delle Compane, the Arch of the Bells, skirted the immense, ornate Renaissance beauty of the Basilica of St. Peter and went up the steps of the Sacristy and Treasury Building, which housed Cardinal Maglione's private quarters. He was quickly ushered into the cardinal's working office.

At precisely 8:30, Maglione entered, his scarlet robes glistening in the overhead lights. He bade Tittmann a good morning, thanked him for coming, and indicated for him to be seated. The room was surprisingly spare of furniture and had a corporate feel to it, like that of a senior financial executive in a large American company.

The cardinal got right to it. "I've just received some distressing news from Monte Cassino," he said in his sonorous voice. "The Germans are at this moment occupying the monastery and removing its art treasury." Marglione was a tall, almost too slender man with heavy brows, a meticulous manner, and piercing black eyes. However, with close friends he exhibited an informality and a fine sense of humor and he personally liked Tittmann, always addressed him by his first name when they were alone.

"That *is* disturbing, Your Eminence," Tittmann said. "But, frankly, a bit surprising. Didn't General Kesselring promise the Holy Father this would *not* be done?"

"Apparently that promise has been abrogated," Maglione said with an ironic twinkle in his eyes. "There's more. Abbot Diamare and his monks will also be removed." Now his gaze took on the deep intensity of a viper scenting the night air. "A better word might be *kidnapped*. More ominously, the abbot's informant strongly hinted that they might even be murdered by the SS."

"Good Lord!" Tittmann cried. "Surely the pope will intercede."

"Sadly, he cannot."

"But, Your Eminence, this outrage—"

Maglione held up his hand. "Harold, you know the delicate balancing act the Holy Father has been forced to play with the Nazis. He can't risk antagonizing them at this moment."

"But this would be barbaric."

"So is it *all*," Maglione countered. He sighed. "You *are* aware that a similar fate hangs over the Holy Father, aren't you?"

"What?"

"Oh, yes. Mr. Hitler has a secret plan to also remove His Holiness and the treasures of the Vatican. To some *undefined* place in the north. For his and their . . . protection."

Again the American chargé d'affaires was shocked. He frowned, shook his head. "I *have* heard rumors. But I never gave them any validity. Such a thing would be *unthinkable.*"

"Nevertheless, it's true." The cardinal leaned forward, placed his elbows on his desk. The light played on his robes, the red shifting to a purple sheen and back again. "So, I'm asking you a favor, Harold. Contact your government immediately, inform them of this, and ask that *they* intercede."

"How?"

"I don't know. Diplomatically, through some neutral nation, perhaps. An appeal from the president. Such efforts and the publicity alone might be sufficient to deter Hitler. I simply don't know. . . . Will you do it?"

"Of course, Your Eminence."

Maglione rose. "Use my office to code your message. One of our couriers leaves for Bern in a half hour."

"All right."

"Please express our gratitude to your president."

"I will, Your Eminence," Tittmann said, his mind already framing the message.

It took nearly twelve hours for it to reach the Encryption-Decryption Division of the navy's Chief of Information Office in Norfolk, Virginia, coming from the U.S. embassy in Bern, Switzerland, since all U.S. embassies and consulates used navy code to transmit their diplomatic messages. Once the CIO did the initial deciphering, the dispatches were then sent directly to the State Department's Diplomatic Relations Division for review and dispersal.

By then it was 2:00 in the afternoon in Washington. Still, it wasn't until 6:00 that evening that Major General Bill Donovan's secure telephone in the headquarters of the Office of Strategic Services in the Pentagon rang. The call was from Admiral William Leahy, chairman of the Joint Chiefs of Staff.

Leahy personally disliked Donovan, considered him a

dangerous maverick with an ego the size of Detroit. During the African Campaign, for instance, Wild Bill had far overstepped his bounds by authorizing the bugging of the Spanish embassy in Washington. That nearly cost him his job. But he was a favorite of the president, who interceded, ordering the JCS, under which OSS operated, to simply "ignore" the breach of federal law.

Leahy wasted no time on pleasantries. "I've just talked with the president," he began in his brusque, charging way. "We've got a pissy situation. The Krauts have occupied the monastery on Monte Cassino. According to the Vatican, they might bump off the abbot, some old geezer named Diamare. At the same time, General Freyberg's making a stink, demanding we bomb hell out of the damned place before he assaults it."

Donovan was silent a moment, thinking. Then: "I don't understand something about this. Why would the Nazis want to kill the abbot?"

"Who the hell knows why that crazy bastard in Berlin does *anything?* It doesn't matter. The whole thing's about to put the president into one damned dicey situation."

For weeks prestigious newspapers like the *New York Times* and the *London Times* had begun questioning the injunctions against destroying religious sites in Italy. Such prohibitions, they rightfully claimed, were responsible for killing too many Allied troops. Some papers even went farther, calling Roosevelt a stooge for the Vatican.

Leahy continued, "The president's getting enough flak over sparing religious sites now. If this abbot's killed by either us or them, the water's going to get scalding." In addition to being JCS chairman, the admiral was also Roosevelt's chief of staff and extremely close to the president, a member of his inner circle called the Map Room Clique. "I've considered an option that might at least defuse this Monte Cassino thing. We send in a team and get that old son of a bitch out of there. Are your people up to it?"

"Hell yes," Donovan snapped.

Donovan was an ex-corporate lawyer and had once fought against Pancho Villa's raiders on the U.S.-Mexican border and was a battalion commander in World War I for which he had received the DSC and the Medal of Honor. Physically, however, he was unimposing, a roly-poly man with thick glasses.

He said, "How much time do we have?"

"Not a helluva lot. It might even be too late already."

"Do we inform the Limey?" Donovan referred to British General Henry Maitland Wilson, who had replaced Eisenhower as supreme commander in the Mediterranean in mid-January so Ike could begin the in-depth planning for the Normandy invasion.

"Not unless absolutely necessary. He'd want to start feasibility studies. We don't have time for that bullshit."

"I'll see that it's carried out, Admiral."

"Good," Leahy said. "Keep us apprised." And he was gone.

Naples, Italy
0241 hours

OSS Major Max Nunn was still half drunk when the phone in his hotel room in the Spaccanapoli District of the city woke him. He'd spent the evening with a group of officers from the 103rd Supply Battalion at a restaurant near the Dante Piazza, some of the officers friends from his lawyer days. It had been someone's birthday, he couldn't recall who.

He sat up, felt a pain like a hot knife pierce his eyes. A young woman beside him whimpered and rolled over. Her name was Chiara. She was delicate, darkly pretty, and had a birthmark just below her belly button that looked like a sailing ship.

He'd picked her up on the Piazza. The whole city was full of women offering sex for anything from silk stockings to cans of food. She told him she was a doll maker, had bathed him gently, and then given him an hour of the roughest sex he'd ever had. He was still sore.

"What is it?" he growled into the antique phone. Its mouthpiece stank of dried saliva. The room was freezing, old with peeling walls and a badly dented brass chamber pot. The call was from the duty officer of the G-2 Section of Fifth Army's occupation headquarters in Naples. He informed Nunn that they had just received a high-priority cipher from OSS Special-Ops Section in Cairo that demanded his immediate attention.

Shivering in the cold, he quickly dressed, gave Chiara ten dollars, and then raced his jeep back through the dark city to the headquarters facility located in the Palazzo di Machiella in the hilly, once affluent Vomero District of Naples.

He read the decode, requested confirmation from Cairo, got it, and began trying to raise his agent in Caprioti. He had a hellish time; the air was filled with storm energy. It was nearly 5:30 when he finally got him, the man fading in and out. He issued his order in code, repeating it three times to be certain the officer got it precisely.

Afterward, he sat at his desk drinking coffee and feeling the tendrils of his hangover coming on strong.

They could have slept for days. But men who have the tensions of combat deep in their minds rarely do so. Blue Team awoke before dawn and sat smoking quietly and listening to the pack mules returning from the high country.

They were in a stone cowshed at a small mule park at the bottom of a range of four-thousand-foot-high stony ridges. The park was bivouacked in a small olive grove. The American officer and his enlisted men who commanded the outfit were part of the 36th Division that had been fighting the Germans for over a month in the mountains east of Monte Cassino. The actual mule skinners were Italian soldiers and they and their animals were from Sardinia.

Each night at dusk a hundred or so animals would carry

supplies to the soldiers fighting up above. The last part of the trip was so steep packers from the engaged battalions would have to carry it the rest of the way. Each day just before dawn, the mules returned with the dead and wounded.

Parnell sat near the gate of the shed, watching them come in. As usual it was raining, a fine, sleety, bone-chilling rain. The mules were small and coughed a lot. Each animal was led by an Italian soldier who went *burrrrr* with his lips to make his mule move. The NCOs wore plumed Tyrolean caps and hollered brutally at their men.

The Italians always refused to lead the mules that carried dead bodies. Instead, an American did it. The corpses were draped over the mules' backs belly-down and lashed with bungee cords. They were unloaded right beside the shed and laid on the ground in a line. There were twenty-one this morning, their faces open to the rain since dead soldiers in combat were never covered, so they could be identified.

Red felt a touch of sorrow lift through his heart, experienced a moment of anger. Yet both were neither deep nor prolonged. He just sat and smoked and watched and after a while Sol came over and sat down beside him. Neither spoke. Speech in the presence of dead men always seemed intrusive.

Dawn light was coming sulkily out of the sky. Mist drifted along the ground and the mules made weary nickering sounds, their legs invisible. The rain carried the smell of pine trees and cargo boxes and Cosmoline packing.

The outfit's CO, Lieutenant Joe-Wayne Burke, came bustling through the trees carrying a large thermos and a box of ceramic cups. He was short and stocky with a pugilist's nose and a fuming energy. "How y'all doin'?" he called cheerily, coming up. "I figured you boys could use some coffee."

Parnell gave him a big smile. "Jesus, you are *so* right."

As Burke began pouring and handing out cups, the men rose from their blankets, which were covered with gas envelopes to add to the warmth. The brew was steaming hot and deliciously sharp on their tongues.

"I finally raised y'all's OSS officer in Cap-a-ratty," Burke said. "Goddamn storms is raisin' hell with our radios. He's gonna call back at O seven hunnert. Wants y'all's AB report."

"Thanks."

"When y'all're ready, come awn down to the depot. I'm scheduled to get in some of them new winter mackinaws and buckle boots today. You boys kin hep yo'selves." Each evening convoys of trucks brought up supplies, crates of ordnance, water, K- and D-rations, medicine, and field kits. They were stored in a "depot" among the olive trees until the pack loads were made up.

Burke squatted. "Looka here, two of my drivers is bringin' me a couple quarts a' Jack Daniel's this mornin'. Y'all's welcome to share some a' that good ole Tennessee sour mash, if you're a mind."

Everybody looked up. "You serious?" Parnell said.

"Hell yeah."

"We're already there, man."

Burke laughed. "Come awn ahead, then." He turned and went back through the trees.

Everybody got up, hurrying, suddenly energized at the prospect of good American whiskey in their bellies. Cowboy Fountain paused long enough to survey his companions. "Damn," he said, "ain't we the sorriest-looking' bunch of goat ropers you ever did see?"

Wyatt chuckled. "Yeah, we sure enough *do* look like we been rid hard and put up wet."

"Talk for yourselfs," Weesay said. "I be looking' good with a *bigot estilo*."

"A what?"

"A mustache, *meng*. Like a fuckin' Jamaica pirate."

"Pirate? What in hail you gonna steal around here, Chihuahua?" Bird said.

"The ladies, baby, what you think?" He made an obscene gesture with the tips of his fingertips, rubbing them together as if he were rubbing coital fluid between them. "These Wop muchachas gonna go crazy I tickle their *casitas* with my pussy bumper."

"Pussy bumper, my ass," Angelo said, smiling. "You know what you look like, Weesay? A goddamn spic bandit."

"Hey, fuck you, *paisano,*" Laguna called back, also grinning.

Blue Team's final acceptance of Angelo Cappacelli had come slowly. No words had been said, no handshakes exchanged. Such things were unnecessary and would have been embarrassing had they been voiced. But it *did* come, Angelo having earned it, that peculiar and immensely deep bonding and trust between men who share their lives in harm's way. Now he was one of them.

They trooped out into the rain, going silently past the line of bodies, and stood around under the olive trees while Lieutenant Burke poured heavy shots of Jack Daniel's into their coffee cups. From the high ridges came the endless sounds of fighting, now so familiar to them they were ignored just as a beachcomber forgets the sounds of surf. A heavy barrage started far downslope, German artillery going after the cargo trucks as they wound their way back down the steep hairpins to the low country.

They were interrupted by one of Burke's radiomen. "Sir?" he called, hurrying through the mist. "I got Lieutenant Parnell's OSS officer on the wire. He says it's chop-chop."

The OSS man was a lieutenant named Eugene Henry. His transmission was thick with static and odd surges that sounded like gusts of wind. Parnell started to give him his after-action report on the Fratoni mission, but Henry began rapidly clicking his key to interrupt him. Red clicked back, said, "Go ahead."

"Did you get Fratoni out or is he dead?"

"He's dead."

"You get a positive ID?"

"Negative. My man was killed. But all indications are it *was* Fratoni."

"Good enough. Get your codebook out. I've got a new mission for you."

Red blinked slowly and felt his tiredness, almost an entity, thickening his body, dulling his mind, lift up through him. He was seated on a wooden ration box inside Burke's radio van, which was icy cold. The duty operator had moved aside so he could get to the radio mike. Now he was leaning on the antenna shaft eating a Three Musketeers candy bar. Red slowly took out his codebook, waited.

The static rushed into his ear. Henry's voice disappeared, then came back slowly, getting gradually louder as if he were approaching from one end of a long corridor. "Can you copy?"

Red keyed. "Go ahead."

"I'm going to code now." He did so, using the three-letter combinations, repeating each one before moving to the next. Now and then he would fade away again, had to repeat the last combination a third time to fix where they had been when he returned. Parnell scribbled on his notepad.

It took eight full minutes to get it all. Henry finished, asked, "Did you fully copy?"

"Affirmative."

"Do you need repeat?"

"Negative."

"No margin for failure, Lieutenant. Good luck to—" Lieutenant Henry vanished into a new maelstrom of static.

Parnell deciphered the message. The van was heady with the rich scent of the radioman's chocolate. His new Tactical Mission Order stated that he would immediately report to the command post of F Company, Second Battalion, 141st Infantry Regiment, which was at a position designated Point 445 near the top of the Monte Cassino Ridge. It was on its eastern flank a few hundred yards from the tiny mountain hamlet of San Onofrio.

From there, Parnell and his men were to penetrate the monastery, locate and bring out Abbot Gregorio Diamare.

Nineteen

Roccasecca, Italy
13 February 1944
0914 hours

The Gestapo captain had an abominable breath, a sourness like horse manure. He toyed with his silver fountain pen
with a death's-head on its crown, all six feet seven of him in
his resplendent black-and-silver uniform. His name was Hel-
mut Schleissner. He sat directly opposite Major Keppler and
casually asked his questions, snide-voiced, feigning arrogant
aloofness. They had been at it now for nearly forty-five minutes.

They were in an ornate room of the medieval Palazzo di
Casamani, which was now serving as headquarters for General
Frido von Senger und Etterlin, commander of the XIV Panzer
Korps. The place was overflowing with clerks and staff personnel. This particular room had gold-leaf accents in the
wallpaper, silver door handles, and fine brocaded window
curtains. Beyond the crystal panes, Keppler could see tanks
and armored vehicles and trucks moving in a vacuumed silence.

"Who exactly killed Dr. Fratoni?" the Gestapo officer asked. He had already worked this point three times before.

"I've already told you. My men killed him."

"Did you order them to?"

"No, they acted automatically. The man was attacking me."

"Did you also act automatically?"

"I attempted to draw my sidearm."

"Attempted?"

"Fratoni's daughter also began attacking me."

The Gestapo man smiled. He had large teeth and a long nose. Perhaps a hidden echo of *Judin* there? Keppler thought viciously. The captain tapped his pen onto the glass-smooth cherry-wood desktop. "I understand she *took* it from you."

"Lies."

"Yes, of course," Schleissner said coolly. He turned his head and looked out the door, watching something out there distantly.

Keppler squirmed, felt his cheeks, the dome of his bald head growing flushed. He shifted in his seat, aware of how filthy his own uniform was. Covered with mud and dried blood, the cloth was beginning to reek.

He had had to wait nearly twelve hours for the Gestapo to show up at San Vittore di Lazio to fetch Dr. Fratoni. They finally arrived in an open-backed light-armored OP vehicle. With it was an Opel three-ton cargo truck and two motorcycle escorts. There was only a single squad of Gestapo police with a sergeant in command. Watching them come up into the town in the deepening twilight, Keppler petulantly wished the enemy guerrillas were still there, to show these arrogant idiots what *real* war was like.

The sergeant spoke very little. Keppler and his men, only twenty-one left of the original forty-two, were trucked to the town of Cassino. They remained all night in the wreckage of the town's train station. Just after dawn, the area was strafed by British Spitfires, wounding two more of his men. Eventually

they reached Roccasecca. Yet even there he was not allowed
time to clean himself.

Captain Schleissner turned back. "How many partisans
were in the attack?" he asked with sudden sharpness.

"I can't be certain. Perhaps thirty."

"I've been told ten."

Keppler tilted his head back slightly, his eyes narrowed
balefully. "Captain, you are deliberately baiting me."

"Does it seem so?"

"Yes. I protest, I *vehemently* protest."

"Then tell me the truth."

"How *dare* you!" The major started out of his chair. "You
forget yourself. You're speaking to a superior officer."

"Sit *down*, Major," Schleissner shouted, his casual manner totally gone.

Fuming, Keppler sat back, aware of the ferocious thudding of his heart.

The Gestapo officer crooked his long arms, leaned forward on his elbows. "You are responsible for the loss of one
of the most powerful Resistance leaders in Italy," he said. He
paused, then added, *"Major,"* his voice low, edged with contempt. "Your security was shabby, your defenses *pathetic*.
You lost half your men to a small unit of make-believe soldiers." He hissed. "You even had your own sidearm taken
from you."

Keppler sat stunned. Yet he couldn't take his eyes from
those of the young captain. He felt a quiver beginning in his
throat, willed it back. He heard laughter from the outer hall.
It seemed to mock him.

Schleissner continued, "Except for the unfortunate fact
that men are needed at the front, you would be dead now . . .
Major."

"What?" Had he heard him correctly? They would have
executed him?

Schleissner took his elbows from the desk, pulled a sheet
of paper to him. He uncapped his pen, quickly scribbled some-

thing, speaking as he wrote: "Be thankful you're not. And also be thankful you're even being allowed to retain your rank." He looked up. "For now." He continued writing for a moment, then turned the paper and slid it across the desk. "That's your new billet."

Keppler picked up the sheet, scanned it. He glanced up, shocked. "But this is merely an artillery battery."

"Yes. Six field guns and thirty-two men."

"But I'm a major!"

"Indeed," Schleissner said. He retrieved a folder from a drawer, began poring over its contents. As he did, he said, "Report to the quartermaster for combat gear and a new sidearm. I suggest you not lose this one."

That was it. Keppler had just been dismissed. By a *captain*. He rose slowly, shakily. He stood for a moment, staring at the top of the Gestapo officer's head. It was an outrage. He wanted to speak, to bellow. He felt the quiver in his throat break free, the thing like a violent tremble beneath his skin. He could not bring himself to brace to attention. There was more laughter from the hall.

At last, he whirled and stalked out.

0953 hours

They could see it from far off and from every point on the Liri Valley floor, the Abbey of Monte Cassino, the huge structure up there on its promontory ridge designated Hill 516 from its elevation in meters, its rows of windows looking down on the plain far below like watchful eyes in the sky.

Blue Team had made a quick descent from Lieutenant Burke's mule park to the valley floor, coming down in one of his supply trucks. They passed the still-burning wreckage of two of his other trucks hit on the road by enemy artillery fire. Now they were at the divisional field headquarters of the 36th Division in the small village of Cosiliatte east of the Rapido River. The place was alive with activity as the headquarters units of the New Zealand Corps were in the process of taking over for the departing Americans.

The overall transition had gone slowly. In this sector, the New Zealander and Indian battalions were still deploying into the hills and scattered elements of the 36th were still in position up in the higher ground, battalion and company level units not yet relieved. Some, in fact, were still so close to the German lines that whenever firefights broke out, they were usually fought with grenades and bayonets instead of machine guns.

Company F, 141st Infantry, was one of these on its Point 445.

A captain named Mathew Voorhees was OSS divisional liaison. He bore an amazing resemblance to the actor David Niven and talked in brusque declarative sentences like those in a Hemingway short story. Parnell reported to his office, a bivouac tent on the edge of a cow pasture. It had stopped raining but the sky was still overcast and the air was numbingly cold with patches of snow lingering in the shadows.

Voorhees immediately had them draw new field uniforms. On this mission they would be going in as American soldiers, he explained, so Abbot Diamare would have no difficulty identifying them as Allied troops.

Afterward, he personally drove Red and his two noncoms to the village church where a young priest, Father Tommaso Leccisotti, described for them the physical makeup of the monastery and its grounds, the structure full of wings and underground passages. He was quite handsome and had been a novitiate at its *collegio* as a boy. He spoke only Italian. Voorhees did not. So the OSS captain stood around looking useless while the three Mohawkers rapidly questioned the father.

It was nearly noon when Parnell and his team left Cosiliatte aboard a requisitioned ammo carrier and headed for the command post of Second Battalion, 141st Infantry, which was up in the hills to the east of Monastery Ridge. They were weighted down with fresh ordnance in their clean chocolate

OD woolen winter clothes with scarves and gloves and American flag patches on one shoulder and the Arrowhead and T of the 36th Division on the other, yet still wearing Burke's mackinaws and clip boots. The stark contrast between their sallow, unshaven faces and their spic-and-span uniforms made them appear like some marauding force that had just plundered a military storehouse.

Three minutes after their departure, a small Piper J-3-SX single-engine recon plane dropped out of the overcast and landed in the cow pasture near the Cosiliatte HQ. As it came to a sliding halt on the soft ground, its 65 Continental engine fluttering to a stop, a British officer in a fighter flying suit and goggles popped out. He was met by the NZ Corps commander, General Freyberg.

The pilot was Lieutenant General John Harding, Alexander's chief of staff. Freyberg had been making so much noise over his demands for a bombing of the monastery, Harding had flown in from Allied Headquarters, Mediterranean, at Caserta to see if he could get the situation resolved.

Harding was a jovial officer who had been an airman during World War I and who grabbed every chance he could to fly, particularly cloth-and-wood airplanes. When he did, he always wore the same ratty leather flying cap and goggles he had used over France.

For the next hour, he studied Monte Cassino with binoculars, went over recent intelligence reports, and listened to the New Zealander's harangue. "I tell you, John," Freyberg rumbled, "I simply *will* not send my lads up that bloody hill while those Krauts are sitting there with their arses safe as sin behind those monastery entrenchments. It would be utter madness."

Harding grunted, scratched at his chin. "General Clark still maintains the Germans *haven't* occupied the monastery. So he feels that bombing such a holy site would be unnecessary and counter to American policy." He shrugged. "All his staff officers seem to agree with him."

"Ach," Freyberg scoffed, the sound like the drawing up of phlegm. "These Yanks are still *amateurs*, man. They deal with war like flamin' Hollywood soldiers. This *policy* of theirs, this preserving of Catholic holy sites, it's absolute rubbish. And they're goddamned wrong about no Germans being in the abbey. My God, John, you've seen the intel reports yourself."

"Mm," Harding said, nodding. At the moment, they were seated in one of the command tents sipping tea laced with cognac. Harding loved the combination and because of that love, always had about him the liqueur's creamy scent. "Nevertheless, this whole cock-up's put Wilson in a damned dicey place, Bernard." He eyed the New Zealander from under his eyebrows. "You *do* realize it appears to be developing into a mere test of wills between you and Clark."

"I accept that," Freyberg snapped pugnaciously. "I bloody *well* accept that. And I'll simply say this, if that publicity-hungry American fool can be comfortable sending *his* men to the mill, *I'm* not."

General Freyberg was a well-loved and heroic figure to the Brits. A strapping six-footer with a barrel chest and enormous prowess that had carried him to two Olympic medals in swimming. He had fought at Gallipoli in the Crimea and again on the Western Front in 1914, which earned him the Victoria Cross.

"How *does* Alexander and Wilson feel about this?"

"Neither one has specifically decided anything yet. But I'm certain Wilson at least is in agreement with your position."

"Then there's hope I'll prevail?"

"I would say so, yes."

"*Bloody* good-oh," Freberg cried, his face unscowling for the first time. He happily freshened Harding's cup with cognac, then glanced up. "But, aye, John, you'd best speed things along. My men are scheduled to kick off in less than seventeen hours."

"I'll get something definitive to you by this evening."

"Fair enough." The New Zealander lifted his teacup. "Bewdy, mate."

"Bewdy," Harding said.

It took Blue Team three hours to get to Second Battalion's CP, constantly winding their way upward through a rocky and barren landscape filled with the debris of combat: burned-out motorized equipment and deep shell holes filled with water that had frozen over and small clusters of graves bearing piled stones for markers.

Always to their left was Monte Cassino, its angle changing as they went higher. Twice they came under light artillery fire, just a few rounds that shuddered the ground and hurled rock slivers. Then it began to snow, heavily. They could no longer see Monastery Ridge as they moved through the vacuum formed by the soundless drift of snowflakes, the rattle and boom of battle seeming suddenly far off and of another place.

Second Battalion's CP was totally different from divisional. It was in a small stone farmhouse where frozen melons still hung along the outside rafters and the floor was dirt. Its tiny rooms were filled with stacks of ordnance crates and medical supplies.

In their gun positions outside, the troopers were dirty, their faces drawn and pale under their growths of beard and their eyes gone dull with that look of slow, emotionless shifting. The battalion's initial complement of 804 men had been diminished to 297 men and eighteen officers.

The commander, Lieutenant Colonel Clinton Kull, was sitting on his helmet in what had been the kitchen of the farmhouse. One wall and fireplace had been knocked down by shell fire and now a canvas covered the hole. Two large maps were stapled to the opposite wall and there was a small mobile telephone switchboard where a battalion clerk sat. Several sleeping bags littered the floor.

Kull was warming his hands over a can of Sterno. He was a husky man with the mangled face of a linebacker. Both he and his clerk wore mud- and bloodstained mountain division anoraks, which were reversible to white.

He watched Parnell duck through the narrow doorway, brace, and identify himself. Tiredly returning Red's salute, he said, "So you're the OSS hotshots are gonna penetrate the belly of the beast, eh?"

"Yes, sir."

"Not an enviable task." He sighed and stood up, picked up his helmet, and pulled it on over his crew cap. They left the house and crossed a dip in the ground where two dozen mules were tethered to lines strung between boulders. Several had dead bodies already bungeed to their wooden pack racks. These would be taken down out of the hills as soon as darkness came. The animals stood with their heads down, their breaths forming bursts of smoke.

They passed two machine gun positions, formed of stones and called *sangars,* then down another dip in the ground, and finally to a small promontory. Below them the snow made it seem as if it were a long drop into fathomless space.

Kull stood with his hands in the pockets of his anorak and pointed with his chin. "F Company's about a thousand yards in that direction. The CO's Lieutenant Josh Tomczyk, damn good man. But those poor sons a' bitches've been up there for two weeks. We have to send their supplies over at night, shoulder-packed." He worked his own thick shoulders like a fighter, looked up at the snowfall. "You're lucky. You'll at least be able to cross in this stuff. The Krauts never shoot at anything they can't see clearly."

"Does the lieutenant know we're coming?"

"Not yet. We can't raise him. Damned sunspots have really fucked up this mountain atmosphere." He thought a moment, then added, "Watch out when you approach his perimeter. Come from downslope. They've got wires out on the upside. Sweet Sixteen's their challenge." Kull chuckled mirthlessly. "I think the lieutenant misses high school."

Parnell squinted out there. The snowfall had decreased his visibility down to about forty yards. "Have you a compass heading to his position, sir?"

"From the farmhouse, it's dead-on 273 degrees."

"How heavily invested *is* the monastery?"

"Hard to tell from here. According to Tomczyk, the Jerries've been rolling men and gear in fast. Mostly Panzer motorized infantry and artillery units. But he also spotted some paratrooper shoulder patches. The bastards are tuning up for those New Zealanders. They know they're coming."

Parnell considered a moment but couldn't think of anything further to ask. "Well, thank you, Colonel." He drew himself erect, saluted. "We'll be moving out immediately."

Kull returned the salute, then said, "One other thing. Tomczyk sent out a probing patrol three days ago. Thing actually got all the way to the abbey's outer wall before it was spotted. You might want to use the same entry route." He looked at Red. He had brown eyes that in sunlight might have been the color of maple wood. Now they were dark and expressionless. "Well, good luck . . . Parnell, is it?"

"Yes, sir. Thank you."

They walked back to the farmhouse. Kull offered Parnell a cup of coffee. It had been made that morning. He brought it to a boil over another Sterno can. It tasted terrible.

Fifth Army Field Headquarters
Presenzano, Italy
1603 hours

Captain George Breuer, air support officer of the U.S. II Corps, couldn't believe his eyes.

Three minutes before, his secure teletype had begun printing out the updated coordinates for the Monte Cassino Ridge Bomb Safety Line, the data coming directly from the Air Mission Coordination Center at Allied Command Headquarters, Mediterranean, in Caserta. As each new coordinate came in, one of Breuer's corporals pinpointed it on the plastic overlay of a huge wall map of the entire southern end of the Liri Valley.

As he watched, a trace was slowly forming, which indicated the parameters of a new BSL. It lay less than five hundred yards beyond the front line of the advanced units of the 34th Division still in their positions on the ridge. It also completely excluded the Abbey of Monte Cassino.

As II Corps' ASO, Breuer's primary job was to establish these bomb safety lines for any planned close-support air strikes within the corps' sector. Any area that was too close to operating Allied units was marked as forbidden ground for the bombers. Until this latest change, his BSLs for Monastery Ridge had consistently allowed a thousand-yard cushion between his frontline troops and the bombers' targets. Also, under Eisenhower's order, he had always included the monastery within that safe area.

Now, even before the full trace was complete, Breuer darted out of his own Quonset and sprinted through a bevy of staff cars and armored half-tracks parked near the HQ's Main Operations complex. It was housed in hastily built Quonsets all painted forest green and scattered in a thick stand of silver pine. To the left of the HQ area was General Clark's personal trailer, also green and with its wheels anchored by fifty-gallon drums.

He approached a senior staff officer, a major named Walton. "Sir," he barked, snapping to attention, chest heaving from his run. "Permission to speak to General Clark, sir."

Walton had been staring at a thick folder open on his desk. The hut was overly warm and smelled powerfully of kerosene from heaters along the wall. He looked up slowly, as if reluctantly being drawn from a fascinating novel. He frowned. "The general's not here."

"Then I must see some other flag officer, sir."

Walton leaned back, crossed his arms. He had a pleasant

but subdued face, like a kindly high school principal who had long since lost his youthful illusions. He smiled wanly. "I take it you just received your new BSL trace?"

"Yes, sir. It's completely garbled."

"No, it isn't. The parameters have changed."

"But they cover our own lines now. And the entire monastery's in the bomb zone."

Walton nodded. "General Wilson just authorized a saturation bombing run on the entire top of Monastery Hill. Mediterranean Air Command's already scheduled it for midnight."

Breuer shook his head, dumbfounded. "We'll be killing our own men, for God's sake!"

"No, not really. They'll be going in with mediums carrying only hundred pounders. The BSL will allow sufficient safety. Besides, there are Diggers and Gurkhas up there now, not ours."

What the hell kind of statement was that?

"Then what do *I* do, sir? I haven't received any clearance from corps or even anything from General Ryder." General Charles Ryder was commander of the 34th Division.

Walton grunted. "Wouldn't make any difference. Nobody but Wilson and Eaker can change things." He gave Breuer a fatherly smile. "I suggest you just log your traces and go have a cup of coffee."

"But, sir—"

"Breuer," he said wearily, "don't sweat it, okay?"

"Yes, sir," the captain said distractedly. "Thank you, sir." He turned and walked to the door, murmuring to himself, "Jesus *Christ!*"

It was like feeling their way through an abandoned rock quarry, huge boulders and sudden, steep sheer faces, the snow pathless and always climbing with only scattered bunches of mountain shrubbery for handholds. It was bitter cold and still and Blue Team's breaths made little clouds of smoke that formed and vanished.

They moved in Indian file, each man close behind the one ahead so he wouldn't get lost in the snowfall, which had thickened. Parnell was on the point, stopping every few yards to check his compass. They came to a ravine with gravel fans along the bottom and then a sharp incline where the men had to feel for solid holds. Through their woolen gloves the stone felt like iron slag and made their fingers numb.

It took them nearly two hours to get across, Parnell angling downslope for the last two hundred yards and then working back up again. Suddenly they heard the solid crack of a machine gun bolt sliding home and a voice called hoarsely, "Who the fuck goes there?"

Red stopped dead. Softly, he answered, "Sweet." He felt the man behind him come up onto his right.

"Sixteen," the voice called back. "All right, come on in. But do it slow, bud."

F Company was scattered over a quarter-acre position, the men in rock *sangars* with canvas tent halves for cover. They were all bundled in blankets and scarves, only their stubbled faces showing, gaunt faces with hollow eyes like those of miners who had been trapped underground for a long time.

A sergeant approached Parnell carrying a Thompson. He watched the rest of the men come in, then quickly brought up his weapon, its muzzle pointed at Red's chest. The other soldiers close by also swung their guns to bear on the team. "You ain't carrying no supplies," the sergeant snapped. He squinted hard into Parnell's face. "Who the hell *are* you?"

"A special OSS force," Red answered. "Where's Lieutenant Tomczyk?"

"OSS force? What the fuck is that?" Before Parnell could respond, the sergeant barked, "Everybody on the ground."

Parnell glanced back, then squatted. The rest of the team did the same. The sergeant said to his men, "Watch 'em close." He turned back to Parnell. "You, come with me."

Lieutenant Tomczyk was asleep in his *sangar,* curled over in the fetal position with a blanket wrapped around his boots and another covering his shoulders. He sat up instantly when the sergeant touched his shoulder, automatically reaching for his submachine gun.

"Him and six others just come in, Lieutenant. They claim they're from something called OSS. They knew the challenge sign."

Tomczyk studied Parnell. The edge of a toilet tissue showed under his jeep cap. He had a round face with a cluster of freckles on his nose and very blue eyes. "What's this all about?" he asked Red. His voice had a high register to it.

Parnell introduced himself and explained the mission. Halfway though, the sergeant quietly moved off. As he listened, Tomczyk withdrew a pack of cigarettes, offered one, then lit both. When Red finished, the company CO shook his head, snorted. "Sounds nuts to me."

"What do you know about the monastery?"

Tomczyk shrugged. "The Krauts've been bringing up heavy reinforcements over the last twenty-four, maybe thirty hours. Infantry and artillery units mostly. Some paratroopers."

"Are they *inside* the monastery?"

"Oh, yeah. That's new. Before, their gun positions were always outside the main wall. They've also been trucking stuff out, lots of crates and flat boxes. Me, I think they're stealing artworks. They've also removed a lot of the refugees who were camped along the outside of the wall. Some monks, too."

Parnell grunted. "Christ, I hope the abbot wasn't one of 'em."

Tomczyk made no comment.

"Colonel Kull said one of your patrols got to the wall."

"Yeah. Sergeant Macwhorter took his squad up." He chuckled. "Crazy Scotsman. He wanted to go right through the front gate and make the whole place surrender to him. But they were seen. Place got hot pretty fast."

"When was this?"

"Three days ago."

"I'd like to talk to him."

"Sure." Tomczyk blew on his fingers through his gloves. "How you figure on getting into that building? Looks like a damn fortress."

"I spoke with a priest down in Cosiliatte, used to be a novitiate at the abbey. He told us about a couple entry points in the monastery's foundation."

"You could use Macwhorter's route in." He nodded his head toward the east. "It runs up a deep gully about a hundred yards out. The walls are steep as shit so you'll have a helluva time in this snow." He squinted out at the flakes silently coming down. "I got a feeling she's gonna slow up soon. Then you'll have bright moonlight." He shrugged. "Take your choice."

"Where're the closest Kraut gun positions?"

"Well, Hans Shit-face's up about 250 yards northeast. We give 'em names. The other one is Rudolph Rat's-ass. He's off our right flank about the same distance."

"Damn, they're in pretty tight, aren't they?"

"Yeah."

"Must be a bitch up here."

Tomczyk nodded. "Gets a little tense now and again. We pop at them, they pop at us. Sometimes we get lucky, sometimes they get lucky." Matter-of-fact.

"How long you been out here?"

Tomczyk pushed the cuff of his jacket up to look at his watch. It was 4:18 in the afternoon. "As of now, eleven days, fourteen hours."

"How come they haven't shelled you off?"

"We exchange mortar rounds once in a while. But they can't bring their big guns to bear on us. We're below their deflection maximum."

"Kull said you've got wire upslope. The Krauts got mines laid, too?"

"No, none in the in-between ground. There's not enough defilade for either of us to lay deep sections. But watch out for trip wires when you get close to their positions."

"What about San Onofrio?"

"No, nothing's there. It wasn't but a little cluster of stone houses to begin with. Now it's a pile of rock." Tomczyk turned and whistled softly. A moment later, Sergeant Macwhorter emerged out of the snowfall.

He was the one who had ordered the team on the ground and brought Red in. His face was hawklike, his stubble thick. He talked rapidly and held Parnell's gaze. He told him about the gully his patrol had used, the ravine almost sheer-walled and very narrow at the bottom. But they'd be invisible to the two Kraut gun positions, he said, until they reached a rise topped by a small stone building about a half mile away. On the maps it was called the Iannucelli House and had apparently been where the abbey's monks meditated in isolation.

Beyond the rise, the ground sloped up gradually to the foundations of the monastery. But along there, he went on, the Germans had blasted caves into the rock and were using them for storing ammunition and sleeping quarters. At the lower end of the gully, below their own position, a narrow mule path led all the way down to the valley floor east of the town of Cassino.

"Don't get caught on that trail in daylight, Lieutenant," Macwhorter warned. "Them Sausage-eaters use it sometimes to sight in their fieldpieces."

Afterward, Parnell huddled with Bird and Kaamanui, went over what Macwhorter had told him. "We'll head out at 1900," he instructed. "Everybody try and get some sleep." The two noncoms moved away.

Parnell hugged himself, blew on his gloves. Still, to him the cold was an old, pleasant friend that made him feel oddly placid. He watched the snow for a moment. Apparently, Tomczyk's prediction was coming true, the snowfall *was* thining out. He could see late afternoon light beginning to filter through it. Diffused, it made the barren landscape glow with a pale incandescence.

Lieutenant Tomczyk had loaned them blankets. Parnell

chose a rock niche and curled down inside it. The stone felt so solid, so deep, as if it ran clear to the center of the earth. He made a pillow of his demo pack and closed his eyes, went over the mission in his mind for a few moments, then picked up other mental images: a log fire and the taste of Jack Daniel's on his tongue again, the heated, urgent sensation of slipping between a woman's spread loins, the feel of . . .

The pictures disturbed him, seemed suddenly too terribly far away from this barren, frigid, stony place. He scrunched around, dug his head deeper into the snow-wet canvas material of his demo pack, and instead focused his mind only on the log fire and the snapping crackle of its flames and the sweet piney headiness of the burning wood.

In a few minutes, he was asleep.

Forty minutes later, fifteen hundred feet above where Red lay, American General Ira Eaker fine-tuned his binoculars and stared down at the huge U-shaped complex of the Abbey of Monte Cassino, slightly hazy from the last remnants of the snowfall. Still, it lay out there exposed on its promontory like a castle in a fairy tale, its walls and cloisters snow-edged and the great robin's-egg-blue dome of its basilica creamily tarnished by the last rays of the sun.

Although Eaker was brand-new to the command of the Mediterranean Allied Air Force, he wasn't happy about his assignment. Previously, he'd been in England, where he had fought the Brits tooth and nail over the most effective way to bomb the cities of Europe.

The British preferred night saturation bombing in which everything within a designated area was hit. However, the Americans, with their more sophisticated Norden bomb sights, insisted the most efficient and deadliest method was to go in in broad daylight and concentrate on specific targets. He'd been sent to Italy before he'd had the opportunity to prove his theories.

With him was Lieutenant General Jacob Devers, another

American who was now deputy to General Wilson. They were aboard a small L-5 Courier aircraft normally used to carry messages between field units. That made a lot of brass in one small plane. But they knew the danger was minimal since German gunners never fired at such insignificant aircraft, fearing to give away their positions to immediate fighter attack.

Eaker whistled appreciatively. "Lord *God,* look at that beautiful target."

"Stands out like a sore thumb, doesn't it?" Devers said.

Because of the furor General Freyberg had created by insisting the abbey be bombed before his assault, Eaker had decided to go have a look for himself. Wilson had sent Devers along for a personal report.

Eaker flipped off his autopilot and brought the plane around for another scanning run. This time he focused his attention on the flat ground and slopes outside the monastery compound, searching out telltale signs of German machine gun and artillery nests. It was difficult, the sunlight fading too rapidly.

At last, he retook the controls and they swung toward the west, Eaker shaking his head. "Those mediums won't be enough," he said flatly. The present makeup for the bombing sortie against Monte Cassino included eighty-six B-25 Mitchell and B-26 Marauder medium bombers carrying loads of hundred-pound bombs. They were scheduled to go in at midnight, less than six hours away.

Devers turned, surprised. "But that's all Freyberg's asked for."

"Too wasteful and inaccurate."

Devers snorted. "Old Jumbo's gonna get pissy if you change up this late." "Jumbo" was the nickname for the three-hundred-pound General Wilson. Under theater-command rules, the only two senior officers who could authorize or change a strategic bombing strike were Wilson and Eaker.

"Damn it, Jake, look down there," Eaker countered. "We send in those mediums at night on saturation runs, they'll put their loads all over hell." He shook his head. "No, we send in the Fortresses first. Right after dawn. Then if it's necessary, we'll put the mediums in later in the day."

Without waiting for comment, he keyed his radio, called, "Milkman, Milkman, this is L-fiver Domino, over." Milkman was the call name for the tower operations at the landing complex just outside Allied Headquarters in Caserta.

They came right back: "L-fiver Domino, this is Milkman. Go ahead, over."

"Notify Concertina BG-Com they are authorized for double-up on two-niner-niner for TS designated Candydrop. Repeat back." Two-nine-nine was the military designation for the B-17 Flying Fortress, which had been the number Boeing assigned to its original experimental model. TS: Candydrop referred to Target Sortie: Monte Cassino.

"Affirmative, L-fiver Domino," Milkman said and repeated the message verbatim. Then added, "Please relay your AC code for authentication, over."

Eaker consulted his knee board. Whenever a senior theater commander was away from his headquarters, he was given an Authorization for Command code in case he had to relay orders by radio communication. It was changed daily. He read off his present code, "Zebra-zebra-zero-fiver-Alpha. Copy?"

"We have authentication. What is your ETA?"

"One-niner-zero-zero hours. Over and out."

"Affirmative one-niner-zero-zero hours. Milkman out."

Eaker turned and winked at Devers. The light in the cabin was dim now. "Wait till those five-hundred-pounders home in on that abbey. They'll blow that whole goddamned ridge down into the Liri." He chuckled devilishly. "Then let's see what the damned Limeys have to say about precision bombing."

At 5:53, Combat Flight Operations for the U.S. Second Bomber Group attached to the Mediterranean Allied Air

Force Command stationed at the huge airdrome at Foggia in southern Italy dispatched two officers and two noncoms to call up the 144 air crews assigned to carry out the bombing sortie on Monte Cassino. Their premission briefings were set for midnight.

The fliers lived in a tent camp inside an olive grove two hundred yards from the approach end of runway 27R. Since arriving at Foggia, they'd improvised a small club, a PX, and a movie theater inside two large man-made caves nearby. Now, amid the ever-present roar of planes coming and going, the B-17 air crews left unfinished drinks and the tail end of *Stagecoah* starring John Wayne to head back to their quarters to check gear and grab some sleep.

Out on the runways, crew chiefs had already assigned their air techs for preflight systems checks on the big bombers; while over in one of the base's four powder bunkers, armament crews were beginning to work up the ordnance loads, carts of .50-caliber machine gun cases and wheel racks of five-hundred-pound demolition bombs.

Unfortunately, two hundred miles away at Allied Headquarters, Caserta, no one remembered to notify Freyberg of General Eaker's last-minute change in the makeup and scheduling of the bombing run on the Abbey of Monte Cassino.

1900 hours

Parnell had awakened several minutes before. He lay listening to the stillness of the night, such an odd thing, not a sound anywhere. The overcast was gone and the barren landscape of Point 445 was now drenched in the brightness of an early-risen moon.

It would be so easy to remain under this blanket, he thought, just stare up at the stronger stars showing amid the moon's light like distant, isolated campfires on a plain. Then he sighed and got up. Bird came up while he was hooking up his demo pack.

"Everybody ready?" he asked.

"All set, Lieutenant."

"Where's Tomczyk?"

"Yonder, where we'll be goin' out."

F Company's CO was standing in a hollow with the rest of the team, everybody motionless, waiting, their hands deep in their jacket pockets. The young lieutenant nodded as Red came up, then turned and looked toward the east.

"This moonlight could give you some trouble," he said. "The snow's amplified it. But you shouldn't have a problem until you get to the stone house. From then on, be careful." He turned back. "You want me to lob a few mortars over there just in case you have to take out those caves? Give you a little cover noise?"

"No, I think we'll try and bypass 'em. Maybe lay in some wire, though. Do they move around much up there?"

"Not really. Mostly guard mount changes. I suspect their radios are as fucked up as ours, so even if you're spotted, it's possible they won't be able to communicate the sighting. If you *do* get exposed, I suggest you take 'em out fast but quiet. A full firefight'll sure as hell bring 'em running."

Parnell settled his pack, looked up toward the monastery, just the highest points of it visible, dark and foreboding. He felt an icy breeze sift up from downslope, scattered across his face like a spray of fine snow.

Tomczyk said, "When you come back in, we'll be using a new challenge. Off Tackle." He extended his hand. "Good hunting to you."

They shook. "Thanks," Red said.

They went out in single file, Wyatt on point, Parnell directly behind him, with Kaamanui taking the drag slot. It was harder moving than when they'd come in, the moonlight and snow so similar in color they merged into a single whiteness. Still, Bird went quite swiftly, his black silhouette etched in the moonlight and the smoke of his breathing fuming over his shoulder and then dissolving.

Parnell checked his watch: 7:15. He hoped to be into the

monastery no later than 11:00. That'd allow them at least four hours to locate and extricate the abbot well before dawn.

Dawn, he thought, another day, another hill, another journey into the dark places. It seemed so endless, everything folding down into identical moments, hours, days. What the hell would tomorrow be anyway? February thirteenth? Fourteenth? Yeah, the fourteenth. Something familiar about that. What? He remembered, chuckled.

What a shitty fucking place to be on St. Valentine's Day.

Twenty

The Iannucelli house was as frigid as an igloo, the insides dense with the feel of tundric isolation, bare stone walls with just a single slit window that let in a needle of moonlight. It was a single room with stone platforms like catafalques where the monks had slept and stone kneeling benches, grooved from the centuries of lonely men lost in torment and prayer.

Squatted behind one corner of the building, Parnell looked up the slope. It slanted up about seventy yards, then flattened out into a small plateau. On the right, the level ground dropped off into a fifteen-foot bluff. He could see the entrances to two caves in the bluff wall, demolition debris scattered out front like shattered pottery.

Beyond the bluff rose the foundation of the monastery, great gray blocks of stone that merged into the main building's walls, looking thick as the world. The structure rose up so awesomely that Parnell thought, *God, it's huge.* There were six long lines of windows in the abbey proper, all gleaming blue white now, some reflecting the moon like giant irises.

Bird came duckwalking in from the other corner. "One

ringstande, Lieutenant," he whispered. A *ringstande* was a small, stone-protected gun nest. "To the left. Two men."

Red studied the up ground closer. The moonlight was so bright it fused objects into a single sheet of glowing white. But, there! he finally spotted it, the barrel of a weapon glimmering softly.

He scanned from right to left, studying the approaches to the gun position. Farther left the corner of the abbey rose, hiding the lower slope beyond. He swung back to the far right to the bluffs and the two cave entrances. Apparently there was only a *ringstande* on this side, the Krauts obviously figuring assault from here was not likely. Still, he realized it was going to be a bitch getting past this position.

Wyatt said, "Look yonder, Lieutenant. Farther left. Ain't that some kind a' groove in the ground?"

The snow made imaginary images, false ground read. Then he saw it, a faint shadow line in the snow, a ditch. Good, that would at least offer some defilade for them to get to within twenty yards of the German gun. Still, crossing the remaining ground would be murderous.

He ducked back, thinking. Finally he leaned closer to Wyatt. "We'll have to draw their fire. Blind 'em with their muzzle bursts long enough to rush the position."

Wyatt nodded.

"Hopefully, the others'll think these guys are just getting jumpy, shooting at shadows. Okay, two men in, two on the far right to draw fire. Tell 'em to watch for trip wires in that ditch. Use knives only, unless absolutely necessary. Once it's neutralized, we wait five minutes, see if anybody else opens on us."

Bird went to the ground and crawled back down to the others.

Cowboy and Angello took the ditch, squirming up slow as caterpillars, Fountain with his gloves off, feeling for trip wires, his fingers getting numb fast. They'd pause every few feet to listen, lying flat in the snow, their scarves pulled up over their mouths to diffuse the smoke from their breaths.

They had advanced about thirty yards when Fountain spotted a wire, tiny silvery thread shining in the moonlight about two inches off the snow. He traced it out, a double grenade set, Eihandtgranate 39s, egg-shaped, each holding four ounces of TNT. He gently explored the one on the right, concentrating hard, making his numb fingers register touch.

The grenade's small metal cap had been unscrewed, exposing the wire loop of its friction igniter. The trip wire was then clamped to the loop so that the slightest jerk on it would initiate the igniter. He took a deep breath, felt his heart pounding. Sometimes, he knew, the Krauts used tension springs on one grenade so that the moment the trip wire was cut it would ignite the other.

He slid to his left, felt out the other one. His fingers didn't register springs. *Okay, okay, here we go.* Holding the wire as gently as he could, he placed his wire cutter across it, the cutting edge directly below so there wouldn't be any pull when he applied pressure. He snipped. There was a tiny click. The grenades were immobilized. A second trip wire appeared three feet farther on. Again, he made a clean cut, defusing the two grenades. They continued on.

They were now within twenty yards of the German gun, could clearly see the soldiers' breaths, two of them, and hear their occasional murmured exchange. Cowboy held up two fingers, then sliced the air. Quietly, each man pulled his knife and lay flat again, heads down, bodies coiled to leap up, all around them the silent whiteness of the wintry night.

It seemed as if a thousand minutes passed, then one of the Germans growled something, a sharp exclamation. There was the loud metallic *chunk* of a breech lock. When the German gun opened up, the explosive sound of the rounds rolled down the slope. A short burst, then ringing silence.

Cowboy and Angello remained motionless, knowing machine gunners always laid out twin bursts first and then traversed, left to right. Another quick burst came. The instant it stopped, both men lunged to their feet and went pounding up the slope, directly toward the gun position, their heads ringing from its blasts and their own adrenaline.

Fountain went over the low stone wall and instantly plowed right into one of the Germans. Growling, he clawed for the man's face, felt helmet, felt eye socket. He dug his numb fingers into them and brought his knife to bear, ramming it deeply into the man's Adam's apple, his carotid surge blowing blood back along Cowboy's knife groove.

He was vaguely aware of Angelo right there beside him and then suddenly he saw him rolling away, Cappacelli and the other German a single shadow and the only sounds in the stony stillness the animal surge of breaths and the deep, throaty, hissing snarls of men in deadly combat.

Once more, abruptly, there was total silence, disturbed only by the drumming of their own blood in their ears, a residual ringing. Both Germans were dead, heavy dead there on the rocky floor of their stone nest, the frigid air reeking of that hot, sliced-skin smell of fresh blood and urine and the packing odor of the canvas tent cover.

Six minutes later, they saw the rest of the team coming up, following the groove in the earth.

A mile to the west, down the long gradual incline of the ridge, elements of the New Zealand Corps continued moving up toward their assault positions. It was now nearly ten o'clock. The heavy snow and confusing orders had slowed their progress.

The assault would include a third of the 1st New Zealand Division and the 3rd, 5th, and 2/7th Gurkha Rifles of the 4th Indian Division, all tough, battle-hardened troops, well rested, and anxious to engage. Their mood was very high, the "Kiwis" and "Johnny Gurks" maintaining precise squad and platoon movements as they always did, their officers strolling casually among them with cheery words and walking sticks.

The assault on Monte Cassino Ridge was set for 4:30 A.M., six and a half hours away.

It was called the Rabbit Warren, a series of cocoonlike holes in the foundations of the abbey. Inside, it was cavelike, all the holes connected, the ceiling low with stone shelves containing rabbit hutches. The cages were all empty. The air smelled of moss and earth stone and sour feces.

The dark, frigid connecting corridor was crowded with refugee families, huddled together in little clumps covered with ragged blankets and cardboard box sides, mostly old men and women and little children, their eyes in Blue Team's vest lights like those of subterranean creatures suddenly exposed. They watched the armed men pass in dead silence, only the thud of their boots resounding along the narrow tunnel.

Suddenly a shadow rose, an old man in tattered black clothing. He called to them, *"Signores, favorimi, grazie."* Red paused. The man came forward. He had a bandage around his forehead. It was stained with dried blood, black with the edges turned yellow. His eye sockets were deep, framed in wrinkles.

"Comé?" Red said.

The old Italian looked at their uniforms and his eyes widened, like someone who has just encountered a miraculous vision. "You are *Americanos!*"

"Sí"

"Oh, Signores! Oh, Dio!" He took Parnell's hand, kissed it. "You have come to save us from the German *malfattori."*

Red pulled his hand away. "No. We come for the Father Abbot."

"Ah," the old man said. The look of sudden hope instantly left his eyes, gone. He slumped, stared at the floor. Then he lifted his head again. "You know where he abides?"

"Do you?"

"Oh, *sí, sí.*" He rattled off something too rapidly for Parnell to follow.

Red turned his head. "Angelo." Cappacelli came up. "What the hell's he saying?"

Angelo and the old man talked for a moment, the man smiling, putting his forefinger to Cappacelli's head, then to his own. "You *Italiano,* no? *Bene, bene, ci ho piacere.*"

"*Sí*" Angelo said, turned back to Parnell. "He says he was a shoemaker, Lieutenant. Used to fix the monks' shoes. He knows the monastery well and believes the Father Abbot's in the Crypt."

To the old Italian, Red said, "You know where this Crypt is?"

"*Sí, sí!*"

"You lead us?"

"*Sí. Grazie tante.*"

"Okay, old man, lead ahead. *Adiamo, adiamo.*"

"*Ora, sí, presto.*" He darted off, the team right behind him.

He guided them through narrow corridors where the air was absolutely motionless and had the feel and stony cold of sequestered centuries. Medieval torch cages lined the walls. The rock below them was stained by the saltpeter and lye that the torches had been soaked in. They formed yellow lines that shimmered coppery in the flashlight beams.

Eventually, they reached a tight, winding staircase that seemed to pass through two stories. It broached out onto a small balcony that overlooked the main cloister. There were lights back under the porticos and on the landing of a huge stairway, men moving about.

The old man pointed down, turned his head, and spat, murmuring, "*Visperettas!*"

Parnell studied the cloister. It was vast and magnificent, marble flooring with inlaid figures and statues standing pure white in the moonlight. Thick columns ringed the cloister and merged into a grand stairway that led to the basilica.

Near the entrance were three 75mm airborne recoiless guns set behind sandbag fortifications, their crews in sleeping bags amid stacks of ordnance crates.

At the other end of the area several cargo trucks were parked in front of the grand stairway. Crews of Italian civilians were loading crates onto their flatbeds and now and then other men came out of the basilica carrying more. Gestapo guards with machine pistols paced leisurely about.

Red drew the old man back. "Where's the entrance to the Crypt?"

"Inside the basilica, *signore*." He pointed to the top of the grand staircase. "There, through those doors."

They'd never get past the cloister. "Is there another way into the basilica?" he asked.

The old man thought a moment, then grinned. *"Sí, signore,* near the Burying Wall."

"The what?"

"The Burying Wall," the old Italian repeated, then explained: "When is All Hollowtide, they make—what you call?—*procession?* From the basilica to the graveyard?" He pushed his palm through the air, indicating the back of the abbey. "Many peoples bring things from the dead. To place in the graveyard. You see? Is great honor for the dead. The procession, she go from the basilica, through many tunnels, and then out. I can show you."

Red nodded, waved him on.

Major Keppler gloomily settled himself onto a water canister. He was in his new underground command quarters, a small blast cut inside a gun crew's shelter located behind their battery. Overhead was a steel ceiling, the rest of it a trench blasted out of the ridge's stone. The walls had drill holes where the dynamite charges had gone and the kerosene-smelling air still held a lingering mist of explosion dust.

Over the last few hours, his rage had finally devolved down

into utter depression. Here he was, a superb hunter of sabo-teurs, a superior *officer* commanding a mere artillery pla-toon. *Ach du Scheisse! Das schweins! It is unspeakable.*

It had taken him nearly ten hours to reach the approaches to Monastery Ridge. Then he had to wait another hour for a vehicle to take him to the monastery itself. An *Oberfeldwebel* or master sergeant named Teufell met him at the main gate.

He led him along a footpath in the snow the entire length of the eastern wall of the abbey to his battery position, two hun-dred yards beyond the rear of the monastery. It consisted of three 75mm mountain howitzers and three 28/20mm antitank cannon set up to fire against infantry. They were in uncovered entrenchments protected only by sandbags and daylight camo netting.

Their field of fire spanned steep rocky precipices that went nearly to the floor of the valley, cut only by goat and mule trails. He stood for a moment and scanned it. The snow-covered slopes showed jagged pinnacles and down about two thousand yards a domed knoll called Monte Calvario with a few deserted stone farmhouses visible on its flanks.

In grim silence, he apathetically inspected each gun, the crews standing at attention in their gray utility field blouses and "dice shaker" boots with canvas blast anklets. They made up Battery C, Second Battalion, 4th Light Artillery, 16th Panzer Division. Afterward, Sergeant Teufell pointed to the ground in front of the guns. It was flat for about twenty yards and then sharply sloped downward, everything covered with snow. Several small red flags were poked into the upper side.

"When you move forward, Herr Major," he warned, "al-ways follow a line straight down from the flags. That area is mined."

He grunted without interest.

If Keppler had known anything about artillery place-ments, he would *really* have been insulted. German defen-sive theory always stressed the Principle of Depth with counterattack as its primary purpose. As a result, the Krauts placed their heaviest guns and most proficient crews in those forward positions where the enemy was most likely to attack. Their job was to halt and hold the initial assault so that fresh reserve troops could then surge through their emplacements in counterattack. The worst gun crews were therefore placed in the rear of the fortification, in positions where attack was not expected.

In truth, Keppler's battery was the worst in the entire divisional Range-and-Fire list.

Now he lethargically took out his pack of brandy-scented cigarettes. There were only four left. He extracted one, lit up, and surveyed his quarters. The room was little more than a closet containing a bunk, a kerosene lamp and warmer, the water canister, and a field telephone in a leather case. Beyond it was a room of like size with a table containing ranging maps. On the other end of the shelter were bunks for two gun crews.

Sergeant Teufell appeared. "Excuse me, Herr Major. Would you like some tea, sir?"

"No."

"Perhaps food, sir?" Teufell had the long, horsey face of a sad clown and hands with extremely bony fingers covered with burn scars.

"Get out!" Keppler shouted. "Just get the hell out."

Teufell withdrew.

The Crypt shimmerd and gleamed in candlelight, a large room, its walls, floor, dome, and ceiling completely covered with Aquileian mosaics of Christ and saints and symbolic stag hunts and winged angels, the glass and stone tesserae, or set pieces, angled so as to create the most reflective light in the perpetual dimness.

There were pedimental niches in the walls holding statues of the Twelve Apostles and a dome of turquoise blue underlayered with silver foil that gave to it the impression of three-dimensional depth, like peering upward into a lake that danced in dappled sunlight.

Below the dome was a huge marble altar with a gold-leafed Christ fallen to one knee under the weight of the Cross. It was filled with candles. Inside the altar were shelves containing four boxes of Jerusalem ebony. These held the relics of Saint Benedict and his sister Scholastica, the Nun of San Sabastian.

Each morning, the Father Abbot said Mass here, kneeling with his monks on the floor. Now there were only four present: Diamare, Dom Matrinola, and two other monks, the only ones still left in the monastery. They had withdrawn to this, the most revered place in the abbey, for refuge and meditation.

Now Matrinola lifted his face and stared at his Father Abbot. He loved the man deeply, was always highly protective of him. After a moment, he said, "Monsignor?"

Without turning, Diamare said softly, "Yes."

"We have to speak. Decisions must be made, and quickly."

The abbot's head moved slowly from side to side. "I've told you, Martino. I will not leave."

"But it's too dangerous now," Matrinola cried. "I believe Captain Sonnemann. These Gestapo intend to *kill* you."

"If it be so, let it be so."

Matrinola put his head down, inhaled, drawing patience. "If you won't think of yourself, then consider this. Once you are killed, the Holy Father will be forced to accuse these Germans before the world. When that happens, Hitler will kill *him,* also."

The old abbot turned and stared at his secretary. His Mass vestments glistened as he moved, the altar candles casting his face into grotesque shadows. "No one would dare commit such insanity!"

"Hitler and these Gestapo *are* insane."

"Martino, I have no choice." It was a cry of pure anguish.

"Yes, you do."

"How easily you forget your own vows."

"My vows, like yours, bind me to the Rule of Benedict. But they also bind me to God. Every good is superseded by a greater good. As Abbot Superior, you are autonomous here. You can cancel your vows for the sake of that greater good. . . . *Oh, Dio,* Monsignor, would you have the Holy Father *murdered?"*

"No!" Diamare wailed. *"Madre di Dio, no!"*

"Then you *must* leave."

They waited. The abbot turned back to the altar, staring up at the Fallen Christ. After a long moment, his eyes closed and he shook his head again, no.

Freyberg quietly stepped from his divisional command tent in Cosiliatte and stood for a moment looking up at the sky. It was washed in moonlight that drenched the entire blacked-out encampment now into glowing areas of blue white and dense shadow.

At last, he lifted his binoculars and looked to the north-west. The Abbey of Monte Cassino immediately came into view, looking like a great block of gray-white granite floating just above Monastery Ridge. To him, the moon's reflection off its many windows suddenly gave it the appearance of something alive, a starship come to reconnoiter the Liri. *An enemy running surveillance.* Even in fancy, the general's thoughts were couched in military purpose.

He took his eyes away long enough to glance at his watch. It was six minutes after 11:00. Returning to his glasses, he scanned the sky, turning slowly until he was looking nearly due east, picturing in his mind's eye those Mitchells and Marauders out of Foggia sweeping in on their bombing runs against that blasted hill. Just forty-four minutes to go. *If* those bloody Americans got here on time.

Someone came out of the tent, a tiny sliver of light showing for a second through the security flap. It was his adjutant, Colonel Paul Bert. Freyberg lowered the glasses, looked at him. "Wot's Meteorology say?"

"The sunburst effects could remain until at least 0600, I'm afraid."

"Bloody things."

All day a vicious storm of powerful magnetic impulses from sunbursts had interfered with communications throughout all of southern Europe. It had gotten worse as night came on. Now, as Freyberg's units moved into their jump-off positions up on the slopes of Monastery Hill, the smaller radios of companies and platoons had become totally useless. Even the larger sets in battalion CPs were fading in and out, drowned by horrendous static bursts.

"Well, no matter," Freyberg said, shrugging his big shoulders. "My boys'll know what they're about without being told. Has there been any contact with those bombers yet?"

"No, sir. I assume they're on radio silence by now." Bert was also a muscular man, fond of surfing and mountain climbing. He looked up. "At least, the moon'll do *them* some good."

The general laughed abruptly, booming from his barrel chest. "By God, Paul, we'll sweep Jerry *this* time."

"Aye, we will indeed, General."

Freyberg turned south again, spoke aloud to the approaching American pilots, "All right, you mad buggas, let's get this bleedin' business started."

Thirty minutes later, at the Foggia Airbase, the Flying Fortress crew officers began drifting into Mission Operations, the men in their high-altitude flying suits and lamb-collared leather jackets with the Eagle-and-Bomb logo of the Second Bombardment Group. They were in good spirits, a general, boyish joshing.

Finally Group Commander Lieutenant Colonel Gil Wyman mounted the platform and brought them to order. A huge aeronautical map of central Italy was on the wall directly behind him along with a 16mm screen.

"All right, gentlemen," he began, extending his telescoping pointer. "Let's get on with it." He turned, put the pointer tip onto Monastery Ridge. "Your target for this run is the great Abbey of Monte Cassino." Men exchanged glances, eyebrows lifted.

The colonel went on, going over the mission flight procedures. There would be four flights of Flying Fortresses each. Takeoff time was set for 0226 hours. Immediately after liftoff, the aircraft would set up in their bombing formation high over the field in what was called the rendezvous. This was to be completed by 3:56.

The flights would then head west on a heading of 261 degrees at 21,000 feet. Since forecasts predicted forty-knot winds at that altitude over the Abruzzi Range, the formation would reach its IP or Initial Point in approximately thirty-eight minutes. The IP was a position mark on Highway 6, which ran from Naples to the Liri Valley. There the road crossed Lake Sepino on a causeway, easily recognizable from the air.

Once achieving their Initial Point, the formation would go to complete radio silence and swing northwest to its approach heading of 315 degrees and gradually increase altitude to 23,000 feet, literally following the highway to Monte Cassino. The Time to Target would take twenty-six minutes, putting them over Monte Cassino just at first light. Once their bomb runs were completed, the Fortresses would immediately swing a ninety-degree turn for the mountain town of Isérnia, then adjust heading for the final leg back to Fóggia.

They killed the lights. A 16mm projector whirred, throwing lines of light and a picture of the monastery onto the screen on the platform. It showed the abbey from about five hundred feet above it, the camera aircraft doing a slow 360. The film was black and white, scratchy, the cameraman jiggling and tilting while down below the huge U-shaped building turned slowly in white sunshine, its gardens and narrow roads and, farther back up the ridge, dense pine woods.

The eastern face of the ridge was a waste of steep rock pinnacles and towers, sharp fissure lines and gullies, mule trails here and there, and the little tram car inching its way up its slender cog line. The western side was smoother, a gradual slope yet just as barren, the rock grayish in the picture with only scattered clumps of grass and mountain shrubbery.

The film lasted three minutes, obviously cut from a longer strip. The lights came on and Colonel Wyman turned the platform over to the meteorological officer who issued the weather forecasts and altitude conditions. He added, "Stay off your radios as much as you can. We're experiencing hellish electric storms from sunbursts that'll probably hold until at least 0600. Your radiomen can use Morse code if necessary. But with this particular sun storm, I think they'll have trouble there, too. I suggest you have your mechs rig power phones aboard for your internal use."

Next was the intelligence officer, who gave estimates of potential flak. "We don't anticipate much from the ridge positions," he said. "The Krauts aren't expecting this kind of air attack there. But once you're spotted, the Liri Valley'll light up quick. We estimate at least moderate flak conditions."

Colonel Wyman returned to field a few questions, then dismissed the men. He did not wish them well or good hunting. To airmen, that was considered bad luck.

It was now 12:32.

Again they were lost, down in caverns of stone, Parnell thinking, *Jesus Christ, do* all *Wops lose their way underground?* The old man turned and turned and agonized over his befuddlement. He'd finally told them his name, Eustacio Soccapetti, a helluva sonorous name for such a little, withered runt.

Still, Red couldn't fault him. The bowels of the monastery were like a gopher city, filled with tunnels and corridors and tiny rooms holding dusty, unrecognizable items, ancient things, and the rooms themselves so sullenly silent and captive, the sensation of time completely gone, as if the surface were somewhere far away and that if they were to emerge into the light, they'd discover Crusaders on their way to the Holy Land or even Roman legions returning to Rome with campaign spoils.

All that bullshit's well and good, Parnell thought, but the goddamned time *was* moving ahead. Rapidly. That Father Tommaso back in Cosiliatte had been one hell of an optimist, making the monastery sound so well planned and laid out, neat as city blocks. Well, either way, they had to *move.*

"Come on, Eustacio," he shouted. "Where in hell is this Burying Wall?"

"Forgive me, *signore. Eh, matto, poveretto.* I try, I try." He thumped himself on the head in self-exasperation.

They explored several more corridors. At last they reached a double-sized one, the walls painted white and the middle of the ceiling marked with dark soot lines from torches moving along the center. Procession torches.

Eustacio cried, "Here is the one. See? See?" He turned to the left, hurriedly shuffled off. The others fell in behind him. The corridor curved to the left, then to the right, and finally came to a wall, twenty by twenty, every inch of it covered with relics of the dead, bits of cloth, eyeglasses, rings, letters, all of them stuck to it by globs of hardened wax: the Burying Wall.

The old man grinned triumphantly, kept turning to wave them forward. They reached a narrow stairway, the overhead completely soot-covered with the dense odor of incense in the air. The stairs went up a flight to a door made of oak planks bound by strips of rusted metal.

Parnell gently pulled old Soccapetti back and pressed his ear against the door. He could hear faint sounds, hammering. He studied the door handle, an ancient thing like a latch. He lifted it, pulled the door open slightly, looked out.

It entered into the back of the basilica, under what was probably the choir loft. The massive expanse stretched off nearly the length of a football field, with great vaulted ceilings and nave pillars all done in black and gold leaf. The altar apse stood at the far end, its foundation at the top of a fan stairway directly beneath the building's dome. A ten-foot crucifix rose from the altar. Beyond it, the curved backdrop of the apse was covered with intricate frescoes and glittering mosaics that seemed to cast a halo of light about the huge cross.

Several Gestapo guards lounged idly beside the altar, smoking, machine pistols hanging from straps over their shoulders.

In front of the altar stair three large klieg lights illuminated an area where a dozen Italian men worked, making wooden crates and cartons. Numerous art objects stood about and there were stacks of new lumber among finished crates and tall, narrow painting cases and barrels for statuary. As he watched, four men came out of a side room that was connected to the altar platform carrying a huge painting. They brought it down the steps and set it down near the workers.

Parnell pulled back, waved Wyatt up. "Check it," he whispered.

Bird peered out for a long moment, came back. "I make five guards, Lieutenant. We can take 'em from the side."

Red nodded and moved back down the stairway, the men following, gathering around him. "We go in one at a time," he said. "Three along the left wall, four on the right. Wait till everybody's in position. Then we take the bastards fast."

Everybody checked their weapons, clicked off safeties, tapped knife sheaths. In single file, they returned to the door, Wyatt in the lead. He eased it open, then shoved it all the way. In a second, he was gone.

Twenty minutes earlier, General Freyberg had finally managed to corral his rage. Now he prowled about his headquarters tent, red-faced and dangerous, his staff and clerks staying the hell out of his way.

He paused beside a radioman. "Goddammit, 'aven't you got that Yank bastard *yet?*" he boomed.

"Sorry, sir. I keep losing signal."

Freyberg cursed and headed off again.

He had given the Yank bombers a good fifteen minutes beyond their scheduled arrival. But still nothing, not a sound, not a bloody bomb. He knew these swaggies were too often late, but *this* was absolutely unthinkable. He'd immediately set his radiomen to contacting the main Allied Headquarters in Caserta, intending to go right to General Wilson. They finally got through to some watch officer who, through surging static and fadeout, said the general was not present.

Next they tried for Harding, again got a blurry message that claimed he was somewhere near the Anzio beachhead. Now they were attempting to reach General Eaker. Crazy cross talk and music came through the speakers amid blowing explosions of static and electronic noise, the security scramblers making voices and tones one huge mishmash of sound coming through like records played backward.

"I have Colonel Climer, sir," one of the radiomen abruptly called out. George Climer was Eaker's chief of staff. Freyberg rushed across the room, scooped up the radio mike. The radioman turned up the speaker.

"Climer?" Freyberg shouted. "Can you read me?"

". . . affir . . . have you, sir . . . Go . . ." Climer's voice, slightly delayed, flashed in and out.

"Goddammit, where the bloody hell are your *planes?*" He closed his eyes, heard the echo of his last words warbling through the speaker as the scrambler ran through rapid tone and pitch changes.

"Say aga . . . Bad con . . . over."

Speaking through his teeth, Freyberg repeated, slower, "Where are your bloody *bombers?*"

There was a powerful splay of static. It rose to an ear-splitting level, drained away, Climer's voice coming up, ". . . altered. General Eaker ha . . . four flight TOT set . . . not notified? Over."

Altered? He looked up at one of his staff officers standing nearby. "Did he say altered?"

"Yes, sir."

"Altered to flaming *what?*" Into the mike, he said, "Say again and explain." There was a long glittery surge of static through the speaker. "I said, say again and explain." Another long slurring rumble of static.

The radioman shook his head. "We've lost him, General."

"Bloody *hell!*" he bellowed and hurled the mike down onto the radio table. "You get that son of a bitch *back.*"

"Yes, sir," the radioman said meekly.

They went one at a time, darting through the shadows, their boots treading lightly over the marble patterning of the floor. The hammering continued, echoing throughout the vast space. The air was less dense here yet carried a heavier odor of incense and newly sawn wood.

Parnell was the last. He ordered Eustacio to remain until he whistled for him. The old man's eyes were wide. He mumbled something, crossed himself. Red slipped through the door and went down along the right aisle. It was rib-vaulted, the walls and window casings done in complex tracery and the stained images in the windows huge and grotesquely shaped.

As he approached the end of the aisle, hidden from the Germans up on the altar platform, one of the Italian workmen spotted him. The man jerked upright and stared. Parnell held up his hand. The Italian looked a moment longer, then returned to his work. But now his movements were suddenly self-conscious.

Parnell looked across the nave, the work lights making huge, bright circles against the dark aisles, throwing solid column shadows. He could dimly make out Bird, Smoker, and Angelo kneeling, their heads turned toward him, Thompsons slung, knives out, the blades catching reflected light. He came back, looked at the others ahead of him, their heads turned, too, watching, ready.

He nodded, once.

The Gestapo men in their black-and-silver uniforms were hardly alive long enough to realize what was happening, seven enemy soldiers suddenly appearing out of the shadows and racing straight at them, knives held down low, plunging swiftly up the stairs in dead silence, only the sound of their boots. Beyond them the Italian workmen leapt away, then stood aghast.

Almost in a chorus, the Germans shouted, an incoherent expulsion of air and shock. But before they could react in any positive way, the enemy soldiers were on them, knives working, slashing, plunging deep into their bodies. The Germans were twisting, groaning wordless cries, and trying frantically to flee but going down instead, suddenly feeling terribly weak, the knives still working, flashing under the lights as their blood splashed against the foot of the altar, dripping, pooling along the floor. Their eyes rolled and took one, final glimpse of the world, which was now dominated by the agonized face of Christ towering high above them.

Instantly, Blue Team dashed for the shadows behind the altar, their Thompsons flipped around, muzzles up, getting blood all over the stocks and trigger guards, panting from the killings. For a second, Cappacelli dropped to one knee, twice made the sign of the cross, then kissed his thumbnail. *Madre Dio, forgive me, at the very foot of God I murder.* At the bottom of the stairs, the Italian peasants were praying, too.

Parnell whistled. A moment later, old Soccapetti came shuffling down the right aisle, repeatedly crossing himself. He struggled up the steps, calling, *"Signore? Signore?"* He half genuflected, then rose as Parnell stepped from the shadows, his eyes slitted.

"Which way?" he growled at the old man.

"La camera, through this way. *Via, signore, subito."* He would not look at the dead soldiers and quickly disappeared into the side room from which the workers had brought the painting earlier.

Parnell hurried to the door, stood beside it, waving the others in. "Go! Go!" Below, the Italian workers were gingerly starting to come up the steps, staring at the dead Germans.

Four members of the team were into the side room when a huge door suddenly slammed open at the other end of the basilica. A voice shouted something in German and a machine pistol opened up way back there, the flashes like sparks off an acetylene torch.

The report slammed into the vast space, bouncing and echoing along the nave and side aisles. Two workers were struck, the bullets entering their bodies with a thudding sound. They fell forward onto the steps. The others immediately scattered, shouting with fear. More bullets slammed into the altar and the foot of the crucifix, hurling wooden splinters.

Parnell instantly fired back. Right beside him, Wyatt began shooting, too, and then Cowboy, their bursts booming up into the dome, the spent cartridges tumbling onto the altar platform.

Keppler was so deep, Sergeant Teufell had to shake him several times before he finally came up out of sleep, into the cold and the hard feel of his bunk, staring up at this strange noncom shaking him.

He scowled. "What is it, you fool?"

"There's been firing from *inside* the monastery, sir," Teufell said.

Keppler sat up, rubbed his hands over his face, blinked sleep away. "Inside?"

"Yes, Herr Major."

They went up and stood looking at the great bulk of the abbey wall, its top etched in brilliant moonlight. No firing now, only a profound altitude stillness. Suddenly Keppler spotted a platoon of soldiers jogging toward the structure along the back road that led to the woods. They came on in perfect double time, their boots hitting simultaneously, battle harnesses jingling, paratroopers coming in from their bivouac in the forest.

"Send a runner out to those men," Keppler barked at Teufell. "Find out what's happening."

"Yes, sir." The sergeant darted away. A moment later, one of the nest gunners ran off toward the approaching platoon.

Keppler paced back and forth. His body, so quickly pulled from the comparative warmth of his bunk, shivered in the sharp cold. The moon had passed its zenith and now in the east there were stars over the Abruzzi peaks appearing like floating sparks from a distant, dying fire.

The runner returned, braced before him. "Herr Hauptfach, the Falschirmjagers have been sent to capture an enemy raiding party in the basilica."

Keppler's head swung around to stare at him. "There are Resistance fighters in *there?*"

"I don't know, sir. The platoon leader just said a raiding party."

He disgustedly waved the runner away. Resistance fighters, he thought fiercely, those scum *here?* Cursing, he started pacing again, wanting suddenly, desperately, to go up there, find them, *slaughter* them as all the bitternesses and insults of the last days came rushing up into his throat like a cast of gall, scalding his tissues.

He stopped, gazed fixedly, helplessly up at the high, impenetrable dark walls, and felt the frustration grip his heart like a sorrow.

As 0200 hours approached, on the other side of Monastery Ridge the last New Zealand and Indian units were finally achieving their final jump-off points along an arcing perimeter about a thousand yards downslope from the abbey.

Unfortunately, now many of the first- and second-wave units were unable to communicate or even see each other despite being only yards apart. The slope's jagged rock fields of huge boulders, scree, and narrow ravines created single-unit isolation. Besides, over the last hour the radio interference had worsened. Now the scattered mortar and machine gun squads and rifle fire teams were completely cut off from their own assault leaders as well as from their field command posts farther down the hill. Since these units were assault troops, no telephone wire had been strung between them and the rear zones.

Now all along the western slope, men hunkered down among rocks cold as alpine peaks and watched the moon and prayed or final-checked their weapons or sharpened their blades or whispered or slept as they waited for 4:30 to come.

Colonel Bert slipped from the tent, squinting to adjust his eyes to the sudden drop of light, from high-intensity tent bulbs to moonlight. Finally he was able to see General Freyberg standing a few yards away, looking angrily up at Monte Cassino. He hurried over.

"Sir, we just picked up something," he said. "It's a coded message in Morse out of Spain."

The general twisted around. "Spain? Wot the bloody hell has Spain got to do with anything?"

"Whoever sent it claims to be relaying for Eaker's HQ."

Freyberg cursed, then both men rushed back into the main headquarters tent. Four staff officers were standing beside one of the radio operators. They made way for the general. The operator handed him a decode sheet. He quickly scanned it, his eyes widening.

It read:

   Fm: 601/AAFCC . . . To:178/1NZCQ . . . SM-143
   Alpha-MC KK . . . SM-144-Alpha-MC IT . . . 299X . . .
   TOT: 0700Z/////////

Translated, it meant:

   From: Eaker/Allied Air Force Command Caserta . . .
   To: Freyberg/New Zealand Corps Headquarters Cosi-

liatte . . . Strategic Mission 143 Alpha Monte Cassino canceled . . . strategic Mission 144 Alpha Monte Cassino initiated . . . B-17s . . . Time Over Target: 0500 Greenwich Mean Time//////

"How'd you get this?" he growled down at the operator.

"It came through a skip channel, General," the operator said, the young man deeply tanned with almost-white blue eyes that formed a stark contrast in his face.

"A wot?"

"A skip channel, sir. Electrical storm bursts sometimes create crazy signal bounce. All of a sudden I began pickin' up this ham operator outta Spain. He come in clear as you please. Claimed 'e was relayin' a message from AAFC in Caserta. 'E was transmitting in the open but knew *our* coded call sign. Even had the correct CSCB." These initials stood for Current Status Code Base, which was changed each day, sometimes each hour, to maintain communications security.

"Could you authenticate?"

"All 'e would say, sir, was he was relayin' from Caserta. I made 'im repeat message twice, sir. Then the channel closed."

Freyberg turned and looked at Colonel Bert and his other staff officers, stared hard at them for a moment, then furiously began pacing. "That blithering Eaker's canceled the air strike," he said through gritted teeth. He couldn't believe it. *My God!*

"Could be a German ruse, sir," Bert suggested.

The general stopped and whirled around, his face suddenly jolted as the full implications of the change in the bombing strike hit him. "Good Christ, man," he bellowed. "What if it isn't? That means the bleedin' Yanks are sending Fortresses in. Our assault units'll be on top of that bloody ridge when they come. Jesus, we've got to *stop* them."

"But we can't get *through* to Fóggia, sir," one of the other staffers said. "It's completely in the black. And even if we could, General, no one but Wilson or Eaker can order a cancelation of a strategic mission."

Freyberg stood there, his entire huge body trembling with fury. Then he reached out, grabbed ahold of the operator's tunic. "Get through to our battalion CPs up on that flamin' hill," he snarled. "I don't care how the bloody hell you do it, just *do* it. Tell them the assault's off. All forward positions are to immediately withdraw to at least two thousand yards from the top of that fucking ridge."

The general swung around to the other operators. "The rest of you, do anything you can to raise Caserta and Fóggia. Shit, try for Presenzano and even bloody *Algiers*. Jus' get somebody, *anybody*, with some bleedin' authority to stop this."

He started pacing again, saying to his staffers, "Get runners up there immediately. Use the quickest men you've got." Everyone but Colonel Bert hurried away. The general looked at his watch: 2:08! He shook his head, looked up, right into his adjutant's hazel eyes. Unspoken images passed between them and Freyberg felt his barrel chest constrict with an overwhelming, icy, electrifying sensation of disaster.

The hunt had been going on now for the past forty-seven minutes. Blue Team scurried through dank, interlocking corridors, a crazy house of stone, laying trip-wired grenades on their back trail, while German paratroopers worked their way methodically into the tunnels, their voices echoing and reechoing, precise, soldier shouts calling to each other, clearing space after space like commandos.

Old Eustacio was lost again. In his terror, he'd led them into the wrong level. He kept stumbling, panting, wide-eyed, mumbling. Half carrying him, Parnell hurried them all along, searching for another stairway.

Suddenly one of their booby traps went off, a double blast. The explosion roared through the corridors, made the air suck back and forth for a few seconds. Two minutes later, another explosion, this one even closer.

They came to an intersection, paused. The old Italian looked this way, that, then pointed to the right. They headed off. Within a minute, they came to a stairway, headed down, Wyatt and Cowboy out front. Before they reached the bottom, two Gestapo officers abruptly appeared at the foot of the stairs. Gunfire erupted, bullets singing and slamming off stone walls, jolting, confined sound.

Both Krauts went down. Bird and Cowboy vaulted them and went to the floor as more firing came from up a long, wide corridor lined with doorways.

Soccapetti tugged urgently at Parnell's sleeve. "*Signore, ecco gia,*" he rasped.

"What, goddammit?"

"The Crypt. Is *there,* the other end, s*ignore.*"

They counted three machine pistols down there, their tinny after-blow sounding like MP-43/1s, garbage guns made of metal stampings and worthless for field combat. Gestapo weapons, all for show, intimidating the civilians.

Parnell descended to the lower step, peered around. Smoke floated, reeking of cordite. A strong light shone from one room fifty feet along the corridor. He caught Wyatt's eye, signaled *bogues,* noncombat troops. *Rush 'em!*

They rolled a grenade down the hall. It bounced like a lemon, fizzing. Before its explosion echo was gone, five men were lunging forward, going low, Parnell and Smoker behind them at the stairs laying in covering fire. They reached and quickly entered the room, firing. A moment later there was silence once more except for the men calling, "Clear."

The three Gestapo troopers were dead. The room was huge, filled with shelves, dust marks showing where hundreds of objects had been. Rolls of paper and twine were scattered about. Four Italian men were huddled in one corner.

Parnell reached the door, started in, then saw slight movement to his left. He swung around, bringing up his weapon. A little girl of about six was standing in the hall a few feet away. She was ragged, dark-haired, with dark oval eyes. A moment later, a little boy peeked around a doorsill, then another. Finally an old woman stepped out, cringing at the sight of his uniform. One by one, others followed, coming slowly, frightened.

In all, there were eleven women and children. Some wore bandages, others were obviously feverish. They had been patients in the monks' cells. Parnell studied them, felt a whisper of sadness, then quickly roused himself. He looked back for Eustacio, who crept cautiously in from the stairwell.

"Get these damn people back into their rooms," Red shouted. He turned, signaled his men. They started down the corridor, dodging around the women and little ones.

There was a tremendous blast. The ground and walls shook as if in an earthquake. Dust rained down from the ceilings. A woman screamed, her shriek blending into the violent rebound of the explosion as it crossed and recrossed through tunnels and corridors.

Gradually, the noise faded, absorbed back into the stones. The woman stopped, too. There was a deep, ground silence in which the air seemed to hold sound, like the last vibrations of a chord gone beyond hearing.

Then another sound came. At first it was a soft, sifting, burbling murmur. Quickly it grew into a hissing. No one moved except for their heads, tilted, listening, trying to identify the thing. *What the hell is that?*

Parnell's mind shifted rapidly through possibilities, caught something. The priest's description of the monastery. It hit him. Distracted, he'd been staring at the back of Bird's head. Slowly Wyatt turned, stared back at him. He knew, too.

Oh, shit!

The Germans had just blown the abbey's main water cisterns and were flooding the lower tunnels.

Twenty-one

Major Nelson Ellerbrock and his copilot, First Lieutenant Joe Ledy, were completing their pre-takeoff check list, Ledy reading off items from a plastic card, the major checking them, calling out, the huge bomber sitting on the taxiway of runway 27L with half of the mission's 144 aircraft lined up behind him, each one stopped at an angle to the one ahead. From the air they all would have looked like big stitches in a garment.

On this bombing strike, Ellerbrock was mission group leader, all the other flights keying on his aircraft, number 616. This was the twenty-third mission for him and his crew of ten. His other officers were Lieutenant Phil Esposito, navigator, and an ex-deputy sheriff from Spearfish, South Dakota, First Lieutenant Bobby Ball, bombadier.

The pre-takeoff list completed, he clicked his power phone intercom to check connections to each of his crew members. His radios, like all of those in southern Italy, were out completely now as were all magnetic instruments. Departure Control was using lights to signal landing and takeoff clearances.

He straightened, arched his back muscles, and settled comfortably in his seat. A moment later, he got the white blinks to enter the active runway. Easing on power to his four Curtiss-Wright R1820-97 engines, the aircraft trembling, he moved forward, braking to make the turn, then braking again to align down the runway.

Revving near full revolutions, he and Ledy made one last engines check, then eased off power and waited for final clearance. There it was, green flashes. Ellerbrock shoved all throttles to full power. The engines roared into life as the huge aircraft began moving, sluggishly at first, everything shaking, but gradually picking up speed, the edge lights starting to riffle past faster and faster as he felt the flight controls coming alive through his wheel. The Fortress seemed to grow lighter, wanting to fly. He let it, easing into the rotation, the nose coming up, and the drag disappeared as they lifted clear of the runway and climbed into the night air.

The door to the Crypt was solid oak with gleaming steel bars holding the planks together. Parnell pounded on it. The sound echoed back up the corridor. It was dim down at this end. Wyatt and Smoker were stationed at the far bend of the hall while Angelo, Laguna, and Cowboy were at the stairs. The water had started coming in three minutes before. Now it was already over their boot tops.

From inside, a man's voice shouted in German, "Go away. Leave us alone."

Parnell yelled back in Italian, "Is the abbot in there?"

"Go away!"

Goddammit. "Don't be afraid. We're here to protect him. We are Americans."

Silence. Then faint German shouts somewhere among the tunnels, the words jumbled as if they had leaked from the stone walls.

"Do you understand?" Red shouted again. "We—are—Americans."

More silence. *Shit.*

"Looks like we'll have to blow her, Lieutenant," Kaamanui said.

Strung out behind them were the refugees and the four workmen, the adults looking frightened and small while the children played in the layer of water on the floor, swishing their shoes to make it spray.

Parnell looked at his watch: 2:35. "Give 'em a couple minutes. But go ahead, pick out the charge points."

Sol stepped around him, began running his big fingers over the heavy door, feeling for weak spots. Parnell put his mouth close to it again, bellowed, "Hurry up in there. We don't have much time."

"It's a trick," the voice called back, this time in English. "You've come to kill us."

"Goddammit, if I wanted to do that, I would have blown this door down by now. Listen to me. Didn't you hear the explosions? The Germans have blown up your cisterns. They're flooding the tunnels." In frustration, he began kicking water against the foot of the door, which was still several inches above the surface. "Look down. See that water?"

Silence again.

Come on, you son of a bitch, open this fucking door.

Tiny tendrils of water seeped through the crack at the foot of the door. Dom Matrinola stared at it, little needles reflecting candlelight. It was true, the Germans *were* attempting to flood the abbey. Or was it just another part of the hoax, to get them to open the door?

Frightened and confused, he tried to make his mind think rationally. The solitude of a monastery made it easy to teach your mind to blot out the rest of the world, the combats of reality. But now he had to think dynamically, filter through options and possibilities and realities. He tried, yet all he could grab onto was the horror that somebody was trying to kill his abbot.

Were they really Americans out there? Or was this just a part of the ruse to trick them to open it? Still, as the man had said, he could use explosives if he wanted, blow it down, and come in easily to do his killing with none to see.

"Dom Martino," one of the other monks cried out. "Come quickly. The monsignor has fainted."

He hurried to Diamare. The little man lay on the floor now like a pile of altar clothing, on his side, his face deathly pallid, his eyes glassy. Martinola put his fingers on the abbot's carotid. His pulse raced. He leaned closer. "Monsignor, can you hear me?"

"Yes," Diamare said feebly. "What must we do?"

He studied the shriveled face, saw no signs of stroke. The old man had had attacks like this before, his eyes going vacant, disoriented, his old heart pulsing with fear. It had always seemed a kind of withdrawing, the man seeking to hide within the protective shell of an isolation deeper even than that of his own chosen life.

Matrinola looked up into the anxious faces of the other monks, saw what he, too, knew. If they didn't get the Father Abbot to safety quickly, he would die. "Open the door," Matrinola ordered.

Meanwhile, ninety-three million miles away, cataclysmic events on the surface of the sun were continuing to throw large portions of the earth into communication blackout.

Periodically massive magnetic changes were occurring within the core of the sun. Coils of magnetic energy called flux ropes created by its differential rotation formed. As the upper loops of these ropes reached the surface, flares of high-energy electrons were hurled out into space at the speed of light. These solar explosions were so powerful, a single, small flare contained enough electrical energy to power the entire world for a billion years.

As this eruption of supersonic electrons struck the sun's

corona, gigantic plasma waves and fast-drift radiation bursts moving *faster* than light were created. In turn, these collided with the sun's chromosphere and were instantly shattered into shock waves, intense radio, microwave, X-ray, gamma, and cosmic radiation pulses. Within six minutes, these pulses would reach the earth, completely disrupting all magnetic- and electronic-operated equipment.

The solar flares of 13–14 February 1944 would eventually prove to be the worst since observations and records were begun in the early seventeenth century. The horrendous rain of charged particles that they sent plowing into the higher latitudes of the earth created aurora borealises as far south as Madrid and Rome and completely destroyed radio and navigational equipment throughout most of Europe, the British Isles, western Russia, and the North African littoral.

The main communications center for the Allied Air Force Command Mediterranean was in the basement of the twelve-hundred-room palace of Charles IV, the eighteenth-century Bourbon king of the Two Sicilies in Caserta, thirty miles north of Naples. The vast space assigned to it had been cut into cubicles and offices by wooden partitions. Now, in its very heart, the Tactical Mission Communications Section, Colonel Climer prowled, constantly checking the row of clocks on one wall.

It was now 3:10.

Ever since his garbled conversation with Freyberg, Climer's sense of panic had been expanding. From what he could make of the general's words, it was obvious the New Zealander had *not* been informed of the changes in the bombing strike against Monte Cassino. An inconceivable screwup. But Climer was experienced enough in the ways of military bureaucracy to know such things were often routine.

It was the *corollary* of that failure that really had his head zinging. If Freyberg actually didn't know, then his scheduled assault on Monastery Ridge at 0430 hours this day was still in effect. And *that* meant there would be Allied soldiers right in the middle of that target zone!

Climer had immediately ordered his radio operators to attempt to raise either Wilson or Eaker, turn those damned Fortresses back. But nobody, not even General Jacob Devers, Wilson's deputy commander, or his staff knew precisely where the theater commander was. With their radios now nearly in total malfunction, it had also been impossible to put out a trace on him.

It was the same with Eaker. The general had personally told Climer that he intended to fly over to Anzio, talk up the possibility of precision bombing runs there. Since his departure, nothing had been heard from him. For all Climer knew, Eaker and that damned little airplane of his could be down with him dead or captured.

Around 2:00 A.M. Climer got a break. One of his operators had suddenly gotten a signal from a ham operator in Spain, call sign SRX99B. The section duty officer asked if they could use him to relay to Freyberg. Climer stared at him. Jesus Christ, a helluva goofy and risky way to transmit secret military information. But what the hell, they had no choice.

They transmitted the coded message, giving the Spanish ham only what was absolutely necessary for him to contact Freyberg's HQ and relay it to them. Now the big question was: had Freyberg received the message?

He paused beside an operator, the man slowly twirling dials. From his speaker came the deafening sizzles and moans of sun-affected atmospherics. The operator looked around at him helplessly. "I'm sorry, sir. The air's completely blacked out on us."

Oh, God, Climer thought, *heads are going to roll over this. And one of them's going to be mine.*

General Freyberg didn't say a word when told that all radios were now completely nonfunctional, not a word. He

merely stared long at the staffer who informed him, then turned
and went outside again. It seemed as if the outside held some
solace against his rage.

The time was 3:18, an hour and twelve minutes away
from the moment his corps would storm up that blasted hill.
Unless his runners got to them first. But as an old soldier, he
knew the obstacles they'd be facing.

He turned to look up at the monastery, the vision of it
changed slightly with the lowering moonlight striking it at
an angle now. He glowered at it across all that expanse of
winter night and tried to will his mind to his boys hunkered
down up there, waiting, watching the minutes tick off as they
brought themselves to that irrational pitch of adrenaline and
pride and just plain stupidity that made a soldier leap away
from safety and charge into the guns that were trying to kill
him. Yet he knew the futility of transmitting his thoughts,
knew that unless his men received verbal orders to stand
down, they would carry out their mission without hesitation.

The general had been correct about the runners. His staff
had dispatched seven, three in Jeeps and four on motorcycles. They had to cover approximately eight miles to reach
the battalion CPs on the lower slopes of Monte Cassino
where other messengers on foot would then have to climb
another mile up to the assault companies.

Most of their run was along the front line. Two motor-
cyclists were knocked out almost immediately, picked off by
fire from both sides of the line. Without radios, none of the
Allied forward companies and picket posts had been warned
that runners would be coming through their sector. As soon
as they spotted objects moving so rapidly and alone across
all that moonlit white, they had opened on them. The Kraut
gun posts did the same thing.

Within thirty-five minutes of leaving the headquarters at
Cosiliatte, two more messengers had been stopped. One of
the Jeeps hit a shell hole and flipped over onto its driver,

while another runner had his cycle shot out from under him. Soon after, a second Jeep, its driver trying frantically to escape enfilading fire, got bogged down in a snowfield and was killed.

That left two.

Smoker Wineberg was thinking, *Christ, we got a fuckin' parade going here.* They were plowing through corridors, the floodwater up to their knees now, freezing cold, their legs getting numb. They heard the frantic chirps of rats that swarmed, making Vs on the surface. Holding his Thompson in one hand, he had a little Italian boy cradled in his other arm. The boy had dark, round eyes and tossled hair and snot dripping from his nose.

Directly ahead was one of the younger monks, Dom Something-or-other, leading them, moving steadily through the water, holding up the hem of his black robe like a shy girl daintily crossing a stream. Behind them, the rest of Blue Team and the other monks, some also carrying children, came on. The tall one, Dom Matrinola, had the limp abbot on his back, the old man's shriveled fingers gripping his cowl.

They were headed for the monastery cemetery. Matrinola told them they could escape down the slope where the tram station and tracks were. He had not seen German troopers in the area, he said. Once down beyond the main slope, they could follow a mule trail down to the valley floor.

Wineberg watched the monk ahead of him curiously. He was the first monk he'd ever seen, such a young man, strong looking, like an athlete. Why in hell would any man become a monk? Wineberg wondered. Lock himself up in a holy prison without family or drink or women. Stupid.

Smoker had never been religious minded. He figured no god, *any* damn god, really gave a rat's ass about him or the routes of his life. Those things were solely *his* concern. If he screwed up, there was nobody else to blame.

He felt the little boy's breath against his cheek. The kid

was sick, trembling yet skin-hot at the same time. He didn't make a sound, simply sat quietly in the crook of Smoker's arm, his big eyes watching with the same distant, vacant look he'd seen in faces all over this country.

Such lack of expression always reminded him of the Depression days back in the States, only those had been *American* faces, hollow-eyed and lean but with that same dull disconnection. Winos coming off two-week binges, shivering in the cold as they waited for the mission houses in south Georgia and west Texas to open; families standing in dole lines just to get a stinking bowl of cold soup and a chunk of bread; bindlestiffs in dark boxcars coming into the icy gray dawn of towns in northern Colorado or Montana . . .

He heard a click. *Oh, Jesus!*

He was partly turned away when the twin grenades went off. Water and pieces of Dom Something-or-other came hurtling back into him. He felt the concussion wave cross through his legs like a sudden burst of heat. He remained perfectly still, heard through the ringing in his ears the others shouting, saw Cowboy and Weesay plowing forward, their guns up to cover his back, Weesay calling, "Easy, baby, come back easy now," and two of the women blubbering incoherently.

The little boy was still locked in silence. Smoker turned his head, looked at him. Some of the monk's blood dripped from the boy's ear, a piece of yellow fatty tissue. He reached over and flicked it off; its presence on the child's skin seemed like an indecency.

Holding the boy high over his head so that his own body would shield him, Wineberg began to retrace his steps, lifting his boots high and then easing them back down with steady deliberateness on the chance the Krauts had strung more trip wires they had somehow missed before.

It took him several minutes to get clear. Two monks tried to get around him, run to their monastery brother. Smoker cursed at them, shoved them away. "Back off, goddammit. Y'all ain't no good to him now." They didn't understand what he was saying, stood there looking and looking down the corridor at the remnants of the body of Dom Something-or-other floating in a pool of blood so red in the flashlight beams, both his legs blown off, one stump bobbing obscenely in the flow current.

Withdrawing back down the corridor, Parnell, Bird, and Dom Matrinola discussed options, the tall monk still carrying his abbot. Matrinola had the sharp-beaked features of a bird of prey and eyes that seemed to carry flames down deep.

"Look, there's gotta be another way outta here, Padre," Parnell said.

"All the corridors converge on the cloister and basilica," Matrinola said. "There will be soldiers there."

Red thought a moment, then turned and waved little Eustacio up. "Tell the padre how we came in."

The little Italian bowed profusely to Matrinola, then explained, "We came through the Rabbit Warren, Dom Matrinalo."

"Can we go out the same way?" Parnell asked.

The monk thought a moment. *"Sí,* I think perhaps we *can* get out there without being seen."

Parnell held the flashlight on his watch: 3:49. "We've got maybe an hour and a half to get out and down that damned slope before daylight," he said. "So, let's get this son of a bitch rolling."

They headed back the way they'd come, Bird out front, Matrinola calling directions. Wyatt had hastily fashioned a dragline, using a loaded clip pouch tied to two rope belts the monks wore, casting it out and then dragging it back along the floor to trigger any trip wires. The men's small flashlights threw tubes of light. The water had reached their waists now.

Eight minutes later, they came under direct machine gun fire.

Strategic Bombing Mission 144 Alpha had completed its rendezvous over Fóggia two minutes ahead of schedule, its four flights layered out in bombing formation. Every aircraft was now on individual power phone communications, the flight leaders issuing formation changes by flasher light.

At 3:56 Major Ellerbrock ordered Lieutenant Ledy to signal his wingmen and flight leaders that he was initiating rendezvous breakout to head for the Initial Point. The flasher light clicked loudly and threw a penumbrial glow onto the copilot's window.

A moment later, Ellerbrock dipped the big B-17G into a left bank, bringing up the nose slightly and easing on power to offset the increased drag of the turn. Around they came, his gyroscope compass indicators swinging slowly. As they approached 261 degrees, he began bringing the aircraft out of the turn until they were level again, engines and atitude stabilized.

Behind them, the entire formation, in perfect synched turns, followed until they were all aligned to their new heading.

At precisely 0405 hours, New Zealand Division's preassault barrage started. Two hundred guns went off simultaneously, their thunder rolling across the Liri Valley. Battalion level 105mm and 155mm towed fieldpieces and airborne 75mm pack howitzers. Farther back, the Corps batteries joined in with their big eight-inch and 240mm fixed howitzers casting two- and three-hundred-pound shells twenty miles.

But with no radio contact to forward observers, the gun crews had switched to time-on-target block barraging, traversing their shells from one coordinate section to the next and then back again. Still, the crew captains were very aware that their own assault units were only a thousand yards downslope of the target zone. They tended to overelevate. As a result, their shells were overshooting the forward part of Monastery Hill and the Abbey, landing instead in the forests behind it.

To make things worse, the moon's light had dimmed drastically as it neared the western horizon. Then dense billows of smoke from the impact explosions and burning trees began sweeping across the entire ridge, completely blotting it from view. Now the gun crews weren't even able to track their hits with binoculars so as to adjust fire.

The first big round that came in over the monastery sounded to Keppler in his dream like a freight train, a big night steamer back in Selesia, pounding through the darkness. He was standing on a hill with his heavy SS coat on, the night freezing and the sound of the train echoing off into forested distances. In the dream, he complained to someone who was there. He couldn't make out who, just a shadow.

When the round actually struck, the concussion wave blowing through solid rock knocked him clear off his bunk and onto the stone floor. He lay there, confused, his mind zipping between reality and dream. He heard men yelling, lifted his head.

Then the entire world began to explode in one, rolling, crashing upheaval of sound, deep in it the sizzling, slurring reverberations of more incoming shells. The steel ceiling of his dugout hummed with vibration, dust rained down. The ground shook and went on shaking. He could feel the intensity of its movements through his body, his head rattling, his mind tearing off in all sorts of horrified directions.

Sergeant Teufell appeared beside him, crawling. He shoved his face at his, shouting over the roaring. "Are you hurt, Major?"

"What is happening?"

"We're being bombarded, sir. Stay down, Herr Major, stay down."

Yes, Keppler thought frenziedly, *yes.* He could not believe the sound. It was like being inside a tornado, a whirlwind gone totally out of control. He felt his stomach lurch with fear. His earlier diarrhea had abated. Now he felt its rushing return grip his insides, vaguely wondred if he would shit in his pants, didn't care, just lay there with his head cradled between his elbows, listening, feeling the sounds of doom coming down on him.

Seven minutes earlier, Parnell and his men had been preparing to assault the Kraut machine gun. It was somewhere around a curve in the tunnel, the gunners ricocheting their rounds against the stone walls, sending lead caroming and whisking through the air and making bubble lines through the water.

People had been hit, Red knew, voices screaming, bodies surging back, trying to flee the savagery of the incoming bullets. Here and there, he saw his men, countering the rush, moving forward toward him, firing back at the curved walls.

He realized the old abbot's face was nearby. The man was staring in utter horror at him, wispy hair pasted wetly to his shriveled scalp. Then suddenly Dom Matrinola popped up out of the water like an avenging Greek sea god.

Sol and Angelo went plowing past him, cleaving water and growling obscenities. German voices echoed back at them between machine gun bursts. Red grabbed Matrinola's limp hood, dragged him and the abbot past him. "Get those fucking women and children back up the tunnel," he bellowed at him. "Get 'em *back*." Then he turned and moved forward.

Someone yelled, "Grenade!"

Everybody went under water. Parnell saw the flash through his eyelids, felt the concussion sweep back through the water. It made his stomach burn as if a shot of poison had hit his intestines. He surfaced. Smoker and Cowboy came up nearby. "Who's hit?" he shouted at them.

"Some of the refugees," Smoker called back. "They killed the kid." His dark eyes were wild. He stood up fully now and let go a long burst from his Thompson just as three others fired too, their muzzle cracks thunderous.

"Grenade the bastards and converge," Parnell hollered.

The machine gun fire stopped, leaving a crazy, thrumming silence. Abruptly a German voice shouted something. Red saw Wyatt twenty feet ahead of him arch up and heave a grenade and then Angelo doing the same. They turned, hid their faces from the blast.

Twin explosions, flashes of light like captured lightning. Then everyone was moving forward, each man laying in suppression fire high overhead, ricocheting and banking his rounds.

Two dead Germans in dark camo battle dress were beside their MG-34, which they had been firing from the waist, heat gloves on their hands. One had no lower face. He floated on his back and water sloshed in and out of the huge bloody cavity.

There was a violent blast far away. The dripping walls of the tunnel trembled. Right after, another blast came and another and another until their percussions became one long, roaring, continuous detonation. The walls and floor of the tunnel shook violently, water rained off the overhead, and the grenade smoke shivered and made vibration lines. Everyone looked up, thinking *What the hell?* like blind men in the presence of thunder.

Finally, Weesay sucked spit through his teeth, turned, and looked at Parnell in stunned surprise. "Chee-sus H Chris', Lieutenant," he croaked. "This fuckin' place is under barrage!"

At 0429 hours exactly, the guns fell silent, all at once, their distant flashings vanished as if they were no longer there, sucked back into the deeper shadows westward, their last rounds still arching in with sizzling, cloth-tearing whispers. Then utter silence, heavy and dense.

Fifty-seven seconds later, the assault companies of the New Zealand and Indian Divisions came up out of their ravines and jagged rocks like dark creatures from out of the earth, surging forward, heavy with weapons and ordnance, howling, rushing, infantry squads and platoons and machine gun and mortar teams moving along a ragged line in the fading moonlight.

They came swiftly at first, dipping and dodging around boulders, leaping rocks, firing as they charged, their lines breaking into scattered segments after a hundred yards, all precision lost as the ground sundered them into isolated groups and individuals. Men shouted to one another, cursed, screamed, others ran in total silence.

Then counterfire came from far up the slope, as the German guns and crews that had survived the bombardment opened up, firing downhill, gravity speeding their bullets, their tracers laying out hot red lines. Soon mortar explosions started blowing gaps in the advancing forward waves.

Bodies and parts of bodies and smoke and patches of fire and rock slivers like whirling knife blades and the *thrupppping* spray of automatic fire rolling down in higher registers and the deep-throated lethal claps and searing whinnyings of bigger shells rocketing through the frozen, near-dawn air.

They advanced to within eight hundred yards of the monastery. The gigantic building was lost in backlit folds of smoke and fire. Moving slower now, they reached the seven-hundred-yard point. Far downslope, the second wave began its lunging, charging advance.

Six hundred yards . . .

The German counterfire thickened, coalescing into a deadly storm that raked back and forth. Sections of the assaulting line began to waver, then stall as men no longer advanced, instead went to ground, seeking defilade. Seconds ticked off, turned into minutes. Now, in the flashes of the enemy guns, troops were visible, a horde coming down between them, dropping quickly along the upper slope and spreading out in full counterattack.

At 4:33, Lieutenant Ball from his bombadier position spotted the IP, Lake Sepino, glowing far down there in the last shards of moonlight. He notified Ellerbrock. A few moments later, he felt the huge bomber swing to the right, the lake coming up now at an angle and the ribbon of Highway 6 visible, a line like the mark a finger leaves in velvet.

He glanced toward the east. From this altitude, he could see the faint glow of dawn far beyond the mountains now, the line of it jiggling as the Fortress began to shake slightly. The headwind they'd been bucking shifted around to come in off their left wing. Finally, number 616 leveled up and then began a gradual climb.

Ahead lay darkness. Earlier, Ball had watched artillery working near the Liri Valley. Now everything had ceased. Yet almost due west, very faintly, he saw other artillery start up near Anzio, flashes like sheet lightning over the sea. He eased back into his chair, flexed his cold hands, and breathed easily through his mask, the smell of rubber and long-dried saliva always there, and looked ahead and waited to go to work.

The German paratroopers had vacated the tunnel works beneath the abbey, abandoned their hunt. Now Parnell could hear fighting, small arms, and mortar explosions far away, as if they were from a war movie coming so faintly from a room far down a hotel hall.

They moved on, past the dead machine gunners, the tunnel narrowing and the water up to their chests. The men had to literally drag some of the refugees with lifeguard carries. Two women and Smoker's little boy had been killed, several others wounded. The women kept screaming and reaching backward, Parnell and Wyatt hollering and shoving everybody along.

They reached a thick wooden door. Dom Matrinola said it opened directly into the Rabbit Warren. They hauled on it but it wouldn't budge. Its ancient wood had swelled from the water. Parnell yelled up to Kaamanui on point, "Blow the son of a bitch."

Everyone except Sol moved back around a corner, waited.

Four minutes later, the sergeant came plowing back through the water. The explosions were muffled. A cloud of smoke and water droplets rolled back through the tunnel. They could hear hissing, water shooting outward, then in a sudden expulsion as the door crashed out. The water instantly began draining away, a current forming, pulling them along.

There were more refugees in the warren than there had been earlier, several hundred cowering back against the corridor walls. When the water hit them, they began to scream and pray, some of those near the door actually getting swept off their feet, sliding along and out the entrance doorways, the water pouring out, smoking as it hit the snowy air.

Abbot Diamare refused to go any farther. Matrinola lowered him to one of the hutch shelves. The old man wept, looking like an ancient, drowning bird, saying he had to remain, to administer to these poor people, *his* people, his *flock*.

Parnell pushed his way back to the two monks. "What the hell's the problem?" he demanded.

"The Father Abbot says he can no longer leave," Matrinola said.

Red ignored that. "Pick him up."

Dom Matrinola turned his hawk face on him. "Neither of us can leave now."

Parnell glared. "No, that ain't the way it's gonna go, fella. My mission is to get this man out of here. That's exactly what I intend to do. Even if I have to tie both of you and *carry* you out."

"But these people—" Matrinola began.

Red cut him off: "They can come with us if they want. They can stay here if they want. They're not my concern, *he* is."

Diamare leaned forward, reached beseechingly to him, saying in Italian, *"Signore tenente,* please, you must understand. I have taken vows to God and—"

Again Parnell interrupted, thrust his face down close to the old man's. "I don't give a shit about your vows, Padre. You hear that out there? This position's under *assault.* From the sound of it, we're *losing*. That attack could kill you, or the Krauts will as soon as it's over. Either way, they'll blame *us* for your murder." He swung around to Matrinola. "No, no way, Matrinola. You got ten seconds to decide whether you come freely or we carry you."

The huge monk stared at him through narrowed eyes.

"Come on, goddammit, which is it going to be?"

Matrinola finally nodded slowly. He turned and lifted Diamare. He and Parnell, the other Mohawkers immediately falling in behind, went through the doorway and down into the snow.

The paratrooper runner came down into Keppler's bunker. He was an *Oberjager*, a corporal. Keppler's gun crews had already left cover, emerging soon after the artillery bombardment stopped. Then as they realized the entire position was under attack, they quickly assembled at their guns, whipping off barrel jackets and shifting ammunition crates, preparing for action. Now they were sitting there, squinting out toward the sound of fire and waiting for orders.

Their position had remained untouched by the artillery. Several fires from the shelling were burning back near the paratroopers' bivouac. Smoke smelling of pine wood kept drifting down toward them and the air was filled with sparks and stone dust.

The paratrooper demanded to see the battery leader. They told him Major Keppler was still in his bunker. The corporal looked at them, puzzled. "Your battery captain is a major?" The men nodded, laughed.

Now, stepping onto the rock floor of the bunker, the corporal called, *"Major, wo ist du?"*

Keppler stepped from his room, growling, "What is it?" His face was pale, his bald head gleaming under the ceiling light. The paratrooper looked at him with open insolence. He did not bother to salute.

"We are under attack, sir," he said sharply. "Your orders

are to contain the reverse slope. You will prevent any attack
that develops on this side. All radios are out so you will fire
at your discretion."

Keppler slitted his eyes. He did not like the corporal's
tone. "Where is this attack coming from?" he demanded.

The paratrooper shook his head. His answer was curt.
"You have your orders."

"How— Wait! You there, stand at attention."

The paratrooper ignored him, whirled, and disappeared
back up the bunker steps.

All their grenade traps had exploded at the caves. Two
dead Germans lay outstretched, blood in the snow and smoke
still filtering out of the rock holes, as Parnell and the others
dashed past. Behind them, several refugees had started down,
too, hesitated, then continued on, following the men's tracks
through the snow. More refugees came down until there were
about thirty people trailing them as they headed down into
the gully.

Parnell paused, hurrying the others past him. Matrinola
lumbered along with the abbot on his back now, refusing help.
When Wyatt passed Red, his eyes were tight, grim. He shook
his head.

Red looked back up the trail. Dawn light was beginning
to fuse into the air, dimmed slightly by periodic clouds of
smoke that drifted over them. He could see the Italians, little
Eustacio with them, dark shadows, coming down, stumbling,
jostling into each other like terrified sheep moving down a
draw, carrying their meager bundles and children.

"Damn it!" he hissed and waved them to hurry.

0456 hours

With aircraft 616 in the lead, the bomber formation had
come straight up Highway 6, past San Pietro and San Vittorio

di Lazio and what the Americans called Million Dollar Hill, which marked the entrance to the Liri Valley, covering in minutes what Fifth Army had taken so many bloody months to traverse.

Below them the earth was merging out of darkness while beyond the Abruzzis, daylight pasteled the eastern sky. Now, directly ahead, Ellerbrock and Ledy could actually see the Abbey of Monte Cassino. It sat out there beautifully gray white on its promontory, alone, high enough to catch the first solid light from the east.

The captain clicked his power phone. "Okay, everybody stay off the wire. We're making the approach . . . Bobby, we've got target visual."

Below and forward of them, bombardier Ball was already peering through his Norden bombsight telescope, watching the Liri Valley come into view. During the actual bombing run, he would be in control of the aircraft, his movements with the telescope automatically being transmitted to the controls of the B-17. Then, using the imput data of air speed, altitude, wind, and bomb weight, the unit would calculate the proper trajectory and drop point. Once that point was reached, it would automatically release the bombs.

But for now, Ellerbrock's eyes rapidly scanned back and forth over his instrument indicators. He had to keep the bomber within precise parameters, particularly its speed at 155 miles per hour. Everything looked sharp.

He clicked his phone: "All indicators on and holding steady. Okay, Bobby, she's yours."

"Roger."

For the next forty-five seconds, Ellerbrock and Ledy were spectators, eased back in their seats, feeling the plane get sluggish as the Norden brought down the bay doors, the unit immediately adjusting controls. They were into the first flak now, puffy bursts of black smoke and flashes on the ground looking like camera flashbulbs. At first the flak was too low, but it gradually rose until the bursts were appearing at their altitude.

Abruptly, Ellerbrock felt the plane lift sharply and its four

Curtiss-Wrights surge as it was suddenly freed of its six-thousand-pound bomb load. He shoved forward, his hands prepared to take over the controls. Through his phone plug, he heard Ball's voice calling out, "All released and away . . . Take her."

His hands gripped the wheel, felt the Norden release, felt the weight of the aircraft come back to him. From the corner of his eye, he saw Ledy's head turned, looking back and down, seconds ticking off, and then the reflections of quick flashes and the faint sounds of distant explosions barely heard over the steady roaring of his engines.

Parnell heard the whistling whine of the bombs before he realized there was a formation of B-17s high overhead, their engines lost in the sounds of the ground fighting, their brown bodies way up there catching sunlight.

He stopped dead, turned to look upslope, saw Wyatt glance at him, saw Cowboy and Angelo and the others farther back suddenly motionless for a fleeting moment. Then they were diving for cover, someone dragging Matrinola and the abbot down with them. Farther up the gully, the refugees remained motionless for a few seconds longer, staring overhead. Then, realizing what was coming at them, they burst into motion and came stumbling, running, screaming toward him, some going into crevices and side holes and under boulders.

The first stick of bombs crashed into the ridge in sudden twin lines of massive explosions. The first ones hit far up the back road in the woods, the others slammed into the ground fractions of a second later. Then more bombs struck. Their detonations were so continuous the spacings disappeared into one roaring cauldron of sound. Concussion waves raced outward and down the slope like a hurricane wind.

Parnell, pressed tightly against a boulder, turned his head slightly. He watched as great billows of gray smoke climbed upward, roiling, filled with huge chunks of sundered ridge rock and masonry, everything hurling upward like rocket

shells and then arching, slowing, falling back, some the size
of Jeeps.

For a moment, his mind stalled, overwhelmed by the horrendous sensual imput. Then like the release of a floodgate,
adrenaline and panic and shock jammed through his body
and he was moving, reacting, legs going seemingly of their
own volition, carrying him back up the gully.

Oh, Christ Almighty, we gotta get these people outta here!

They were about four hundred yards down the slope. Fortunately, most of the bombs were striking off target, to the
back of the monastery and toward the western side of the
ridge. The clouds of smoke now came rolling down toward
them. He saw his men coming down, too. Some were lug-
ging refugees, gripped at the waist, flung over shoulders,
dropping down crazy-fast, headlong, their faces jarred, gone
white.

The smoke and rock dust caught them, instantly enveloped
everything in a whirling, pressurized cloud of dense gray
mist. A monk appeared beside him. Parnell grabbed him,
shoved him forward, whirled, grabbed at someone else who
emerged suddenly out of the gloom, Eustacio. He shifted his
weight, propelled him down and away. All around him the
air and mist and dust seemed energized with a continuous
upheaval of sound, the roaring, crashing, crescendo of explosions.

The enemy bombers were long gone.

Keppler prowled among the wreckage, pausing now and
then to study the reduced walls of the monastery with awe,
nothing standing upright anymore, only great rubble piles
that seethed smoke and flicks of fire, the smoke smearing
across the entire sky, giving the new morning light a dirti-
ness, the color of dried sewer on cement. Soldiers climbed
and probed and called out among the ruins, the place already
taking on the mantle of ancient violence.

The corpses of his lost men had already been laid out in a

line. The others walked about with stunned, remote faces, not holding his gaze when he looked at them. Several of the battery's guns had been destroyed. Sandbags and ammo crates and unfired shells were strewn down the slope, the weapons themselves torn and upended. Smoke sifted along the ground like a gell, filling craters and bunkers and spider holes. The firing from the other side of the ridge had dissolved down into sporadic bursts, scattered and feeble like the last weightless punches of an exhausted boxer.

Earlier, while still in his bunker, Keppler had heard the bombs coming down and then they were there, quick as a blink. The entire ridge shook with such a tremendous jolting that it had instantly halted his mind, all thought and reflex gone, only the sensual absorbing of the shiftings and lunges of the earth and the bunker walls and the thunderous *crack-crack-crack* of the bombs striking with tiny spacings between them, almost too rapid to detect.

He felt the concussion waves hurtle overhead, felt the air in the bunker get sucked up through the stairway, hiss out seams in the steel plating of the ceiling. His ears burned. He tried to stand, couldn't. Instinctively he looked up, saw the steel plates vibrating so violently it was as if his vision were blurred. They gave off a high-pitched whistling. Smoke began pouring down into the bunker until it was choking with the stuff, dense with the acidic stink of expended explosives and rock dust.

He became aware of a warmness and realized, oddly without horror, that he had crapped in his pants.

Suddenly the other side of the bunker came crashing down. Sounds magnified, roarings, avalanches of stone. His mind came back, instructed him with precise urgency that he must get away. He began to crawl, his head held close to the bunker floor. He vaguely heard men yelling somewhere overhead. He kept on, panting with terror-effort, whimpering. He reached the stairway, stopped for a moment, unable to continue. He drew his knees up, felt chunks of rock striking his bald head, his shoulders. He huddled there.

The thunder and motion seemed to go on and on and on.

Now he stepped gingerly among the remnants of his command. He couldn't remember how he had come out of the bunker, how long he had been here. He held the folds of his great SS coat tightly about him lest the others see the soiling of his trousers. He could faintly smell the sourness of his own excrement when he moved, feel the slimy grossness between the cheeks of his ass.

Now, for the first time, he realized he was standing in sunshine, a break in the clouds of dust and smoke. At his feet, some of the snow had melted from the heat of the bombardment. Little rivulets made lacy webbings through it.

He looked out over the Liri Valley. Through the haze he saw fields, a river like a winding crayon line and roads and tiny villages, all of it so peaceful looking, distance hiding the signs of war. His gaze swept eastward, to the foot of Monastery Ridge, a landscape of jagged stone precipices and wash gullies in dawn shadow.

He spotted movement, a thousand yards downslope near the knoll called Monte Calvario. He leaned forward, squinted, finally made out little ant figures moving in a line along a mule trail. He shouted for someone to bring binoculars. A gunner came down, silently handed over a pair.

The figures leapt into human form through the lens: Italian refugees, men and women, some children. He watched them toiling down. Filthy, brutish things, he thought. And suddenly he wanted their blood, demanded it, *deserved* it. He whirled around. "Prepare to fire," he bellowed. He pointed. "Down there. See? *Kill* them!"

The surviving gunners looked up at him, then, one by one, they pushed to their feet and moved down to two of the antitank cannon still serviceable. There was the clean crack of breech wedge blocks sliding back and the sleek, heavy sound of fresh shells banging and the blocks slamming forward again. The guns' traversing gears made soft hums as their muzzles inched around into firing position.

A gun captain, peering through his ranging scope, called out. "Sir, all I see are peasants."

"Kill them."

"But, Herr Major, there are children and—"

Keppler viciously turned on him. "You have been given an order, you imbecile. Now fire on those people. *Fire!*"

The twin discharges of the weapons made strange, screeching blasts as the shells were rammed through their tapered barrels, sending the compressed 28mm rounds out at tremendous velocity. Keppler watched the shells make two double lines of bluish smoke as they rocketed down the slope, saw sudden geysers of dust appear on the mule trail, people scattering, heard the impacts coming back two seconds later.

Again and again the guns fired off. As the rounds struck, heavier smoke and dust rolled out and up into the new sunshine. Keppler felt a shout of pure joy, of retribution, leap from his throat: "We *have* them," he screamed. "We *have* them."

He ran forward.

Someone yelled a warning.

His mind absorbed it and he paused, suddenly realized what the cry meant, went cold as he tried desperately to draw back his leg. Too late. The trip wire tugged so gently at his right ankle. There were two sharp explosions just beside him. He felt himself being lifted by an invisible force. Blood spewed all around him. He somersaulted in the air, the earth and sky revolving. Excruciating pain jammed through his body, up from his legs, into his torso, his chest, his brain.

The last thing he saw as he hit the ground were the two bloody stumps of his thighs, his trousers ripped off, the stumps grotesque and jagged and pulsing. He screamed. Shock hit him. Slowly, the pain began to seep off and then the light, too, until his vision was dim and it was as if he were in a thickening, soundless darkness filled only with spirals and shafts and tendrils of light like phosphorescent sea creatures moving through the deep.

Then he was gone.

* * *

The instant he heard those tapered-barreled shells slamming through the air, Sol Kaamanui knew precisely what they were and what they were coming at. His muscles were already projecting him to the side of the mule trail when they struck twenty yards ahead of him. He went down into rock scree, the impact explosions singing in his ears, stone slivers zinging over his body.

He and Cappacelli had been in the middle of the line of refugees, everybody hustling quickly, knowing that the moment they were on the other side of Monte Calvario, they'd be home free.

Now he lifted his head, called out, "Angelo, you okay?"

"Yeah . . . Jesus!"

The rounds had landed in the middle of several men and women. They were strewn about among smoking chunks of rock, their bodies lying in contorted positions on the ground, some without limbs. From behind him, women began to moan, a strange, keening sound, rising up out of the stone landscape. A single wail rose above the others, knifing through the lower sounds.

Sol turned hs head. A little girl came running along the road toward the impact craters, which were still fuming tendrils of smoke. Her face was streaked with blood but her eyes were bright. He shouted, began to come up to intercept her. Angelo beat him to it, rising quicker, coming up into a full sprint instantly like a runner out of the blocks, going low, arms outstretched, reaching to scoop up the child.

There was another sundering of air and the screel of incoming rounds. *"Angelo!"* Sol bellowed and came completely to his feet. But he was off balance. He tried to dive forward, instead went down on one knee, rose, started forward again just as one of the incoming rounds struck Cappacelli directly in the back.

Sol actually saw it go searing through him, making a gaping hole through which he could see light, the round going at such high speed that its impact didn't even hurl him forward.

Angelo's blood fumed after it, tendrils and lines of flesh, exiting his body to explode directly in front of him. The sundering crack and upsurge of earth instantly engulfed the little girl. A second later, it swept over Sol, heat like the sudden opening of a furnace door.

He felt something hit him, powerful as a solid punch into his right side. It threw him back. He fell down, slid across scree, and lay for a moment, looking up at smoke crossing over him. It made the sunlight oily-looking.

Then the pain struck, his entire torso flaring with fire. *Oh, Christ, I'm hit.* He tried to rise, was distinctly aware of his blood running out of him. It was almost as if he could hear it, like a siphoning through tubes. *Jesus, I can hear myself bleeding to death,* he thought.

Silly, silly. Despite the pain, he wanted to laugh at the absurdity of it.

Death.

That thought wasn't so funny. He experienced a thundering surge of terror and panic go through him. He blinked repeatedly, thinking crazily yet methodically that if he blinked fast enough, he could beat his own insides from leaving him. Smoke drifted. It had no smell. He saw a shadow. Parnell, peering down at him, touching his face.

He tried to smile. But then Parnell faded away.

Aftermath

It was far from over.

The New Zealand Corps, like the others, had been driven back down the western slope of Monastery Hill with heavy casualties. Many in the first assault wave were killed by the American bombs. Freyberg was stunned. Not only by the losses but also by the bitter irony that the Germans had used the bombing to turn the abbey, now merely a mountain of sundered rock, into a nearly impregnable defensive position.

But determined to take "that bloody hill," he regrouped and hurled his battalions back up the slope. This time it was an even worse slaughter. Some of his line companies lost 60 percent of their men within the first fifteen minutes of engagement. Still, the others doggedly hung on for three whole days before finally being withdrawn.

It would take two months more before Monastery Ridge was finally occupied. On 18 May, the Krauts pulled out to head north. That afternoon, the Polish Volunteer Corps, made up of survivors of both Soviet and Nazi massacres in Poland and under the command of Lieutenant General Wladyslav Anders, made it all the way to the top across a landscape scattered with decaying bodies and bright red poppies bursting forth among the bones.

Seventeen days later, on 4 June, Rome was taken. Unfortunately for the men who had given their lives and their blood to get there, the victory was quickly blown right off the front pages by the more dramatic start of the invasion of western Europe, Operation Overlord, on 6 June.

As for the remainder of the Italian campaign, it would be another year before units of the U.S. Fifth and British Eighth Armies would cross the River Po and occupy the last German stronghold in the mountains of northern Italy on 14 April 1945. It would occur only twelve days after the death of President Roosevelt and six days before the suicide of Adolph Hitler.

Naples, Italy
22 February 1944

The sun made Colonel Dunmore's glass of *limoncello* glisten like molten gold. He and Parnell were seated at a tiny table outside a café located in a narrow alley in the Spaccanopoli section of the city. It was cobblestoned. The walls were yellow with faded green shutters. The two other tables were occupied, an American sergeant with an Italian woman and two French sailors in their red-tufted caps. It was nearly noon.

Dunmore studied his companion. Red was drinking Sasso beer from Tuscany in a earthenware bottle. "You look like hell, John," he said finally.

"I expect I do, sir." Parnell took a long pull, looked up the alley. The day was cool but with the feel of early spring in the air. The previous night, he had been in a fight in a café somewhere off Vico Donnaromita, the main drag of the section. He was half drunk when a big, beer-bellied lieutenant of supply started giving him a batch of shit about his Mohawker patch, the guy saying, "What the hell outfit is that, fella? I've never seen that insignia before. What, you Indians that got drafted? Hey, whyn't you give us a dance around a fire, make the goddamn rain go away?"

Parnell hit him. He was solid despite his gut but he went

down like a dropped steer with Red right on him, going for his eyes, then breaking his nose and finally his elbow. Red's right hand reached, slapping for his boot knife, which fortunately wasn't there since he fully intended to kill the son of a bitch. MPs pulled him off, hauled him to a police barracks inside the Palazzo Marigliano until they could figure out how many courts-martial offenses they could lay on him.

"Good thing you weren't armed," Dunmore said. "You would have killed that poor bastard."

"Yeah."

The colonel smiled quietly. "Your instincts are still sharp. You'll be okay."

Parnell looked at him, said nothing.

"How's Kaamanui?"

"All right, sir. So far. He's getting shipped back to England this afternoon." Sol had been seriously wounded, a chunk of shell debris taking out two ribs, part of his gallbladder, and a hefty slice of side tissue. Except for Angelo, the rest of the team had gotten away without any major hits. Seven refugees were also killed, several more wounded. They'd quickly field-dressed Sol and the others and got them back to an Allied battalion aid station south of Cassino. From there, Kaamanui was transported to a general hospital in Naples.

Dunmore nodded. "Good. We can stop and see him before he leaves. . . . Sorry about Cappacelli."

"Yeah." *Sorry, everybody's always sorry.*

Dunmore sighed. "Some of the other teams have taken casualties, too. In fact, we lost *everyone* on White Team, either killed or captured. A combined op with the First Commando in Norway. Then Red Team lost three men in Greece."

White Team, Parnell thought, Lieutenant Dick Mellow. They'd bunked together during Mohawker training, Dick with the big snore and the big laugh. *Shit.*

Both men fell silent. Finally, Dunmore said simply, "They've given the Mohawkers back to me."

Parnell glanced up. "Oh? That's good, sir. Congratulations."

"Patton put a word in with Ike. They were both very impressed at your extraction of Diamare." He chuckled. "Even that little prick Nunn was surprisingly gracious when I told him. Hell, he even helped get you out of stockade."

Parnell had never met Major Nunn. But apparently the man had also been pleased with the Diamare mission. Through one of his OSS field agents, he'd ordered the remnants of Blue Team off the line and back to Naples for two weeks of rest and recuperation.

Dunmore leaned closer. "How are your men?" he asked softly. "Truly?"

"They're fine, sir," Red answered and thought, *Here it comes, the next mission. Another day, another hill.* It seemed suddenly as if there had never been a beginning and would never be an end. He finished the last of his beer, eased the bottle down. "Where?" he asked.

"France. Operation Overlord. The invasion of western Europe." Dunmore spoke so softly, Parnell had to lean in to hear him. "You'll go in just ahead of the 101st Airborne as Pathfinders. Then you'll link up with the French Resistance and move inland."

Parnell nodded.

"I'll bring in two replacements from Green Team for you. OSS sent them back to the States as instructors."

"No," Red said quickly. "No replacements, sir. Five men'll be enough."

Dunmore's eyes narrowed. "Will you be able to retain your force capability?"

"Hell yes, sir."

Dunmore considered that, inhaled, let the air out slowly. "All right. I'll cut your orders immediately. You can spend another week here." He grinned. "Just stay out of fights."

"Yes, sir."

"You want another beer?"

"No, sir."

Presenting . . .

A sample chapter from Charles Ryan's

next exciting Recon Force thriller

Storm Front

Coming from Pinnacle in 2005

Decision

Supreme Allied Commander General Dwight D. Eisenhower eased back his heavy chair from the long, green baize-covered conference table, rose, and walked to a series of tall windows across the room. He stood there a moment, then eased the thick blackout curtain aside slightly and silently gazed out.

In the darkness, he couldn't see the long stretch of neatly groomed lawn that went down to steep chalk cliffs that then sloped to the densely packed homes and buildings of the city of Portsmouth. Yet even if it had been day, everything would have appeared misty as rain, hurled by forty-five-knot winds, slammed against the French crystal panes.

He was in the library of Southwick House, his D-day headquarters. Seated behind him at the table were six of his senior commanders. On one side were his fellow Americans, Generals Omar Bradley and Walter Biddel-Smith, along with British Admiral Sir Bertram Ramsey. Across the table were

British Air Chief Marshall Sir Arthur Tedder, Ike's deputy commander, Deputy Air Chief Marshall Sir Trafford Leigh-Mallory, and General Bernard Montgomery in his usual corduroy trousers and roll-neck sweater.

Since the first of June, these men had met here twice a day, primarily to receive weather updates from their chief meteorologist, Group Captain J.M. Stagg, a dour but brilliant Scotsman who now was already two minutes late for this meeting.

Ever since March of 1943, the massive preparations for the invasion of western Europe and the opening of the Second Front against Nazi Germany had been under way. Now nearly a quarter million soldiers, sailors, airmen, and merchant seaman, with millions of tons of equipment and over a thousand ships in assembly ports from Felixstowe on the North Sea to Milford Haven, Wales, were on hold, waiting for the word to cross the English Channel.

D-day had originally been scheduled for 4 June. But then a violent low front, designated L5, had swept across the British Isles. Strong winds and drenching rain quickly turned the Channel into a cauldron. Eisenhower was forced to order the invasion postponed for at least forty-eight hours.

A light tap sounded at the library door and a young major came in to inform Eisenhower that Captain Stagg had arrived. The Scotsman swept in briskly, snapped to attention, and curtly apologized for his tardiness. He waited for Ike to return to his chair, then moved to a large weather map on an easel in front of a wall of books.

He quickly went over the latest weather reports from the three primary stations in Britain: the BFC office at Dunstable, the USAAF station in the Thames Valley, and the British Admiralty, London. Things didn't look good.

He then moved on to his own team's analysis of the situation. "Although it is admittedly quite dicey at this point," he said in his heavy accent, "I do believe we have a window. L5 has reached its dissipation cycle and another low front is behind it, L6. However, I believe this one will issue from the north, off the Greenland coast. L5 originated off Norway in the east." He indicated the areas on the map. "This difference will allow us a break during four and five June. It should last for at least eighteen hours."

Montgomery interrupted in his piping, squeaky voice, "How firm is your forecast of break, Captain?"

"I believe it is *very* firm, sir," Stagg anewered. "There *is* disagreement, I must admit. Both the Admiralty and Dunstable believe it will come in from the east. The Americans, however, agree with my analysis."

Eisenhower asked, "Is eighteen hours optimistic or a stretch?"

"l believe it would represent the median, General. A bit less, a bit more."

For the next twenty minutes, the commanders worked Stagg over with sharp, blunt questions. Tedder, Leigh-Mallory, and Admiral Ramsey were particularly concerned over ocean conditions as well as cloud cover above the French coast that could badly hamper air strikes. Montgomery challenged the meteorologist's conclusions, asked when the next opening would come. Stagg said 15 to 17 June. Eisenhower listened quietly while the captain tenaciously held his ground.

At last, Ike dismissed him and he and the others spent the next half hour discussing probabilities, opinions, and the feasibility of postponing until the next solid weather window. Opinions seemed evenly divided.

Eisenhower finally took a table vote. Tedder, Leigh-Mallory, and Ramsey were hesitant and called for continued postponement. Bradley, Bidell-Smith, and surprisingly, Montgomery, considering the harsh way he had gone after Stagg, voted to utilize the forecast break and launch the invasion immediately.

Eisenhower again rose from his chair and went to the window. No one spoke. The final decision was now on his shoul-

One

They were volunteers, Pathfinders from the 501st Parachute Infantry Regiment of the 101st Airborne Division. Yet, except for Blue Team and three noncoms transferred from the 82nd, which had already seen combat in Sicily and Salerno, they were all green and untested.

Standing forward of the open door, the stick jumpmaster, Lieutenant John "Red" Parnell, gave the men lined along both sides of the Douglas C-47 *Airtrain* a close study. He wasn't a part of the 501. Instead he was leader of a five-man unit designated Blue Team, which was part of an elite recon force called the Mohawkers.

All the team members were combat veterans from North Africa, Sicily, and Italy. Two of the original team had been lost at Monte Cassino, one killed, the other badly wounded. Now, besides Parnell, the unit consisted of Sergeant Wyatt Bird and three corporals, Cowboy Fountain, Weesay Laguna, and Smoker Wineberg.

Once on the ground with the drop zone secured for the main force of paratroopers scheduled to come in at 0130 hours, Blue Team's Task Mission required it to leave the other Pathfinders and move cross-country to link up with a circuit, or cell, of the French Resistance. Together, they would assault the German garrison guarding a small farmer's bridge across the River Pointe, a small tributary of the Douve, to prevent enemy reinforcements from reaching the DZ and the invasion beach designated Utah two miles beyond. They were then to quickly proceed due north, recover a cache of heavy weapons and explosives dropped the previous night, and assault a four-gun battery of German 155mm field howitzers emplaced above a coastal cliff near the town of Ravenoville, four miles north of Utah beach.

Parnell had deliberately scattered his own men and the three 501 noncoms among the jumpers on the chance somebody might freeze during the drop. Now as he scanned, it was easy for him to spot the combat vets, sitting quietly, some apparently even dozing, everybody with their faces blackened by camo-paint, which accentuated the whiteness of their eyes. The new men, however, kept shifting uneasily in their seats, stared a bit too long at the deck, or continuously fidgeted with their equipment.

Each man carried nearly 150 pounds of gear: T-7 chutes— no emergencies now since they would be jumping from only three hundred feet—weapons, bandoleers, and clip pouches of spare ammo, grenades, Hawkins mines, blocks of TNT, three days of K- and D-rations, smoke grenades, and signal flares. In addition, several had small bags roped to their legs that contained Eureka radar sets to mark out the three drop zones, A, B, and C, assigned to the 101st. Farther southeast, the 82nd Airborne Division was also deploying their own Pathfinder teams to light up *their* three DZs.

Parnell checked his watch. It was four minutes after midnight. They'd be over their jump point in six minutes.

Precisely three-quarters of an hour earlier, they'd taken off from the RAF base at Greenham Common, England, a flight of six aircraft from IX Troop Carrier Command. At first, they'd gone southwest, then turned due south and headed straight for the Cherbourg Peninsula, below them the ocean momentarily calmed and sparkling in brilliant moonlight while the plane's airstream hurtled past the open door filled with the roaring and smell of hot metal from the starboard 895-kW Pratt and Whitney engine.

Holding on to the static line cable overhead, Parnell shrugged his big shoulders boxer-style and settled into his bulky chute harness. Right then he felt the first tension begin, combat coming, down in his belly and chest, the adrenaline starting, the sensation not particularly unpleasant and somewhat like the butterflies he remembered before a football game: that anticipatory eagerness, joy even, to get on with the damned thing. Only now his feelings were controlled, quieted by the knowledge of his own deliberate professionalism, which had come after having been in similar situations so many times before.

The red light behind his head flicked on.

Parnell bellowed, "Stand up."

Everyone rose, their boots shuffling on the aluminum deck as they lined up in the center of the aircraft, facing him. He gave the order to hook up. Sharp metallic clicks as the men clipped their static lines to the overhead cable. He waited a moment, then called out, "Run your equipment check." Each man quickly checked the equipment of the man in front of him. Finally Red shouted, "Count off." The response was rapid, each trooper calling back in sequence: "Seventeen okay." "Sixteen okay." "Fifteen okay."

He glanced out the door, saw land suddenly appear, first a narrow strip of bright white beach, and then the dark of earth, everything flashing past just below them. Lights began to appear on the ground, bright flashes as flak and multicolored tracer rounds came up toward them, moving so slowly, arching like Roman candles. He caught the faint clatter of explosions over the roar of the engines.

The aircraft veered sharply to the left, held for a moment, then jinked back to the right, the pilots nervously dodging flak bursts. All the men swayed back and forth, grabbing for support. Parnell leaned forward slightly, looked straight down. The ground was now a sheet of white, fog down there, only the tops of trees showing, jetting past. Shrapnel began hitting the outside of the aircraft. It sounded like heavy rain and made the C-47 jostle and buck.

He glanced at his watch: 12:09. "Coming up on one," he called out.

There was a *bang* and a heavy jolt, then the hiss of incoming air. A hole the size of a basketball had been punched into the right side of the aircraft's fuselage, back near the tail. The C-47 shook violently. Men cursed, frantically tried to remain upright.

Red turned, looked up at the red light. *Come on, you son of a bitch,* he thought, *we're gonna overfly.* He could vaguely hear the radioman shouting time and position reports to the pilots through his intercom.

The red light snapped off and a green one came on. Parnell bellowed, "Go! Go!"

The first two out were Bird and Wineberg, point men, the most dangerous position in a drop, the others, coming forward hurriedly, shuffling, and going out, their bodies twisting to face the tail as the slipstream hit them, their static lines whipping back.

There was a sudden, loud *crack* and a bright burst just outside the door. Shrapnel flew in, slammed into the other side of the fuselage. Red felt the concussion wave hit him and the body of the trooper who had been in the doorway crashed into him and knocked him to his knees. He realized he was covered with blood and bits of clothing and bone and unfired cartridges. The trooper had taken the full force of a German 3.46-inch Pak/Flak shell. It had blown his head and right shoulder completely away.

For one miniscule moment, Parnell went nearly motionless under him, only his head swiveling. He saw the faces of the others glowing green in the jump light, everybody else frozen too as the C-47 rocked and rolled crazily. Little flecks of fire leaped and twisted on the fuselage bulkhead.

Then he was moving, his mind pounding at himself, *Get them out!* He bodily lifted the trooper's corpse and hurled it through the doorway, letting its weight pull him fully to his feet. The man's static line snapped back. He turned, saw a young face staring at him, reached out to grab a handful of battle tunic, screaming, "Jump, goddammit, *jump!*"

Slowly the aircraft leveled. By now, the line of men was moving again. He heard Weesay's voice and that of two of the noncoms cursing them on. They came past Parnell, some slipping on the bloody deck but going out and away, until finally Laguna appeared and was instantly gone.

Red slammed his own static line buckle over the cable, braced his hands on the doorway. It was slimy, the metal ripped and jagged. He lunged forward and out, his arms automatically snapping against his chest, his head down, turning himself in the air as the blast of the slipstream hit him like a hurricane.

Cowboy Fountain had been glad to get out of that C-47, leaving it before the flak hit. He'd always hated getting shot at up there, like most paratroopers terrified of getting nailed in the balls, flat gelded with his boots on aircraft aluminum. The T-7 chute gave him its usual crotch-crunching jolt as its Ramtex cotton panels blossomed open, a canopy-first deployment unit made for low jumps. This one *damn* low, only time enough for two oscillations before he hit.

Coming down, it had looked like the Fourth of July, fireworks going off everywhere except out over the swampland to the east that lay shining in the moonlight like a huge lake. He landed in an open, grassy field, fog-layered and mushy. *Well,* he thought, *at least I missed them damn swamps.* In their premission briefing, they'd been informed that Rommel had flooded the swampland in ten, fifteen feet of water. Any paratrooper going down there with so much gear on would drown, sure as hell.

He was halfway out of his harness when he saw one of

the C-47s take a solid flak strike. He stiffened. Goddamn, it was his! He stood there, saw men dropping, their chutes looking like mushrooms in the moonlight. How many out? He'd lost count. Then the aircraft was on fire, moving off to the left, banking steeply. It continued, straight down into the ground, exploding in a huge ball of flame.

He felt a frozen chill ripple through his body. *Jesus Christ, the lieutenant and Weesay were the last ones in line.* He cursed, then forced that thought from his mind. Hurriedly recovering his chute, he unbagged his Thompson submachine gun, charged it, and moved off stealthily, scanning the misty ground and horizon, a tree line visible on his right, a solid, dark line, a hedgerow, in the other direction.

The firing stopped abruptly and the drone of the aircraft faded off into silence. Around him the night seemed suddenly remote. His boots made slushy sounds. The air smelled of grass and field flowers, lilac and hyacinth, old-lady odors. He continued back along the line of the jump, searching for the rest of the stick.

After leaving Naples, Italy, Blue Team had been flown straight to England, to what would be their first training base, a onetime cricket pavilion outside Nottingham that was now used by the British Special Air Service, the SAS.

But first they were given a four-day leave. Fountain spent most of his time with a girl named Edie Fowler, blond and buxom, a spotter-predictor with the town's Auxiliary Territorial Service. She talked a mile a minute, fucked like a mink, and raved about his Western drawl, said he "sounded like Wyatt bloody Earp."

Afterward, in quick succession, he and the team trained at several bases. Initially, at Nottingham, where the SAS gave them a rush course in French, taught them updated demo techniques using the new PE 808 RDX plastic explosives, and supplied them with captured German small and medium

field arms to strip and test-fire. Next, they were sent to
F-Section of the British Special Operations Executive in
Maidstone for classes on the French Resistance and its operational systems. Finally, they spent three weeks making ultra-
low insertion jumps with the Second Battalion of the 501st
at Chilton Foliat.

Three minutes later, Fountain was challenged, the tiny
chirp of a metal "cricket." Each trooper of the 101st and 82nd
had been issued one of these toy clickers just before takeoff
so they could identify each other on the ground. Cowboy
stopped, frantically searched for his own. It was gone. The
cricket chirped again, the clicks ominously faster this time.
A thought occurred to Cowboy. He called, "Jimminy."

There was a pause, then a voice came back: "Cricket." A
shadow rose from the grass and approached. It was one of
the 501 noncoms, Sergeant Glenn Briggs, who snapped,
"Where in hell's your clicker?"

"I lost it."

Briggs dug one from his battle tunic, handed it over.
"Was that our transport got hit?" he asked.

"Yeah, I think so."

"Shit! Okay, let's go."

Soon they encountered Bird, Wineberg, and two other
501 troopers, one with a Eureka unit. Briggs sent one man
back along their track to see if he could find any other members of their stick while he and the radar man began setting
up the unit and their signal lights.

Bird, Smoker, and Cowboy silently moved off to reconnoiter the entire DZ, the three of them going without words.
Far off, the blaze from the C-47 crash had died down until it
was now merely a faint glow like that of the firepit of a near-
dead volcano.

*   *   *

Weesay Laguna had crashed through a tree and then into swamp, rocketing straight to the mud-thick bottom in ten feet of water. All the way down with his gear suddenly like a lead anchor, he was thinking, *Jesus y Maria, I'm gonna fuckin' drown!*

As soon as he had left the C-47, he knew he was in big trouble. Below him, the ground was *glistening,* for God's sake, moonlit water in all directions. The damn pilot's jerking around back there and the flak hit had put them beyond the DZ, right out over the flooded swampland.

Still, he didn't have too much time to think about it before that tree sitting on a bank was looming up at him, its leaves etched with moonlight. He went through it like a cannonball and into the water, not particularly cold, alive with shafts of moonlight all shattered and distorted by his plunge. The bottom was about two feet of slushy mud.

He felt for his boot knife and began cutting his harness. He felt tension on his risers and realized the chute had caught in the tree's branches. Frantic, his cheeks puffed and straining to hold in every tiny whisper of air, his heart pounding wildly, he began to climb hand-over-hand back up the risers. Jesus, he felt as if he were lifting a car, his body weight doubled. The risers jerked, started to slip. Moaning in his throat, he sped up: *reach, pull, reach, pull. . . .*

He broke the surface and kept right on going until he was up among leaves, everything dripping, the folds of his chute and the risers entangled all over him. Panting, he listened, heard men screaming, violent splashing. He looked out, tried to pinpoint their positions, couldn't. The water's surface was covered with scattered patches of thin fog.

The screaming stopped.

He cut himself loose and climbed down out of the tree, dropped to the bank. The tree was on the side of a narrow berm. Thickets of pussy willow and swamp grass covered the ground except for a narrow foot trail along the top of the berm. He quickly unbagged his weapon and lay with his head just below the trail, scanning.

Something moved way off to his left, a man running. He stiffened. The figure came on. He put his muzzle right on the center of it, worked the clicker with his left hand. The figure stopped. There was an answering clicking. The man came up. It was Lieutenant Parnell. They squatted beside the tree. He could smell the cloying odor of fresh blood on Parnell's tunic.

Red asked, "How many landed out here?"

"I heard at least three, Lieutenant."

They listened. Total silence. "Damn it!" Parnell hissed.

They waited several minutes. Another figure came along the causeway. He was limping, hobbling along like a gnome. Both men challenged, got answering clicks. The man was a private from the 501. Parnell asked him about the others.

"I know they was at least three ahead of me, sir," he said, breathing hard. "And Sergeant Meisell. But I couldn't find nobody."

"How bad you hurt?"

"Ankle sprain, sir. I can move okay."

"All right, you two wait here. I don't get back in five minutes, head out." Parnell rose, glanced up at the tree. "Get that chute outta there. Shows up like a fucking neon sign." He went sprinting off along the causeway, going low, back in the direction from which the private had come.

They cut down the remnants of Laguna's chute and buried it in the bank mud. Then they waited, their eyes constantly sweeping the landscape. It was eerie how still the night was, no breeze, no night birds. Yet they did spot a crane flying across the moon, way up, a stick figure struggling on long wings.

Weesay said, "What's chu name, *meng?*"

"Foley." The private sighed, his shoulders shuddering as if he were cold. "Shit, I heard them poor bastards drowning out there. You know?"

"Yeah," Laguna said.

Parnell returned, shaking his head. "They're all gone. Let's move."

They headed back along the jump line, going as fast as Foley could manage.

Captain Joe Lightfine, the name translated from Norwegian, put his tiny vest light onto the rubber terrain map spread on the wet grass. Lightfine was chief jumpmaster for the two Pathfinder sticks assigned to Zone A.

He and Parnell had trained together back at Chilton Foliat. One of the things they had done there was study sand tables made from aerial photos of the jump area. Then someone had gotten the brilliant idea of molding out rubber terrain maps from the sand tables so the unit officers could take them along and quickly orient themselves once they were on the ground. Now Lightfine's map looked like a tiny landscape, the flashlight casting its hillocks and headgerows into shadow-relief.

"We're right here," he said to Parnell, pointing. "Just south of those hedgerows."

A few feet away were two troopers. One was setting up a Eureka unit from which he would transmit a homing frequency to a so-called Rebecca unit aboard three of the lead aircraft of the 101st's main contingent of paratroopers. The other soldier carried an S phone pack, a new invention that would allow Lightfine to communicate directly with the troop carrier pilots.

"Your perimeter secure?" Parnell asked.

"Yeah. There hasn't been any enemy response yet." He grunted. "Looks like we fooled the bastards." After dropping their sticks, the C-47s had headed inland to give the impression they were on a bombing run.

"Did you lose any?"

"Nobody dead but four injured." The captain shook his head. "I'm sorry about your guys, John. Thank Christ, *we* didn't come down in those goddamned swamps."

Red made no comment. He leaned in, ran his eyes along a series of low berms on the rubber map, which were three hedgerows two hundred yards south of their position. Good cover for rapid movement, he thought. He followed the hedgerows northwestward, the land rising slightly, here and there patches of crinkled rubber indicating woodland. To the east toward the coast were the squares of the hamlets of St. Germainde Varreville and Ravenoville. The Pointe River Bridge was due southwest.

Their DZ, code-named Zone A, was the northernmost of the three 101st's main jump sites. Zone B was four miles to the south outside St. Marie-du-Mont, and Zone C was near the key rail junction of Carentan. To the east were the three DZs of the 82nd, the first of which was between the smaller junction town of St. Mere Eglise and the Merderet River.

Both men consulted their watches: 12:43 A.M. The main drop was now only forty-seven minutes away.

"You'd best head on out, John," Lightfine said.

Like Parnell, Lightfine had been an outstanding football player in college, at Michigan State, where both he and his twin brother, Jerry, had made All-American mention. Red had twice received All-American honors at the University of Colorado and then went on to play pro ball with the Detroit Lions.

Jerry Lightfine was now a pilot with the Ninth Air Force flying B-26 Marauder tactical bombers on night strikes over France. Twice he'd come up to Chilton Foliat and the three of them had gotten drunk in the local pubs, debating the ability of Colorado to whip Michigan, the two Lightfine brothers identical-looking, big men with the broad, open features and the faintly Norwegian-tanged speech of their Minnesota farmer rootstock.

"Watch yourself," Joe added. He smiled. "I got a bottle of Crown Royal waiting on us back in England."

"You're on, Joey." They shook hands.

Parnell signaled his four men, who had been patiently squatted down a few yards away. Together they quickly, silently moved off toward the hedgerows.

* * *

There were three Maquis at the rendezvous, the place chosen a quarter mile downstream of the Pointe Bridge near a farmhouse where three haystacks had been set out to form a triangle.

Parnell had flashed his recognition signal, three groups of the letter S in Morse code with his vest flashlight: S . . . S . . . S. They were quickly countersigned. He and Wyatt went in while the others maintained cover.

The leader was a tall, rangy man whose code name was Lucas. His real name, Parnell would later learn, was Vaillant Duboudin, a famous French race car driver. He, like the other two, was dressed in a black leather jacket, dark trousers, and a fisherman's cap. Each carried a British Sten MKII machine pistol.

Duboudin shook Parnell's hand, grinning. *"J'ai Lucas, Lieutenant. N'hesitez pas a France."*

"Merci."

The French Resistance movement was composed of over 300,000 members. The two main groups were DeGaulle's BCRA or Free French, and the French Forces of the Interior, the FFI. In between these were numerous, independently acting units called circuits, some with as few as two to six members. They referred to themselves as the Maquis, which meant scrubland. Many were violently opposed to each other, yet had momentarily come together to fight the greater enemy, the Nazis.

Lucas immediately launched off into a rapid appraisal of the situation, speaking in French. Red listened for a few moments, getting about half of it, then held up his hand. "Whoa, hold it," he said in English, then in French, "My French is no that good."

The leader tilted his head, surprised. "I was told you spoke it well."

"No well. *Un petit.* If you are speaking slow, I am possibly to understand."

Lucas shook his head, grunted. One of the other Maquis

quickly stepped forward and said in pure American, "Actually, your French rather stinks, Lieutenant."

It was a woman.

Parnell turned to her, surprised. "You're American?"

"Of course." She laughed, a soft, merry, tinkling sound. "Anabel O'Keefe Sinclair, Chicago born and raised. Look, fella, let's just use English. It'll be a damn side simpler."

She explained the layout: "The bridge has a single pill-box, on the eastern side. Usually four men, two MG-34s. Their bivouac's two hundred yards farther on in some trees. All told, there're about twenty men and a radio unit."

Parnell listened. Anabel Sinclair had a nice way of gesturing, very feminine. He couldn't see her face clearly in the moonlight and her hair was tucked up under her hat. But now that he knew, he could see the obvious curve of female hip in her trousers.

"We have fourteen men in our circuit," Sinclair went on. "Armed mostly with Stens and handguns and a few captured MP-40s." She nodded toward one of the haystacks. "There's a German antitank rifle for you in there. A 7.92 Panzerbuchse .38. You take out the pillbox, we'll handle the bivouac. I suggest you do it quickly. As soon as our weapons fire off, the Krauts will send troops from St. Mere Eglise, posthaste."

He said, "You're Flapper, aren't you?" Back at the SOE briefings at F Section in Maidstone, agents' names had never been mentioned. But in the final, premission data he'd received, there were the code names of the three agents he'd be meeting in France: Lucas, Alain, and Flapper.

Except for a handful of key leaders, none of the rank and file of the Resistance movement knew the specifics of the coming invasion. This included Sinclair and the others. As far as they were concerned, this American team of elite specialists was here simply to conduct specific sabotage raids.

"That's me," Anabel said perkily. She pushed back the cuff of her jacket to look at her watch, then turned to Lucas and the other man and rattled off something in French, way too fast for Red to follow. She came back to him. "Any questions, Lieutenant?"

"No."

"Till later, then." The three Marquis moved away quickly and were soon gone from sight beyond the farmhouse.

Wyatt chuckled quietly. "I guess we'all got our orders, ain't we, Lieutenant?"

Parnell snorted. "Sure as hell sounds like it, don't it?"

They were able to approach to within sixty yards of the bridge's German pillbox, crawling through a field of spring wheat almost ready for harvest, the spickletts smelling strongly of germ-oil. Bird, who would be firing the Panzerbuchse rifle, carried it in the crook of his arms, the telescoped barrel of polished carbon steel freshly oiled. Weesay brought the two-legged mount and Cowboy the saddle magazine that fitted directly onto the weapon's breech.

The pillbox was an old-fashioned Type 630 modified by emplacing a tank turret over a sandbagged pit. One machine gun was visible through a sqaure embrasure that faced the bridge. The other was higher, open, with a steel plate welded to the turret. It was camouflaged with tree branches and tufts of river grass. A German soldier was standing beside it, smoking.

The Pointe Bridge itself looked old, formed of stones and double arches with no railing. It looked to be wide enough for two horse carts to pass abreast. The river was narrow, perhaps thirty yards across. It appeared languid, yet in the moonlight small ripple lines were visible in its center, indicating a current and a decent depth to it.

By signal, Parnell deployed his men. He gave Wyatt a clear line of fire to the machine gun's embrasure while the others took up positions along the riverbank so as to shoot around the steel shield on the second gun. Quietly, Bird assembled the antitank rifle, affixing the mount and clipping on the magazine. Then he stretched out, fitted the padded butt stock to his shoulder, and took a bead on the target through the weapon's big O-ring sight.

They waited, Parnell laying beside Bird. It was 0121 hours. The ground seemed alive with tiny bugs, mosquitoes droned about their heads. High up, the moon had passed its zenith, in the clear night air looking flat-round, bright as a vanilla-colored balloon caught in a spotlight. Across the river, the German soldier had finished his cigarette and returned to the pillbox.

It came as a low drone at first, so faint it might have been a distant wind. It grew in volume until it was a roaring of many, isolated engines. The night began to light up, flares and pink, green, and white tracers going up, the staccato chatter of machine guns and the deeper booms of flak guns opening up. The whole night erupted in sound and flashing, arching light, the motionless brightness of the moon suddenly diminished.

Parnell's hand tapped Wyatt's shoulder. A second later, the Panzerbuchse fired off with a deafening slam. Again and still again, the rounds rocketing across the river, shattering the air. The small pillbox exploded in a shower of white-hot metal fragments as Thompsons came into action, their low, throaty, slow-steady raps sounding hollow beside the anti-tank gun's muzzle blasts.

Parnell's ears rang. He looked over at Bird. The sharp smell of cordite smoke drifted among the wheat stalks. They both smiled icily at each other. Wyatt had just fired the first American round, ironically from a German gun, to start the invasion of Western Europe.

DON'T'MISS CHARLES RYAN'S

FIRST RECON FORCE THRILLER

LIGHTNING STRIKE

ISBN# 0-7860-1564-0

In the dark days of World War II, a special unit was commissioned by Lieutenant James Dunmore, an intelligence officer on General George Patton's staff. Made up of the toughest and bravest volunteers the army had to offer, the unit had only one purpose—to hit first, hit hard, and kill without hesitation. This band of elite warriors would become known as the Mohawkers—and the last thing the enemy would see would be . . .

Recon Force
Lightning Strike

For their inaugural mission, the Mohawkers are sent to the African coast ahead of the Allied invasion to take out a battery of railroad-mounted artillery. Led by the relentless Lieutenant "Iron John" Parnell, the ragtag band of soldiers must fight their way past a bloodthirsty corps of French Foreign Legionnaires, outwit an arrogant Luftwaffe captain, and grab the guns. Surrounded by enemies who'd gladly end their first mission before it begins, the boys know there's no room for mistakes—and they'll have no mercy for anyone who gets in their way.

ABOUT THE AUTHOR

Charles Ryan served in the United States Air Force as a senior airman and munitions system specialist in the armament section of the 199th Fighter Squadron based at Hickam AFB, Honolulu. He attended the Universities of Hawaii and Washington, and has worked at numerous occupations, including judo instructor, commercial pilot, and salvage diver. He's written for newspapers in Honolulu and San Francisco and magazines, as well as being the author of seven novels. Ryan currently lives in northern California.